ABINADI

ABINADI

a novel by

H.B. MOORE

Covenant Communications, Inc.

Top cover image: © Covenant Communications, Inc. Middle cover image: *Vintage Paper* © Royce DeGrie, courtesy of iStock. Bottom cover image: *Plate VIII: General View of Las Monjas, at Uxmal,* by Frederick Catherwood, *Views of Ancient Monuments in Central America, Chiapas and Yucatan,* 1844, London: Archivio White Star.

Cover design copyrighted 2008 by Covenant Communications, Inc.

Published by Covenant Communications, Inc.
American Fork, Utah

Printed in Canada
First Printing: November 2008

15 14 13 12 11 10 09 08   10 9 8 7 6 5 4 3 2 1

ISBN 13: 978-1-59811-654-0
ISBN 10: 1-59811-654-1

PRAISE FOR
H.B. MOORE'S BOOKS

"In *Land of Inheritance* . . . Moore persuasively renders as must-read historical fiction the rich (and growing) body of scholarship about ancient life in Mesoamerica. I highly recommend this exciting, well-written, faith-centered and faith-enhancing novel."

  —Richard H. Cracroft, *BYU Magazine* columnist, former chair of BYU English Department, and former dean of BYU College of Humanities

"In the first three volumes of her Book of Mormon historical fiction series, Heather B. Moore showed that she could create a view of an ancient world that combines the best scholarship with a lively imagination. She does a fine job of walking the tricky line of faithfulness to the scripture and creative storytelling. She opened up the hearts of her characters in ways both remarkably touching and authentic. In this fourth and final volume she does all of that, as well as writing one of the most exciting adventure tales that I have read in a while."

  —Andrew Hall, Reviewer for Association of Mormon Letters

"H.B. Moore may be the most exciting new writer in the LDS genre. In *Out of Jerusalem*, Moore takes characters from thousands of years ago and breathes life into them. I look forward to reading more from Moore."

  —Richard Paul Evans, #1 *New York Times* Bestselling Author

"Moore takes us into the thrilling world of Lehi and Nephi and brings the women onto center stage with remarkable effect."

  —Peter Johnson, Motion Picture Producer & Director

"A great read . . . H.B. Moore will take you on a journey worth every minute you spend with Out of Jerusalem. I highly recommend her series."
    —James Michael Pratt, *New York Times* & *USA Today* Bestselling Author

"H.B. Moore's *Land of Inheritance* lives up to the grand proportions of the scriptural epic tale found in the Book of Mormon."
    —Jennie Hansen, *Meridian Magazine*

"A conscientious researcher, Moore brings to a genre that I usually find heavy and boring a fresh voice and an imagination that creates believable characters and situations that belong to a time and place far removed from our own."
    —Charlene Hirschi, *The Logan Herald,* columnist

"This last book in the Out of Jerusalem series certainly does not disappoint. H.B. Moore brings the Book of Mormon to life through her meticulous research and creative talents. Moore helps us to read "between the lines" of Nephi's account and gives us a stronger connection to early prophets through this compelling book."
    —Dayna Davis, LDSfiles.com Staff Reviewer

"H.B. Moore skillfully and engagingly leads us into the group's triumphs and challenges as this small colony struggled to establish itself and to forge a new identity on foreign soil, inescapably far from their beloved Jerusalem. This book is a terrific read."
    —S. Kent Brown, Director of the Laura F. Willes
    Center for Book of Mormon Studies, BYU

For the women of faith in my life—my many sisters:
Karilynne, Julianne, Shoshauna, Jill,
Melissa, Laura, Amy, Hailee, and Suzanne

Acknowledgments

Just like a manuscript, the acknowledgments are a work in progress—often being added to right before press deadline. That is because many people have a hand in a writer's work from the beginning to the very end.

I'd like to thank my supporting cast—my husband, Chris, and our four children. They know when I put on my lipstick that I'm off to another speaking engagement or book signing.

Thank you to my taskmasters who don't let me get away with a comma splice or point-of-view shift—my "enduring to the end" critique group—Lu Ann Staheli, Michele Holmes, Annette Lyon, Jeff Savage, Stephanni Meyers, Lynda Keith, Robison Wells, and James Dashner. Thanks also to Josi Kilpack for her early advice on the prologue.

My parents, Kent and Gayle Brown, were the first readers of my manuscript and offered many helpful insights. Also, I'd like to thank my father for answering all of my pesky emails about the minutest details.

Special thanks to my father-in-law, Lester Moore, who continually supports my work and offers valuable insights to my writing. A special thank-you also goes to Karen Christofferson, marketing advisor and champion of my work.

In addition, I readily admit that I am not a scholar in any fashion—although in writing this book I have read certain chapters in the Book of Mormon more times than I should admit. My heartfelt gratitude extends to the scholars of the Book of Mormon and the archaeologists of Mesoamerica for publishing their research. I would not have been able to build upon their expertise and create a story if it weren't for their lifelong dedication.

My publisher has been wonderful, and I can't thank the Covenant staff of editors, marketing personnel, and design team enough. I have a hard enough time coming up with a simple title, and they make the finished product shine. Special thanks to my main editor, Kat Gille, for her many talents, and to managing editor, Kathy Jenkins, for her continual support and encouragement to start a new series. I have been bugging Kathy about a book on Abinadi since 2006, so she is probably glad to finally get it out the door! Also, thanks to the finest editors I could ask for, Angela Eschler and Christian Sorensen, who picked up where my critique group left off. Thanks also goes to copyeditor Jennifer Spell.

I'd also like to thank the readers of my Out of Jerusalem series. I have received many tender thank-you emails and letters, which I save and cherish. Writing is solitary work and takes incredible motivation to move forward bit by bit each day. Without your support and enthusiasm, my dream of continual publishing wouldn't be realized.

Sincere thanks goes to Andy Livingston, my vigilant map designer, and Phill Babbitt, talented website designer. Last, but never least, thanks to my "writing family"—the LDStorymakers.

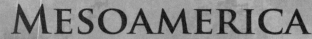

MESOAMERICA
The Late Preclassic Era
300 B.C. — A.D. 250

GULF OF MEXICO

Bay of Campeche

M E X I C O

Narrow Neck of Land

Wilderness of Hermounts

Valley of Gideon

Chiapa de Corzo

▲ *Hill Amnihu*

Land of Zarahemla

R. Sidon

Narrow St

GULF OF TEHUANTEPEC

● Izapa

Salinas

UNITED STATES

MEXICO

N

SOUTH AMERICA

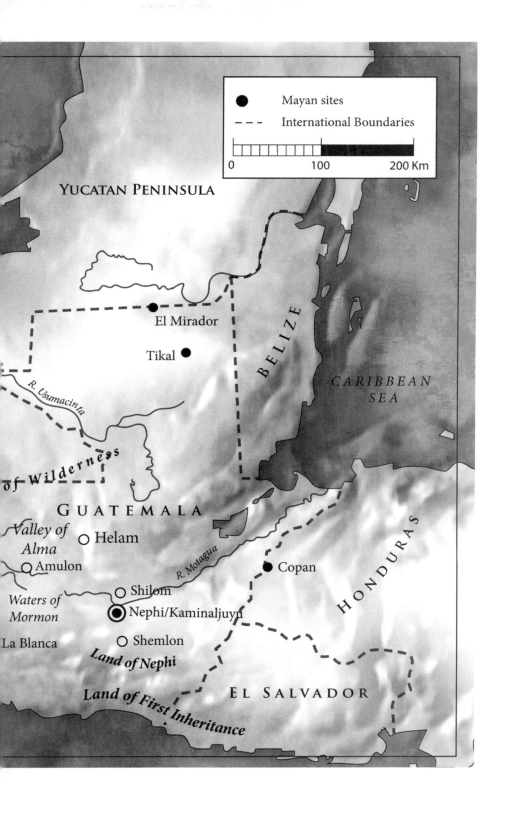

YUCATAN PENINSULA

● Mayan sites
- - - International Boundaries

0   100   200 Km

El Mirador ●

Tikal ●

BELIZE

CARIBBEAN
SEA

R. Usumacinta

of Wilderness

GUATEMALA

Valley of
Alma   ○ Helam

○ Amulon

R. Motagua

Copan ●

HONDURAS

Waters of
Mormon   ○ Shilom

◎ Nephi/Kaminaljuyu

La Blanca   ○ Shemlon

Land of Nephi

Land of First Inheritance

EL SALVADOR

Preface

Within the passage of Mosiah 11:20 through 17:20, the life of a remarkable prophet emerges. Abinadi steps into the scriptural text with little introduction, evidently a descendent of a small group of Nephites who had returned from Zarahemla to repossess the city of Nephi. Abinadi, known for his martyrdom in King Noah's court, makes a grand stage entrance with his first, and seemingly failed, attempt to call the people in the city to repentance.

Traditional LDS artists, such as Arnold Friberg, depict Abinadi as an aged man, possibly at the end of his years, facing his execution as ordered by King Noah. In this volume, I have chosen to portray Abinadi as a young man who is in his twenties when he receives the first call from the Lord. Before starting to write, my first question was, "Is there any information within the scriptural text that hints at the age of the prophet Abinadi?"

Scholars such as Robert J. Matthews make it clear that there is no indication in the Book of Mormon text as to how old Abinadi was. "We know nothing of Abinadi's early life," Matthews states. "We find nothing in the record to indicate whether he was old or young, large or small. What we do find . . . is a man of courage with an agile mind, a profound knowledge of the gospel, and a strong personality" ("Abinadi: Prophet and Martyr," *Ensign*, April 1992, 25).

After starting the first draft, I came upon a painting of King Noah's court called *Abinadi Had Testified*, created by Walter Rane. As I studied the characters—King Noah, Abinadi, and possibly the high priest Alma, I noticed something very interesting: Rane had clearly depicted Abinadi as a young man.

I decided to place Abinadi at the age of twenty-seven in the opening scene of this book, with a specific purpose behind doing so. I wanted to expound on a story—a story that has been passed down from generation to generation—of a man who sacrificed everything for what he believed in. I didn't want

Abinadi to be a man at the end of his natural life or a man who'd lived a life full of happiness with children and grandchildren. I saw Abinadi as a man who still had many years ahead of him—one who stood to lose a lot more than just his life.

Also introduced in this volume is the high priest Alma. When I first started to characterize him, I considered the swift rise and fall of wickedness within the community he grew up in. Under King Zeniff's rule, the law of Moses was correctly observed and remained upright. The very next generation, however, almost effortlessly fell into abhorrent wickedness, ignoring the ten commandments, worshipping idols, and stooping to harlotry in the palace. Alma's internal character arc mimics the rise and fall of the city's changing values, starting with a strong foundation in his childhood, falling into temptation as he serves in the court, then eventually clawing his way back to the truth.

The Mesoamerican culture is complex, colorful, and genuinely engaging. Some of the research information was horrific, other parts simply beautiful. In the chapter notes at the end of this book, I've detailed elements of the Mayan culture that surrounded the Nephites and Lamanites during the late-Preclassic Era (300 BC–AD 250).

The Kaminaljuyú area of Guatemala is one favored location for the land of Nephi. John L. Sorenson notes that the Zeniffites, a group of Nephites led by Zeniff, returned to the land of Nephi to find the Lamanites occupying the region (*Images of Ancient America: Visualizing Book of Mormon Life,* 198). The Zeniffites lived under Lamanite rule for some time before fighting and gaining their independence around 165 BC.

The chronology of this book is patterned after the timeline found in the appendix of *Voices from the Dust,* by S. Kent Brown. This places the coronation of King Noah around 140 BC, and Abinadi's first appearance in 130 BC (see Mosiah 11:20).

The prophet Abinadi's teachings were bold and could not be misinterpreted, not even by a court filled with conniving high priests. Abinadi emphasized the laws of Moses as "types of things to come" (Mosiah 13:31). The Atonement took dominance in Abinadi's speech when he taught the court members that salvation does not come through the law, but through the Lord (see Mosiah 13:28). According to Robert Matthews, "Abinadi is the first to speak specifically of the first resurrection [in the Book of Mormon] and to discuss the general resurrection in detail" ("Abinadi," *Ensign,* April 1992, 25).

Abinadi declared that "the time shall come that the salvation of the Lord shall be declared to every nation, kindred, tongue, and people" (Mosiah

15:28); we see the initially harvested fruits of that prophecy among later prophets of the Book of Mormon. Ann Madsen points out that although Abinadi's life was cut short, his influence reached far and wide. On the day of Abinadi's execution, only *one* believed—the high priest Alma. Yet Alma was the one to escape King Noah and write down the words of Abinadi. Madsen notes that "more than 60 years later, Alma the Younger testifies of his father's eye witness account" ("Abinadi Interprets Isaiah," *Journal of Book of Mormon Studies,* 10:1 [2001], 14). Abinadi's influence was felt far and wide, indeed.

It is with humble admiration and deep gratitude that I present to you the story of a man who patterned his life after the Savior's, even until the very end.

Prologue

Till I die I will not remove mine integrity from me.
(Job 27:5)

128 BC

A rat scurried across Abinadi's legs, and he tucked his feet beneath him, wrapping his arms around his knees. The air inside the prison cell had blossomed into ripe humidity, sending rivulets of perspiration down Abinadi's back. Gazing with effort at his dim surroundings, he wondered about those who had been in this cell before. He'd spent only three days here, but he'd heard of those who had been imprisoned for years.

A thin beam of muffled light filtered through the corridor beyond. The absolute dark was softening with the morning. Anxiety pulsed through Abinadi as he anticipated the guard's arrival. He should be here any moment with the next instructions.

The previous night had proved sleepless as Abinadi crouched on the earthen floor, his back against the cold stone wall. There was nothing to lie upon, nowhere to sit except the dank ground. Standing was too exhausting and lying would have made him bait for the two rather large rats occupying his cell—the hard round of bread thrown in the night before had immediately become the varmints' property. Despite his protesting stomach, Abinadi did not care about the food or the spilled vessel of water that darkened the dirt near his feet—courtesy of the rats. His thoughts left his physical environment as they replayed the day, little more than two years earlier, when he'd received the call to be a prophet.

He had been only twenty-five years old when the Lord asked him to preach repentance to His people. Abinadi's entire life had changed in that instant. And now, here he was, caged like an animal, awaiting his final sentence. The sounds of his not-so-distant past seemed to fill the prison cell—his son's bubbly laughter, his wife's comforting whispers during restless nights, the voices praising God during Sabbath services in his home. Closing his eyes, Abinadi reveled in the sweet memories and let the salty tears fall.

From the Lord's first instruction, Abinadi's wife had understood that he *had* to preach the Lord's words. But would she understand *this*—that she might have to raise their son alone?

In his heart, Abinadi had already made his choice. He would finish the Lord's errand with the same determination with which he'd begun it.

The echoes from his memory blended with new sounds. *Chanting.* It seemed to fill the entire cavern. Abinadi listened as the rhythmic words grew louder. Somewhere . . . outside . . . people were condemning him. His pulse quickened, and he took a deep breath.

"O God," he prayed through cracked lips, "with Thy strength I will pass through the valley of death."

The low chants seemed to envelop him. The heavy door of the cell opened, and Abinadi lifted his head, ready to face the guard. But two men entered instead, their finely woven cotton capes thrown on haphazardly. They were high priests from the king's court—some of those who had accused him. Abinadi smelled stale wine on their clothing, undoubtedly from a night of indulgence.

"Have you had enough time to reconsider?" one of the priests asked. Abinadi knew him as Amulon. The man was tall; his physical presence alone made him powerful. He wore a coat of jaguar skin and a belt of fine, beaded cloth. In one jeweled hand he gripped a long obsidian dagger.

"I am not afraid of death," Abinadi said, gazing up into the man's eyes. "Christ will break the bands of death, and the grave will have no victory."

Amulon blinked, his face unresponsive.

But the priest next to him laughed. "Everyone knows that if you die you go to the underworld." He guffawed and slapped Amulon's shoulder.

"Enough," Amulon growled at the other priest, then he narrowed his eyes at Abinadi. "You are foolish to speak against the king." He took a step closer, but Abinadi didn't move. "He asks for your presence once more. If you value your life, you'll recant your words and ask for his forgiveness."

When Abinadi didn't respond, the unnamed priest reached down and grabbed him by the arm, sneering. "I say you've had your chance."

Abinadi stumbled as the men jerked him to his feet then pushed him into the corridor, steering him along the narrow underground passage. The darkness had lifted, signaling that dawn had come and gone. But that didn't keep the damp from settling beneath his skin. He had been here once before, on another mission . . . but that seemed so long ago, another life-time. As they ascended the stone steps, morning light pierced through the eastern prison entrance. Abinadi blinked against the brightness, and when he emerged above ground, two guards immediately seized him, relieving the priests.

Abinadi's skin tingled in the warmth of the sun while they walked. It was a beautiful day. The stoic trees that lined that pathway to the main temple were reverent somehow, as if something tragic were about to occur.

Abinadi and the guards arrived at the central plaza, where the revered ceiba tree stood—some thought it was the center of the universe. It shaded the surrounding area with its leafy, long-reaching branches. Several smaller temples with altars were spread out from the plaza—which created a lively scene on the Sabbath when the priests gathered to make sacrifices. Abinadi nearly tripped as one of the guards prodded him with a staff. Amulon and the other priests followed behind, laughing intermittently. Every step brought Abinadi closer to the judgment of the king. According to the laws that King Noah had established, Abinadi *was* guilty of blasphemy, and now he would meet his punishment.

Protect my family, O God, Abinadi prayed, *for I know what I must do.*

He looked about him at the surreal beauty of the early morning, expecting a hollow void of helplessness to consume him. But it did not. His soul was quiet, his mind at peace. The Lord had wrapped His arms around him.

They came to the temple grounds, where Abinadi was surprised to see a crowd waiting. It silently and fluidly parted as the guards shoved him along. Abinadi recognized some of them—men he'd worked alongside in the fields or purchased goods from in the market.

He'd spent his youth as nothing more than a simple farmer, paying his one-fifth taxes to the king and trying to provide for his ailing mother. Life had been trouble-free, although filled with hard labor. But he'd been content to move through the days, unobtrusive, unassuming. Until he met the Teacher, a man who led a group of elders in the old ways of their Fathers—Lehi, Nephi, Jacob, Enos . . . It was then that Abinadi started to question the teachings of King Noah's priests. He started to desire more—happiness, freedom, equality.

Abinadi left the sullen crowd and climbed the steps to the temple, sorrowing at the way King Noah had allowed it to be desecrated. Stone idols of nature gods lined the stairs and stood sentry at the entrance. Stepping into the cool interior, Abinadi caught a glimpse of the bright-colored idola-trous murals on the walls as his eyes tried to adjust to the semi-light. He soon came face-to-face with the raised platform of judgment seats. The king and his priests lounged upon them—as if a common thief were being brought before them instead of a prophet.

Abinadi stood for several uncomfortable moments, guards on both sides, as Amulon took his place on the right side of the king. The two men leaned their heads together to speak. Amulon was clearly older than the king, but Noah looked haggard from much indulgent living. His skin glistened with oil, and his beaded cowl looked too tight upon his neck. His feathered cape didn't quite cover his girth, and as he tipped his head closer to Amulon, his elaborate headdress slipped. With one hand, Noah righted it, but the perspiration on his forehead caused it to slip again.

The king was so elaborately adorned that he looked like a moving pageant. At least a dozen jade bracelets pinched the flesh of his arms, while the rings on his fingers, alternating between gold and jade, made his gestures cumbersome. The cape over his shoulders had intricately sewn feathers, and his kilt was dyed in the popular turquoise. Two young women stood on either side of him, waving reed fans, although it didn't seem to be helping much.

Finally, King Noah struggled to stand and gazed at his prisoner. "Abinadi," the king said in a loud voice, his smile twisted. "How was your visit with the rats?"

The priests' laughter roared through the room.

The king's eyes glinted with delight, but his voice was harsh. "We have deliberated your case for three days. Because of your blasphemous words against me and my people, you have been found guilty. Your crime is worthy of death."

Although Abinadi expected as much, his body shivered at the words.

Noah rubbed his meaty hands together, his face pulled into a stern glower. "And, unless you retract your destructive words, we will have no choice but to follow through with your punishment. This is your last chance."

Abinadi stared at the king until the monarch glanced uncomfortably away. Then Abinadi looked at every priest, saying, "I will not recall the words which I have spoken, for they are true. I have come here, knowing that I would be punished. I accept death if that is your demand." He knew he *was* willing to die in the name of the Lord. With every part of his soul he believed that true salvation came through the Lord. It was true. *All of it.* His mortal life had no great significance in the realm of eternal life with God.

His gaze found the king's again. Noah's face had darkened, and Abinadi's voice rose almost as a clap of thunder. "But know this: if you slay me, you will be shedding innocent blood." Warmth now surged through him as he felt the sure presence of the Lord in the room. He spread his arms wide, pulling from the guards who clasped them. "Your deed—my execution—will stand as a testimony against you at the last day." Abinadi's gaze bore into each person on the platform. "Against *all* of you!"

The guards recoiled, and the priests fell quiet as if they, too, could feel the sudden power pulsing through Abinadi. No one spoke. No one moved.

Noah shrank back a half step, his expression one of mixed astonishment and fear. For an instant, he appeared bewildered. He turned toward Amulon, who rose and deferentially whispered in the king's ear. The priest on Noah's other side, rising energetically to his feet, also bowed slightly and whispered to the king.

A spark of hope ignited in Abinadi's chest where none had burned before. Maybe Noah would recant his sentence and Abinadi would see his wife and son again. Perhaps this was a test—like Abraham's of old.

At the far end, two of the priests broke from their trance and stood from their chairs, one shouting, "He has reviled our king!" The other lifted a fist and yelled, "Kill him!"

The horrible words pierced Abinadi's heart, but he kept his gaze on the king. Noah nodded to the two priests at his side, his eye growing bold again. Amulon moved away from the king, his arms crossed, a sneer on his face. One by one each of the priests stood and joined the chanting. "Kill him! Kill him!" Their voices thundered in the temple, reverberating against the walls.

After what seemed an eternity of jeering chants, Noah lifted his arms for silence. In the sudden quiet, it seemed as though even the once-holy walls held their breath.

King Noah's voice was calm, clear, and full of authority. "Let it be done."

One

And thou shalt love the Lord thy God with all thine heart.
(Deuteronomy 6:5)

THREE YEARS EARLIER

A breeze ran like a tremor through the green stalks of maize, bending the matured plants in the heat of the sun. It was as if they bowed to acknowledge the melancholy sound of the conch shell, which was announcing another marriage for King Noah.

At least the sound was melancholy to Abinadi. A Nephite girl born beautiful and noble had little choice in her destiny. He thought about all of those women for King Noah's court alone . . . Abinadi lifted his gaze and stared across the neat rows of crops planted in the field at the northern edge of the city of Nephi. This was his homeland. He had been born here, four and twenty years ago, during King Zeniff's reign.

His family had once owned this parcel of land under Zeniff's rule, but when the king's son Noah took over the kingdom, the people were so heavily taxed that eventually most sold their homesteads to the king just to survive. Abinadi focused once more on carrying his load up the path. The bundle on his back was strapped to his head, held in place with a band that stretched across his forehead. The bundle was packed with ripened maize, ready to be sold at the market. But first he had to stop at the king's treasury to pay his one-fifth part in taxes.

On the way to the treasury he would pass *her* house—a young woman whose beauty exceeded that of most of the ladies already at court. As he moved forward at a labored pace, Abinadi's pulse involuntarily quickened beneath the heat of the sun. Whisperings throughout the town had said that she was close to becoming betrothed, so Abinadi had been relieved to hear that the king's new wife was a different woman. The king seemed to marry at least twice a year—the number of his wives totaled a healthy dozen already. At least for now Raquel was saved from the greedy king.

Raquel. The name hovered in his mind, although he dared not speak it. Just saying it aloud might somehow allow another to discover his thoughts. He had watched her from afar over the past year. Although she was outwardly beautiful, he was drawn to more than her appearance. He'd seen her wander the market, stopping to help an elderly person or young child. It was as if her beauty and kindness radiated from within and she couldn't help but share it.

If only he had a chance to make his feelings known . . .

Abinadi scoffed at himself, stopping in his path. How could he entertain such a possibility or expect a woman like Raquel to do so? He had nothing. He labored in the fields day after day, with no wealth to show for it, only food on the table for his elderly mother.

And his home was a lonely one. His two sisters had long since married and moved into their in-laws' homes. His older brother, Helam, lived in a secluded settlement organized by a group of elders—former priests in Zeniff's court. His brother preferred seclusion, for his face made many uncomfortable. When Helam was twelve, he and his father had cleared a field for planting. They'd burned the debris, and the intensity of the fire had gone out of control—Helam was surrounded by the flames and suffered severe deformities. Usually Abinadi helped with crop-burning too, but that day he'd been ill. Their father never recovered from the guilt and abandoned both his family and the city of Nephi, never to return—leaving Abinadi with an equal burden of guilt. He thought that if he'd just been there to help, he might have been able to somehow prevent his brother's injuries.

Abinadi's thoughts returned to somewhat less painful subjects, settling, of course, on Raquel. She lived in close proximity to Noah's court in a stately home, her father a high priest and military commander. Abinadi was far below Raquel's class, so her family would never take an offer of marriage seriously. What was he next to a military commander or a high priest? Just a quiet, poor farmer . . . no one significant.

"Abinadi, the Teacher sent me to find you."

He turned to face the young boy who ran toward him along the dusty path. Abinadi smiled as the lad came to a swift stop. "The Teacher knows I'm selling at the market today, Ben."

The boy's breathing came heavily, and his thin chest expanded and sank with each gasp. He glanced quickly about him, then whispered, "There's a meeting tonight among the elders from the city, and the Teacher wants you to discuss the plan."

Abinadi nodded and placed his sweaty palm on the boy's shoulder. "I'll be there," he whispered back. The boy took his task very seriously, and Abinadi was grateful for it. Though he couldn't help but smile at Ben's enthusiasm for keeping a secret, Abinadi also knew that there would indeed be real danger if the meetings were ever discovered. Every month the "Teacher"—an elder named Gideon—came from his secret settlement to the city in order to meet with the elders who still lived within the land of Nephi.

Abinadi handed the boy an ear of maize and received a gapped grin in return.

"You've lost more teeth?"

"Two more." A grave look passed over Ben's face. "But I can still eat this." He waved the golden vegetable in front of him.

"Very good." Abinadi refrained from laughing. "Be on your way, then."

With haste, Ben turned on his heel and ran back in the direction he'd come. It seemed the boy had another message to deliver—with equal discretion and enthusiasm.

If only everyone could be as pure and eager to learn as Ben, Abinadi mused. He'd heard stories from his mother about how things used to be, before the reign of King Noah. People like his brother, Helam, would not have become outcasts. The poor, the ill, and the crippled were taken care of under Zeniff's rule. Perhaps, if that were still the case, his father would have stayed. *Perhaps.* Yet, as Abinadi neared his twenty-fifth year, he had an increasingly difficult time understanding how his father could have deserted his family—guilt-ridden or not.

I could never abandon the ones I love, no matter what the reason. Abinadi pushed forward again, stretching his neck against the weight of the bundle. The activities he'd participate in tonight would be another deterrent to someone like Raquel. If the secret meetings were ever discovered, Raquel's father would be the first to prosecute Abinadi.

I might as well forget about her now. But it was too late for that. As he rounded the final stretch of maize, he saw the outer courtyard that belonged to her home. Since it was late afternoon, he assumed she'd be inside, far away from his curious eyes. Yet he couldn't help but wonder what she was doing inside those walls. Then his step slowed, and he nearly lost his footing.

She sat in the courtyard, alone, working at a freestanding loom. Her back was to him, but he knew it was Raquel. Her ginger-colored hair spilled over her shoulders, intermingling with the delicate iridescent blue and green feathers that adorned her exquisite cape.

Abinadi didn't know whether to creep past her without a sound or to increase his pace and rush by. Before he could decide, he heard her humming. The sound stopped abruptly as he neared, and he glanced over at her, just catching a glimpse of her profile. Her lashes were lowered over her dark eyes—eyes that contrasted with her golden skin. She did not lift her head, but continued her methodical weaving of the fine cottony thread from a ceiba tree.

Abinadi's stomach tightened at the sight of her slim fingers deftly working the loom. He wished he could sit on the outer wall and simply watch her.

Since she gave him no acknowledgment, he continued silently, knowing it would be impolite to interrupt her work with a greeting. Raquel was stoic as he passed, not even casting a wayward glance in his direction. It was as if he were as invisible as he felt. He focused his gaze on the path as he leaned forward and put more strength into carrying the bundle.

This is the last time I'll pass by this place. Raquel was likely to be betrothed before the end of the year, and his heart would need to be well turned from her when it happened.

"Farewell," he mouthed. But he still couldn't bring himself to utter her name. *Farewell, dear . . .*

* * *

Raquel kept her head down until Abinadi passed. She hoped he hadn't noticed the tremble in her hands as she wove the shuttle through the kapok threads. When he was a good two dozen paces away, she raised her eyes. She could only see the back of him now, but that didn't change the memory of his face in her mind—the deep, sorrowful eyes, amber-colored complexion, heavy eyebrows, and angular chin. He was tall, far taller than her father and other men who came around the house. And he was younger, probably in his mid-twenties, than those men who continually cajoled her as she explored the herbs at the market.

She'd heard the women discuss him at the well in the center of town, but she'd always kept quiet. He was not the most handsome man in the city, but he had a commanding presence, one strangely combined with humility. Yet he was so quiet that Raquel couldn't recall ever hearing him speak. She knew without asking what her father thought of him. He was associated with the tribe of elders, a dying breed who had been part of King Zeniff's court, and although Abinadi was much too young to have advised Zeniff, any association with the elders immediately put a black mark upon a man in her father's eyes.

Late at night, she'd lain awake listening to her father's plans to discover the elders in some act of defiance or treasonous activity against King Noah. Then they would be hauled off to the court. Only one punishment was handed down to the treasonous: death by fire. They would burn for their beliefs—beliefs that were contrary to the laws of the land. Beliefs that made Raquel think more than she should. But whenever she asked her mother about God or about their ancestors' beliefs, her mother quickly reprimanded her by saying those were things only the high priests knew about.

Raquel's aching hands slowed their pace, and she realized that she'd been absentmindedly working for several moments. "Oh no," she muttered, looking at the threads she'd missed. She'd have to undo part of the weaving.

From her position in the courtyard, she heard occasional joyous shouts and equally joyous singing. King Noah had taken another wife today—Maia, a girl younger than Raquel by a full year. Not that Raquel was old at seventeen, but most of her friends were at least discussing marriage with their mothers. Raquel could never bring herself to mention such a thing, although she knew her parents talked about it when she wasn't in the same room.

That could only mean one thing, she knew. They would choose someone she didn't like—someone old or short. Or even a man who had a brood of children but no wife to care for them. *It would probably serve me right,* Raquel thought. She hadn't exactly been the devoted daughter that she should be. Maybe in deed, but not in mind. She wondered if any other daughter in the city felt so disgusted with her surroundings.

With a tug, Raquel tightened the shuttle and began weaving again. She knew she was ungrateful and spoiled. She wore luxurious clothing, ate the finest food, and had servants to do the heavy chores. In fact, her mother didn't even like her to weave, but Raquel insisted that it was better than embroidery. She never could get her clumsy hands to cooperate with a small bone needle and such thin thread. Fortunately her mother didn't bother her if she was weaving or spending time in the garden cultivating the herbal plot—though that was also something her mother thought a waste of time. Growing and collecting herbs had been her grandmother's passion, and now it was the only way Raquel could hold on to her grandmother's memory. The herbal practices were said to have been handed down from woman to woman all the way back to one of the daughters of Father Lehi.

This is why Raquel visited the market to ask questions of the Kaminaljuyú tribal women who came to sell their herbal remedies. They had solutions for everything from a painful tooth to childbirth pains.

During the afternoons when Raquel wasn't in the garden, she sat in the courtyard, mindlessly weaving blocks of fabric. She didn't know where they went when she finished, and she didn't care. The activity gave her peace and quiet away from the household to think about her secret. The secret that she knew she could die for, no matter who her parents were.

* * *

That evening, when Abinadi slipped out of his childhood home, his mother had been asleep for quite some time. He moved silently through the fields that led to the city.

In the distance, torches blazed, surrounding King Noah's expansive home. The palace sat upon a hill near the reconstructed temple that had originally been built by their ancestor Nephi. The newer walls topped the crumbled ones. It was a scene of contrasts: the wicked had survived and flourished; the righteous had fallen into decay, almost forgotten.

Almost.

The thought sent Abinadi scurrying across the final path, and he breathed a sigh of relief as he reached the last rows of maize. As on many previous nights, he found it easy to blend in with the crops—easier than trying to fit in with the people of King Noah.

In the thin light of the moon, Abinadi made his way through the rows. The breeze had cooled enough that he drew his cloak about his waist and fastened it with a sash. In his mind he went over the new things he'd been taught over the past several moons—specifically the plan of salvation. It made more sense than any doctrine he'd heard from Noah's priests. And tonight he would recite it for the elders. A shiver traveled along his arms. He knew that the words of God were true, but he wished he didn't have to speak in front of others. Helam was the one with the gift of speech—yet he rarely appeared at public meetings, preferring to study alone or with the elders only. He also remained hidden in the elders' settlement, away from curious stares. But the few times Abinadi had heard his brother teach had been astonishing.

Abinadi's own belief in God was personal, sacred, quiet. He'd rather toil in the fields all night long than preach in front of other people about what was most dear to him. Abinadi moved more quickly, as if running faster would calm his nervous heart. As he reached the edge of the maize field, he moved upward along the sloping hill. He hurried as fast as he dared through the agave vineyards, not wanting to attract attention from the guards. Noah valued his agave wine so much that he'd positioned guards day and night around the spiked plants. But it seemed no guards were in place tonight—a rare occasion possibly due to the marriage celebration.

The smell of the sweet honeylike nectar of the agave accosted Abinadi's senses. For an instant, he nearly sympathized with Noah's passion for abundant wine. The sweet aroma made Abinadi want to languish among the plants and let the night slip away uninterrupted. But he pressed forward and soon cleared the heady vineyard. When he entered the line of trees he breathed a second sigh of relief. He was now well out of view of any guards or the odd soldier on the king's errand.

He slowed when he neared the cave entrance that wasn't noticeable to the casual observer. But Abinadi knew what he was looking for, so he soon spotted the outline of the narrow opening through the foliage. Quietly he moved to the entrance. Then he picked up a pebble and threw it into the long shaft—the customary announcement of his arrival. He waited for the small rock to be thrown back, a sign that he could safely enter.

A minute passed, then two. Abinadi's heart started to pound as he thought of reasons why there would be no return pebble. He picked up another and tossed it into the interior, hearing the reverberation of the rock against stone. But no return signal came.

Straining to hear any sound or movement, Abinadi waited several moments, wondering if they'd left. Or perhaps he was early. His pulse drummed as he thought about the final possibility: they'd been discovered and ambushed. What if one of the elders was injured with no one to help?

With his heart thumping against his chest, Abinadi took a few steps into the cave. The sudden cool was expected, but tonight it prickled his skin, seeming to seep into his bones. He spotted a crumpled head covering. As he picked it up, his stomach twisted. Someone had fled this cave quickly. He moved forward again, and a half dozen paces ahead, the walls glowed with firelight. He hoped he was wrong and they just hadn't heard his signal. With a more confident step, he continued forward, thinking the elders had moved to the blessings. That would explain the delay in signaling him to enter.

The cave was more of a vault, said to have been originally constructed by Fathers Nephi and Jacob to conceal the Liahona, the sword of Laban, and the brass plates. Since then, the vault had been widened into a cavern that could hold several dozen people—perfect for secret meetings. Each time Abinadi entered, he felt as if he were somehow walking on hallowed ground.

As he rounded the bend that opened into the cavern, Abinadi stopped short. A small fire crackled in a pit in the center of the room, but the chamber was empty. Various mats surrounded the fire pit as if they were waiting for their occupants to return. Abinadi spun around, searching for clues.

Abinadi circled the fire, glancing around the empty room, trying to understand where everyone had gone. He crouched against the ground and studied the footprint patterns, seeing nothing unusual. Then he saw a spot of color on the other side of the fire pit. A brilliant green feather lay on the ground. None of the elders or the apprentices wore anything as costly as feathers, which meant that it belonged to an outsider—a wealthy Nephite or . . . a Lamanite.

Abinadi snapped his head up at the realization, then he retrieved the feather and tucked it into his sash, out of sight. With swift strokes he kicked dirt over the fire, then, feeling his way through the new darkness, he moved out of the tunnel toward the fresh night air.

He exited the cave, finally straightening his tall frame outside the low opening. A thud echoed in his ears, and he felt a tremendous pressure on his neck, squeezing so hard that he gasped for air. It took him a second to realize that a pair of strong hands was choking him. He brought his own hands up in defense and tried to wrench away from the assailant. A voice hissed in his ear. "Make another sound and this blade will cut out your heart."

* * *

Raquel knew she shouldn't do this week after week, yet as she tied a turban over her head, covering her hair and part of her face, excitement coursed through her. She wore a rough-sewn tunic common to the young boys of the city. She tied a pouch to a rope around her waist—just in case she came across any useful plants. Once a week, Raquel joined the group of shepherds who tended her father's flocks. Thinking she was just another hired servant, none of the shepherds ever bothered her. And when they spoke to her, she merely answered with a masculine grunt.

It was her one escape from the mundane lifestyle she had to endure day after day. Only her cousin Seth knew her secret. He was the one who'd made the suggestion in the first place after growing tired of hearing her complaints. Her father's flocks grazed the land just north of King Noah's vineyards. Typically the flocks required only two or three shepherds to watch, but since a recent raid by the Lamanites, the number of shepherds had doubled. Seth had been called in to help, and Raquel went with him. The threat of the Lamanites only made the adventure more exciting, she decided. Spending time with her younger cousin on a quiet hillside wasn't nearly as thrilling as listening to the shepherds' stories of past battles. And now, with the added danger, the shepherds spent most of their time predicting what might happen.

Seth had warned her against coming tonight because of the celebratory nature of the king's court—the streets would be filled with drunken and brazen men. But Raquel was sure that none of them would bother her if she were dressed as a shepherd boy. A smile, concealed by her scarf, widened across her face as she moved through her parents' courtyard. All she had to do was make it to the road and no one would be able to tell where she'd come from.

Before leaving the house, she crept through the rear garden and stopped at a small hut that housed the tools for gardening and her herbal collection. She pulled open the reed door, splashing moonlight and illuminating the baskets and jars filled with dried herbs and plants. Raquel's practiced eyes scanned the contents to see if she was low on any one particular herb, evaluating the groupings of dried hibiscus, apple leaves and magnolia tree leaves, dried papaya, and leaves from the sour orange plant. She peered inside the jar of willow bark. Only two strips left. She'd have to remember to search for more of the pain-relieving bark along the way. Listening for any stirring within the house, she quietly slipped through the garden, around the house, and into the courtyard.

Sticking to the side paths, Raquel hurried along, enjoying the freedom that the lightweight men's tunic gave her. Her beaded and feathered clothing left at home, she felt as if a burden had been lifted. She only wished that her hands and feet were calloused like the shepherds'. As it was, her feet throbbed with blisters, which she would carefully tend to by applying her homemade guava paste when she returned home from the fields.

Loud laughter rang out a few paces ahead, and Raquel came to an abrupt stop. She hesitated, wondering if she dared pass by the two people who seemed to be embracing. She turned right and made her way through a narrow passageway between two houses. This part of the city was known for its riotous living. She had overheard stories from the servants, and now she marveled to herself, thinking about what her mother would say if she were caught.

"Come inside, young man, I have something special for you."

Raquel whirled to face the speaker. She was startled to see a tall, beautiful woman standing in front of her. An easy smile crept to the woman's face.

"Ah, you are inexperienced." The woman's eyes took in Raquel's appearance. "Tonight will be my gift to you."

Raquel opened her mouth in shock then closed it quickly. She managed to mutter in a deepened voice, "N-no thank you." She hurried past the woman, her pulse wild with fear. It wouldn't take much for her identity to be discovered—and to be found in such a place would definitely anger her parents. She shuddered, grateful that the woman didn't pursue her or send someone after her. Raquel started running, passing the sounds of laughter and music coming from the surrounding buildings.

She nearly vowed not to take this chance again, but still she did not turn for home. If this was to be her last time out, she'd make it worthwhile.

Two

I have gone astray like a lost sheep.
(Psalm 119:176)

Music from the flutes, panpipes, and drums pulsed through the throne room, causing the hanging drapes to sway as if keeping time. Alma stared at the surroundings and soaked in every detail. An elaborate bamboo cage housed a fine collection of quetzal birds—some larger than he'd ever seen. In the center of the room, King Noah sat with his new bride as a troupe of magicians displayed their latest tricks. The king's laughter boomed over the music, and the wedding crowd echoed his laugh. Against the walls, low tables held varied dishes of spicy food—meats, tamalitos, quail eggs, pears, nuts—piled high on silver and gold platters.

Alma smiled, hardly believing he, a simple carpenter, was here in the center of the king's weeklong wedding festivities. He was only twenty, and yet he had been invited as a personal guest of the king. If his parents had been alive, they would have been truly shocked. They had been a part of Zeniff's court, but after the old king died, everything at court changed. Alma's father, Cephas, had been Zeniff's intellectual advisor, a meticulous scholar. But now a new king was in power, and the old ways of the previous king had been put to rest.

Alma gazed about the room, seeing that there was nothing intellectual going on in this festivity. He looked at his hands, strong and hardened through his occupation. Crafting furniture could never compare to his father's scholarly abilities.

Trying not to let the memory of his parents ruin the evening, Alma focused on the new bride. No one could argue against her beauty. Her dark hair shimmered like copper, even in the dull glare of the torchlight. Her skin was flushed, yet it had no blemish or dark spot of any kind. But it was her melodic voice that had entranced Noah when she'd first come to sing at court.

Alma smiled. On that day, a few weeks earlier, it seemed every man had fallen in love. Alma had just delivered a newly constructed judgment-seat to the palace when the singer was led into the throne room. Her voice carried throughout the halls, and Alma hovered in the entryway, listening in fascination.

The mere fact that Alma was Maia's distant relative had brought Noah's attention to him, and suddenly he was the favored citizen—the man to secure the betrothal. It hadn't been hard, at least not after he'd presented the bride price to her parents. The young virgin had urged her parents to take the gold and silver. They would be able to live the rest of their lives in comfort, and the only cost was for their daughter to marry the king.

The chance of a lifetime.

And now at the wedding, Alma tapped his foot in time with the rhythm. The final magician created a haze of smoke and disappeared. Noah clapped loudly, and Alma joined in with the others, bringing his calloused hands together. Then everyone grew quiet as the young bride stood. Maia cast a smile upon her king—now husband—then gazed over the audience. For an instant, Alma's eyes locked with hers. He was surprised to see not delight and gratitude, but a deep melancholy just beyond her thick lashes. However, the impression was quelled in the next moment as she opened her mouth and sang.

The beautiful words of a traditional wedding song seemed to fill his entire being. The melodic prose was haunting and soft, soon growing in strength and power.

The most alluring moon has risen over the forest;
It is going to burn suspended in the center of the sky
To lighten all the earth, all the woods—shining its light on all.
Sweetly comes the air and the perfume.
Happiness permeates all good men.

The girl smiled as she sang the sweet words about a man and woman's joyous coming together. Alma smiled in reply, although he knew the girl sang to her new husband. While the singing was beautiful, the lyrics left him unsatisfied in a strange way. He lifted the jeweled goblet to his lips and drank heartily of the free-flowing wine. As the sweetness coursed down his throat, it became easy to ignore the sense of the girl's sadness and to believe in the good fortune that any girl had in marrying a king. He watched her smile at her new husband, and Alma decided that Maia had made a good future for herself. When she finished, the gathering broke out into another song.

A hand reached through the crowd and squeezed Alma's shoulder. He turned to see Amulon, a giant of a man, already staggering with drink. His chest was bare, but over his shoulders hung a coat of jaguar skin. Jewels dotted his fingers and earlobes. The elaborate headdress he usually wore was replaced with a band of gold. The man was at least forty, but his muscular physique made him look younger than their thirty-five-year-old king. Amulon slung an arm around Alma and gave him a friendly embrace. "You are on the record, my friend."

"What?" Alma asked, not sure he'd heard correctly over the singing. He'd had enough wine himself not to be offended by the man's foul breath.

"The king's record. We discussed your name last night." Amulon jabbed Alma with an elbow. "This union, this marriage"—he held his goblet in the air, sloshing wine over the brim—"is all because of you. And the king doesn't forget those who help him."

What's the record for? Alma wanted to ask, but Amulon had joined in the bawdy singing that made speaking impossible. A young boy sidled up to them and refilled their wine goblets. *I've had enough*, Alma thought. He looked around, seeing that everyone else continued drinking, not seeming to care how much they consumed. He took a few more gulps as the song finished.

"And now, my new friend," Amulon said into his ear, "the female guests leave, and the real entertainment begins."

Alma craned his neck to see a group of ladies lead the bride out of the room. The crowd thinned as the other women also took their leave. Alma's heart thudded in anticipation. One part of him said that now would be a good time to slip away, but the other part was too curious. After all, he was a personal guest of the king.

Noah commanded his priests to join him in the center of the room. Cushions were brought in by servants, and the men took their places around the king. Amulon grabbed Alma's tunic and pulled him along. "You're invited, too."

"I'm not a priest," Alma started to protest.

"Don't worry about that, my friend," Amulon said with a hearty laugh.

They pushed through the crowd, and when they reached the king, Alma suddenly felt the excess agave wine rebel in his stomach. His vision wasn't as clear as usual, and his head felt like it floated above his body. Noah smiled at the two of them and waved them over to a pair of cushions. Amulon settled next to Alma. "See what I told you? You'll be made a priest soon enough."

Priest? A priest of King Noah? Alma could hardly believe the words. His besotted mind tried to mull over the changes it would bring to his simple life. Everything would change. He stared at the goblet in his hands, watching the varying color of wine illuminated by the flickering torchlight. Being a priest meant duty, power, honor, residence at court . . . *gold*. He would be equal to his father at last . . .

An image flashed through his mind—the face of his father and a clear picture of his disappointment as Alma served an impious ruler.

Wild clapping caused Alma to look up from his goblet and shake his reproving thoughts away. His parents were long buried and no longer held any power over him. This was another time, a different king, and altered rules. Blinking rapidly to clear his vision, Alma stared at the scene in front of him. Several veiled women had entered the room. They slowly danced, circling the king and each priest. Apparently they weren't aware that Alma wasn't one, because he received a good deal of attention. Somewhere from the other side of the room, he heard low music, but his senses focused on the girls.

What would Noah's new wife think? Alma wondered, realizing at the same moment why she'd been taken out of the room. Did she know what was going on here? Alma's stomach rumbled loudly, capturing his attention. The lightheadedness returned as one of the girls moved very close to him. Close enough to touch. He kept his hands gripped on the goblet, noticing that the other men didn't refrain from touching the women. Some of the priests stood and moved with the women as the others shouted encouragement. Alma glanced at Amulon—the man's eyes were glazed in pleasure, perspiration beaded on his face and torso.

Instinct told Alma to leave the room and get away from this carnal scene. The stories he'd heard of King Noah's court were now confirmed.

But then a feather touched the back of his neck, and he turned. He looked into the large, beautifully painted eyes of a woman. She took his hand and pulled him toward her. He reluctantly stood, feeling embarrassed. But the others didn't seem to notice his hesitation. His face heated as he thought of excuses for why he couldn't dance with her. Amulon's laughter cut through his uneasy thoughts, his voice sailing over the pulsing music. "Relax, my new friend. Enjoy your success."

Alma's mind reeled as the woman's hands caressed his arms. She guided him into sensual movements, and he found himself following. He closed his eyes, thinking maybe it would all go away like a strange dream. But the music continued, and the dancing continued, and the wine . . .

Oh no, Alma thought as his stomach pierced with pain. He tried to mutter an apology to the woman before dropping to his knees. In an instant, all that he'd eaten or drunk that night was lost.

* * *

Everything hurts, Abinadi thought. There was probably not one part of his body without a bruise. Even so, he was grateful to still be alive. He stared into the darkness at his surroundings. The attacker had left him in a clearing with several other victims. Some of them weren't moving at all, and he heard pitiful moaning coming from one nearby. Even with his arms and legs tied, Abinadi was able to struggle into a sitting position. In the moonlight, he barely made out the groaning man's features—and the clothing that identified him as a shepherd.

Scooting closer, he said softly, "Are you all right?" When the man turned, Abinadi saw that he was young—perhaps twelve or thirteen.

The boy said, "I'm better off than the rest." His eyes shone with unshed tears. "It's my cousin I'm worried about. She planned to meet me at the fields tonight."

"She?"

"Yes. It's dangerous enough for her to go against her father's wishes, but now I have no way to warn her." His pleading gaze met Abinadi's. "They killed some of the shepherds already."

"Who did?" Abinadi asked.

"Lamanites," the boy said, his face registering surprise at the fact that Abinadi didn't already know. "They've been closing in on the borders for weeks. But I didn't think they'd attack us."

Abinadi nodded, his questions falling silent. He'd known about the extra military force along the borders of the land, but for Lamanites to come as far as the grazing fields was unheard of. "What part of the city are you from?"

"South of the king's palace. My name is Seth." He looked around as if worried someone might overhear. "I'm not really a shepherd. I'm just helping with my uncle's flocks."

So he's not a commoner like me if he lives south of the palace. "I'm Abinadi."

"I thought I recognized you," Seth said.

Abinadi stiffened, wondering if that were good or bad. He had never seen this young man before.

"I've seen you with Ben," Seth added.

It was as if a knife pierced Abinadi's chest as Seth spoke the name. He'd forgotten that the boy should have been at the meeting too. He inhaled sharply as myriad thoughts passed through his mind. "Yes, I know Ben," he finally said, wondering how much he should reveal. Nothing that wasn't necessary. "He was supposed to meet me tonight. Have you seen him or heard anything about him?"

"No," Seth said. "I doubt the Lamanites would bother a young boy."

I hope he's right, Abinadi thought. Ben was only eight years old, but he had the intellect of a much older boy. Abinadi prayed the child was smart enough to stay clear of the enemy. He looked at Seth again. "How much time do you think we have before the Lamanites return?"

"Not long. I think they're probably raiding the wine presses," Seth answered.

"I hope they'll drink themselves into a stupor."

Seth nodded. "Except they might be even more ill-tempered then." He scooted to Abinadi's side and peered at him closely. "If you know Ben, you're probably one of *them.*"

"Who?" The hairs on Abinadi's arms stood. Such a statement had never led to anything positive.

"The religious ones—I don't know what you call yourselves—but the king keeps a close watch on your leader . . . what's his name? Gideon?"

Abinadi's heart sank. This young man knew more than he should. The Teacher was in fact Gideon, but not many knew that. "How do you know him?"

Before Seth could answer, the piercing cry of a howler monkey cut across the clearing.

They're coming. Adrenaline sliced through Abinadi as he waited for the first appearance of the Lamanites. The dozen or so living captives instinctively edged toward the center until they became one mass. It probably wouldn't make a difference, but for a brief moment, it gave them a small sense of security.

Three

And it shall come to pass, that whosoever shall call on the
name of the Lord shall be delivered.
(Joel 2:32)

The fields were empty—too empty. Raquel strained to see through the darkness. Where were the sheep? The men? A whisper of warning touched her back, and the hairs on her neck stood. Instinctively, she crouched and placed her hands on the steady ground. What was going on? Where was Seth?

She was sure he'd told her to meet him here at the north field by the agave presses. Her breathing had slowed after her mad sprint through the city, and now she could hear the wind as it stirred the nearby branches. She glanced uneasily at the forest south of the pasture. No matter how reckless she'd been in coming here by herself, she wouldn't venture there alone—in the dark.

Raquel wrapped her arms around her knees, hugging them tightly against her chest. She couldn't just wait here all night, but she didn't want to return home yet. She looked around wondering if Seth had tricked her. Even as she thought it, she laughed at herself. He had just told her the wrong field by mistake. But what if . . . what if something had happened to her cousin? No, she decided, the sheep would still be with the other shepherds. She rose to her feet, ignoring the touch of fear that slid along her arms.

She waited as long as she could stand it, her courage ebbing into boredom, then anxiety. She could search for some plants and herbs, but most of them grew near the line of trees, which loomed a little too dark. There was nothing to do except return home. But this time, she planned to keep to the outskirts of the city to avoid any more unsavory encounters.

Just as she rose to her feet, she saw something black scurry between two trees. Raquel covered her mouth to silence her own scream. Maybe it was an animal, perhaps a wild boar. Heart pounding, she walked toward the rows of maize, careful to steer clear of the edge of the forest.

Suddenly, the dark shape burst out of the trees and hurled toward her. Raquel froze in place, staring, unbelieving, as it grew closer. "Help," it cried.

Help? Animals didn't talk.

The shape was too tall for a boar, and it had two legs. *A child.*

"Help!"

The child didn't slow as he reached Raquel, but plowed into her, knocking both of them to the ground. Stunned for an instant, Raquel finally pushed the child off of her. The young boy's eyes were large with panic.

"What's wrong?" she asked, grabbing his arm.

Tears rolled down his cheeks as he stared at her. "Help."

Raquel peered at him in the moonlight. He looked slightly familiar, but his round face and brown clothing didn't give any clues. "What's your name?"

He took a ragged gulp of air. "Ben."

"All right, Ben," Raquel said, feeling sorry for this boy while at the same time becoming increasingly worried for Seth.

"They're following me," Ben whispered. "They caught the Teacher, and they tried to catch me." He started to tremble.

"*Who's* following you?" she asked.

"The Lamanites."

A shot of dread coursed through Raquel. She looked at the tree line, trying to see any hovering forms there. Her skin crawled to think of blood-thirsty men hunting down a young boy. Or girl. "You must come with me, and we'll find help," she whispered. She stood and pulled Ben alongside her. "We'll keep cover in the stalks, and when we reach the city, we'll find someone to help."

He was already shaking his head. "No—they'll kill the Teacher and his elders."

Raquel let out a low breath. The "teacher" must be their leader. "If your friends live in the city of Nephi, they'll be protected under the king," she said.

"No." Ben's voice was scarcely above a whisper. He looked at the ground and shuffled his feet. "He's not favored by the king."

"The king will overlook your friends' beliefs to fight the Lamanites," Raquel said. A shade of hope was restored to the young boy's face. "Come on, Ben. If we are to help your friend, we must hurry." Then another thought occurred to her. In spite of what she had just told Ben, Raquel knew that chances were slim that the king would send his men to save religious zealots. But if the shepherds were attacked, the king might be roused to action. A new shard of fear pierced Raquel. The life of this teacher, and perhaps Seth, might depend on her actions after all. "Do you know Seth?" she asked.

"I . . . don't think so. Is he an elder?"

A wry smile crossed Raquel's otherwise anxious face. "No. He's my cousin. But he was out here with the sheep." She gazed over the empty fields, her heart telling her that something bad had happened to him. With greater urgency, she said, "Let's go."

They plunged into the maize and started running. Adrenaline propelled her forward, and she ran as fast as she dared without losing Ben. She couldn't believe this was happening. Mixed fortune had brought her here tonight. She just hoped she wasn't too late to get help for Seth and the others.

Ben tugged at her robe, and she looked over at him. He slowed to a stop, his thin chest heaving. "I can't leave the Teacher behind."

"We're not leaving him—we're finding help," Raquel said. She'd never met anyone so obstinate. "If the Lamanites have captured our people, King Noah will send an army and rescue them." At least she hoped Seth or the other shepherds would be reason enough for the king to take action.

"I must protect the Teacher from the Lamanites *and* from King Noah," Ben said, his eyes fearful.

"How?" Raquel asked. "You're just a young boy."

His expression hardened. "I made a promise to the Lord."

Raquel bent forward and placed both of her hands on his shoulders. "You'll keep that promise by coming with me. We'll get help, but we have to stay together for our own protection." She wanted to shake some sense into the child.

The boy still hesitated. Then he did something very strange. He knelt on the ground and bowed his head.

"What are you doing?" Raquel whispered. "We've got to hurry." She leaned down, ready to grab his arm, when she heard his soft words—pleading and supplicating.

"O God of our righteousness. On this night, spare the Teacher and all the men who are in danger. Show us the way. We are indebted to Thee for Thy kind mercies, O Lord. Amen." The boy opened his eyes. "All right. I'm ready."

Raquel shook her head in shock. "Only the king and the priests can pray."

"No," Ben said, his eyes locked with hers. "Everyone can pray. The Lord will hear and answer prayers, no matter who asks—"

"Come," Raquel said, fighting the urge to laugh. She'd never heard such foolishness. As if the great God of the universe would pause in His work to listen to a little boy in the middle of a maize field. Besides, it was completely unnecessary since the priests said prayers in behalf of the community.

They zigzagged through the fields until they reached the main road to the city. Ben kept up with Raquel, but every so often, crying wracked his small frame. Raquel kept his hand in hers as they hurried along the road, first so that he wouldn't slow her down, and second because his pitiful crying was difficult to bear. She hushed him over and over, but to no effect.

Finally, she stopped and took his shoulders firmly. "Ben, you're slowing us down. You need to stop this crying. The sooner we find help, the better."

"But if I tell them the location of the Teacher and the elders . . ." A tremor of emotion passed over his face.

At once, Raquel understood his dilemma. "You won't be betraying your friends. This is a matter of life and death," she said, trying to calm his trembling body. She removed the turban from her head, and her hair tumbled past her shoulders. "My father is part of the king's court. I can speak with him and the king. If it makes you feel any better, I'll take the blame."

Ben stared up at her, clearly startled by her hidden identity. "Y-you will?"

"Of course," she said with a smile, realizing that she truly meant it. "You can trust me."

"All right," Ben said as they started again, his pace noticeably increasing.

The road widened, stretching toward the city. On the slopes that rose from the center of town, torches still blazed around the royal courtyard.

The wedding, Raquel thought. She'd almost forgotten. It would be perfect. All of King Noah's chief officers would be there. She and Ben could inform everyone at the same time. She swallowed the hard lump in her throat, knowing all she needed now was courage—courage to disturb a king on his wedding night.

They wove their way through the streets until they reached the outer wall of the king's residence. A guard rose unsteadily to his feet and leered toward her. "Come to j-join the d-dancing?"

The odor of sour wine emanated from the man. "No," Raquel breathed, taking a step back. "I need audience with the king. The Lamanites have crossed the borders."

The guard stared at her for a moment, then swayed slightly. He looked past Raquel and Ben toward the empty road. "I don't see any L-lamanites."

That's because you're drunk, Raquel wanted to retort. "They've breached the vineyards and captured some shepherds," she tried again. She squeezed Ben's trembling hand. "The king needs to be warned."

"All-ll right," the guard slurred. He staggered to his post and took a long swig of wine from a jug. Wiping his mouth with the back of his hand, he mumbled, "Come with me."

At last, Raquel thought. They followed his slow steps through the torch-lit courtyard, and she squinted against the brightness. As they neared the main hall, the music grew louder, mixed with bursts of laughter and conversation. A couple of men lounged outside the curtained entryway. They gazed at Raquel with unbridled interest, but she tried to ignore them.

"A m-message for the king," the guard announced, rocking on his heels.

"Ah," one of the men said with a greedy smile and moved toward Raquel. "I'll take her in."

She recoiled as he reached for her arm, "*We* have a message," she said, practically crushing Ben to her side.

The man looked at the boy in confusion.

"I am not a dancer," Raquel clarified.

The man's expression drooped, but his eyes stayed inquisitive. For an instant, Raquel wished she had replaced her turban. Her unbound hair was a symbol of her unmarried status. She didn't want to be rude to these men, for they certainly knew her father.

The other man joined them. "The king will not be pleased." They walked through a great hall, sounds of music and laughter growing louder. Then the man stopped before a large curtain. He pulled it aside, and Raquel stepped into the glittering interior.

Confusion hit as she stared into the massive room. A crowd of men and women were dancing—*together*—something that shouldn't happen between those who weren't married to each other. Raquel stared at the sight for a moment, then turned toward the men who had let her in. One of them grinned and motioned for her to enter. The crowd broke apart as Raquel and Ben walked across the room. In the center of the action, the king sat upon a pile of cushions. Several women dressed in next to nothing surrounded him. A priest sat near the king, with just as many women hovering over him. Then to her surprise, Raquel recognized the priest. "Father!"

A dark cloud passed over the priest's face as he registered who the girl in boy's clothing was. He shoved away the woman who leaned against him and stood. He took two strides toward Raquel, then stopped. "What are you doing here? You should be home."

Raquel tried to swallow her shock at seeing her father with all these women—as if he enjoyed it—and said, "I"—she glanced at Ben—"I have a message for the king."

Her father's eyes narrowed. "Not tonight, Raquel."

"Amulon," King Noah's voice boomed over the music, "bring the children forward."

Slowly, Amulon turned to face the king, but not before throwing Raquel a warning glare. She knew she'd just tasted her last night of freedom. Her punishment would undoubtedly be severe at best.

Gripping Ben's hand, she stepped forward and bowed low, Ben following suit. She'd never seen the king this close before. He was near enough to touch. His headdress, in the shape of a large bird, was intimidating, and the cape over his shoulders was a vibrant green. Noah's heavy jowls lifted into a smile. "I don't believe I've ever met your daughter, Amulon. You've neglected to tell me how fair she is."

"She's only seventeen," Amulon said, a strange pleading in his voice.

Raquel sensed he was furious. Her stomach twisted. Maybe her father was embarrassed that his daughter saw him in the company of other women.

But she would worry about that later. She had urgent news. "The Lamanites are here," she burst out to the king.

King Noah lifted a dark brow and leaned forward. "Lamanites?"

Raquel couldn't tell if he was mocking her or if he always wore a half-smile when receiving grave information, but she forged ahead. "They've breached the north border and captured some of the shepherds."

She cautioned a look at her father. His face was drawn into a scowl. "Seth is missing too," she said quietly.

Her father's face seemed to harden further, but he turned to the king with a slight bow. "My brother's son."

Noah's eyes finally grew serious. "Ah. Family then." He rose to his feet with some difficulty, causing the surrounding women to scatter.

Nearly everyone had stopped dancing to listen, and the soulful music ceased. Then a fleeting thought passed through Raquel's mind. Where was the king's new bride?

The king raised his hand for quiet, and the whispers turned silent. With his eyes locked on Raquel, he said, "Amulon, take thirty soldiers with you to the north border and find those shepherds."

Murmuring filled the room. Amulon grabbed his daughter by the shoulder, ready to haul her off, but she said, "Wait! There's more!"

Everyone looked at her. Her father's face reddened with sure anger.

Raquel glanced at Ben then at King Noah. "The elders of Zeniff's reign are also missing."

Noah jerked his head up and crossed to Raquel and Ben. "Who?"

Was he trying to trick her? Or did he really not know? Raquel stammered, "They—they are no longer elders, your highness, only former patrons of King Zeniff's court—"

"I know who the elders are!" Noah bellowed, his face scarlet. "Tell me their *names,* girl." The king circled Raquel and Ben, sputtering, "And never mention my father's name again in my presence."

Blood rushed to her head as she imagined all sorts of horrible punishments this great king could order upon her. Why wasn't her father stopping his ranting? She didn't know their names, and somehow she didn't think *Teacher* was sufficient. Regardless, she'd keep her promise to Ben. As far as King Noah knew, Ben was just another shepherd.

A small but strong voice spoke up. "No matter their beliefs, they've been captured by our enemies."

Noah leaned close to Ben and hissed, "Give me their *names,* boy!"

Ben dropped Raquel's hand and tilted his chin upward. "Their names are Gideon, Ezra, Timon, Nathan, and Abinadi."

Abinadi . . . The name rocked through Raquel. She had only ever heard of one man named Abinadi, so it could be no other. Seth, and now Abinadi, were in the hands of the Lamanites. Forget her father and his thirty men. She would fight herself. Pulling herself from her thoughts, she saw that Noah's gaze was focused on her, as if scrutinizing her every feature. Her face and neck grew warm until he finally looked away.

"Amulon, I need fifty men!" Noah called out as if he could read Raquel's mind. "Capture the Lamanites and throw them into the cells! Then bind the elders and bring them here."

Like an instant thunderstorm, everyone burst into action. Raquel kept Ben at her side and tried to dart out, but her father was quicker. He grabbed her by the arm, steering her out of the palace. "Go home, now!" he commanded, signaling to a guard.

Raquel nodded, tears burning beneath her eyelids. She hurried across the courtyard with Ben at her side. Outside the gate, they said a hasty good-bye and, with a forlorn look, Ben stared after Raquel as she went in the opposite direction. No one bothered her this time as she raced through the streets toward home. At least she'd delivered the warning to the king, although she might pay for the court intrusion for the rest of her life.

Four

He that sacrificeth unto any god, save unto the Lord only,
he shall be utterly destroyed.
(Exodus 22:20)

Abinadi instinctively moved in front of Seth. The short time they'd spent speaking was long enough for Abinadi to know that protecting the boy would be advantageous. Seth knew a surprising amount about the elders. Abinadi hoped to keep the alliance friendly.

As the first men stepped into the clearing, Abinadi heard the sharp intake of breath come from Seth. "Gideon," the boy whispered.

Sure enough, the unmistakable form of Gideon was thrust forward, his arms held by two burly Lamanites. Anger flooded through Abinadi as he watched them twist the Teacher's arms painfully behind him. The other elders came into view—all propelled by about a dozen Lamanite warriors.

"They're going to kill us," Seth whispered.

Abinadi nodded. He'd never seen Lamanites in full warrior dress, but the men who had started to surround them were clearly battle ready.

"Move to the center," one Lamanite shouted, obviously the leader. The front part of his head was bald, shaved clean, and two plaits of hair extended to his shoulders. His arms and face were painted a dark color—almost black. And he wore a breastplate over his torso. He wielded a huge sword the length of five hand-spans. Its wooden blade was stained a dark red—the blood of many victims. Protruding obsidian spikes edged the sword, giving it an even more deadly appearance.

Behind Abinadi, Seth tried to stand. "Wait," Abinadi said under his breath. "They haven't brought all the prisoners yet."

More Lamanites entered the clearing, the rest of the elders in tow. Abinadi scanned the men, knowing each and every one. Nathan, Ezra,

Timon . . . Then he stopped. Where was Ben? The young boy wasn't with the others. He hoped this was good news.

The elders were forced to the ground. They crumpled down with the shepherds, and Abinadi caught the stoic gaze of Gideon. There was no fear in the man's eyes as the Lamanites proceeded to tie everyone's feet together. Then the warriors stood at attention, swords trained on the huddled mass of prisoners as the Lamanite leader paced before them with a smirk on his face.

Every so often he shouted an order to one of his men, but it amounted to nothing more than moving a prisoner from one side of the circle to another. Two of the warriors were clearing brush and grass, turning over the dirt in a wide oval then outlining the shape with rocks.

When Abinadi realized what they were doing, a horrible ache took over his stomach. At the same time the thought passed through his mind, Seth spoke. "They're making a sacrificial mound."

Abinadi nodded. When warriors were traveling and didn't have access to one of their graduated and elevated temples, they created mounds of earth instead. After an enemy was caught, the warriors would sacrifice the strongest prisoner—by offering his still-beating heart to their god.

The Lamanite leader wasn't randomly moving prisoners about. He was assessing them, trying to determine who was the strongest.

The next person to be moved was Seth. A Lamanite ordered him to stand, then roughly pushed him until he took his place at the opposite side from Abinadi. With a sinking heart, Abinadi saw that only he and Gideon remained at their end. It was between the two of them. Abinadi was no soldier but had probably been picked because of his size and physical condition. *I'm not a fighter,* he thought, *just a simple farmer.* But if he could protect Gideon's life this way, then tonight he'd stand as the strongest warrior.

Before Abinadi could state his case, Gideon jumped to his feet. "I'm the leader here, take me!" he shouted.

Several Lamanites lunged toward Gideon, grabbing his arms to restrain him. But it wasn't necessary. Abinadi recognized the passive look in the elder's eyes. Gideon was going as a lamb to the slaughter.

A couple of the other elders stood to interfere in Gideon's path, but they were quickly shoved aside.

Abinadi stared at Gideon's retreating back. Their leader was closer to God than any other man Abinadi knew. Gideon was a never-ending well of wisdom and compassion. To lose a leader like this was to lose contact with God Himself. Without another thought, Abinadi rose to his full height. "He tries to protect me. Here am I. Take me instead."

Gideon whirled, oblivious to the Lamanites jockeying for position. He stared at Abinadi in surprise, which he quickly covered up with determination. "No, *I* am the leader of these people. This man is but a guard."

The Lamanites laughed. The leader strode to the two men and stood between Gideon and Abinadi, looking from one to the other with interest.

Abinadi moved forward, meeting the gaze of the Lamanite leader. "I am younger and stronger. My heart will pay your tribute."

The Lamanite folded his arms across his broad chest, the many scars on his shoulders radiating in the moonlight. "You both want to die?" A grin stretched across his face, and for a brief instant Abinadi thought both he *and* Gideon might be sacrificed . . . all their bravery for naught.

But the Lamanite leader took a step back and clapped his hands together. "You will fight for it. If you lose, your heart will be cut out tonight." He gave a curt nod and cut the ropes that held Abinadi.

"And the one who wins?" Gideon shot out.

"Will be the leader for one more day."

I'll lose the fight, Abinadi thought. *Then Gideon will continue to teach the people.* He turned to face the Teacher, but another man stood in his place. Apparently he and Gideon were each to fight their own fight. There would be no advantage gained by intentionally losing; he needed to fight for his life. Abinadi looked up at the huge warrior. It wasn't often that he met someone taller than he, but this man was enormous. His head was completely bald except for one plaited lock at the nape of his neck, and strange circular scars marked his face, as if they had been carved there on purpose. Abinadi wouldn't be surprised if he wrestled the animals he hunted to the ground, killing game with his bare hands.

The Lamanite grunted, his nostrils flaring. Then he leaned forward, moonlight glancing off the knotted muscles in his shoulders. His expansive chest heaved with anticipation. The man held no weapon. *I was right,* Abinadi thought with no satisfaction. Before he could take any sort of defensive position, the first blow landed. Abinadi reeled, his jaw smarting. He brought a hand to his face and took a step backward. The Lamanite lunged again. Abinadi leapt sideways and avoided the worst of the attack, but the Lamanite caught hold of his legs, and Abinadi dropped to the ground.

Vaguely, he heard yelling, or cheering, coming from the shepherds. Or was it the Lamanites? He managed to kick free of the bulky fighter. He scrambled to his feet, his mind spinning. The offender's black eyes didn't hesitate, and Abinadi twisted to avoid another blow to the head. They stumbled to the ground again, and the Lamanite managed to get one arm securely locked around Abinadi's neck, the other wrenching his right arm backward.

With his left hand, Abinadi reached for the man's head and yanked his long plait. The Lamanite's head snapped back, giving Abinadi just enough room to smash his forehead against the man's nose. The warrior screamed out in pain. Abinadi used the instant of agony to angle his knees and push the man off of him, then pin him to the ground. Intuition kicked in, and he pressed his full weight against the man's neck. The Lamanite slipped into unconsciousness.

The sounds of the men came into focus and Abinadi looked up, surprised to see the shepherds and elders hooting and hollering. Two legs stopped in front of him—the Lamanite leader grinned. "Care to join my army?"

Abinadi started shaking his head, then heard an awful, high-pitched cry. Everyone turned to look toward the trees as several dozen Nephites stepped into the clearing from all sides. They were surrounded.

Relief surged through Abinadi. He rose to his feet, his body trembling from both pain and exertion. They were saved.

Someone shouted, "Amulon!"

A mighty man stepped forward, decorated in military dress—breastplate, headgear, and a shield. He held a long sword in front of him. Abinadi glanced from Amulon to the Lamanite leader. The fear was plain in the Lamanite's eyes. They were outnumbered at least three to one. Amulon cocked his head to the side, and every Nephite took one step forward.

The Lamanites edged toward each other, looking to their leader for instruction. The Lamanite leader kicked the warrior who'd fallen. "Get up." But confusion was apparent in the fallen man's eyes. He staggered to his feet, his chin and neck bloody from his broken nose. But it took only an instant for the man to see the surrounding Nephites.

The warrior panicked and took several steps backward, then turned and ran, plowing right into two startled Nephites. Mayhem broke loose. The Lamanites tried to run—some of them escaping—but most of them were subdued quickly by Amulon's men. Once the king's men had transferred the ropes that bound the shepherds and elders to the Lamanites, Amulon stood before the group.

"On the order of King Noah, we'll escort you back to the city."

Abinadi had moved back to Gideon's side. They shared one look that forged an indestructible bond of kinship.

As the former captives started to follow the soldiers, Amulon said, "Wait." He moved toward the group of elders. "The king commands an audience with you tonight. Your hardships are not yet over."

A faint chill touched Abinadi. The elders were not favored by the king; in fact, some of the practices they performed had been outlawed in the city of Nephi. Never mind that the elders didn't actually practice their religious beliefs within the city.

As the Nephite soldiers pressed them forward, dizziness engulfed Abinadi. If only he could drink some water and rest for a moment. He reached for the person who stood closest to him. Then everything went black.

* * *

The first hint of morning light splashed through the narrow window of Raquel's room. She opened her eyes, startled that she'd slept at all. For several moments, she lay still, listening to the sounds of the house and surrounding courtyard. Everything was quiet—almost too quiet. Her father hadn't come home the night before, undoubtedly leading the campaign against the Lamanites.

Raquel let out a soft moan and turned onto her side. What had happened to Seth? Was he all right? Sorrow twisted her stomach for her cousin, her best friend. And what about Abinadi—the quiet man who intrigued her for reasons she couldn't explain? Had her warning come in time? Had her father assembled the soldiers quickly enough? Raquel let out a sigh of frustration and wondered how many Lamanites had breached the border.

Her father could be in just as much danger as any of the others. Then another image crossed her mind—that of King Noah's very inquisitive eyes studying her. Suddenly uncomfortable, she rose from her pole-frame bed and slipped on her sandals, then pulled a cotton cape over her shoulders. She doubted her mother was still sleeping—not with the tension of the unknown hanging in the air.

Raquel crept through the narrow halls, not wanting to disturb any of the servants. She hoped for an audience alone with her mother. Raquel stopped at her parents' room and hesitated in the entryway. Her mother was alone, sitting on the raised bed. She was hunched over and rocking slightly, murmuring something. Raquel froze, wondering if she should back out of the room and return later. If she didn't know better, she'd think her mother was praying like that little boy, Ben. But that was impossible. Her father was a priest of King Noah's court, and personal prayers were strictly prohibited. The community worshipped together, not individually.

Raquel took a shuffling step backward as her mother suddenly straightened and turned her head. Surprise flickered across her mother's face for an instant, then was gone.

"Come here," her mother said.

Raquel entered the room, trying to avoid her mother's all-knowing eyes. Itzel was a small woman, but very skilled in running an elaborate household. The only thing that Raquel wished her mother would do more was stand up to her husband. Itzel never questioned him and was always quick to obey—which just proved that she couldn't possibly have been praying.

Raquel held her breath, waiting for the chastisement.

Instead, her mother took her hand. "Where were you last night?"

She finally looked at her mother. Had she not heard the servants' gossip yet? But her mother's expression was sincere.

"I had to warn the king. I know that it was an inconvenient time, and that Father was upset I . . . interrupted the wedding celebration." She glanced away, feeling disgust as she thought about the women who had surrounded her father.

"I'm not concerned about your visit to court. I want to know where you were before that."

Raquel lowered her head. "I was going to meet Seth."

"By yourself? At night?" her mother asked in a shocked voice. She stood and crossed the room. From a corner she picked up the boy's tunic that Raquel had worn the night before. "Anything could have happened to you."

Raquel nodded numbly.

Itzel waved the rough-woven fabric. "You not only put yourself in danger, but you brought out questions of your moral character." Her eyes darkened. "Your father and I are working on a marriage match for you. If there is any question about your virtue, your chances could be lost."

A hot tear splashed onto Raquel's cheek. It had all seemed like a daring game before, but now she realized it was much, much more.

"As a high priest in King Noah's court, your father is sworn to uphold the laws of the king even when they apply to his own family." Itzel hesitated, her expression softening. "*Especially* when they apply to his own family. You don't want to be punished as an example."

Raquel sniffled in the quiet moment. Her mother's hand touched her shoulder, and Raquel wished she could lean against her mother's softness for comfort like she had as a little girl. "I hope Seth and the others are all right . . . I wish I could have—"

"There's nothing you could have done. You're not responsible for what the Lamanites do or for Seth's actions." Itzel pulled away and tilted Raquel's face toward her. "None of this is your fault."

A man's shout came from outside.

"Your father!" Itzel said and fled the room. Raquel hurried after, following her mother into the courtyard.

Raquel's father had just entered the gate, and now he called out to his wife. "Itzel!"

Her mother crossed the courtyard. "Amulon?"

Raquel's eyes widened at the thought of her mother flinging herself into her husband's arms, but Itzel stopped short of such a display. "Come in and eat."

Amulon followed his wife inside their home, barely acknowledging Raquel with a brief glance. She knew better than to ask him any questions when he had an empty stomach. She decided to wait in her room until she was summoned. But as she turned to go, her father said, "Stay here, Raquel."

Slowly, she turned around and faced him, but he wasn't looking at her. He continued to eat as if there were nothing else to attend to that day. Raquel looked at her mother, but she discreetly kept her expression blank.

Finally, her father finished his meal of tamalitos, beans, and roasted squash, and after a long drink of agave wine, he raised his eyes to Raquel. "Seth is safe. So are the other shepherds."

Relief burned hot in her chest. "And the elders?"

Amulon stood and stifled a yawn. "All safe. We delivered them to the king, along with a half dozen Lamanites."

Questions tumbled through her mind, yet she knew she'd been lucky to get that one answered.

Amulon looked from Itzel to Raquel. "That was over two hours ago. On the way back, I stopped at Eli's home. He has made his intentions clear."

Clear? About what? Raquel's mind raced. What could be relevant about Eli? He was nearly forty and a widower. His first wife had died a barren woman. He was a scribe for Noah, and Raquel had seen him several times on his way to court. The man was always bent over a scroll of bark, muttering to himself. He'd let his beard grow wild, and his appearance was in need of a woman's attention. She snapped her head up.

Her mother wore a serene smile, although it didn't seem to reach her eyes. "At last. It is settled." She crossed to Raquel, her hand outstretched, but Raquel backed up.

"What's settled?" She looked from her mother to her father. She knew she had to be punished for her escapade, but what did her father mean about Eli?

"Tonight, Eli will come for supper. He will officially extend his offer of marriage to you," Amulon said, his gaze piercing Raquel. "I suggest you ready yourself to make the best impression."

"But he is so old," Raquel protested. "And—"

"And he is wise, knowledgeable, has a very nice income from the king, knows how to care for a woman . . . all things that will give you the security and—" Amulon cut himself off, looking at his wife. "And the supervision that you need."

"I thought I'd be betrothed to someone I *liked* . . . or at least to someone who was close to my *age*." Raquel bit her lip hard, trying to keep the tears at bay. She thought she saw her mother's chin quiver.

Her father laughed. "He likes *you*, very much, and that will be enough for now." Amulon took a step forward, towering over his daughter. "Last night I realized I've let you play a little girl far too long. It's time you become a woman, grow up, and take responsibility—do what you were made to do."

"What's that?" Raquel whispered.

"Bear sons," her father stated. "Care for a man and keep his house."

Raquel shook her head, a pit of desperation forming in her stomach. "But I'm not ready."

Her mother placed a hand on her arm. "The betrothal will be the customary year. You'll be eighteen, nearly nineteen, by the time you marry—plenty in age."

"No," Amulon interrupted. His wife and daughter stared at him. "She'll marry before the second moon. Since last night, I've felt a sense of urgency in this matter that I've not had before."

Her mother's hand slipped from her arm, and Raquel's tears couldn't be held back any longer. Her vision blurred as she turned and hurried out of the room. It was no use appealing to her mother. The woman didn't have a chance when her father had made up his mind. And her father's tone told her that he already had.

She ran through the hall and flung herself on her mat. She was sure a deluge of sobs would rack her body instantly, but it was as if she couldn't believe what had just taken place—her mind wouldn't let it become reality. The sobs were mysteriously absent. Then something amazing happened.

Her mother started arguing with her father.

Raquel sat up, listening.

"It will take many months just to sew the bridal wear," Itzel said.

Amulon's voice was defensive. "You can alter what cousin Carina wore."

"My daughter will have her own things. Her father is a high priest in the king's court . . . It would be disgraceful for her to wear second-hand clothing!" Her voice rose in pitch. "And our family members must be notified. We'll have to prepare our home for many guests. It will take many days just to contact them all . . . two or three moons before they can assemble. They'll find it impossible to travel until after the harvest."

"You don't understand, Itzel," Amulon said, his voice at full volume now. "You should have seen the way *he* looked at her—as if she were a prize quetzal that could be bought with a few pieces of jade."

Her mother gasped. "The king?"

Raquel brought a hand to her mouth.

"Yes. It was as if a torch had been lit. I saw the . . . *desire* in his eyes," Amulon said, his voice harsh.

Raquel held her breath as her heart pounded furiously. There was silence between her parents for several seconds. Then her mother spoke. "Tell me everything."

Dead quiet stretched into a full minute.

Raquel couldn't move, couldn't breathe. Was it possible that the *king* was interested in her? *King Noah?* He was old, close to her father's age, although still younger than Eli. Why would a king, who could have any woman, wife, or concubine he wanted, want *her?* She had been dressed as a shepherd, but still he was interested? Her body felt cold all over. He had just married. He had just met her . . . on his *wedding* night.

She didn't believe it. The king's oldest son, Limhi, was about her age. Maybe the king had been thinking of her as a match for his son instead. Her father must be mistaken. But his next words stopped her.

"He was amused at first," Amulon said, his tone reticent now. "A girl and a young boy interrupting the festivities with such 'important' news. It was as if he looked to them for further entertainment. Perhaps he thought to humiliate them and throw them into prison—just for enjoyment."

Raquel left her room and carefully moved closer, down the hallway. She didn't want to miss one word.

"But she was wearing a shepherd's robe," her mother said.

"That's what makes it so ironic *and* so extraordinary. When I first saw her, I was reminded of you . . . when we first met." Her father's voice had softened.

Raquel's face heated. She'd never heard her father speak this way before. She felt like an intruder on their quiet moment.

"She captured everyone's attention just by her presence," Amulon continued. "Until that moment, I hadn't realized how beautiful my daughter was and how other men might regard her."

"What did the king say?"

"He commented on her beauty and . . . he said I had neglected to tell him how fair my daughter was."

"Oh no," her mother whispered.

"Then he became angry at something she said."

"What?" Itzel asked, sounding horrified.

"She said the other missing men were elders of Zeniff's court." Amulon took a deep breath. "He yelled a bit but calmed quickly. It was as if he actually *enjoyed* her outspokenness."

"She challenged him, and he let her leave?" Her mother's voice trembled.

"He ordered more soldiers to be sent for the rescue," Amulon said.

A moment of silence passed, and Raquel could hardly stand it. Her father either knew a lot more about the ways of men than she, or he was absolutely wrong. She'd seen none of this in the brief encounter.

"Pray that Eli is not too late," her mother said.

He's coming tonight. How can that be too late? Raquel wondered. She hurried to her room, trying to understand all that her parents said. Lying on her platform bed, she stared at the reed roof above. *Eli or King Noah?* The king was . . . overwhelming. She'd just be another girl in his harem. What about his new wife? Surely he was enraptured by her and wouldn't think twice about Raquel's visit. The king couldn't possibly think *she* was beautiful like all of those elegant women at court. Her mother had told her many times that she was too outspoken—too much like her father. Raquel was far from demure—a definite requirement in order to please the king day in and day out.

A pebble landed on her mat, causing Raquel to jump. She crossed to the high window and peered out. The leaves of a cashew tree blocked her view, so she threw the pebble out the window and waited. A moment later, it came sailing back in.

"Who's there?" she hissed, trying to see past the greenery.

A shuffling sound, then a young boy appeared.

"Ben!"

He bobbed his head and smiled at her. But Raquel detected the sadness beneath the smile. She remembered the plight of the elders, including Abinadi, and was seized with worry. What had Noah done with them?

"Is something wrong?" she asked.

"Nothing," he whispered. "I wanted to thank you."

"You're more than welcome," she said. He looked at her with such sincerity that she wondered if her heart could melt. His brown eyes were so sweet, so innocent. "How are your friends?"

His expression lightened for a moment. "The king let them go." Then he looked down, shuffling his feet.

"That's wonderful," Raquel said. "I told you that you could trust me." She said it in jest, but she realized by the sorrow that filled his eyes that it was the wrong thing to say.

"I do trust you, but . . ." Ben looked from side to side, then moved closer to the window. "Abinadi is injured."

Raquel's pulse quickened. "What happened?"

Ben lifted a shoulder. "He has bruises and welts all over his body and face. His mother says he'll mend in a few days, though she's having trouble keeping him resting."

Raquel wanted to smile. The news of his survival was sweet to her ears. But she couldn't let Ben know it.

His mouth tugged into a pout. "The others have left me behind."

"What do you mean?"

"Gideon was ordered out of the land by King Noah, and the other elders took their families and left with him. I tried to go, but the Teacher was insistent that I stay in the city. He said that I could do much good among the wicked, but I can't tell anyone about God." He wrinkled his nose. "I just have to be a good example."

Raquel stifled a laugh, even though the boy's words touched her. He was so serious about it. "What are you? Eight or nine? Of course you have to stay with your family."

"I don't have a family."

Before Raquel could respond, he added, "Abinadi invited me to stay with his mother. But he'll be leaving to help build up Gideon's settlement as soon as his mother lets him out of bed. So I'll be alone again—except for his mother, I suppose." He rubbed his face as if he were seriously considering it.

"Of course you should stay with his mother. Perhaps . . . Abinadi . . . will return soon."

"I don't know about that," Ben said. "But maybe if I stay with his mother, they'll know where to find me."

"Definitely," Raquel said, then added one more thing. "And I'll know where to find you too."

The boy's face brightened. "Will you come and see me?"

"When I can," Raquel said softly. "I'm in a bit of trouble right now, but the next chance I have to pass by, I will. Tell me, where *is* Abinadi's home?" She hoped Ben hadn't noticed the excited tremor of her voice.

"The last house at the crook of the river before the maize fields," Ben said.

Raquel thanked him, and after he hurried away, she settled onto her mat. At least the elders had left the city and were no longer in danger from

King Noah. At least Abinadi wasn't seriously injured. He'd be joining the elders soon—safe from the king. She stared up at the ceiling again.

The next time she saw Abinadi, if ever, she'd probably be a married woman.

Five

Turn ye not unto idols, nor make to yourselves molten gods:
I am the Lord your God.
(Leviticus 19:4)

The heat of the day finally stirred Alma awake. He lifted his head and took in his surroundings. He was in his small, dark room, the walls lined with colorful fabric and the floor with intricate rugs. A faint breeze sailed in through a solitary window, and a couple of flies buzzed their way in the glowing pillar of light. Alma sat up on the cushions and rubbed his head. It felt like he'd been hit with a boulder. With a groan, he remembered the events of the night before. It all blurred together—the wine, the music, the dancing, the women.

His stomach churned for a moment, and Alma wondered if the wine was still sour in his stomach and he'd have to rush outside. But the sensation passed. With a sigh, he lay on the cot again. The woman he'd danced with, or rather who had danced with *him,* had been beautiful on the outside. But in their brief encounter, he saw something beyond her physical appearance. Something dark in her eyes, something strangely appealing yet appalling in the same breath.

A temptress.

Alma raised his head, wondering where the idea had come from. King Noah had no need for harlots; his palace brimmed with legal wives and concubines. But the more Alma thought about it, the more he was sure those dancing women *had* been harlots. He turned over on the cot and faced the wall, closing his eyes in understanding. The rumors he'd heard about harlots in the king's palace were also true. The image of his father's eyes plagued his mind. It was as if he'd let down his parents, even though they were in their graves, by the simple act of dancing with a harlot. Alma folded his arms, trying to push away the ridiculous thought. His parents were as dust and had no influence on him now.

A shuffling sound came from outside the room, and Alma turned just as someone entered. He stared, unblinking, at the young woman who carried a tray loaded with guavas, cherries, cheese, and wine toward him. She was younger than the women from the night before, but her expression was far beyond her years. *Another temptress?* Alma sat up and cleared his throat. His face flushed hot as he realized his odor was probably foul and his appearance disheveled. Then he wondered why he cared.

The woman—the girl—knelt before him and held out the tray of food. The wine in the goblet sloshed against the brim. Alma hesitated, glancing at the girl, but her eyes were lowered. His gaze stalled on her high cheekbones and full lips . . . graceful neck . . . He tore his eyes from her and focused on the tray. His throat was parched, so he reached for the wine and took a small sip. Surprisingly, it calmed his stomach. He took another sip, followed by a long drink.

When the goblet was finished, the girl smiled and started to pour more wine from the narrow jug. But Alma put up his hand, stopping her. "Let me," he said. He poured wine into the goblet. Before he knew it, he'd finished the second cup. The girl still waited quietly.

"Thank you," Alma said.

She nodded and motioned toward the food.

He took a cherry from the platter. "What's your name?" he asked, unable to keep his curious gaze from her face.

She shook her head slightly. "You can call me whatever you like."

Alma straightened, staring at her. "You don't have a name?"

She stared back, amazement flickering in her eyes. "I . . . the king calls me Jahza."

"All right, *Jahza*," Alma said, wondering why she wouldn't tell him her true name. "Thank you for the wine and food." He waited for her to rise and leave, but she remained. "Is there anything else?" he finally asked.

"That's why I'm here," Jahza said in a soft voice. "The king sent me to serve you." She slid closer to him and placed a hand on his arm.

He was so surprised, he didn't move. Slowly, she slid her hand along his arm until she reached his shoulder. She was close enough that he could smell the faint odor of jasmine on her hair. Her other hand reached for his neck, and she pulled herself toward him.

Alma flinched. He removed her hands and gently pushed her away. He knew his face was scarlet, but he had never been this close to a woman before. Seeing the look of discomfort on her face, he stood and took several steps away from her. "I'm sorry, Jahza. Perhaps King Noah meant for you to visit someone else?"

"No," she said, her smile covering up the unease in her eyes. "The king said it would be your . . . first visit." She stood and walked to him, standing very close. "That's why he sent me. The king thought you'd feel more comfortable with someone young."

The two goblets of wine had done more than help Alma relax. The girl before him was becoming more and more enticing by the moment. He let out a low breath. It was all here before him for the taking . . . ordered by the king, no less.

Jahza touched his arm again, her fingers trailing to his hand. "As a soon-to-be-ordained priest of the king's court, you'll enjoy every pleasure and privilege that you desire."

Was he really going to be made a priest? Amulon had said so, and now this woman seemed to think so too.

She brought his fingers gently to her lips. Alma closed his eyes. Her skin was so soft, supple. He opened his eyes and gazed at her. She smiled at him, her eyes accepting.

"I'm sorry," Alma whispered. He dropped his hand and turned away. He moved to the door and opened it before he could change his mind. Then with a swift backward glance at the crestfallen girl, he escaped into the hallway.

He realized his hands were trembling, and he felt as if his chest would explode. It was unbelievable—the king had sent him a harlot. And he had refused her. Sure as the sun would set that day, Alma knew he'd just forfeited his chances of becoming a priest. But if it entailed all of this . . . He shook his head and quickened his pace. From the small room, he'd seen a garden just outside. He was grateful the hallway was empty so he didn't have to encounter anyone of the court—and try to explain why he had refused Jahza. Slipping through a door to the garden just beyond, he finally let his emotions surface.

His face burned with embarrassment. Any moment now, Jahza would make her report to the king. Alma could well imagine the laughter, the humiliation, and the ridicule that would follow. Or even punishment. After all, he had turned down a gift from the king. Alma's breath grew still as he remembered the king's easy wrath. When the man wasn't being entertained, he was usually in a foul temper. Perhaps the king would be more lenient the day after his latest marriage.

Alma made his way through the garden, stopping to stare unseeingly at the climbing bushes of flowers and buzzing insects. The early morning

brought a promise of blooming humidity, but at least for now the temperature was sweet with coolness. He found a boulder to sit on and thought
about the girl he'd just rejected. The look in her eyes pulled at his heart. He
wished he could apologize to her again but feared he'd never get the chance.
She *had* a name, he thought—a name taken from her by the king. What
happened to her birth name? Was a woman—a harlot—so inconsequential
that her name was taken from her upon arrival at the king's palace along
with her virtue?

A soft sound reached him, and Alma held his breath, listening. He
wasn't alone in the garden. Someone was crying. Perhaps a child? *Perhaps
Jahza?* He rose and moved through the garden, walking toward the sound.
He passed under a group of overhanging trees, then stopped and stared at
the sight before him.

The trees opened into a secluded courtyard, surrounded by a circle of
foliage. In the center was a carved bench of fine wood. A woman sat on the
bench, her head bent so that the cascading hair covered her face, her shoulders trembling with quiet sobs.

Alma knew instantly that the woman was Maia, the king's new bride.
Why was she here alone, crying? Why wasn't she with her new husband in
his royal rooms?

He took a quiet step backward, ready to leave the woman to her privacy,
when Maia lifted her head. Their gazes locked, and Maia's eyes widened.

They spoke at the same time.

"Alma," she said.

"I'm sorry to intrude," he said. He offered a stiff bow, then turned to
leave.

"Wait." Her voice was soft yet melodic at the same time. She was next
to him in an instant, her tear-stained face peering up at him. Her chin trembled as she spoke. "I am very happy, and the king is a wonderful husband."
She looked away. "I don't want you to think I'm dissatisfied in any way."

"Of course not," Alma said, knowing that her eyes betrayed her words.

"I miss my family, that's all," she whispered, looking down at her
clasped hands. Then she smiled up at him, her eyes brightening for an
instant. "I have been blessed to come here."

Any woman would consider herself fortunate to marry a king, Alma
thought, trying to convince himself. Even so, how could the bride miss her
family so much after only one day? He sensed that something else was
wrong. He opened his mouth to ask if he could help her with anything, but
she stopped him.

"When you see my family next, tell them that I . . . I love them."

"All right," he said.

She turned away again, but not before he saw new tears brimming. She moved past him and quickly left the garden, leaving Alma alone. He left the secluded courtyard and searched for an outside gate. It seemed the garden was completely walled in. He'd have to go back through the hallway and risk running into someone—perhaps Jahza.

He took a deep breath and strode purposefully through the garden, trying to dispel the image of Maia's haunting eyes and the misery he saw in them. As soon as he entered the hallway, a rush of footsteps joined him. A familiar voice boomed out, "Alma!"

"Amulon," Alma said, feeling his stomach sink low. Did the man already know about his failure with Jahza?

"Feeling better?" Amulon asked.

Alma searched for the man's meaning, then realized he referred to the events of the night before. "Yes, thank you. I slept well."

"Good," Amulon said, grinning. "What do you think of your new room?"

"My room?" Alma said. "It's mine?"

"As a priest, you'll have many benefits."

Alma nodded, thinking. A room wasn't all he'd been given. He wondered if he could trust Amulon. It seemed that the man had gone out of his way to befriend him. "I'm afraid the king may not be pleased with me."

"The king is more than pleased. He just enjoyed a wedding night, defeated some Lamanites, and banished the last of his father's elders." Amulon laughed. "You slept through the whole thing."

Alma stared at him. "How did all that happen?"

The two men walked along the hallway as Amulon caught him up on the events that had transpired. They weaved their way through the various rooms of the palace until they reached the throne room. Alma relaxed a little, feeling at ease with Amulon's easy nature.

"I must confess something." Alma lowered his voice. "The king sent a woman to my room . . ."

Amulon nodded. "Which one?"

"Jahza."

"Ahh," Amulon said. "She's the new one. Was there a problem?"

"I—I turned her down," Alma said, avoiding his friend's gaze.

"I see," Amulon said quietly. He looked past Alma for a moment, then said, "It's not my business, but I know what your concern is."

"You do?" Alma said, hope filling his chest. Maybe he wouldn't be ridiculed by the whole court after all.

"You need to lay down the law with your wife. Tell her about your new lifestyle. It's part of being a high priest." Amulon winked and slapped him on the back. "Let's get in there. They're waiting for you."

Before Alma could explain that he didn't have a wife, guards threw open the doors, and a shout rose up in the hall.

King Noah stepped from his throne. "There you are!" He swept forward, perspiration beading on his forehead as if he'd already worked a full day. But there was no work in sight, just a feast of fruits, breads, and sweets laid out on low tables, and a crowd of people. Didn't anyone ever sleep? Alma recognized a few of the priests from the night before. Some of the women were the same too.

King Noah embraced Alma, then turned to the crowd and said, "Now that Amulon has brought Alma, I will make the announcement."

A hush fell over the crowd, and all eyes focused on Alma.

"Alma will be anointed high priest at sunset," the king said.

Cheers erupted around him, and Alma blinked at the celebrators. They hardly knew him. People massed around him, congratulating him and pressing gifts into his hands. Everywhere Alma turned, someone else complimented him.

"Let's eat!" the king shouted. The crowd moved as one toward the platters. Flanked by the king and Amulon, Alma was continually offered food and wine; he was suddenly ravenous, so he accepted.

Entertainers came forward, all bowing before the king, then to Alma. Jugglers had come in from a nearby village. The Kaminaljuyú men arranged themselves into a semicircle, playing drums, while a juggler took the center. The juggler twisted and turned, keeping a carved stick in the air.

Alma sat in amazement—it was as if he were royalty. At one point, Jahza slipped by his side and sat ever so close. There was no disappointment in her eyes now. She simply stared at Alma as if she adored him, and the king seemed more than happy to make room for her.

The hours wore on, passing with little acknowledgment from Alma. The wine and food kept coming, and it was easy to indulge. He was so relieved to still be in the king's grace, he joined with the other priests in celebrating. After all, it was for his own ordination.

Finally, at the command of the king, the priests staggered to their feet and the group made its way toward the king's main temple. The numbers had thinned considerably from those who'd been present at the feast. Alma realized that only the priests were invited to this particular event.

They exited the palace and followed a wide path to the temple walls. Just beyond the temple, a newly constructed tower stood—higher than any building in the land. It gave the king a full view of the lands of Shilom and Shemlon. Amulon stayed at Alma's side, pointing out the architectural features of the surrounding buildings.

"The doors of the main temple are made of fine wood," Amulon said. "The walls are strong—reconstructed during Zeniff's time." He pointed to small idols. "These ornaments are gold and silver. Of course, King Noah added these after his father's death. Makes things more interesting, eh?"

Alma gazed at the intricate idols with interest. It seemed that everything Noah built was the finest in the land. This temple was the largest and sat the highest on the hill. They ascended the steep stairs, then entered the temple, and the cool interior of the large hall greeted them. Abinadi immediately noticed the fine wood and the intricate workmanship. He slowed his step, breathing in the fragrant aroma of the heady incense that filled the air. Then his gaze was drawn to the end of the room. A row of seats was elevated above the floor. One of the seats was the same that he'd been commissioned to build. But over his woodworking, gold had been laid. The gold ornamentation glowed in the dim light, quiet and majestic. Two of the priests lit the torches that lined the room, and the gold leapt to life. It twinkled merrily in the light as if promising a life filled with pleasure. A low wall had been built in front of the row of seats, and Alma watched the other men take their places and lean against the breastwork, waiting for what was about to take place.

A sense of awe entered Alma. This was the place where judgments were handed down to the people. This was where the king ruled the city of Nephi.

Noah waited for all the other priests to be seated, including Amulon, then turned to Alma and motioned for him to kneel.

"In honor of your duty to the kingdom in bringing me a new wife, I have decided to ordain you a high priest of my court." The king raised his sword. "The vacant seat of the high priest office will be filled tonight." Noah leaned toward Alma and whispered in a loud voice, "Just remember the first rule: Stay away from my wives."

The priests laughed, the sound filling the spacious room. One priest shouted, "What about your concubines?"

King Noah sputtered, then roared with laughter. Alma smiled, relieved that it was taken as a joke and not a foolish comment that might land someone in prison. Then Noah lowered his sword over Alma's bowed head and spoke the prescribed words of ordination.

It was all over in a matter of seconds, and Alma stood and blinked. The high priests were on their feet, cheering for him. He walked around the low wall and received the congratulatory pats on the back. Amulon pulled him into a fierce embrace. "Welcome!"

"Let us move to the altar," King Noah commanded after a short time.

Everyone filed out of the temple and surrounded the elevated platform. Amulon handed the king a finely shaped obsidian dagger. The hilt was encrusted with jade and gold. The king turned to Alma and held out the dagger. Alma stepped forward with a bow and took the weapon.

"And now, our new high priest will consecrate the altar with his blood."

Alma's stomach lurched, but Amulon had prepared him in advance, explaining that King Noah had "restructured" the laws of Moses to better serve the growing kingdom. Swiftly, Alma drew the blade across the palm of his hand, then placed his hand squarely on the altar. This was not following the laws of Moses that his father had practiced, but Alma told himself that it was a new king, a new law. The other priests bowed their heads and murmured a prayer in unison.

After the prayer, the king said, "Every sacrifice made before the next moon, be it animal, clothing, or autosacrifice, will all be in commemoration to our new high priest, Alma."

The group moved across the courtyard and back into the palace.

In the throne room, Alma sat on the golden seat that had been reserved for him. Disbelief surged through him. A few days ago, he would never have imagined being a part of King Noah's court. His father had been the one in the family who was a king's man—the revered scholar—not Alma. Yet here he was, being given power to judge a man's fate, wealth beyond his imagination, and the prestige and respect of the leaders in the city.

I could become accustomed to this, Alma thought. *What was I so worried about before?* The king made the laws here. Noah ruled the people. The traditions of Zeniff and of Alma's father had died with them. It was a new land, a reconstructed temple, and a new people.

And I am a new person, Alma realized.

The king sent an order for his children to be brought in to meet Alma. The priests reassembled in the throne room, and a short time later, a line of more than two dozen children entered and stood in order—from the eldest, a boy named Limhi who was on the verge of manhood, to a babe in a midwife's arms.

Alma marveled that one man could have so many children—but the number of wives explained it all. He watched the eldest boy with curiosity. Limhi was thin and quite pale, looking out of place in a room full of brazen men. He looked around the room furtively, not making eye contact with anyone—seemingly uncomfortable in his father's presence.

Noah walked toward Limhi and clapped the boy on the shoulder. "This one spends too much time in study with the scribes. I'm sending him on a very long hunting trip next week. He needs to become a man!"

The priests clapped their hands. Limhi looked away as if he were embarrassed. As soon as the king allowed it, he hurried out of the room after his siblings.

Amulon left at dusk, but the celebrations continued through the night, and by midnight Alma was completely exhausted. He excused himself to his quarters, much to the dismay of the king. But this time Alma had held his wine, and although his journey along the palace corridors was somewhat staggered, he managed to find his new room. The oil lamps burned softly, welcoming him, and a tray of fresh fruit and another jug of wine sat in the corner. Alma smiled. He would sleep well tonight on the soft cushions— dreaming of new adventures and of being one of the most powerful men in the land.

A movement on the cushions startled him. "Who goes there?" Alma said, reaching for the dagger at his waist.

A slender woman rose from the cushions. Her dark hair flowed over her shoulders, and she wore a wrap that left her arms and shoulders bare. In her hand, she held a goblet of wine.

"Jahza?" Alma said.

She smiled at him in the dim, warm light but said nothing, merely raising the goblet to her lips and taking a sip.

Alma hesitated in the doorway. Yes, she was beautiful, and he was a high priest now . . . deferential only to the king. He had no wife to betray. He took a step forward, and Jahza's eyes flashed with excitement. Alma turned and gently shut the door. Then he looked at Jahza. He would not abandon her a second time.

Six

Honour thy father and thy mother, as the Lord thy God hath commanded thee.
(Deuteronomy 5:16)

The day had been filled with routine tasks, but Raquel's thoughts were anything but mundane. Her father had returned to court to celebrate the ordination of a new high priest, and her mother had spent the day embroidering, her lips pursed against any open conversation.

Raquel worked at the looms in the courtyard, wishing that the fading light would slow for just a little while longer. At dark, Eli would be here, and Raquel dreaded seeing his eyes upon her . . . and knowing what he came for. She tried to imagine what it would be like marrying such a man— a man for whom she felt no love, only duty. Was that how her marriage would be? One of duty filled with dreary tasks day after day? Other girls her age planned and speculated about who they'd be betrothed to. Their fathers listened to their suggestions—but alas, her father was not so inclined. His duties lay first as a high priest in the king's court. Duties with the family had to be in line with what met the king's approval.

She didn't want to resent her father—her parents. But it was *her* heart. Didn't that count for something? Couldn't their love for her transcend public expectations of who she should and shouldn't marry? She sighed, realizing that some might envy her nice home and luxurious clothing. Little did they know, her heart was far from content.

She wished she had someone to talk to—about Eli, about the king, and especially about Abinadi. She missed her new young friend, Ben. He seemed intelligent beyond his years, but he was still vulnerable, with no family, no mother, to take care of him. Raquel's heart warmed to him at the thought. As every hour passed, she became more concerned for Ben's future and worried about Abinadi's health. She thought idly of her cousin, Seth. But her new secrets would be too much of a burden for even her best friend to bear.

One secret was almost too much for *her* to bear—that of seeing her father enjoying another woman's company. Raquel wondered if her mother knew anything about harlots at the king's court; somehow Raquel had never pictured her father as being a part of it. Should she say something to her mother? *No.* Raquel's heart sped as she thought about approaching such a forbidden topic with her own mother.

Dusk took a firm hold on the land, and the fading light forced her to stop weaving. She looked at her handiwork with surprise—she'd completed almost twice as much work as usual. As she rose from the stool, she wondered why her mother hadn't called her in to help oversee supper preparations. Her mother no doubt had the servants scurrying through the cooking rooms, getting ready for their special guest.

Delaying another moment, Raquel walked through the courtyard to the outside gate. She gazed along the road, looking north toward the king's palace, then south, toward the river where Abinadi lived. His home was certainly a simple place compared to the grandness of the king's home.

It's not like I can choose anyway. She'd soon be married to Eli—a scribe. A man who'd had a wife before her. A man who'd want children. Perhaps she'd be happy. She could grow rows of herbs with no one to fuss over how she spent her time. She'd immerse herself in the care of her children and not think of what her life could have been like if . . .

A whistle sounded, and she snapped her head up. Someone was coming. Before deciphering if it was her father, or even Eli, she fled from the gate and hurried inside. The front room had been swept clean and incense burned on a low table. Sounds of instructions came from the cooking rooms, but Raquel bypassed them and went straight for her bed chamber. At any moment, she expected to hear her father's booming voice. He'd call for her and insist on inspecting her appearance.

Raquel took off her work tunic and picked up the one that she wore on special occasions. Briefly she fingered the delicate weave of the cotton. It was a deep indigo color. Her mother had spent weeks embroidering the tiny leaves and flowers on the edges of the garment. Raquel splashed scented water onto her face, neck, and arms—water that had undoubtedly been ordered by her mother. Quickly she slipped on the tunic, feeling the coolness of the luxurious fabric against her skin. She'd have more clothing like this made before she was married.

Still straining to hear her father's voice, she was surprised when no one called for her. She untied her ginger hair and combed through the snags until it was sleek and smooth. Then she twisted it to one side and threaded a dark blue strip of cloth through it. Finally she lifted from a small wood box a jade necklace that her parents had given her on her last birthday.

She turned and gazed into the length of polished metal propped against the wall. She looked her best, so at least her parents couldn't complain about her appearance. Raquel moved into the hall, wondering where her father had gone. Perhaps it had been Eli, and he was already seated for supper. Her palms grew moist at the thought. Could she really marry this near-stranger? Could she ever come to love him? Was he like the other men at court, with concubines? Her face burned as she now counted her father among those men.

When she entered the gathering room, she found her mother standing alone, facing the square window and holding a rolled parchment in her hand.

"What is it?" Raquel asked, walking toward her mother. "Where's Father?" She didn't dare ask about Eli, lest she seem eager.

Her mother turned, her expression a mask of stone. Slowly, she looked at the scroll in her hands. Then her voice trembled as she answered. "It's from the king. He sent a messenger to deliver it."

"What does it say?"

Her mother shook her head helplessly. "The messenger didn't read it. We'll have to wait until your father gets home."

Raquel's hands ached to hold the scroll and peek inside. She'd learned a few words from Seth, but she could never admit that to her mother. A girl knowing how to read would be frowned upon. "He gave no indication?"

"No," her mother whispered. The anticipation was clear in her eyes, bordering on fear.

"Father should be here soon, right?"

Her mother's gaze wavered. "I don't know." She turned away.

"But we're expecting Eli for supper this evening," Raquel said, not understanding why her mother didn't know such basic information as her father's time of arrival. Surely hosting their future son-in-law was important enough to leave yet another celebration at court.

"I don't know much of anything," her mother answered. "Only what he wants me to."

Raquel stared at her back, wondering if she'd heard right, or if she was *supposed* to hear her mother's words. A dull sense of sorrow descended upon Raquel. She saw plainly for the first time the coldness of her home. Her mother wasn't happy. Previously Raquel had assumed it was her mother's nature to be quiet and overly submissive to her father. Now she saw differently.

Her father didn't need to tell his wife about activities at court—Itzel knew. As Raquel looked at her mother's withdrawn figure, she saw a lonely woman whose bloom of beauty had long faded into domestic chores. Her mother didn't shop the markets like the other priests' wives or take pleasure in new fabrics, exotic foods, and exclusive perfumes. Costly apparel and a beautiful home provided no joy for her mother—not when inside her soul was empty.

And it will be the same for me, Raquel thought. *I, too, will be surrounded by every comfort, but empty without love in my home.* She stepped toward her mother, wondering if she could offer any comfort. But before she reached her, her father burst into the room.

"Itzel, I passed the king's messenger along the road," Amulon said, staring at his wife.

She turned to him and held out the scroll.

He took the scroll and opened it.

Raquel held her breath, but no one asked her to leave. In fact, her father didn't seem to notice her presence.

"It's just as I thought," Amulon said. He kept his eyes on the scroll, reading the words over and over.

Itzel covered her mouth with a trembling hand. Raquel wanted to demand an explanation, but she was afraid she'd be sent out of the room.

"When?" her mother asked.

"Tomorrow morning." Amulon raised his eyes to gaze at his wife. "What should we do?"

Raquel looked from her father to her mother. This was the first time she'd ever heard her father ask for her mother's advice. His eyes were hooded, his expression troubled. Those eyes flickered to Raquel's. She flinched as his voice boomed.

"Well, what do you have to say?" he practically yelled.

"I—I . . . What is the message?" Raquel asked, seeing her father's anger seep red into his face.

He glanced at the bark leaf parchment in his hand. "The king requests your presence at court tomorrow," he said. "He'd like a formal introduction." He looked at her, and Raquel was surprised to see a hint of worry in her father's eyes. He'd never been afraid of anything before.

"What does he want?" Raquel asked, although she could very well guess the answer.

Amulon let out a sigh and handed over the scroll to his wife. Then he turned from the women, falling silent for several moments. Finally he said, "The king is interested in you, Raquel. I've seen this happen over and over.

The king sees a young woman whom he finds beautiful, and soon she becomes his wife or concubine." His voice had dropped into a harsh tone.

Hearing this firsthand came as a shock. This wasn't some conversation between her parents that she'd eavesdropped on. Her father was speaking to her like she was a grown woman. "Maybe he won't find me attractive after all," she said, hope budding in her chest.

Her father turned, sadness in his eyes. "It's too late for that." He glanced at his wife, then back to Raquel. "The fact that King Noah sent a messenger and didn't just tell me at court today means that he's serious. He's going to make the visit official. He wants me to *present* you." His voice wavered. "*Present* you like a gift, an offering, free for the taking."

Raquel tried to pull herself out of her numb state. "But if I'm betrothed to Eli—"

"The king knows you're not. He saw your fingers free of any symbol of commitment last night. And he has . . . spies who report to him . . . especially when his interest is focused. He probably knows about Eli's visit tonight. He'll know the outcome before we ourselves know it." Amulon crossed the room and stood before Raquel. "Tonight you will be pleasant to Eli, although no promise will be made. Tomorrow you'll go before the king. If he desires you, you'll live in luxury the rest of your days. Your children will have every privilege. Your . . ." He looked quickly away.

She thought she saw the glimmer of a tear. Then her father did something that he hadn't done since she was very small. He kissed her on the cheek and patted her head. "Prepare the table for our guest."

Her mother guided Raquel by the elbow to the cooking room as if she were something fragile. They helped the servants make the final preparations for the plentiful meal. Raquel tried to focus on the boiled beans on maize tortillas, cassava, dried fish, and tomatoes, but every so often she caught her mother looking at her—not as a mother looks at her daughter with concern and worry, but as a woman looks at another woman. Assessing, comparing, wondering.

Raquel hovered in the cooking room when Eli arrived. She'd be presented to him following the meal, after the two men of the household ate first. She kept busy shelling peanuts. Her mother was quiet as usual, and snatches of the men's conversation reached them, mostly about the health of the flocks, the recent Lamanite attack, and Eli's work at court.

When the meal was finished, the servants bustled into the room and gathered the half-empty dishes. Quickly, the women ate the leftovers in the cooking room. Raquel picked at her tortilla, not hungry.

As her mother stood, Raquel knew it was time to be officially presented to Eli. She rose and smoothed several strands of hair from her forehead. Her mother stepped forward and pinched her cheeks, bringing in a flush of color. Raquel lowered her eyes and followed her mother to the gathering room. When they entered, Eli was standing with her father in deep conversation. Both men turned when the women approached.

"Ah, my wife, Itzel," Amulon said.

Eli bowed, smiling at Itzel. "It's a pleasure to meet you. Thank you for the delicious meal."

Itzel nodded and said in a soft voice, "You're welcome."

Raquel looked up quickly, studying Eli. He was a full head shorter than her father, making him just a tad taller than she. He was quite portly, and his clothing looked frayed—which surprised her, since he was a man of the court. Perhaps it was due to lack of mending. His normally wild beard had been trimmed. At least the man had made an effort. With dismay, Raquel noted fine streaks of gray in his beard, signifying his forty-plus years in age. *Maybe I'll be a young widow,* she thought, then immediately felt ashamed for thinking it.

Her father's voice cut through her thoughts. "And this is our daughter, Raquel. She'll be eighteen this year."

Eli's large eyes beneath thin brows feasted on her, and he grinned. He stepped forward and bowed. "It's a pleasure to meet you formally."

Raquel responded as politely as possible. "Thank you for coming." Her voice came out just above a whisper, which prompted her father's sharp glare. "W-welcome to our home. I hope you will be pleased . . ."

Her father nodded slightly, and relief surged through her.

The four of them settled onto cushions. Raquel and her mother listened to the men continue their conversation. As they talked, Raquel tried to imagine what marriage would be like to such a man. He seemed to carry his excess weight delicately, as if he were comfortable with his size. His face was pale, probably due to the long hours spent indoors writing. Raquel wondered if he might teach her more words to read. Probably not, she decided. He seemed like the type to follow rules.

Despite his size, Raquel couldn't help but notice his long, slender fingers. He gestured with them extensively as he spoke. His voice was soft, almost feminine, and he used some words that she hadn't heard before. *He must be very educated,* she thought, feeling even more awkward. His gaze kept flickering toward her, his eyes alight with interest. The conversation stalled, and Eli shifted several times on his cushions.

He's waiting, Raquel realized, *for Father to bring up the topic of marriage.*

"Raquel has received an invitation from the king," Amulon said.

Eli's eyebrows shot up, and he visibly straightened. "Oh? How . . . wonderful."

"Yes," Amulon said in a careful voice. "She is to be presented tomorrow."

As a man of court, Eli surely knew of Raquel's visit to the court the night before. Several emotions flitted across his face. If the reason was so obvious to her father, it would be so to another man.

Eli regained his placid expression. "I'll be interested to know how the . . . presentation goes."

Amulon dipped his head in acknowledgment. "I'll bring you word."

By the look on Eli's face, Raquel knew he was coming to the same conclusion her parents had. She shivered involuntarily. She wished she could erase the events of the past two days and revert back to her carefree self—to the Raquel who only worried about escaping to the shepherds' field at night without being caught. That concern had no merit now. It had been a child's game. The game she was in now was not for children.

After a few more moments of stilted conversation, Eli rose to leave. Raquel smiled at him for the first time, but his return smile was less enthusiastic now. He looked past her and offered a few farewell comments. Amulon thanked him again and escorted him through the courtyard.

Raquel stood in the front room with her mother for a moment, not wanting to think about embarrassing Eli, yet at the same time, relieved that perhaps she would not be made his wife. She left her mother waiting for her father and made her escape to her room.

She paced in the darkness, the events of the past two days blurring in her mind. She thought of little Ben and his desperate eyes—so afraid of being left behind by the elders. And finally she sank onto her platform bed and allowed herself to think of Abinadi. She didn't know him at all except by sight and a few comments she'd overheard from other girls. Why was she so drawn to him? Just because he was different from the other men she had observed? Then she realized the reason—he was everything her father was not.

When she'd seen her father at the king's court with another woman draped on his arm, she hadn't allowed herself to internalize it. But now she couldn't deny that her interest in Abinadi perhaps stemmed from his resolve to follow the old traditions, to defy the king, in a sense—a king who was selfish, lustful.

Raquel covered her ears and squeezed her eyes shut. If her parents ever learned of her thoughts . . .

She knew nothing of Abinadi's beliefs, but in the quiet of her room, she sensed they made him the man he was. Quiet, stoic, compassionate. She had a sudden desire to find out what he believed in. How was his god different from those that Noah worshipped? Did Abinadi's god allow married men to entertain harlots and concubines?

Raquel lay on her mat, staring at the dark ceiling. Tiny pricks of light came through the thatched roof from the moon. The sounds of her home quieted, and she was sure her parents were in their beds, asleep. But instead of falling asleep herself, she just lay there as anxiety pressed against her chest, making rest impossible.

Tomorrow she'd be presented to the king. Tomorrow Abinadi would be gone. Tomorrow she would be betrothed to one of two men. Tomorrow her fate would be decided by someone else. If she didn't act now, it would be too late.

Her heart thudding, Raquel rose from her bed and pulled out her dark blue cape. There would be no shepherd's disguise tonight. She'd travel as herself. Carefully she crept through the house and out the back door. She crossed the garden and stopped at the hut containing her herb collection. From her beloved herbal jars, she grabbed a bundle of wild tobacco leaves. Then she crept through the garden again, staying close to the outer wall as she reached the courtyard. Once she had exited through the outer gate, she started running.

Seven

And I have filled him with the spirit of God, in wisdom,
and in understanding, and in knowledge.
(Exodus 31:3)

Abinadi watched his mother bustle around the stark room. "You need your rest too," he said. This was the second time she'd risen in the middle of the night to check the heat of his forehead. Thankfully it had subsided significantly, and he'd be able to leave in the morning. His mother had lit an oil lamp and insisted on warming a thick broth.

In the next room, Ben slept. Abinadi was at least grateful the boy hadn't awakened during his mother's pilgrimages to his room. Ben would be safe here, and perhaps in time, when the elders had built up the homestead, they'd be able to fetch him and offer to house him and other believers.

Abinadi rose on one elbow, wincing but then quickly masking the pain on his face. His mother worried too much and could be very insistent, but the steaming broth did smell good. He removed the rug his mother had placed on him. It was really too warm to be covered with it for long. Red welts dotted his bare chest, but there had been no infection. In the dim light of the lamp, he saw that the swelling had already lessened from earlier that evening.

Since their home was quite small, Abinadi usually slept outside. Tonight he was stationed in the cooking room, with his mother and Ben sharing the only bed chamber. He knew he'd been fortunate to be excused from King Noah's court with only reprimands. Although he wasn't the leader of the elders, any one of them could have been prosecuted for treason. The jubilation of victory over the Lamanites had put King Noah in excellent spirits. Perhaps his new marriage had helped too.

But it was imperative that Abinadi leave the city as soon as possible. Morning couldn't come too early, and if he hadn't promised his mother he'd wait until then, he would have disappeared already.

His mother crossed to him and handed over the bowl of hot soup. Her dark hair, streaked with gray, was pulled into its customary knot at the back of her neck. Her tunic hung loose about her thin body, but her hands were thick and strong. She was still able to do quite a bit of work, although Abinadi was constantly telling her to rest.

"Thank you," he said, noticing that the age lines about her eyes seemed more pronounced. "You should get some sleep. I'll snuff the lamp when I'm finished."

She settled on a low stool. "I can sleep later." She focused her honey-colored eyes on him and watched him closely as if she were making sure he ate every bit of the soup.

He sipped it slowly, trying to avoid a scalded tongue. After several moments, he gave his mother a stern look. "Really, Mother, you can return to your bed chamber. I'll be fine."

She pursed her lips and shook her head.

Abinadi let out a heavy sigh. "All right then. I need to leave at dawn. There's enough stored food to last you and Ben several weeks. I'll return before then and replenish the supply."

His mother clasped her hands tightly together. "I don't care about the supply, son. I worry about your safety. I want to go with you. It's time I fussed over Helam too."

Abinadi gave her a lopsided smile. "You know he'd hate that. He can't stand pity in anyone's eyes—especially his mother's. Besides, only a few women live at the settlement, in the most basic huts. It's a hard life." His voice was gentle. "You have a comfortable home here, and Ben can do the chores. He'll keep you company."

A smile reached his mother's eyes. Then she said, "Ben will be heart-broken to find that you've left."

Abinadi noticed the faint tremor in her voice and wondered if she were speaking more of herself. He set the bowl of soup down and reached out his hand. His mother came forward and took it, resting her cheek on his palm.

It pained Abinadi to leave her, but she was in more danger if he remained. He didn't know what to expect once he met up with the elders. They hoped to build up the settlement enough so that it would be fit for people like his mother to live in.

She lifted her head and placed her other hand on his cheek. "Ben and I will be fine. Don't worry about us. Just take care of yourself and give Helam my love."

Abinadi had opened his mouth to reply when a knock sounded on their hut. His mother pulled away in surprise. "Who could that be?" she whispered.

It was well past midnight. The only person that Abinadi thought might make a visit was one of the elders, coming to tell him that the meeting place had changed. Or a messenger from Noah's court, saying that the king had changed his mind.

Abinadi rose gingerly. "Stay here," he whispered. His mother grasped his arm for a moment, then nodded and released him. He didn't bother to pull on a tunic over his bare torso. If he was to meet his fate, it didn't matter how he was dressed. He crossed the room and, just before lifting the skin door covering, he glanced at his mother. Her expression said everything: fear.

Exhaling, Abinadi threw open the skin. It took him a moment to comprehend who stood there.

"Raquel?"

She looked at him with wide eyes, as if she were scared herself. Perhaps she brought bad news learned from her father. Even so, Abinadi's heart thumped at seeing her—but not with fear.

In a flash, his mother was at his side. "Come in, come in. I'm Esther, Abinadi's mother." She drew the girl inside and lowered the skin against the blackness outside.

Abinadi and his mother stared at Raquel, waiting for an explanation. Raquel looked back and forth between the two, then finally her gaze faltered. She reached inside her outer cape and removed a small satchel. Her eyes flitted to Abinadi, resting for an instant on his bare chest and the welts turning to bruises. "Here," she said, holding the satchel toward him. "These leaves are excellent for treating bruises and abrasions."

If Raquel had announced that fifty men were on their way to ransack his home, he couldn't have been more surprised. *She brought me healing herbs. In the middle of the night.* Somewhere in the back of his mind, he remembered Ben talking about her—how she'd taken him to King Noah's court and informed him of the Lamanite attack. It was obvious that Ben had told her about his injuries and whereabouts.

Raquel still held the bag of herbs toward him, but before he could come up with a response, his mother took the bag. "Thank you, dear." She opened the fabric and examined the dried tobacco leaves. "Do you make a poultice with water?"

"Goat's milk is more effective." Raquel's eyes were still on Abinadi.

If she stares at me any longer, my fever will return, Abinadi thought. Well, at least there was no doubt that she knew of his existence—although she might only be here at Ben's insistence. The boy tended to exaggerate, and no doubt he'd told Raquel that Abinadi was on his deathbed. Why else would a young, unmarried girl risk leaving her home in the middle of the night to help a stranger? And a daughter of one of King Noah's priests, no less. His stomach twisted at the thought of Amulon discovering what his daughter had done. She could be punished.

"I also brought this." She produced a thick leaf. "It's from the curaiao. I picked it fresh. Inside is a cooling gel that will ease the pain immediately." Her eyes strayed back to Abinadi as she handed the leaf to his mother.

"Do your parents know where you are?" he asked.

Her already dark eyes grew black. Abinadi instantly realized that it was the wrong question to ask.

"Of course they don't," she said. "They wouldn't have let me come." She finally shifted her gaze to his mother. "I had to fetch the herbs from the hut in the garden, so they didn't see me leave . . ." She flushed. "If you heat up the goat's milk, the stalks will soften quickly."

Esther nodded and took a step backward. "I think I have some milk left from this morning." She turned and crossed the room to the small cooking fire she'd used to heat the soup.

As his mother busied herself, Abinadi wondered what he should say. Finally, he thanked Raquel and offered her a cushion to sit on.

She shook her head. "I must go now." Yet she remained, glancing about the room. Her gaze stopped on the pile of rugs that made up Abinadi's bed. "You sleep here?"

He nodded, a burst of embarrassment surging through him. Raquel's home was many times larger than his. But when he looked at her, he was surprised to see her smiling.

"I must have startled you when I knocked," she said.

It was more of a question than a statement. "I thought the worst."

Her expression immediately sobered, and Abinadi had a hard time tearing his eyes from her honeyed skin and ginger-colored hair.

"Ben told me you're leaving in the morning," she said in a quiet voice.

Ah, so it *was* Ben. "Yes," Abinadi said. "The king has allowed Gideon to leave the city untouched. Many of the elders have chosen to leave with him and live in his settlement."

Raquel nodded, the sides of her mouth pulling into a frown.

Every part of Abinadi wanted to ask her why she was *really* here. Maybe her father had put her up to it after all and wanted to find out which of them was leaving the city.

"I think I can stay for a few more minutes." She turned, crossing to the pile of rugs, then glanced over her shoulder. "Tomorrow my life is changing."

Abinadi stared at her, not sure how to respond. What did she mean?

"That's why I'm here. I want to learn," Raquel said, facing him.

Learn? "Learn about what?" he blurted, then watched her settle onto what had been his sleeping quarters. Abinadi wished he'd straightened up the corner before letting her in. But how could he have known?

She looked up at him, her expression open, curious. "About your god, of course."

For the third time that night, Abinadi was stunned. The preparation sounds coming from his mother fell silent. He grabbed a cape that hung against the wall and pulled it over his shoulders. Somehow he felt exposed. Raquel had come to talk about the Lord. Incredible. If her father found out, Abinadi would surely be punished. No, killed.

When he looked at her again, she was gazing at him, her expression completely serene.

She's ready.

Abinadi looked up, wondering where the voice, or thought, had come from. He argued with himself. *She might be ready, but am I ready to share what I've so recently embraced?*

His tongue felt thick, and suddenly he was extremely thirsty. He didn't know if he could explain so that she'd understand. *I'm a coward. Here is this girl*—he glanced at her—*no, this woman who is asking to know the truth, and I'm too afraid to open my mouth.* He squeezed his eyes shut, knowing that he probably looked ridiculous. But he had to dispel the image of her glowing beauty if he was going to think rationally. How did one even begin to explain the magnitude, the power, or the love of God? *O Lord, help me, let my words be pleasing unto Thee. Let me share Thy gospel so that it will edify Raquel's life and not bring her grave consequences,* he prayed silently.

When he opened his eyes, she was still watching him, the edges of her mouth lifted in a small smile. He cleared his throat and sat on a cushion across from her. She folded her hands together, waiting.

"It's extraordinary, really," Abinadi started in a low voice. "From the first moments I learned about the true nature of God from the elders, my life has changed."

Raquel nodded. "Did you meet the elders in our city?"

He shook his head. "My brother, Helam, became a part of their community, then tried to convince me to meet the man we call the Teacher, Gideon. When I finally met with him, I asked many questions, and the answers changed my life." He sensed his mother listening. "Like our fathers of old, the elders practice the true ordinances of the gospel—like repentance and forgiveness. They keep the commandments of God, worshipping only the Lord . . . taking only one wife."

His eyes locked with hers, and for a charged moment, neither spoke.

"Ahem," Abinadi's mother interrupted. She glanced from her son to Raquel, her eyebrows raised.

Abinadi looked at his mother, hoping that the sudden warmth flushing his face wasn't noticeable. In her hand she held a bowl with the salve made from Raquel's herbal leaves. Raquel's gaze was still intent as she said, "I don't understand why the king needs so many wives and concubines. What do the elders teach about this?'

"Father Jacob taught that taking multiple wives and concubines is abominable before the Lord unless the Lord Himself commands it for His purposes," Abinadi said. "Regarding our people, Jacob quoted the Lord by saying, 'For there shall not any man among you have save it be one wife; and concubines he shall have none.'"

A smile lit Raquel's face. "I am pleased to hear that. I wish my father . . ." Her voice trailed off as her expression turned serious. She looked away.

After an awkward silence, Abinadi continued. "Under the Lord's plan, we learn to serve others. We're accountable for our deeds. We need to strive to be a peaceable people. If we keep the commandments of God, we will be blessed in this life and saved in the next."

Raquel nodded, her gaze back on Abinadi. "King Zeniff upheld the Lord's commandments. But what happens in King Noah's court is the opposite of all that you've said. Our king has no regard for anyone but himself."

Abinadi's mother let out a small gasp.

But Raquel didn't seem to care. "Everything is bought and sold at court for a price. Slaves, property, women. The high priests can do as they please with no accountability, no thoughts for how their rulings might affect others."

Abinadi stared at her. These were bold statements from the daughter of one of the high priests.

She rose to her feet and spread her arms. "Why is it that in the most humble of houses I feel at home?" She raised her hand to stop any answers. "I know. It's not the place you live in . . ." She looked from Abinadi to his mother. "I've thought about this a great deal the past couple of days. There's something different about you people." She folded her arms across her chest. "And I want to know what it is."

Esther stepped toward Raquel and placed a hand on her arm. "I know what it is."

Abinadi looked at her in amazement.

"It's the Spirit of the Lord, Raquel," she continued. "You're feeling His Spirit in the presence of those who obey His laws."

"I knew it," Raquel said in a quiet voice. "It wasn't something that I could reach out and touch, but . . ." She looked at Esther. "The Lord is real, isn't He? You can feel His presence too?"

Esther nodded and Raquel smiled. She reached for Esther and the two women embraced.

What just happened? Abinadi wondered. He'd never seen anyone accept the message of the Lord so readily. Was it genuine? The look on Raquel's face told him it was.

"I now know what I must do," Raquel said. She clasped her hands together, looking at Abinadi. "I'm ready to come with you."

His mouth fell open.

"I know the risks." Raquel rushed on. "I've thought them out carefully. No one will know what happened to me. They'll never connect the banishment of Gideon with my disappearance—"

"Are you sure?" Abinadi interrupted. "You'll have to give up everything and leave your family."

"I know. But my father loves the things of court more than his family." Raquel bit her lip. "My mother is miserable, and I—I want to find true happiness." She lowered her head. "It doesn't exist where I live."

Esther touched Raquel's arm. "Don't you think your mother would be more miserable if you left?"

"And your father will send an army looking for you," Abinadi said. "This time he won't spare any elders." *Including me.*

Raquel looked at him, her eyes bright with unshed tears. She could see now that she hadn't considered the risks as carefully as she had thought. "I hadn't thought of that." She shook her head and gave a moan. "I just can't go back to them." She sank onto a cushion and buried her face in her hands.

Abinadi looked helplessly at his mother, who set the bowl down and slowly knelt by Raquel's side. "How old are you, dear?"

"I will turn eighteen this year."

"All right then. You're of marriageable age. I'm sure that soon enough you'll be betrothed to a nice man and you can maintain your *own* home," his mother soothed. "You can create your own happiness away from the pattern of your parents' lifestyle."

Raquel shook her head, freeing tears. "You don't understand. In the morning, I'm to be presented to the king."

Esther threw Abinadi a sharp look.

"What?" he mouthed.

Esther patted Raquel's back. "Perhaps you can speak to your mother, and she can petition your father in your behalf." She turned Raquel's face toward her. "Your father is a close advisor to the king, and certainly he can make the king understand your wishes. But I'm afraid that if you don't show up, the king will take it as a personal offense. If he finds that you are in any way seeking learning from the elders . . . well, you know the consequences."

Raquel sniffled and wiped her eyes. "Of course, Esther. I have been selfish, and I can see that my hasty actions will affect far more people than I realized." She rose to her feet, inhaling deeply. "I'll go now. I wish you a safe journey." Her eyes rested on Abinadi briefly. "And a lifetime of peace."

She crossed to the entrance as Abinadi watched her, dumbfounded. Just before she exited, she said, "Rub the herbal paste on every wound. Let it dry, then apply a second layer. It will reduce the pain." She disappeared through the doorway.

Abinadi rose from the cushion wondering if he should call her back.

"Let her go," his mother said. "She's still under the rule of her parents. It's for the best."

Abinadi turned, feeling suddenly cold, as if a warm light had just left the room. He wondered if they *had* done the right thing. "Did you see how miserable she looked?" he said, though more to himself. He looked at his mother. "And she seemed to really feel the Spirit of the Lord. Maybe we acted too hastily."

His mother tilted her head. "It's just as I thought."

"What is?"

"You care for her."

Heat burned behind his ears. "I . . . don't think—"

"And she feels the same." Esther moved to her son's side and looked up at him. "But I'm sorry, son—unless her father is a man of convincing words and a soft heart, when she's presented to the king in the morning, she'll likely become his next wife."

"What?" Abinadi almost shouted.

"Shhh, you'll wake the boy," his mother said. "When the king asks for a young woman to be 'presented,' it means he's considering bringing her into his court—one way or another. With her father being a powerful high priest, she'll come in at no less rank than a wife."

Desperation squeezed Abinadi's chest. "Then we have to do something. I can speak with her father, explain that not all women are meant for the king."

"No," she said. "The danger is too great. Her father would take great offense."

Abinadi knew his mother was right on one level, but on the other . . . he'd never allowed himself to think that Raquel might care for him. If it were true, that changed everything. Like his mother said, she was of marriageable age. But he didn't know her true feelings. If not the king, he was sure Amulon had plenty of men who would be highly interested in his daughter. But what girl wouldn't want to be married to a king?

"Come, let's see if this salve works," Esther said, leading him to the cushions.

As his mother applied the warm paste, Abinadi wondered about Raquel. She'd been driven to come to his home tonight for a reason. He couldn't think it was just because of him. She was afraid of the meeting with the king. But she'd been brought up in a royal household, her father and mother adorned with every privilege. Why would she want to leave all that behind?

He knew the answer. It was simple. The Spirit had whispered to her. Somehow she'd felt the Lord's power and sought a better life. It had nothing to do with *him*. She hardly knew him, but her soul yearned for more than the surrounding debauchery.

His mother's quiet voice interrupted his thoughts. "The young woman must make peace with the life she was born into. If she defies her parents now, her future will be forever ruined and her chances of a good marriage tarnished."

Abinadi agreed, but that didn't make it right. For a wild instant he imagined arriving at Amulon's home with a few sheep and turkeys and offering them to the high priest as a bride price for his daughter. Amulon would be insulted. Abinadi would be cast out, and Raquel would be embarrassed. Yes, it was better that he slip away in the morning and let Raquel live the life that had been mapped out for her.

His mother's gentle hands had done the trick, and before she doused the oil lamp, Abinadi felt the relief of subsiding pain, and almost against his will, he faded into sleep.

Eight

He that troubleth his own house shall inherit the wind.
(Proverbs 11:29)

Raquel crouched in the courtyard of her home for several minutes, listening to the sounds of the night. When she was certain that all were asleep, she crept inside to her bed chamber without being discovered.

She should have been exhausted, but her mind wouldn't rest. Her thoughts tumbled as she pondered the powerful yet few words that Abinadi had shared about the Lord. His mother, Esther, had been right. The difference was the Spirit of the Lord. She had felt it—as if it were a tangible thing she could snatch out of the air. Yet it seemed to elude her when she reached her home. The peace and safety that she'd felt in Abinadi's house were gone. It was as if she'd stepped from a warm patch of grass into a cold shadow. She wanted that warm feeling back.

Raquel pulled her cape tighter across her torso. She hadn't bothered taking it off, and now the extra warmth seemed to ward off the coldness of her home. She closed her eyes and let her thoughts drift to Abinadi. He wasn't exactly handsome in the traditional sense, but she was drawn to him. Was it his goodness, his purity? Perhaps . . . but when he'd let her inside the hut and she caught a glimpse of his injuries, something tugged at her heart. She didn't necessarily feel sorry for him; it was more that she wanted to care for him. To prevent him from ever being hurt again. To stand between him and men like the king.

Men like my father.

Her cheeks heated with shame. Abinadi must think she was an ungrateful child, prancing around the city in the middle of the night—no respect for her parents, for protocol. No decency. He'd probably looked on her with repulsion, knowing that she was about to be presented to the king. No doubt he assumed she'd become a part of the king's court, just as her father. He'd seemed so surprised when she'd asked him about God. She hoped he knew just how sincere she was . . .

She must have fallen asleep, because the next thing she knew, her mother was shaking her shoulder.

"You must dress in your finest clothing," her mother's voice said from somewhere above her.

Raquel's body felt heavy as a fierce headache started. Then her stomach rumbled, reminding her she'd eaten very little the night before. She opened her eyes. By the brightness of her room, she realized the sun had risen well over two hours prior. She'd slept much later than usual. That meant Abinadi had probably left the city already . . . and it was almost time for her visit to the court.

Her mother was sorting through her things. She held up a set of iridescent quetzal feathers. "Wear these in your hair with your turquoise and red tunic. Wrap it tightly so your figure shows."

Raquel opened her mouth but was too surprised at her mother's words to answer. Her mother *wanted* her to impress the king! Raquel looked at her mother's face. Itzel wore a tight, pinched look—very task-oriented. She showed no emotion in preparing her daughter for this event. It was simply a duty.

Anger flamed in Raquel's chest; she felt betrayed. Her parents had feared the invitation from the king, and now her mother seemed to accept it— embrace it even. That meant that her father had ordered it so. Hopelessness descended on her as her mother started combing through Raquel's tangles. Soon her hair would shine like copper. Suddenly she had the urge to run from the room and cut off all her hair. Surely the king would lose his interest then.

There was no love, no consideration for her feelings in all of this. It was as if her parents cared only for the king and would do anything to please him. Even if it meant sending their only child to live at court—a place filled with concubines, harlots, and lustful men. Had she been brought up only to serve a man in such a way? Was there no dignity left in her life? She was to be paraded as a new species, an exotic flower that would become as the rest in no time at all.

What about the king's new wife? What did she think? Her husband's bed was still warm, yet he was already looking elsewhere. Raquel's stomach churned so loudly that her mother heard it.

"You must eat before we go," her mother said matter-of-factly. "It will not do to have you look pale and piqued." She hurried out of the room.

Alone again, Raquel slowly dressed. Her hands trembled slightly as she imagined the king's eyes on her—assessing, desiring. If only she hadn't stolen out the other night to the fields and returned to court with Ben . . . If only . . .

But they'd saved lives in the process.

Yet the price for doing so had suddenly become very high.

She threaded the red feathers into her hair as her mother had instructed, then she looked at her reflection in the polished metal. Staring back at her was a pair of troubled eyes.

Moments later, her mother reentered the room with a round of flat bread. "Here, eat this quickly."

Raquel chewed on the bread as her mother cinched the tunic tightly about her waist then fastened it with a colorful sash.

"Let me look at you," she said, turning Raquel around. She examined her daughter's appearance for a moment, then said, "Very good. Now, be sure you look pleased to see the king."

Inside, Raquel wanted to scream, but instead she nodded obediently. "Aren't you coming?"

"No," her mother said. "Your father will be here at any moment to retrieve you."

Raquel's face flushed at the thought of following her father through the city streets, with everyone and anyone allowed to gawk at her. It would be easy enough to guess where she was headed, and the gossip would start in no time.

The sound of her father calling from the courtyard reached Raquel's chamber.

Raquel stiffened at her father's voice. Her mother called back to say she was ready. "There he is now," she said, making final adjustments on Raquel's appearance. "Go."

Raquel glanced over her shoulder at her mother, wondering if she'd be a betrothed woman the next time they saw each other.

She stepped into the hallway and walked as slowly as she dared to the gathering room to meet her father. He turned as soon as she appeared. For a long moment, he studied her appearance, then he nodded. "Despite what we may have discussed before, this is an opportunity that any family should be honored to have. The king is bestowing a personal favor upon us, which in return will elevate our status and privilege in the community." He hesitated as if struggling to accept the words himself. "We need to make haste."

Her father walked quickly, and Raquel had to scramble to keep up. She knew if her mother were with them, she'd make a comment on the need to prevent Raquel from perspiring so much—but she also knew that her heavy breathing came more from her nervousness than from the speed of their travel.

Her father turned once or twice to urge her to move faster—a look of resolution in his eyes.

"Father," she said. "Have you and Mother changed your mind? Do you *want* me to please the king?"

He stopped and faced her. "You don't understand, Raquel. If we do *not* please the king, then our lives will be in jeopardy. He is the king of this land—to whom we pay allegiance, no matter what." He touched her arm, his expression one of regret mixed with determination. "You must represent our family well even if it means leaving us to join the court . . ." He looked away and shook his head. "It's not my choice." Then his eyes bore into hers. "Our family's honor is at stake."

He dropped his hand and started walking again. Raquel hurried to catch up. Tears stung her eyes, but she stubbornly refused to let them fall. Her father wanted her to impress the king. By the set of his shoulders and the firm line of his jaw, she knew there was no changing his mind now. Like he'd said, it was a matter of family honor.

Still she hoped that somehow her father might be able to prevent the king moving to the next step. Perhaps it would turn out to be just a friendly visit, and she'd return home free to marry Eli.

Raquel exhaled. Was that what she really hoped for? She didn't want to marry Eli either, but she couldn't let her thoughts wander too far right now. The only man she could imagine herself with had left the city, and she'd likely never see him again.

"We're here," Amulon said, his voice more gentle now.

Raquel snapped her head up as they passed the guards at the gate. Her father led her through an elaborate courtyard surrounded by a beautiful garden. Raquel stubbornly stared ahead. She wouldn't let luxury or beauty persuade her. They passed another set of guards at the top of the steps then entered the massive hall. She was surprised to see it empty. The last time she'd been here, it was filled with wedding attendees, music, tables of food, dancing . . .

Her father hesitated, as if he didn't know what to do next. Then a servant scurried from a side hall toward them. He bowed his nearly bald head before speaking. The man reminded her of Eli. Maybe this man was a scribe too.

"The king is waiting in his chambers."

"Not in the throne room?" Amulon asked.

"He specifically requested privacy," the servant said, his gaze landing on Raquel for the first time. His eyes narrowed, and Raquel wondered what he was thinking. Did he disapprove? What did he know about her already?

Amulon thanked him, then glanced at Raquel. Without a word, he turned and led her down the same corridor where the servant had just disappeared. It twisted several times until they reached a flight of stairs. At the base, a guard rose from his stool, his gaze sliding over Raquel briefly. He nodded to her father, and they passed without a word.

Upward they climbed, and with each step, Raquel's chest grew tighter. But at least she wasn't to see the king in front of his court, which was a relief; it would take away any public embarrassment.

Soon they stood before a heavy reed door. Her father knocked, and a man's voice bade them enter. Amulon opened the door and ushered Raquel inside. When Raquel stepped into the room she was struck by two things. First, she'd never seen such display of wealth—gold chairs, embroidered cushions, long drapes, and a cage containing a pair of quetzals. Second, the king was absolutely alone.

He rose to his feet and clasped his hands together. In two strides he was at Amulon's side and pulled him into a fierce embrace. "You're here at last." Noah released him and grinned. Then ever so casually he looked at Raquel, still smiling.

Amulon touched her arm and propelled her forward. "O Highness, this is my only child and daughter, Raquel." He bowed his head.

Noah took her hand and brought it to his lips, his eyes locked on hers. "Welcome to my home. Any member of my high priest's family is like my own."

Raquel let out an inconspicuous sigh of relief. He looked on her as family, a child. Perhaps this was just a friendly meeting, nothing more. His gaze wasn't probing or calculating. If nothing else, it was kind, which caught her off guard. He was about thirty-five or so, not nearly as old as she had first thought. The king's face had a boyish quality about it, although it was apparent that he enjoyed his food and drink.

He waved toward a table stacked with fruits, cheeses, and various jugs of wine. "Would you like something to eat?" He smiled at Raquel. "I grow tired of servants doing every single thing for me. So I excused them all to enjoy a little peace." He crossed to the table and piled food onto two plates, then handed them to Amulon and Raquel.

Her father looked just as surprised as Raquel felt. They took the plates and Noah said, "Be seated, and make yourselves comfortable. Enjoy the food."

His behavior was definitely not what Raquel had expected. Holding the plate, she sank onto a luxurious set of cushions, almost feeling relaxed. It was so quiet here. Calm and . . . beautiful. Although they were surrounded by massive amounts of elaborate decorations, the king seemed genuine. He and her father spoke for several minutes about court business while Raquel nibbled at the food on her plate. Maybe the king wanted her as a servant to one of his wives or a nurse to his children. She relaxed a little more.

Noah rose from his spot and poured three goblets of wine. He served Amulon and Raquel again, to her surprise. She sipped the wine—it was better than anything she'd ever tasted. Then she realized the king was still standing, watching her. "Do you approve?"

He was asking if *she* approved of the wine? Raquel nodded.

He sat again, but this time turned his attention to her. He asked question after question—about how she spent her days, what her favorite foods were . . . Raquel answered hesitantly at first, but when her father gave her a hard stare, she tried to relax and speak more freely.

Noah encouraged everything she said and seemed truly interested. This was different from the deference Eli had paid her, and Raquel found herself second-guessing her reluctance to be presented. It wasn't hard at all.

She had questions of her own, but she bit them back. She was sure her father would disapprove. Then suddenly Noah turned to Amulon. "Can I have some time?"

Amulon flinched, astonishment evident on his face. He cleared his throat and seemed to compose his answer. "Certainly." He stood and bowed.

Raquel wanted to run to her father and beg him not to leave.

With a final glance at her, Amulon turned, his shoulders slightly hunched. He left the room without a backward glance.

Raquel's pulse accelerated at being completely alone with a man—a king, no less.

She kept her eyes lowered as he crossed to her, settling on a nearby cushion. All of her previous fears returned at high speed, magnified. She tried to keep her breath steady as she examined the food on her plate. Carefully, she took another sip of wine. The king studied her and seemed to be waiting for her to say something. But she couldn't. It was as if her throat had closed. The expression on Eli's face when he'd found out about the presentation flashed across her mind. Then the ugly welts on Abinadi's chest . . . Here she was, surrounded by immense wealth, but all she felt was a tortured stomach.

"My sweet Raquel," the king breathed. He touched the hair that fell down her back. She nearly jumped. Her heart hammered with trepidation. "You are like a beautiful blossom. Radiant. Delicate . . ." His hand continued to thread its way through her hair. "You are a flower, ready to bloom."

Raquel let her eyes close. Why did her father have to leave? Was he really so afraid of the king? Was she to become the king's harlot now? Was there no respect for the daughter of a high priest? What about his new wife of only two days?

Noah's hand moved to her shoulder, then along her arm. Her heart pounded with fear. She thought about the words of Father Jacob that Abinadi had quoted—*For there shall not any man among you have save it be one wife; and concubines he shall have none.*

A shiver ran through her as the king's hands found her waist.

Propelled by an unseen force, she pulled away from the king and stood. She didn't look at him as she crossed to the table of food. She put down her plate then turned to Noah. "I'm sorry."

His face had reddened, and in one swift movement he was on his feet. Raquel sensed the anger that was about to spew forth. Fire flamed in his eyes. He opened his mouth, but his words seemed to falter for a moment, and Raquel took the opening.

"What am I to be, then?" she said in a rush, a little louder than she'd intended. But once she started, she couldn't stop. "A harlot? A concubine? Or perhaps I'm good enough to be made your wife—one of many, to be shoved aside when the next maiden captures your eye."

Noah's face darkened; his hands clenched. "Watch your tongue, girl. Your father—"

"Isn't here, and he didn't leave me here to be exploited by you. He brought me here today at your request." Her voice shook, but she plunged on. "I would rather die than become a tainted woman of your court. Only because I honor my father am I here." She moved away from him, sliding closer to the door. "If you do not honor me, I will leave—"

"You dare to insult a king?" Noah sputtered. He crossed the space between them in two steps. She backed up against the door, suddenly worried that he might strike her. He grabbed both of her arms roughly and shook her. "You do not speak unless I allow it. You do not make assumptions, ever. You do as you're told!"

She tried to pull away from him, but he held firm. Raquel was certain her father hadn't gone far and was likely listening on the other side of the door. Why didn't he come in and save her? She glared at the king, her anger multiplying as she realized her father had indeed left her to be fodder for the king. Some honor. Noah's gaze bore into hers, his intentions plain.

She tried to wrench from his grasp again, but he only held tighter. Suddenly she grew still, her expression cold. "Then you'll have to force me," she spat.

The king stared at her, his grip relaxing. He threw his head back and laughed.

Raquel's eyes widened as she watched him—this man was out of his mind.

When his laughter died, he grew serious again. But the anger was gone. Something else reflected in his gaze—a steely determination. He leaned toward her until his mouth was next to her ear. "I have no problem with force, but first I will make you my wife. Your father can marry us right now. We wouldn't even have to wait."

Suddenly his lips were on her neck, hot, greedy. She stiffened. This was not what she expected. She hoped he would cast her out of his court— disgraced, yes, but free of him. His fingers wrapped behind her neck and pulled her closer as his lips moved to hers, and she thought she would suffocate. She wanted to scream.

It's now or never. One act would change her future so she could never return. She'd have to leave everything behind. Her father might pay a price, but the price she was paying now was too high. With all her strength she kicked Noah's shin. He cried out, startled. It was the instant she needed. She twisted from him and opened the door.

She ran past her father who stood just outside. Barely keeping her balance she stumbled down the stairs and past a stunned guard as the king's voice bellowed against the stone walls.

"Capture her! And when you do, I'll need more guards at my door to keep her in." His laughter drowned out the pursuing footsteps.

This was a game to him, and she was the hunted. A conquest.

"Raquel!" Her father's voice almost stopped her, but *he* was the one who had brought her here. She would no longer listen to him.

She ran through the corridors, wondering which way she'd come. She had no idea which direction she was going or where she'd end up. At any moment, the guard could catch her and drag her back. That thought alone kept her moving faster. She skidded around a corner and ran down a long hallway. At the end, the corridor divided in two. Taking the right, she passed a large room full of people. She hesitated, and several of them turned. Some pointed, others just stared.

She turned and ran from the room, coming to the corridor again. She went left this time and ran down the narrow hallway, trying doors as she went. Most of them were locked. One opened into a small storage area, another into someone's private chambers.

Finally she broke through a door and found herself in a small garden. She ran along the paths, searching for a gate. She couldn't find one and was about to scale the wall when a woman's voice spoke behind her. Raquel whirled and came face-to-face with a young lady with dark copper hair. Obviously a resident, she wore a bright cotton wrap and a feathered cape.

"What are you doing?" the woman asked. Her wide, grayish-green eyes studied Raquel with curiosity.

Raquel tried to catch her breath. Something about the woman was familiar. Regardless, the woman could alert the guards and it would all be over. Then Raquel realized who she was. She had known this woman when they were young girls. She was the king's new wife. "Maia?"

The woman narrowed her eyes, so Raquel said, "I'm Raquel, daughter of Amulon."

The woman's gaze refocused, and a slight smile touched her lips. "What are you doing here?"

Horror clawed at Raquel's stomach. The young woman was a year younger than herself and already her husband was straying—not that he'd been a faithful man from the beginning. If Raquel were caught, she'd have more in common with this dark-haired girl than she ever wanted.

"Please," Raquel began. "I need to leave without anyone knowing. My father and the others are looking for me." She took a deep breath, wondering how much she could tell without revealing her treason. "I've offended the king."

The light shifted in Maia's eyes, and she grew very still. "He wants you for a wife," she said in a soft voice as she assessed Raquel. After a moment's hesitation, she said, "No one understands more than I your need to escape. Let me help you over the wall." She moved to Raquel, her gaze still fixed on her childhood friend.

Raquel saw a depth of compassion there—it was as if for a brief moment they were as close as sisters, sharing each other's lives, and ready to keep the deepest of secrets.

Maia interlaced her fingers, creating a foothold for Raquel. Maia was strong and easily supported Raquel as she reached for the top of the wall.

After a bit of scrambling, Raquel perched on the top. "Thank you," she whispered.

Maia lifted her hand in farewell, and for an instant Raquel thought she saw longing in the woman's eyes. Here she hovered on the threshold of freedom, leaving Maia behind in a garden prison. Raquel hoped the woman wouldn't be punished for helping her. She clutched at the vines that scaled the stone as she maneuvered her way down the other side of the wall. Once she landed on the ground, she paused, trying to calm her breath, and crouched, partially hidden by a mature cashew tree.

This side of the palace bumped against a steep slope. Above she saw the beginning of the forest. She just had to make it there before anyone spotted her, then she could run . . . where, she didn't know.

Hearing nothing from the inner side of the wall, Raquel took a deep breath, then plunged upward, grabbing onto roots and rocks to hoist herself up the hill. The sash that her mother had so carefully tied had come undone, and she took a second to retie it. She didn't want any evidence to point her direction. The rocky slope scraped her hands and knees, but she didn't care. Her clothing became wet with perspiration, and the feathers in her hair jostled.

At the top of the rise, she took cover behind the first patch of trees. She waited for a moment, her heart hammering as she looked over the palace grounds. For a moment, she couldn't tell if there was any unusual activity. A couple of people milled around by the side gate, and the garden from which she'd escaped was barely visible. Then she saw a flash of copper hair. The top of Maia's head. Maia stood in the middle of the path, but she was still alone. Raquel sighed with relief. That meant the guards hadn't come to search there yet.

Backing into the forest, Raquel tried to think of a plan. She had nothing with her. No extra clothing, food, or anything to carry water with. The settlement was surrounded by fields, vineyards, and sheep territory, and beyond that was the threat of Lamanites. She shuddered at the thought of coming face-to-face with ferocious men. But she was more frightened of becoming King Noah's wife. If nothing else, the look on Maia's face had given Raquel a glimpse of the life she'd have.

For a moment, she wished she could return home and gather some quick supplies, but she knew it would be impossible. Her father was probably on his way there to alert her mother. He might also send some men to look for her. He'd be furious, so it was that much more important that she put some distance behind her. Raquel started walking, not really knowing which direction to take, except for moving away from the palace. She'd eventually reach someone's field, and she'd have to determine her direction from there.

Although the air was cooler beneath the shade of the trees, her back prickled with perspiration as she walked. She tried to keep a brisk pace, grateful that her night wanderings had given her the endurance to walk long distances. When the sound of a rushing river reached her, she moved quicker and arrived at a small waterfall. It cascaded and twisted to the right, then slowed and meandered along the hills that ran east of the palace. If she followed the river, it would lead her around the entire city of Nephi, then eventually past Abinadi's home and several other homesteads before it would take her into Lamanite territory.

Raquel paused in her step. *Abinadi's house.* Maybe she could gather some supplies there. A waterskin, a rug to sleep on . . . But it might be risking too much. Yet no one knew of her association with his family, and chances were that no one knew that Ben lived there too. Decision made, Raquel plunged ahead, hurrying alongside the river.

Nine

But the path of the just is as the shining light.
(Proverbs 4:18)

Raquel stayed close to the river, knowing it would keep her within sight of the city in case she met with real danger. It took most of the day to skirt the homes and outlying fields. She moved carefully, keeping a wary eye and ear out for anyone within the city—or without. Every so often she waded in the river so her trail would be harder to follow. Her father, among others, was known for his excellent tracking skills. So were the Lamanites. She stopped to pick an avocado. The water and the fruit kept her going.

By late afternoon, she'd made it to the lower reaches of the city where the slope to distant farms and orchards became more steep. It was possible that the king had set up guards to watch the main road. But as Raquel found a place to survey the road, it was eerily empty. She remained still for several moments, watching the road. She was surprised really, and wondered if they'd given up the search. Regardless, she didn't dare step onto the road. She stayed a good distance away since the trees had thinned considerably and there was no cover near the road. She passed through a field of maize, grateful the stalks were tall and mature this time of year.

She connected with the river again and followed it to the beginnings of the southern forest. There she saw Abinadi's home. In the daylight she could better see its makings. It was a modest hut made of long sticks with a thatch roof. Although it was small, it looked tidy and well cared for. She half expected to see Ben running around scattering chickens and Esther sitting in the yard grinding maize or mending something. But everything was quiet. She walked up to the entrance, covered by a skin that, just the night before, Abinadi had stood on the other side of. She paused for a moment, wondering if she should involve these good people in her disappearance.

What if the king's people questioned them? Why should she expect them to risk protecting her secret?

She knocked on the side of the hut anyway, out of options as she was. She thought she heard a scuffling sound come from within the house, but no one came out.

"Ben? Esther?" she called out. "It's Raquel."

Another sound, then the skin-covering opened. Ben's small face came into view. He burst through the opening and leapt toward her, throwing his arms around her legs.

"Hello there," Raquel said, wrapping an arm about him and patting his head with her other hand. She smiled at his enthusiasm, but when he pulled away, he looked upset. "What's wrong?"

He waved her inside, and Raquel followed him. "Where's Esther?"

Once she was inside, he spoke. "She went to sell at the market as she does every day. She didn't want anything to seem different with Abinadi gone." He looked about the room, his nose wrinkled. "She told me I had to stay out of sight. There's nothing to do here."

Raquel stifled a laugh. So he was bored, not upset. "When will Esther be home?"

"Hopefully in time for supper." He shrugged.

This time Raquel laughed. "Would you like me to fix you something?"

Ben's face lit up as he smiled. "Could you?"

Raquel moved about the tiny cooking area and found a grinding rock. She set Ben to work grinding while she lit the fire in the stone oven. With the water from a storage jug, she quickly made a paste, then dumped the batter onto the hot flat stone above the flames. She had little skill in cooking but had watched the servants in her home plenty of times. Soon the batter bubbled and her stomach grumbled in anticipation. When the two cakes were ready, she slid them off the stone with a flat stick and onto plates. Ben started to eat his as steam still rose.

After they'd finished eating, they waited for Esther together, Raquel wondering if she should say anything to Ben as to why she was really here. They talked for a few minutes about the elders when she finally said, "Do you know where they are staying?"

Ben lowered his voice as if someone might be listening. "Abinadi said they were meeting at their headquarters. From there they'd decide when to travel. Only a few outsiders know where the settlement is. I think it's the empty strip between the river and the first set of mountains."

"Are the elders safe?" Raquel wondered aloud.

"They have the protection of the Lord," Ben said.

Raquel looked at the boy, realizing that she believed him. It was incredible, really. She wished she could understand life as he did and enjoy such simple assurance. "Tell me about their headquarters. Is it someone's home?"

"Oh no," Ben said. "It's like a cave, but it was built by our ancestors—Father Nephi and Father Jacob. The elders have expanded it from a storage place to a large room where they can hold meetings."

"And they'll be there a few days?"

"They might be gone already, now that Abinadi is with them," Ben said. He wore a wistful look. "When they get settled in their new land, they'll come for me."

Raquel's thoughts tumbled. The cave seemed like the perfect hiding place until she decided what to do next. But she'd still need supplies. The shadows had grown long in the room, and she didn't want to be wandering too deep into the forest at night. She'd have to leave soon.

"Where is the cave?"

Ben looked at her sharply. Raquel saw that she'd gone too far. This young boy was no fool. But it seemed he was unaware of her visit the night before, so perhaps . . .

"You didn't just come here to see me," he said in a flat voice.

Raquel wrestled with her answer, trying to think up a quick story. But she couldn't wait much longer, and she really did need supplies. She'd have to explain to Ben so that he could explain to Esther. "No, I didn't just come to see you." She smiled. "Although that is part of why I am here."

Ben crossed his arms, eyes narrow.

She took a deep breath. "I—I ran away from my home . . . from the palace, to be exact. The king wants to marry me." She lowered her eyes, feeling the impact of her actions. Had she made the right decision? It seemed so foolish to run from a life in the king's court.

"Abinadi wouldn't like that."

She snapped her head up. "I know. It was foolish of me to do."

"No," Ben said. "Abinadi wouldn't be happy if you married the king."

A jolt passed through Raquel. She tried to keep her voice steady as she asked, "What do you mean?"

A mischievous smile crossed Ben's face. "I heard them talking about you last night."

Raquel stared at him. "What did he—did they—say?"

"His mother knows and I know . . . that he likes you." He covered his mouth and laughed at his own words. Then trying to keep his face straight, he said, "But he won't admit it. His mother says he's no smarter than an alpaca."

Raquel smiled but didn't really dare to hope. Abinadi hadn't actually admitted anything. Besides, if he knew what had happened between her and the king—that awful kiss—Abinadi would be repulsed. He was so pure. She was far from that.

"The king will be angry when you go back," Ben said in a knowledge-able whisper.

"I know," Raquel whispered back. "That's why I'm not going to return."

Ben's eyes widened. "You're really leaving?"

"Yes," Raquel said, swallowing her resolve with finality. "I really am. And I need your help."

Ben nodded eagerly.

"I need to take a few things with me," she said, removing the feathers from her hair. She looked down at her clothing. "If there is a plain tunic that Esther can spare . . ." She held out the feathers. "If you could give these to her as payment . . . And I need to know where that cave is so I can hide."

Ben jumped to his feet. "I'll come with you. I know the way, and I can protect you." He pushed out his chest, his eyes gleaming with excitement.

"No," Raquel said, thinking fast. She couldn't risk this boy's life too. Plus, Esther needed his help. "You need to stay here with Esther like you promised Abinadi." She pressed the feathers into his hands.

He took them without a word, his expression dejected.

"If I see Abinadi or any of the elders, I'll tell them you're waiting patiently."

"All right," Ben said, his face brightening a little. "You'll need to take an oil lamp—it's dark in the cave." He rummaged through the house until he found a piece of parchment and a stylus. He drew a rough map for Raquel. "Here are the hills. If you travel over the first one, you'll see a clearing."

Raquel watched his finger trace the line, her heart pounding at what she was about to do. The location of the cave was right on the border of wild territory. There could easily be Lamanites camping in the area.

She changed her clothing and gathered the supplies Ben brought, tying everything together into a bundle. She thanked Ben and embraced him. She would miss his enthusiasm and simple faith. As she stepped outside of the house, she noticed the lengthening shadows of the approaching evening. Ben had assured her that it would take less than an hour to reach the cave. She should make it there before dusk.

As shown on the map, Raquel followed the river, feeling refreshed after eating and spending time with Ben. Now that she'd come this far, she allowed her thoughts to turn to her mother. A twinge of guilt passed through her—no, it was more than a twinge—but for now she pushed it away. She couldn't let sorrow slow her down. She'd had no choice. Her mother would eventually understand.

According to her map, she was almost there. She scurried up the ridge. From the top she saw the clearing. She'd be able to finally rest and perhaps sleep in a secure cave for the night. And then tomorrow—she wasn't sure. But tonight she'd be assured that Ben was safe, Abinadi was safe, and she was free.

Something whizzed past her, and a sharp pain hit her shoulder at the same time. She gasped at the intense burning sensation. Turning, she looked for the offending insect. With horror she saw blood trickling down her shoulder. A lot of it. She staunched the blood with her hand, taking a few steps backward. What had bit her? Then she saw an arrow on the ground a few paces ahead.

Her chest seized with panic. Someone had shot her. She looked behind, trying to capture a glimpse of movement within the surrounding trees. Her legs threatened to give out, but she half ran, half slid down the other side of the ridge. Her shoulder ached, and she started to feel lightheaded. At least the arrow hadn't pierced her, though it had left a pretty good gash in her skin. She tried to stay low to the ground, looking for anyone chasing her and hoping she was running in the right direction toward the cave.

On she ran, her stomach sinking with nausea. *Just a little farther,* she urged herself. Finally she arrived at the clearing. No one was in sight. Perhaps whoever shot her had lost her trail. She moved along the outside of the clearing, staying hidden, her stomach roiling and her head throbbing. Quickly she scanned for the hidden entrance Ben had told her about. Straight ahead she saw a line of heavy brush.

She worked her way toward the cave, trying to stay concealed in the trees. When she reached the tangles of the brush, she pushed her way through it. She had found the opening. She hovered inside the entrance to catch her breath and wait for her eyes to adjust. Her shoulder throbbed, and she clutched it, willing the bleeding to stop. For a few moments, she listened for anyone who might have followed her. At every slight sound, panic seized her chest again. Then, before she could explore the cave, she stumbled, pitching forward before everything around her went black.

* * *

Raquel didn't know how long she'd lain unconscious, but when she awoke, her shoulder burned so that tears sprang to her eyes. She thought with irony of the herbs she'd risked so much to get to Abinadi . . . what she wouldn't give now for a poultice to ease the pain. She maneuvered to a sitting position, trying not to move her right shoulder. Then she became aware of a new pain. Her hand flew to her face and touched her forehead.

"Oh no," she groaned. Her fingers came away wet. She grabbed for the waterskin, then scooted to the wall of the cave entrance and leaned against the cool surface. She closed her eyes, the pain coming in bursts against her temple. She had to make the bleeding stop. With trembling hands, she ripped a length from the hem of her tunic, then wadded the fabric and held it gingerly against her forehead.

After several moments, she tore a second strip of fabric and tied it around her upper arm, just below her shoulder. She poured water on the wound, then with another strip, wrapped her shoulder. With the bandage, the pain seemed to isolate itself and no longer pulsed through her entire arm.

She used some of the water to clean the blood off her face and neck, then took a long drink and rose to her feet, hoping the cave had some provisions stored. She lit the oil lamp Ben had given her and walked slowly, the lamp in one hand and her other hand running along the rocky walls for support. After several paces, the cave opened into a large cavern.

Her dim light didn't reveal the entire space, but Raquel sensed it was quite large. She walked carefully around the room and found a spring of water in the center. Kneeling by it, she washed away the remaining blood.

The sound of falling rocks startled her. She hovered over the lamp, wondering if she should extinguish it. What if the person who shot at her was here? Or some wild animal? A jaguar that had seen her light? Then, distinctly, she heard footsteps. She blew out the lamp and crept to the far wall.

The light of a torch flared up just inside the tunnel. "Who's in here?" a voice demanded.

Raquel covered her mouth to stifle a scream, but then she lowered her hand. "Abinadi?"

He stepped into the cavern and raised the burning torch.

She moved from the shadows. "It's Raquel—"

"Thank heavens," Abinadi said. He crossed to her and examined her face. "Are you all right?"

"Yes, I probably look worse than I feel." *How did he know I was here?*

"I saw you running through the trees—and there was blood on your clothing." He peered at her. "Your head . . . what happened?"

"I—I fainted." She touched her shoulder. "And an arrow brushed me. I lost some blood."

Abinadi's face crinkled in concern. "You were shot?" He crossed to the wall and lit another torch wedged in a crevice. The room brightened considerably. He turned to her. "Let me take a look."

She held her breath, anticipating the pain as he removed the bandage.

"We need to clean this more." He took her other arm and led her to the pool. "Wait here. There might be something we can use stacked in the corner."

Raquel knelt and dipped her hands in the water, then touched them to her wound while she waited for Abinadi. She was amazed that he'd found her, and just when she needed him. It was as if someone was looking out for her.

In a moment, Abinadi was back with a clean strip of cloth. "We'll have to look outside for the curaiao plant."

Raquel nodded. The curaiao would take the sting away and speed healing time. As he rewrapped her shoulder, she closed her eyes. The pain seemed to lessen just with Abinadi's presence—knowing that she was no longer alone. But what would he think when she told him what she'd done?

"Finished," Abinadi said. His gaze was on her, warm in the torchlight. "Now tell me why you're so far from home . . . and how you knew about this place."

She lowered her eyes, suddenly feeling nervous. Not because of what her explanation would be, but because she was having a hard time looking at Abinadi without her heart hammering. He'd surely notice the scarlet of her face, the sound of her heart in this much-too-quiet cave.

"Ben told me about the cave," she said. "He also gave me a rug and a waterskin from your mother's home." She finally looked at him, seeing the surprise in his expression. "I gave him some feathers in payment."

Abinadi nodded, his gaze still locked with hers. "Why do you need supplies?"

She took a deep breath, willing her voice to stay steady. "I left home."

He furrowed his brow. "You *left?* Meaning . . ."

"I ran away," she said, her breath catching. "I couldn't bear it. I couldn't . . . let the king take me as his wife. I—" Her voice broke and hot tears budded. "When he tried to . . . I knew I had to get away. They were chasing me, but I escaped the palace—"

"They *chased* you?" Abinadi said.

She could only nod. He stood and walked a few paces away.

Raquel covered her face with her hands. She hated crying, and it was all the worse in front of *him*. He must think she was a foolish girl. He'd send her back. She knew it.

"Mother was right," he said in a quiet voice.

She lifted her head and wiped her eyes. "What?"

"My mother said the king wanted to marry you—that's what being 'presented' to him meant." He watched her from a distance. "An arrow wound may be the least of your concerns."

He crossed to her and crouched. Taking both her hands in his, he stared at her intently. "Listen carefully. I don't want to alarm you, but just before I saw you running through the forest, I saw someone else. Actually, *several* others."

"Lamanites? They shot me, didn't they?"

"No," Abinadi said. "The men who shot you weren't Lamanites."

Raquel squeezed his hands, trying to understand.

"They were Nephites," he said. "They were wearing feathered head-dresses."

"They're from the king's court, then."

He nodded and said, "At first I thought the king had sent out a hunting party, but then I saw your injury." He held her gaze. "I think you're their prey."

Her mind reeled. "But if they're trying to kill me, that means the king . . ." She shook her head, unable to voice the thought.

"Issued the order," Abinadi finished.

"What about my father? Couldn't he change the king's mind?"

Abinadi released her hands and rocked back on his heels. "It seems too late for that now."

Raquel dropped her head as despair consumed her. The king was not only *looking* for her, he wanted her dead. What did her mother think? What about her father? What did *he* think? Was this just another order to be followed by King Noah? Obviously it was no longer a game for wooing her. It was now a matter of life and death. If her mind had not been completely made up before, it was now. Even if she wanted to, she could never return.

"We have to get you out of here," Abinadi said, cutting through her thoughts. "It's not safe. You may have left a trail of blood. If not, it still wouldn't be hard to track you."

She opened her mouth to refute him, then closed it. She probably *had* left an easy trail. How long had she been in the cave? *Too long,* she thought. "Thank you for helping me." She stood, surprised that most of her strength had returned. She picked up her bundle and waterskin. Her plan was to head north until she found a settlement to live in or until she reached the sea. She had always wanted to visit the great waters. She could probably find a tribe to join and weave to earn her keep.

Raquel looked at Abinadi one last time. "Tell Ben that I'll miss him. He's looking forward to your return, and your mother will be happy to see you again." She turned away, not trusting herself to say another word. She felt emotion building again and didn't want him to think she regretted her decision.

"Raquel," Abinadi said, but she kept walking.

She'd find a curaiao plant for her shoulder wound, and then she'd travel for a couple of hours to put more distance between herself and Noah's men. It shouldn't be too hard to find a place to sleep.

She reached the tunnel and moved between the close-set walls.

"Raquel."

She slowed, realizing that Abinadi had followed her into the tunnel. He touched her good shoulder and turned her around. The light from the cave entrance was just enough to make out his features. She began, "I'm sorry I have nothing to give you for your kindness—"

"I'm not looking for payment. I'm coming with you."

"You can't." She shook her head. "I've already brought you enough danger. If they track me to this cave, your hiding place will be revealed."

"Nothing here is of value anymore. We've moved to another location." A smile tugged at his lips. "You don't think I'd let a young woman face the jungle alone?"

She lifted her chin. "I can't expect you to put everything aside for some young woman and lead her around the country."

Abinadi opened his hands. "I'd never forgive myself if something happened to you." A slight smile touched his mouth. "Besides, I'm a fugitive just as you are, except *I* was cast out, whereas *you* cast yourself out."

Raquel stared at him, overwhelmed. He was too generous. But what better excuse could she give him? Apparently the threat to his life wasn't enough. "I . . . I don't think it's proper for me to be escorted by an unmarried man . . ."

He laughed, and Raquel found herself smiling. Suddenly, he grasped her hand and gave her a quick bow. "I promise I'll be more than proper."

Her skin burned at his touch. He must have thought . . . She wanted to disappear with embarrassment. Everything she said around him seemed to come out wrong. "I didn't mean . . . of course you would—are—proper." She covered her mouth just to stop herself from speaking.

Abinadi looked at her with those amused eyes. "Wait here. I need to gather a few things."

While he was gone, Raquel debated whether to flee. She hated putting him in danger. If she met her fate, so be it, but she didn't want responsibility for Abinadi's life upon her shoulders too. But if he were determined, he'd find her easily enough. Or someone else would. Fear thumped through her as she thought about running into one of the king's men. Even the Lamanites seemed mild compared to them. Finally she decided that if they were captured by Noah's men, she'd make them release Abinadi in exchange for her going along with their wishes. Instantly she felt better.

Abinadi walked out of the darkness. He carried a bundle over his back. "Ready?"

"Yes," Raquel said. She let him lead the way. They emerged from the cave silently where rays of the sunset poked through the foliage surrounding the cave entrance.

Abinadi brought a finger to his lips, and Raquel held her breath as they listened together. Then, ever so quietly, he took her hand and guided her through the maze of trees that dipped and rose with the terrain. Occasionally the howl of a monkey or cry of a bird startled Raquel, but overall their journey was uneventful. She collected curaiao leaves on the way. Several times she nearly stumbled under the weight of her pack until Abinadi insisted on carrying her rolled pack and waterskin.

He had to release her hand, and she concentrated on keeping up with his long strides. Soon darkness was thick upon the land, and Raquel was grateful when Abinadi slowed his pace. The jungle masses grew denser the farther north they traveled.

"We're almost there," he whispered. They reached a manmade clearing in the middle of a mass of vines and trees. Three tents stood side by side, illuminated by a cooking fire. As the two stepped into the open, the men crouched around the fire looked up.

"It's me," Abinadi announced. The older one who was clearly the leader, Gideon, rose to his feet and crossed to them, his gaze on Raquel. He towered over her, his dark hair and swarthy beard intimidating at first. A long, jagged scar ran from his shoulder to just below his elbow—probably from combat. Yet his eyes were kind.

"This is Raquel, daughter of Amulon," Abinadi said. Gideon simply nodded and asked about Abinadi's journey.

Raquel sensed the elder's curiosity, but his politeness prevented him from immediately satisfying it.

"Are you hungry?" Gideon asked.

"Yes," Raquel said before she could stop herself. She felt embarrassed to have blurted it out so suddenly.

"Come this way, then. We are nearly ready." He introduced her to the other elders—Ezra, Nathan, and Timon—then fetched a rug that she could sit on. "I'll take your things." He waved his arm toward the first tent. "You'll sleep there."

Ezra stood and started clearing out the tent.

"Wait," Raquel said. "I don't want to take your places. I can sleep anywhere."

"You'll be more comfortable inside the tent." Gideon's voice was kind but tinged with authority, like a man not usually crossed.

So Raquel stood by while they prepared the tent, then served a simple meal of dried fish and fruit. Food had never tasted so good. After she had finished eating, Gideon inspected her shoulder injury. He blended the curaiao paste and applied it to her shoulder.

When Raquel crawled onto her mat, her tired body heaved a sigh of relief. She listened to the quiet voices around the fire for a while, then finally drifted into sleep, content for the moment and hoping that the hunt for her had ended.

Ten

But he was wounded for our transgressions, he was bruised for our iniquities.
(Isaiah 53:5)

The sun hung large in the sky as Alma ran through the field toward his home. His father, Cephas, was coming to take him to the Sukkot Festival today. His mother, Ruth, had spent two days preparing food for the journey. Although his father served as high priest for Zeniff's court, his family lived on a large homestead outside of the main city. As Alma pumped his eight-year-old legs, he waved to the laborers. His father employed a dozen men and their families, but on his leave from court, he could be seen working alongside the men. These were the times that Alma loved the best—when his father left the long hours of study and moved among the people, working in the fields.

Today Alma had a special surprise for his father. He'd been working on a wood carving—spending hours each day to get the figure just right. He loved carving, and each night he brushed the shavings under his platform bed so that his mother didn't know he spent his time with wood instead of learning his letters.

He burst into the house and ran through the myriad rooms. "Mother!" he shouted. He found her in the cooking room, bent over a pot of steaming stew. "Is he here yet?"

His mother raised her face, her round cheeks dimpling with a smile. "No, son. I'll be sure to tell you when he arrives." She wiped her hands on a cloth and chuckled softly.

But he couldn't wait. He skidded into his room and carefully removed the wooden carving from under his bed. It was nearly as high as his hips, so he used all his strength to carry the piece through the house. Once he reached the court-yard, he set it in the middle and stood back to admire it.

Just then he heard his father's voice, calling that he was approaching. Alma ran out the gate and down the path. His father looked so regal as he strode up *the path, his dark cape flying behind him. When his father reached him, he smiled and tousled Alma's hair. "Greetings, son."*

"Father," Alma burst out. "I have a surprise for you."

His father's face broke into a rare smile as he removed the traveling bundle from his back. Alma grabbed his hand and tugged him toward the courtyard. Just then his mother came out of the house. Instead of rushing to her husband, she watched father and son with amusement.

Alma pointed proudly to his statue. "See? I carved it myself."

His father just stood there, staring, saying nothing. Alma looked at his mother. The light had gone from her eyes. What was wrong? He'd done all his chores, worked hard at his learning . . .

"You carved this?" his father asked, his voice sounding strange.

"Yes. It's a quetzal bird. I added the scales of a snake—that was the hardest part."

"I know what it is," his father said. He glanced at his wife, then turned to Alma. "Why did you choose to make a bird like this?"

"The blacksmith had one in his shop," Alma said.

His father glanced at his wife again, his face reddening. "This is an idol, son. This is the feathered serpent that is a pagan god. This image is offensive to our Lord and defies His holy name."

Alma stared at his creation. He'd spent months carving it, bit by bit. How could he have known the small statue he'd seen was a pagan god?

"We must destroy it," his father said.

Alma stared at his father, blinking hard. Destroy it?

His father strode toward the carving and picked it up as if it weighed little more than a leaf. He took it to the road outside the courtyard.

Using a piece of chert, he started it on fire, and within minutes, the statue was consumed in flames. Alma tried not to cry as he watched it burn.

His father came up behind him. "You have a talent, son, but you must put it to good use. You need to spend your young years learning, not carving animals and birds." He took one of Alma's hands and turned it over. "My son should have calluses from bringing in the harvest or caring for the flocks, not from idly chipping wood."

His father left the burning site and returned to the house.

Alma sank to his knees, watching the wood char. He'd thought his father would be so pleased, so impressed with his hard work. The one thing that Alma loved to do—and now his father wanted to take it away. Alma wiped at the furious tears that ran along his cheeks, vowing to never show his father any of his carvings again.

Alma awoke to pitch darkness and heard a commotion coming from somewhere inside the palace. He raised his head and winced at the throbbing. For the past day and night, he had continued to drink with Jahza by his side. He ran his hand over the empty cushions next to him. She must have slipped out while he was sleeping. For a brief moment, he wondered where she'd gone. A twinge of envy pulsed through him as he thought of her with another man.

He rose to his feet and stumbled toward the jug of wine. Another sip and his mouth wasn't so dry. He lit one of the oil lamps. The shadows leapt back, revealing a disorganized room. Rugs and cushions were scattered about, wall hangings haphazard, wine spilled on the elaborate rug. Alma's head spun as he thought of what had taken place over the past day. It was like he lived in another world. No accountability, no expectations, no honor . . .

But now I am a high priest, Alma reminded himself.

Running footsteps sounded outside his door. He walked to the door, steady on his feet, and threw it open. He signaled a servant who was passing by. "What's happening?" Alma called.

The thin man turned. "The king is sending out a new batch of men to find her."

"Find who?"

"The girl—the one who rejected him."

"What are you talking about?"

"You really haven't heard?" the servant asked in a half-mocking voice.

"I—never mind, tell me from the beginning." Alma listened as the servant told him about Amulon's daughter, Raquel, rejecting the king's proposal of marriage, then fleeing the palace. An earlier search party had nearly shot and captured her, but then she'd disappeared. Now, even though it was the middle of the night, Noah had ordered the best trackers in the city to band together and find her.

Alma's mind was still fuzzy, but he shuddered at the cruelty of tracking a girl. He'd heard stories of the king's ruthlessness toward treasonous soldiers, but this was against a young girl . . . He'd seen Raquel that night at court; she couldn't be more than sixteen or seventeen. He wondered if Amulon would take responsibility for his daughter's insolence. Alma reentered his room and splashed water on his face from a basin Jahza had brought in earlier. Feeling slightly refreshed, he left his room in search of Amulon. The man had been a friend to him, and perhaps he needed support.

It didn't take long for Alma to find the king and the other high priests gathered in the throne room. As always, Amulon sat next to the king. *At least there doesn't seem to be a breach between the men,* Alma thought, as he watched them laughing and pointing. Then a snapping sound drew his eyes to the spectacle in the corner of the room. Two men, with their hands and feet bound, were facing the wall. A burly servant was whipping them, alternating between the two. Their backs displayed bright red stripes, and blood ran down the length of their bodies.

One of the tortured men whimpered with each strike; the other remained silent. Alma felt sick, wondering what these men had done. He looked at the king and caught Amulon's eye.

"There you are, my friend," Amulon said, motioning for Alma to join them.

Alma strode across the room, flinching each time the whip sounded. He tried to maintain a nonchalant expression as they smiled at him.

"Welcome back," Noah said with a gleam in his eye. He slid over and made room for Alma on the cushions next to him.

Once Alma was seated between them, Amulon leaned over and said in a loud voice, "I heard Jahza had to return to her chambers to rest." He winked at Alma.

The king bellowed with laughter and jabbed Alma in the ribs. "Well done."

Alma forced a laugh, his face flushing. The court seemed to know *everything* almost as soon as it happened. "What's going on here?" he asked before the conversation could fully focus on him.

Amulon drew a breath in, his eyes flitting over to the king, then said, "Those men were sent to find a girl, and they failed."

"Your daughter?" Alma asked.

Amulon took a long drink of his wine before answering. "I no longer have a daughter."

A chill passed through Alma as he studied Amulon, seeing outright fear in the man's eyes. So this was how his friend endured the ordeal. Amulon was siding with the king in order to prove his loyalty to the throne—and most likely to save his own life. But to disown his very daughter?

Noah slapped his thigh and chuckled. "The young woman who insulted my throne will regret the moment it entered her mind." He stood, using Alma's shoulder for support, and shouted to the general court. "Do you hear that? Anyone who defies me will be hunted down and killed!"

Amulon raised his goblet of wine, his eyes determined now. "We hear you!"

The others in the room raised their goblets and drank to the king's proclamation. A jolt passed through Alma as he raised his own goblet to his lips and obediently drank.

Noah pointed at the two tortured men. Their backs were bloody, their breathing ragged. "Take them from my sight. I'm tired of looking at such useless men. Throw them in prison until I decide their fate." His gaze surveyed the crowd. "Where are the dancers?"

A couple of priests leapt to their feet, calling for the women. People scurried about, some leaving the room, others taking their places to watch the upcoming performance.

Alma glanced at the king. A smile was plastered on his face, and wine stained the front of his beaded cowl. As several veiled women came in, Amulon clapped and cheered. Everything had turned carefree again—as if no men had been tortured just moments before. A collection of instruments started up with lively and inviting music. The women swayed toward them, and one by one, they removed their veils. Their haunting eyes seemed to capture Alma. He was trying to push out the thoughts of an abandoned and disowned girl running for her life, so he focused on the dancers, standing alongside Noah and Amulon and swaying to the music.

He scanned the women quickly, not seeing Jahza. Perhaps she had indeed gone back to her chamber to sleep. Amulon drained his goblet then refilled it. Alma could certainly understand his friend's need to drink heavier than usual. Amulon rose to his unsteady feet and picked a dancing partner. The man didn't seem to have any qualms about dancing with other women even though he had a wife at home. It was just part of their callings as high priests in the greatest court in the land.

A slim hand reached for Alma's arm, and he turned. A woman near his age stood before him, her eyes and smile welcoming. She was beautiful, yes, but in a different way than Jahza. She drew him toward her into a slow dance and whispered in his ear, "Hello, it's nice to finally meet you. I'm Bethel."

Alma drew back a little and met her gaze. "I was just recently made a high priest."

"I know." The woman's laughter tinkled like bells. "We *all* know." She lowered her lashes as if she were suddenly shy. "You are much sought after."

It was Alma's turn to laugh. This dancer was far from shy, in spite of her pretense. He knew the game now. In her arms it was easy to forget the things weighing on his mind—his father's integrity, his mother's modesty, what might have caused Amulon's daughter to run away . . . And for a moment he even forgot about coming across Noah's new bride sobbing in the garden.

An hour or two passed; it was difficult for Alma to keep track of time. His mind was muddled with wine again. He had learned to merely take small sips—that way he wouldn't become sick again. The woman he'd first danced with, Bethel, had stayed by his side. From time to time he wondered about the whereabouts of Jahza. Maybe she already knew he'd moved his attention to this new woman—after all, it seemed that word traveled fast in court.

The evening meal was served. Alma still wasn't used to the extravagant display of food—papayas, guavas, varieties of squash, mushrooms, quail eggs, avocado, deer and rabbit meat, cacao drink, honeyed sweets—it was luxurious. As he seated himself next to Bethel, a pair of warriors entered the room. Each of them wore a feathered headdress, signifying their important status. Their white cotton capes were soiled and dirty. Thick jade earrings adorned their ears and both wore gold armbands. A hush fell over the people.

One of the warriors raised his fist, holding several quetzal feathers. He bowed to the king, then said, "We have found these feathers that belong to the daughter of Amulon. We traced her to a hut near the river—and a boy named Benjamin was there."

Alma cast a furtive glace at Amulon, whose face was reddening.

Noah stood, adjusting his cape of quetzal feathers across his broad shoulders as if preparing for a fight. "Bring him in. We will question him now."

One of the warriors left, returning almost immediately with a young boy. Alma guessed he was around eight or nine years old. The thin child struggled against the warrior's thick hand. The boy's hair was wild and his clothing too big, as if someone had handed it down to him. His feet were bare, tanned, and calloused.

Alma cringed as the large men shoved the child to a kneeling position, his bony knees knocking against the floor. Their hands dug into the boy's shoulder, forcing him into submission. Benjamin kept his mouth clamped shut, but his eyes took in everything. For a moment, his gaze rested on Alma, who felt a strange sensation. He was ready to feel sorry for the boy, as he had the men who were whipped, but this boy's expression stopped him. It was not only defiant—it was as if he welcomed his capture. Alma doubted he'd seen greater courage than that displayed in this small boy.

Noah grinned and hitched up his snakeskin belt across his broad waist as he strode to the collapsed child. Amulon leapt to his feet, and the other high priests joined him. They formed a circle around the captured boy. Alma followed reluctantly, repelled yet curious at the same time.

The king removed his sword and playfully fingered the obsidian protruding from the wooden club. "Where is she?" he boomed.

The boy's shoulders flinched, but he simply stared up at the menacing king. One of the warriors grabbed a fistful of hair and yanked Benjamin's head back. "Answer his Highness," he growled.

Benjamin licked his dry lips, his gaze still focused on the king. But he remained silent.

Noah chuckled and circled the boy, turning his sword over in his hand again and again. Alma and the other priests watched breathlessly. "It's all right," the king said in a soft voice. "He'll talk soon enough." He extended his jeweled hand with the sword. "The whips."

Alma's stomach lurched. Whipping a man was one thing, but this was a child. It took every ounce of Alma's strength to remain an observer. At the king's first strike, his eyes involuntarily closed. The boy's chin trembled, and a tear escaped.

The wine Alma had consumed did nothing to soften the king's brutality. Another strike and a muffled groan escaped the boy's lips. More tears, but still the boy didn't talk. He brought his hands to his face as his shoulders shook.

Amulon stared at the child, his eyes glazed over. It was as if he hadn't registered this extreme torture of a young child. How far would Amulon go—or allow the king to go—in pursuing his errant daughter?

On the third strike, blood from the stripes had soaked through the boy's clothing. Alma winced and took a step back, surveying the gathered men. The dancing women had slipped out of the room at some point; so had many of the usual crowd. It seemed that the only ones who'd remained were the warriors and high priests. For a brief instant he saw these supposedly great and powerful men of the court as men simply ruled by fear. Noah brought the whip down upon the boy's back again. The boy was openly crying now.

"Where is she? No girl is worth this pain! Tell us where she is and you will be spared!" Noah continued to shout, but Benjamin refused to answer.

Finally, the king crouched in front of the boy and said, "Are you foolish enough to die for Raquel?"

The boy nodded, nearly choking on his sobs.

Noah straightened and wrinkled his nose, as if he were disgusted by the smell of blood. "Tie him up with the others."

The boy was dragged away, and the high priests meandered back to the meal. Alma hesitated. The women were gone, the music had stopped, and suddenly he didn't feel well. Perhaps the wine had caught up to him after all. He would have to sleep off the tortured image of Benjamin. The boy had amazing tenacity and endurance. And there had been something else in his eyes, something Alma couldn't explain.

He asked for leave from the king, and Noah gave him a knowing smile. Alma stumbled along the hall to his quarters. The room had been cleaned, the cushions replaced, and the jug of wine refilled. Was it Jahza or the new woman, Bethel, who'd cleaned his quarters and brought the wine? He settled onto the cushions, fully dressed, expecting to fall asleep immediately.

His body relaxed as he hovered between the state of wakefulness and dreaming. The beautiful eyes of a woman filled his mind—but they didn't belong to Jahza or Bethel. He tried to push Maia's image out of his mind.

Then he heard the door open and shut, followed by the soft tinkling of an anklet or pair of bracelets. A moment later, a warm body slipped beneath the covers next to him.

Eleven

O give thanks unto the Lord; for he is good; for his mercy endureth for ever.
(1 Chronicles 16:34)

The early morning rain had soaked Abinadi thoroughly, but he was grateful that at least Raquel had a dry place to sleep as well as privacy. He rose just before dawn, not being able to stand the wet any longer. He entered Gideon's tent and found a dry tunic, then peeled off his wet one. A quick glance told him that the welts on his chest were nearly healed. Exiting the tent, Abinadi decided to start the morning fire. Everyone else was still asleep, but it would be nice for them to wake up to a warm meal of maize cakes. He had yet to perfect his cooking skills, but by the time they fetched his mother and Ben, he was sure his mother would be duly impressed.

Striking the chert together to start the fire, Abinadi thought about the near miss Raquel had had with King Noah's men. If they were out to kill her, they wouldn't give up easily. In fact, stopping to camp might have been a poor decision. They should have traveled directly to Gideon's new homestead—a wild patch of wilderness that bordered Lamanite territory.

Abinadi lifted the waterproof skins that covered the basket of maize and the bag of maize meal. There wasn't quite enough for everyone, so he ground more maize kernels, then added water to make a ball of dough. He slapped the rounded forms flat and set them near the fire. Just as the first cakes started to sizzle near the heat, a motion caught his attention. Raquel had stepped out of her tent. Abinadi tried not to stare. It wasn't the gash on her head or the bulky bandages on her shoulder, rather the way her ginger hair set off her dark eyes, making her look like a wide-eyed fawn. His mother's observation flashed through his mind: *You care for her.*

But I shouldn't, Abinadi tried to tell himself as Raquel's gaze settled on him and she smiled. Even though she'd left her family, her home, her luxuries, there was something about her that seemed unobtainable. She was someone who needed to be taken care of in the proper manner—a fine home, servants, nice clothing. None of which Abinadi could provide. It would take months just to build permanent homes at the new settlement and many people to reap profitable crops that could be traded for other goods. Until then, life there would be meager at best.

Raquel approached the fire and crouched opposite of Abinadi, extending her hands toward the warm flames.

Abinadi ignored the string of thoughts that ran through his mind. Before he knew it, he'd have their entire future planned. "How are you feeling?" he asked.

"Sore, but I slept well." She stifled a yawn. "The cakes look good."

"Anything looks good when you're hungry," he said with a muffled laugh.

She looked at him. "I suppose so."

"Well, I'm sure they're edible," Abinadi said in a teasing voice.

Her face flushed. "Of course they are . . . I didn't mean . . ."

"After all," he continued, "how hard can it be to mix maize meal and water and cook it? Women do it all the time."

Raquel's eyes narrowed as she caught onto his teasing. "Not hard at all. It's something even a man can do."

He smiled and held her gaze until she looked away.

After a moment, she said, "In truth, I'm not used to men cooking for me or cooking at all. But I'm sure the cakes will taste fine."

"Hmmm," Abinadi said. There it was again. The difference between them. She probably had servants to do the cooking. She must be laughing at his pitiful attempt. "I can assure you that these will taste just fine."

"I believe you," she said in a quiet voice. "I hope you'll be the one doing the cooking since I was banned from my mother's cooking fire long ago."

"Banned?" Abinadi asked.

She lowered her eyes. "Ever since I caught my best feathered cape on fire, my mother's given me tasks that have nothing to do with heat or flame."

"Oh, I thought . . ."

Raquel tilted her head, studying him. "I can guess what you thought, Abinadi."

As she spoke his name, a shiver ran the length of his arms.

"And I can assure you that you thought wrong," she continued.

He stared at her, not entirely catching her meaning.

"I'm not who you think I am. I might appear an indulged, selfish girl, but I've rejected that life now, although I never did care for it." She waved a hand at their surroundings. "I like it out here, and I'll learn how to cook if it'll earn my keep."

Abinadi opened his mouth to answer, but she plunged on.

"I heard the elders discussing me last night. I won't let you *or* Gideon return and plead for my emancipation from the king. Even if I had his pardon and didn't have to marry him, I still don't want to live in the city of Nephi. My home is no longer there." She folded her arms, her eyes dark with stubbornness. "And if you try, I'll just leave again."

"All right. All right," Abinadi said, trying to keep the smile off of his face. He admired her tenacity.

"Good," Raquel said with a firm nod. "So tell me about who lives at the settlement . . . you mentioned your brother."

"Helam," Abinadi said. "Although you probably won't see him much. He keeps to himself when he's not working or studying. When he was twelve, he was helping my father burn old crops. He was caught in a fire ring and suffered severe burns. Although my brother recovered, my father never forgave himself for not being able to prevent the injuries. And I—it took a lot of prayer to feel like I had been forgiven."

"For what?"

"I was sick that day—I should have been there to help my brother." Abinadi looked away as a shiver passed through him. "About a year after the accident, my father left. He never returned."

Raquel stared at him. "It was a horrible accident. Nothing that you or your father could have prevented."

"I know," Abinadi said in a quiet voice.

"And your brother? He's all right now?"

"In a sense. His skin is deformed, so he insists on covering his body. His condition doesn't bode well for friendships or . . . marriage and children. When Noah became king, people like my brother became automatic outcasts. That's when Helam started living in the elders' community."

"I'm so sorry," she whispered, her eyes filled with tears. "My family is not the only one that has suffered under the king's rule. I wish there were a way I could change what's happened."

On her final word, Abinadi heard something snap in the trees behind him. He lifted a finger to his lips. "Shhh!"

Her eyes widened as she held his gaze.

He pointed toward the tent, mouthing, "Get inside."

Raquel seemed to understand the alarm in his eyes, and she rose and backed away toward her tent. But she wasn't fast enough.

A man leapt from the trees just as Abinadi turned. He had only an instant to prepare himself for the attack. Lunging to the right, he narrowly avoided the man's dagger. Raquel screamed.

This startled the attacker. Abinadi took the moment's hesitation to dive for the man's legs. The attacker's knees buckled, and he fell forward. Quickly, Abinadi released the man's legs and lunged again, throwing his full weight onto the man's back. He grappled for the sword and pinned both of the attacker's arms down.

Gideon and the other elders rushed from their tents. They immediately seized the man, who looked stunned.

As the elders tied the man's legs and arms with a length of rope, Abinadi studied his attacker. The man was well-dressed in a tunic of fine cotton, his cape had rows of long feathers, and his long dagger had a hilt of gold. Abinadi wiped his bloody lip, feeling the throbbing tenderness. He looked at his hand. It was bleeding too. Raquel ran over to him. "Your hand!" She examined his palm. "You must have touched the obsidian on his sword."

While Raquel went to find a binding, Gideon set in on the questioning. "Who are you? And where are you from?"

The attacker looked at them. "I'm Izehar. The king sent me."

"You didn't know you were outnumbered, did you?" Gideon said.

The man shook his head.

"Is there anyone else with you?" Abinadi said.

Izehar remained silent until Gideon yanked the ropes tighter. "We separated a while back."

"And what gives us the pleasure of your presence?" Gideon asked.

The man's eyes shifted to Raquel, who had just returned. She ignored him and crossed to Abinadi. She started wrapping his hand. When she finished, she turned to Izehar. "You can give the king a message for me—"

"Raquel," Abinadi cut in.

But she continued. "Tell the king that the only way I'll return to the city of Nephi is on a bier with my eyes closed in death."

Abinadi touched Raquel's shoulder. "I think that's why this man is here."

Izehar laughed. "Too late for passionate threats, woman. The king already wants you dead." His amused eyes stayed on Raquel. "I can understand the king's obsession with you, but it's not enough to keep you alive." He lowered his voice to a harsh tone. "You may think you're free, but someone else is paying your price."

"What do you mean?" Raquel asked.

"A boy named Benjamin. He rots in prison because he refuses to give information." A sneer crossed his face. "You and the boy are a stubborn lot, but that won't get you anywhere. The king has vowed to put the boy to death if you aren't found by the new moon."

Abinadi's heart thumped. The new moon would rise tomorrow night. He saw Raquel clench her fists. Ben didn't deserve to be imprisoned. He was only a boy. Then a new fear coursed through Abinadi. If they'd found Ben, what about his mother?

"We need to break camp *now*," Gideon said, looking at Timon and the other elders. "Guard him while we prepare."

Timon watched Izehar while the others struck the tents and packed belongings.

Abinadi crossed to Gideon. "We have to go back for him."

"We will," Gideon said. "We need to figure out what to do with Izehar first."

Raquel came up behind them. She had her pack slung over her shoulder, a maize cake in hand. "I'm going." Her face was pale and drawn, but her eyes determined. "It's my fault Ben was captured. Only my return will release him."

"No," Abinadi said. "It will be your death."

Raquel swallowed. "I know." She gave him a searching look as tears brimmed her eyes.

Abinadi grabbed her arm and steered her away from Gideon and the rest of the camp. He stopped just outside the clearing, concealing them in the tangled foliage, away from anyone's hearing. He relaxed his grip but still held onto her. She stared at him, her expression stubborn.

"You came all this way," he said, "encountered all this danger, just to return like a lamb to the slaughter?"

She nodded, a tear rolling onto her cheek. "I must. I won't be able to live with myself if I don't."

"I know," Abinadi said. He touched her chin so that she looked at him. "We're going to put together a plan to get Ben out. But you have to leave it to me and Gideon. In the meantime, we can't have you running back. We love Ben just as much as you do."

Her gaze softened, and he knew she was really listening to him. "And when we return with him," he said, "we won't let him out of our sight again." He smiled gently. "We'll even fetch my mother, and she can teach you about the fine skills of cooking."

A smile touched her lips. "I'd like that."

"Me too," Abinadi said, his heart thudding. Now that he had her cooperation and assurance that she wasn't going to throw herself at the mercy of Izehar, he realized how alone they were—and how secluded.

Raquel seemed to sense it too, but she didn't move. For a moment, they just looked at each other. She leaned toward him, their bodies a breath apart. "Be safe," she whispered.

"I will," he said.

"Catch him!" Gideon's voice tore through the trees.

Abinadi turned toward the sound. Someone ran through the underbrush not far from them. Then Gideon appeared. "He escaped!"

Timon caught up. "I'll find him."

Abinadi looked from one to the other. "I'll go too."

"No," Gideon said. "You and the others look after Raquel. Stay north until you reach the first river. I'll meet you there."

Abinadi hesitated for a moment. "All right."

Gideon and Timon took off in the direction the soldier had gone. Abinadi stepped away from Raquel. "Follow me." Together they walked into the clearing. The packing had been organized into bundles they could carry upon their backs.

Silently, the small group loaded the bundles onto their backs and started their journey.

*　*　*

They traveled silently through the dense foliage. Every so often, Raquel felt Abinadi's gaze on her, and her heart soared. In the brief secluded moments they had shared, she sensed something powerful between them. Abinadi was so different from King Noah, from Eli. But it was more than that. She felt comfortable with him—safe, protected. She didn't care that they were traveling to an unknown place with scarcely food or supplies. They'd join in growing crops with the other settlers and live off the land. If Abinadi was at her side, she knew she could be happy. As the sun dappled through the trees, Raquel wondered what Abinadi thought of her. Had he felt the same powerful feelings?

She pursed her lips together, pushing away the doubts that fringed her mind. She knew Abinadi must think she had been indulged—and she had—but she'd prove to him that she was changed and that she didn't miss her former life. If only Ben and Esther were here, then everything would be right.

The conversation between Abinadi and the elder named Ezra floated in and out of her mind. They were talking about some things Raquel had never heard of. *Resurrection. Atonement. The coming of the Lord.* What did they mean? She focused on the conversation, listening carefully. They kept referring to Isaiah. Who was he?

Her curiosity kept building, and finally Raquel turned to face the men. "Please tell me who Isaiah is."

Abinadi looked at her with surprise. "He was a great prophet. His words have been passed down on the brass plates that Father Lehi brought from Jerusalem."

Ezra nodded and moved ahead of them.

Raquel knew of Jerusalem and how the families of Lehi and Ishmael traveled across the high seas to reach this place. "What are the brass plates?"

A smiled played on Abinadi's face as he stepped closer to her. "Only recently have I learned the truth surrounding the brass plates."

"Oh?" Raquel asked, very intrigued.

"Remember the cavern I found you in? The place the elders used for their meetings?"

She nodded, slowing her step to concentrate better.

"In the first years of the establishment of the city of Nephi, the prophets Nephi and Jacob built the beginnings of that cavern as a place to keep the brass plates and other items like the steel sword of Laban and the Liahona," Abinadi said. "They have stayed safe for centuries."

"I thought those things were only legends made up by people who followed King Zeniff. You're saying they're real?"

Abinadi lowered his voice. The others were ahead of them now, mostly out of hearing range. "I have seen them myself, but as an elder, I cannot reveal their new location."

"You *saw* them? In the cavern?"

"I did." He looked at her. "Those legends are *true.*" He took a deep breath. "Many people have believed in the wrong things for a long time. God has never changed. His plan has always been the same—centuries ago and in our time."

She frowned. She'd overhead discussions between her father and other men about the archaic practices of their ancestors. Her father had explained more than once that the tangible gods of the earth were what should be relied upon, not some god that no one could see or hear. Water, earth, the sun . . . anyone could see those; anyone could see how much respect they deserved. The sacrifices at the temple were made to please the jaguar god and the moon goddess, Ix Chel.

But these gods didn't grace their people with guiding commandments like Abinadi's god did. The only one who issued commandments in the land was King Noah. "Tell me your version of Lehi's journey," she said.

As Abinadi spoke, Raquel remained quiet most of the time, concentrating on her footing through the undergrowth and asking a question here or there. She was amazed at the differences in the versions that she'd heard. But one thing still bothered her. "Why didn't the Lord give Laman the call to lead from the beginning? Wouldn't that have prevented so much hatred and fighting?"

Abinadi stopped and pushed a branch to the side, letting her pass by him. "When Laman was given jurisdiction over his group of people, they lived in such iniquity that the Spirit was taken from them. They cursed themselves because of their own failings. If Laman had been given that same leadership while the family was still together and wandering the desert, the curse would have prevented the Liahona from working, and they wouldn't have found Bountiful or eventually arrived at the promised land."

"Maybe Laman would have been more righteous if he didn't feel threatened by his younger brother," Raquel suggested, her breath coming short as they started up a hill.

"He had opportunities to prove his faithfulness over and over, but he continued to commit vile acts of near-murder, and on the ship he expressed his pagan ideas," Abinadi continued quietly. "He wasn't the one who prayed to the Lord to understand the things that Lehi saw in a vision."

A shiver passed through her body. "Nephi was the one who asked?"

"When Nephi tried to explain his vision to his brothers, he told them, 'Do ye not remember the things which the Lord hath said?—If ye will not harden your hearts, and ask me in faith, believing that ye shall receive, with diligence in keeping my commandments, surely these things shall be made known unto you.'"

"You know what Nephi actually said?"

Abinadi nodded. "I've read his writings."

She stared at him. Was it true? It seemed so fantastic . . . yet so simple at the same time. "So what did his brothers do? Did they ask the Lord?"

"No," Abinadi said. "They told Nephi that he'd spoken hard things, and those things were too much for them to bear. But they humbled themselves for a short time."

"Yet they didn't ask the Lord to know for themselves?" Raquel asked. "Why not?"

Abinadi slowed his step, breathing hard. The others had already reached the top of the hill and had started down the other side. "It might seem simple for others to do it, but when I prayed for the first time, it wasn't easy." He glanced at her. "What about yourself?"

She looked away. *What about me?* She'd seen Ben pray—but he was a child. "I—I wouldn't know what to pray about. It's not as if Nephi told me his vision or my father is Lehi."

"Of course not," he said in a soft voice. "But *I* wanted to know for *my*self—to know if the Lord was real. That's why I'm here now."

Raquel's eyes burned. Abinadi's words touched her to her very core. It was as if a powerful, unseen force enveloped her and made her feel warm and strong at the same time. But she couldn't deny the inviting peace she felt around Abinadi and the elders. Was it because they believed in this specific God?

"If . . . if someone does believe, what would he or she do?" Raquel asked, stumbling on her words. "How much would they have to change?"

They reached the top of the hill, and Abinadi paused. "Some people wouldn't have to change much. It's really about having faith in Christ and His Atonement, then making a commitment—to live the commandments, to obey His laws, to repent and forgive others."

Each word seemed to weigh on Raquel's shoulders. They started down the hill as Abinadi continued to explain the commandments, repentance, forgiveness, then the law of sacrifice that would be fulfilled with the coming of the Lord. Raquel thought about each one. Could Abinadi overlook the fact that she'd dishonored her parents? But more importantly, could the Lord? She had blatantly broken that commandment. Of course she could justify it, since marrying the king wasn't a *righteous* decision. Still, the thought troubled her. She resolved to ask Abinadi about this later.

When Abinadi finished his explanations, she had one more question. "What if the people don't repent, don't accept the Lord?"

His expression clouded for a moment. "Those who knowingly rebel against God and don't repent will not enjoy salvation and will not be a part of the first resurrection." He glanced over at her. "The Lord wants us to be happy. His plan allows for us to become so. We must trust in the Lord and let him inside our hearts and truly accept Him—just as He has already accepted us."

Raquel nodded. Her heart told her he was right. But if she were to accept all of the Lord's teachings and follow *all* of the commandments, would she have to return home?

Abinadi lowered his voice as they neared the others. "Raquel, knowing what kind of man the king is—a man who would imprison a small, innocent boy—you made the right decision to leave."

She stared at him, surprised at his insight, a glimmer of hope touching her heart. "I—thank you for telling me that. I want to do the right thing. But I'm afraid the consequences might be too great . . . for Ben and for me."

"The counsel of your parents was unrighteous," Abinadi said. "You can still honor your parents without obeying them in this regard."

Raquel sighed. But if she *had* followed her parents, none of this would be happening. And what about when Noah kissed her? That was something she could never tell anyone—it was too horrible to think about. As they continued to walk, the sounds of a river grew louder.

"We're almost there," Abinadi said.

The group ahead had stopped near the bank to wait for Gideon and Timon. Raquel and Abinadi joined them, and as the time slowly passed, Raquel grew more anxious. What would Abinadi and Gideon face when they returned to the city of Nephi?

When the sun sat high in the sky, they heard someone slashing through the trees. Gideon and Timon came into sight.

Abinadi rushed to them. "What happened?"

Gideon wiped his forehead with the back of his hand. "Lost his trail. He's probably made it to the city by now . . ."

Timon turned away, deep disappointment on his face.

"We can't wait another moment," Abinadi said.

"I know," Gideon said. "I would have continued to the city, but I knew you'd want to come."

"Yes," Abinadi said. "Let's go."

Without another word, he and Gideon shouldered their bundles. Gideon riffled through a couple of the packs, finding clothing items and stuffing them into his bundle. As Raquel watched the preparations, panic swelled in her chest. What if they were killed? What if she never saw Abinadi again? What if it were too late for Ben?

Abinadi lifted a hand in farewell, and Raquel waved back. Their eyes locked for a moment, and she was tempted to beg him not to go. But there was no other option. One of them had to go help Ben.

Ezra stepped forward and said, "We'll pray for your success."

Abinadi nodded. "And I will pray for yours."

Ezra set his mouth in a grim line. "You will find us camped a half day west of here."

Abinadi cast one final look in Raquel's direction. Then he and Gideon turned away.

She stood watching for a moment, wondering if the Lord would hear *her* if she prayed for Abinadi. Then she turned toward the others, who were already preparing to cross the river.

Raquel plunged into the meandering water with Ezra close to her, supporting her elbow. Once on the other side, she sat in the sun to dry while the men made several trips back and forth carrying supplies high above their heads so the bundles wouldn't get wet.

Was Abinadi right about her not following her parents' desires? If she had, Ben wouldn't have been imprisoned. Abinadi and Gideon wouldn't be racing back to the city—into the threat of danger. She closed her eyes as she thought about Abinadi and their stolen moment in the forest. She certainly seemed to amuse him. But beyond the teasing, she'd seen something more serious in his gaze before he left for the city. Something that made her smile.

She bit her lip and opened her eyes. It would do her no good to let her mind wander about a man such as Abinadi. If he knew about the king kissing her, Abinadi would be far from amused, and he would probably view her with disdain.

The packs were organized again, and Raquel rose from her place. She pushed Abinadi to the back of her mind. But try as she might, he resurfaced in her thoughts time and again as she followed behind the elders.

Twelve

The Lord . . . heareth the prayer of the righteous.
(Proverbs 15:29)

The two men traveled hard and fast. Once they came within view of the city of Nephi, Abinadi said, "I hope you have a plan."

"I do," Gideon said, smiling. "You know me."

"Yes," Abinadi said. "That I do. So I assume we aren't going to present ourselves to the court and dazzle the king with our intellect."

"No. Follow me." Gideon pointed to the north, along the edge of the fields. On the northern end of the city, the king's agave winepresses worked day and night above the rows and rows of waist-high plants. The laborers toiled without much reprieve this time of year. As Gideon and Abinadi drew near, the sweet, intoxicating scent wafted toward them.

Abinadi inhaled deeply and sighed. The perfume of the agave nectar was heavenly as usual.

"The men at the presses know who I am, so you'll have to go in as a wine merchant." Gideon lowered the pack off of his back and withdrew several onties of silver from it. He handed them to Abinadi. "Tell them you want the pure wine—undiluted. Tell them you're on errand from one of the king's priests or concubines."

Abinadi frowned as he took the silver. He'd never held this amount of treasure at once. "It costs this much?"

"No," Gideon said. "But any questions will be stopped by generosity. Then meet me on the hill of the last sheep field." He reached for the bundle on Abinadi's back. "Let me take your things so the taskmaster won't suspect you've traveled far."

Abinadi relinquished his pack and was about to ask why they needed the very expensive wine, but when he turned, Gideon had already disappeared into the trees beyond. He walked to the first press. Men worked over hot fires, heating the agave juice. Several boys carrying jugs ran back and forth between the presses and a hut. Another group of people worked among the plants, scooping out the juice from the hollow of the piñas.

As Abinadi approached, he looked for the taskmaster. One of the workers looked up and immediately crossed to him. The man's body was covered in perspiration. "What do you want?"

"I need to speak with your master," Abinadi said.

"I am Caton, the taskmaster," the man said, his eyes narrowing. "Who are you?"

"Servant to the king. I've come to purchase a jug of undiluted wine on behalf of his favorite concubine."

The taskmaster's face pulled into a frown. "It will delay production and take us too much time to make up for it."

Abinadi held out an onti of silver.

Caton's face brightened considerably. "Ahh. It will be just a moment." He turned and hurried inside the hut.

The errand boys stood in their places, watching Abinadi with curiosity. Much to his relief, he didn't recognize any of them.

The taskmaster returned, and the exchange was made. Abinadi lifted the skin covering and smelled the opening of the jug. Sure enough, the strong odor of agave pulque reached his nose.

"It's the very best," Caton said with a grin. Then his gaze turned curious. "What did you say your name was?"

"I'd rather keep the gift confidential for now."

"Yes, but—"

"Thank you. I'll send your good wishes to the court." Abinadi turned away. He couldn't go in the direction that Gideon had, so he headed east, toward the city. As soon as he was out of sight of the wine presses, he turned north again, heading for the fields. When he spotted the first flock of sheep, he was surprised to see a half dozen shepherds with them. Usually just one or two could handle a flock in the daytime. He skirted the field, keeping in the shadows of the surrounding trees. It didn't take him long to clear the fields. Once he reached the meeting place, Abinadi concealed himself in the forest.

As the sun made its western journey, he waited for Gideon. The hours dragged until evening arrived, and only then did Abinadi start to worry. Gideon hadn't shared his plan, and Abinadi didn't understand what was taking the man so long.

Then he saw something that chilled him despite the warm night. A militia of soldiers exited the city in rows of tens. Abinadi scanned the soldiers, estimating at least two hundred men. They crossed the fields below him and moved into the forest. Fear entered his heart as he thought about Raquel. Maybe Izehar had made it back to the city and Noah was sending out his forces.

After a moment of reasoning, Abinadi decided that even Noah wasn't foolish enough to marshal his army just to capture a lone woman. Abinadi moved deeper in the trees until he could barely glimpse the moon-splashed fields.

Suddenly, something grabbed his arm. He whirled and came face-to-face with Gideon—and the man's huge smile.

"Didn't hear me coming, did you?"

Abinadi had been so focused on the militia's movement that he'd forgotten to watch his own back. He answered as nonchalantly as possible. "Where have you been?"

Gideon cocked his head, the grin still on his face. "The Lord has answered our prayers."

"What do you mean?"

Gideon pointed to the forests beyond. "With full force, Noah is attacking the Lamanites scouting the borders. The court is in an uproar. Soldiers running everywhere, Noah shouting commands . . . No one will notice two drunk men stumbling down the prison steps."

"This wine is for *us?*" Abinadi asked. "I don't think—"

Gideon laughed. "I hope you're a good pretender. We'll act like we're drunk and generously share with the prison guards. Tonight we'll be their best friends." He rustled something out of his pack. "But first, put this on."

Abinadi stared at the fine capes Gideon produced. The rich luster of the colored feathers shimmered in the moonlight. "They'll think we're noblemen." Gideon pulled out two turbans and handed one to Abinadi.

Once both men were newly attired, they moved quickly to the city where the soldiers had recently exited.

The city was eerily quiet. Although oil lamps burned in most homes, the sloped streets were all but empty. Regardless, Gideon insisted that they walk slowly, stagger, and sing loudly. If anyone was questioned later, they'd be identified as two drunk men.

As they moved past the palace, Abinadi kept an eye on the lazing guards. For a night of military adventure, the guards didn't seem caught up in the excitement. At the sound of Gideon's singing, one started laughing.

They cleared the palace and continued around the sturdy walls until they reached the back hillside where a cave had been made into a prison.

A guard rose immediately as they came into view.

"Greetings!" Gideon shouted. "We are celebrating our victory over the Lamanites."

The guard frowned. "But the soldiers just left. Is there a victory already?"

"We'll have victory in no time . . . so why not celebrate now?"

Abinadi staggered toward the guard, extending his hand and the expensive wine. "This was a gift from the king. Smell it—usually reserved only for royalty."

The guard leaned forward and smelled it. "Hmmm. I see what you mean."

"The taste is even better," Abinadi said, pretending to take a swig. He wiped off droplets from his face, then held out the jug again.

The guard looked around furtively, as if expecting the king himself to appear at any moment. "I guess I'll have just a taste."

Less than half an hour later, jug nearly empty, the guard sat at his post, his head lolling as his snores filled the night.

"Let's go," Gideon whispered. They left the jug of wine at the guard's feet and descended the steps into the prison cave. Beyond the glow of torchlight was only steep darkness. Gideon took the torch in hand and led the way.

The prison walls were damp, dripping with putrid water and slimy mold. Abinadi involuntarily shivered, grateful for his cape. The odor was a mixture of rotted food and human waste. He glanced at Gideon, who was covering his mouth and nose with the edge of his turban. Abinadi followed suit.

They came to the first cell, and through the wooden slats the trembling glow of their torch illuminated a huddled man. As the light reached the prisoner's face, he rose in a flash and dove toward them. He thudded against the slats, only to be restrained by his bindings. Abinadi jumped backward as the man screamed, "I'll kill you!"

Gideon grabbed Abinadi and tugged him along. They passed two more cells, both containing delusional men begging for release—promising their daughters, wives, or homes in return.

Abinadi's chest clenched in both horror and sadness. He had no idea what these men's crimes were, but their wretched conditions were sickening to witness. No one deserved such treatment. They arrived at the last cell. It appeared empty, then through the thinning dark, a shape moved.

"Ben?" Abinadi called out in a soft voice.

The boy's head snapped up and turned.

If Abinadi hadn't known it to be Ben, he would have hardly recognized the boy. He was covered in dirt and filth from head to toe, and his body seemed terribly frail and thin. Where were the bright eyes and contagious smile?

"We're going to get you out," Gideon whispered. "But we don't have much time."

Achingly slow, Ben stood. His hands were tied behind his back. He walked toward them. Abinadi reached through the slats and grasped the boy's shoulder. "We're here to take you home."

Ben's large eyes blinked in response, but otherwise he didn't respond.

Gideon and Abinadi lifted the heavy wooden bar that fastened the door.

Ben practically fell forward into Abinadi's arms. His tunic was ripped and stained with blood and dirt. Abinadi grimaced. "We must get him something to eat and drink," he said, casting a furtive glance back into the cell. It didn't appear that there was any food inside. He used his dagger to cut the bindings from Ben's wrists.

"Let's go!" Gideon hissed. Abinadi gathered Ben in his arms and with Gideon ran back through the corridor, ignoring the calls of the still-imprisoned men.

Carrying Ben was effortless, but Abinadi still wished he could do something for those they left behind. They scurried up the stairs, away from the stench, away from the awfulness . . .

"Stop right there!"

Abinadi nearly collided with Gideon. At the entrance of the prison stood three men, torches held high. The one who had spoken wore an ugly scowl. Beyond the three men, the guard was still snoring at his post. One of the others held the jug of wine in his meaty grip.

Abinadi tightened his hold on Ben as the boy twisted to see what had stopped them. He squirmed, and Abinadi let him to the ground, still keeping a fierce hold on him.

"Identify yourselves," the leader ordered.

Gideon withdrew his dagger with barely a nod to Abinadi. The message had been passed. Almost instantaneously the two of them leapt forward and attacked. With one arm wielding his dagger, Abinadi rushed the leader, gaining an advantage for several seconds. He knocked the torch out of the man's hand, then brought the edge of his dagger to the man's throat.

"Get behind me and hang on," Abinadi told Ben. The boy did as he was told. Abinadi gripped the dagger with both hands, pressing forward slightly.

The leader spread his arms as if in self-defeat, but his eyes were not reconciled. Gideon was circling with the others. Abinadi kept his gaze level and dagger poised at the man he had cornered.

"Watch out!" Gideon shouted just as powerful arms wrapped around Abinadi's torso.

Abinadi threw his head back and found his target as he connected with the other man's nose. A blood-curdling scream filled the air as the man fell to the ground, clutching his face, but Abinadi didn't lose his focus on the leader. Ben scurried away as Gideon continued to struggle with the other man.

"Ben!" Abinadi yelled. He couldn't lose the boy twice. A loud crash sounded. Abinadi stared as the leader sank to the ground. Ben had smashed the abandoned jug of wine over the leader's head.

Abinadi turned to help Gideon, and within seconds they had the third man subdued. He turned to Ben. "Can you run?" he asked. Ben nodded.

After quickly stripping the men's swords and daggers, they hurried from the prison. Instead of taking the main road, they angled through the fields. If anyone had been searching for them, they would have been easy targets to spot. The moon hung bright and full, clearly showing the two men and the boy darting along the landscape. Once they reached the cover of trees, Gideon came to a full stop. He knelt next to Ben and examined him, wincing when he saw the welts on his back. "Are you all right, son?" Gideon asked.

Ben nodded, his chest heaving.

"Once we find the bundles we hid in the forest, we can clean you up and get you something to eat," Abinadi said, touching the boy's shoulder.

Ben nodded again.

"It's not much farther," Gideon said. "We'll have you away from here in no time."

"What about Raquel?" Ben asked, his breath still coming short.

Abinadi smiled. "She's waiting for you."

The boy smiled for the first time since the rescue. The three moved quickly through the trees, stopping every so often to listen for any pursuers or cry of alarm from the city. Finally they reached their hiding place. Ben gobbled the dried fish and peanuts that Abinadi found in his pack. Then he guzzled most of the water from the sheepskin. The rest he used to wash the dirt from his face.

"Easy," Gideon cautioned. "You don't want to overdo it."

The boy handed the sheepskin back to Abinadi, who sighed. "There are going to be a lot of people glad to see you. But first, we have one more stop."

They headed south, toward the river and Abinadi's home, Ben walking in front of Abinadi. On the way, Ben explained how the soldiers had come looking for Raquel. Esther hadn't been home yet, and Ben couldn't hold off their questions. When the soldiers saw the quetzal feathers Raquel had left, they knew.

"When was this?" Abinadi asked.

"The day after you left. The soldiers came after supper."

"So it was nearly dark," Abinadi said. "And my mother wasn't home?"

Ben shook his head. "She had gone to the market but hadn't returned."

Worry built inside Abinadi. His mother was always home before the sun set. He hoped she was just delayed. A new fear consumed him. Most people in the city knew she was his mother . . . What if . . .

"Let's hurry," he said to Gideon. Immediately they increased their pace. The wind had picked up since Ben's rescue, and they pushed against it now. Abinadi smelled the coming moisture, signaling the impending rain. They walked near the trees, keeping cover when they could. By the time they reached Abinadi's small homestead, the rain had turned to a ferocious downpour.

Abinadi took the lead, telling Ben to remain outside the courtyard. He and Gideon approached the dark hut. It *felt* empty. Although it was possible his mother had gone to sleep already, he doubted it.

His dagger was drawn before he reached the doorway. Slowly he lifted the skin, Gideon right beside him. "Mother?" he called. "Esther?"

The men moved quickly through the two rooms. It didn't appear as if anything had been disturbed. Abinadi's mat had been neatly rolled as if Esther were waiting for Ben to return.

Something smelled unpleasant, so Abinadi surveyed the cooking corner. He found a jug of sour milk, nearly curdled. His skin bristled with fear. His mother would never waste a thing—especially food or drink.

"She hasn't returned since she left Ben," Abinadi said in a quiet voice as Gideon joined his side. "This milk is at least two days old."

"Where would she go?"

Abinadi shrugged. They had no close relatives in the city and few whom they could call friends.

The two men stepped into the rain. Abinadi stared hopelessly into the dripping trees surrounding the home. His stomach twisted at the thought of his mother alone somewhere, possibly hurt or ill . . . or worse. He turned to Gideon. "Take the boy to the others. I'll wait here overnight and see if she returns."

Gideon placed a hand on Abinadi's shoulder. "You say she hasn't been here for at least two days. What makes you think she'll return tonight?"

Abinadi tried to swallow against the lump in his throat. "I don't know . . . I just can't leave. Not yet."

"We can stay with you," Gideon said, his grip tightening on Abinadi's shoulder, offering support. "If Noah's men return, it's better there are two of us."

"Yes," Abinadi said. "But there are three of us—and it's the third one I worry about most. He needs to get away from here as soon as possible. He's far from safe here."

"You're not safe either," Gideon said.

But Abinadi had turned away. He walked toward the trees. "Mother?" He saw nothing and heard nothing. Where was she? Had she returned to find Ben missing and gone in search of him? After a few minutes of hearing only rain pelting the trees, Gideon stepped up beside him.

"We'll stay with you and help you search in the morning."

Abinadi shook his head. "No. You must get Ben out of here now."

Gideon grimaced but finally nodded. "We'll leave then."

"Be careful," Abinadi said. "And . . . give Raquel my best."

"Certainly," Gideon said. "I left your pack inside the doorway—with the extra cape and turban." He turned and joined Ben.

Abinadi watched the two leave the clearing. The rain still came, the house was still empty, and his mother was still gone, but the thought of Raquel warmed him from somewhere deep inside. Slowly he walked back to his home to wait out the rain. He lowered the skin against the moisture and decided not to take the risk of lighting a lamp. So, in the damp darkness, he knelt by his former sleeping corner. Then he did the only thing that was left to do. Pray.

* * *

The rain continued on and off all night. Raquel knew because she couldn't sleep. She'd expected the men to return at least by midnight. But when the hour was long past, she gave up on trying to rest. She couldn't leave her tent because of the rain, so she didn't know if the other men were as anxious as she. Anything could have gone wrong with Ben or with either of the men. She felt so helpless. She couldn't make a poultice or cook a meal or do anything to fix the problem, and she also couldn't leave; the very least she could do was keep her promise to Abinadi and remain where she was.

She stooped in the low tent and paced as much as she was able, irritated at the weather. It would make travel more difficult. Growing chilled, she sat again and pulled the rug about her shoulders, thinking about Abinadi. Though she doubted he'd ever see her as more than a runaway girl, she saw him as more of a man than King Noah, Eli, and even her father. She closed her eyes, picturing Abinadi's deep-set eyes, his amber complexion, heavy brows . . .

Pray for me, his eyes had seemed to say. But she didn't even know *how* to pray. Watching Ben in the fields had been her first witness of a "believer's" prayer.

She continued to pace in the small tent, growing hot, then cold. The rain finally petered off, and Raquel threw open the tent flap to let in the night air. A glow of a lamp came from Ezra's tent. Apparently he couldn't sleep either. For a moment, she considered speaking with him. Maybe he could explain the method of praying to her. *No,* she decided. *He'll think me foolish.*

A tear slid down her cheek as helplessness consumed her. Was this how the Lord felt when he looked down upon the cities full of people and saw their stubbornness? Yes, she'd been stubborn—and now she was too stubborn to even ask for help with *how* to pray.

The sound of snapping branches reached her ears. Someone was coming through the trees. Raquel drew back inside her tent and lowered the flap. She hoped it was Abinadi, but at the same time fear spread throughout her body. What if Noah's men had finally caught up to them?

"Gideon!" someone said.

Raquel flew out of the tent and came to a stumbling stop. There were only two figures—one was Ben, the other Gideon. She ran to the young boy. "Ben!" He threw his arms around her waist and she laughed, embracing him. "You're safe!"

He turned his face upward and smiled. "You're safe, too."

"You are an excellent map maker . . ." Her voice faded as she looked around, her gaze stopping at Gideon. "Where's Abinadi?"

Ben released her legs. "He went to find his mother."

Gideon's expression was sober. *Something isn't right,* Raquel thought. "What happened?"

"Esther never came home," Gideon said in a quiet voice.

Ben leaned against Raquel again, and she put an arm around his shoulder, pulling him close. "You mean from the time I saw Ben until now?"

Gideon nodded. The other elders murmured among themselves.

"But it's not safe for Abinadi to . . ." Raquel fell silent as Gideon shook his head. She shouldn't upset Ben, so she ruffled the boy's hair and said, "Come with me and tell me all about your rescue." She tried to keep her voice light, but her heart felt heavy.

Abinadi hadn't returned. His mother hadn't come home. Ben was safe, but Raquel couldn't rid her mind of worry.

Inside her tent, she made a comfortable spot for Ben. When she wrapped an extra rug around his thin body, he shied away.

"What's wrong?" she asked.

His expression clouded.

Raquel felt a jolt in her heart. "Are you hurt?"

When Ben didn't answer, Raquel knew that he was. "Let me see," she said in a quiet voice.

He turned his back to her and pulled his tunic down over his shoulder.

Raquel stared, hardly believing what she saw. Ugly, red welts stood out on his shoulder. She lifted the cloth and saw that they ran down his back. "They whipped you?"

He nodded.

Raquel blinked back her tears and reached for her pouch of herbs. "How could they be so cruel?"

Ben turned to look at her, his expression placid. "The king was angry that I wouldn't tell him where you went."

Raquel froze. Her chest felt as if it would burst with sorrow. "You were whipped because of *me?*"

He shook his head. "The king still would have whipped me even if I had told."

"Oh, Ben." Raquel leaned over and stroked his cheek with a trembling hand. "I should have never run away. None of this would have happened."

Ben smiled his brilliant smile. "We're safe now. You should have seen Abinadi and Gideon fighting the king's guards."

She smiled back, but her heart ached even more. While she prepared a paste made from willow bark, Ben told her about Abinadi and Gideon showing up at the prison, then how they fought off some of Noah's soldiers. They had traveled to Abinadi's home to retrieve Esther, but there was no sign of her.

"Does she have relatives in the city? A sister or a cousin perhaps?" she asked as she applied the paste.

Ben lifted his shoulders, wincing. "I don't know. Abinadi was searching the forest around their home."

Raquel's stomach dropped.

Ben stifled a yawn. "You should sleep now," Raquel said, finishing the application of willow bark. "You've traveled all night."

"First I have to thank the Lord," he said. He knelt on his mat and bowed his head.

She felt compelled to follow suit, if only not to stare at him. She listened carefully to every word. The words seemed so simple, yet so foreign at the same time. Ben thanked the Lord for his safe rescue and pleaded for the Lord to preserve Abinadi and his mother. When Ben concluded, Raquel wanted to say *Amen* too, but she didn't dare.

He climbed beneath his covers. Raquel lay in the darkness, listening as his breathing relaxed and became steady in sleep.

Praying seemed natural for Ben. But even as she thought about the simple words he'd said, she didn't know if she could follow suit. It was one thing to refuse marriage to King Noah, but another to participate in something that had been forbidden in her household. Raquel stifled a chuckle. She'd probably already chosen the more rebellious of the two. Praying couldn't possibly get her into more trouble now.

The rain started again as Ben's breathing turned into light snoring. Dawn was only a couple hours away, but still Raquel couldn't sleep. Somewhere out there, Abinadi was searching for his mother . . . and somewhere out there, men were searching for her. A fine pair they made.

Thirteen

Make you a new heart and a new spirit.
(Ezekiel 18:31)

The first thought that entered Abinadi's mind was that the rain had finally stopped. The morning light seemed to ebb and flow as the wind moved through the trees outside. His neck and shoulders ached. He'd fallen asleep praying, and as he adjusted his position, he immediately began to pray again for the safe return of his mother. With the dawn, he'd be able to search for any evidence regarding her departure.

When he finished his prayer, he searched through his mother's things again. It appeared that she hadn't taken anything with her. Not a good sign. He wished he could write her a message, but she wouldn't be able to read it. Instead he moved his bedding into her room. No one else would notice the difference, but his mother would. He donned the cape and turban.

He grabbed a waterskin and tied a rug into a bundle to carry on his back. He hesitated at the doorway, reluctant to leave the memories behind. He gazed at the room again. He didn't know if he'd return, but it was empty of life without his mother there. Without her, it was no longer his home.

The door-skin flapped behind him, and he strode through the courtyard. Nothing but leaves and sticks were strewn about. He circled the homestead, stopping every so often to examine a piece of rope or a scrap of cloth. For the larger part of the morning he trudged through the wet undergrowth surrounding his home, hoping to find some evidence of where she'd gone.

By midday, he knew the search was fruitless. He might have known it from the beginning, but he hadn't wanted to leave without trying everything possible. Finally, he started the walk back to the city. He'd have to pose as a merchant of some sort if anyone asked.

The market was teeming with life when he arrived. Everything from bleating sheep to the finest jade jewelry was up for bargaining. A Kaminaljuyú man waved him over, pointing eagerly to the intricate jade necklaces arranged on a mat.

Another merchant shouted, "Quetzal feathers from the high mountains—fit for royalty." He lifted a brilliant tail feather, reflecting green and gold in the afternoon light.

Abinadi walked past the vendors and spread-out mats, listening to snatches of conversations around him.

Two men lazed near the collection of spices. "The king says his fifty can go against the Lamanites' thousand," one man said.

The other laughed. "All the better, since you won't catch me putting away my trade to become a soldier."

"Amulon is receiving a high honor for his clever command—an unprecedented slaughter, I hear," the first man said.

Abinadi bent over the display of spices and dug his hand into one of the sacks, pretending to examine the quality.

"Yes, so I heard." The second man lowered his voice. "It's a good thing he let out his wrath on the Lamanites and not his daughter."

The first man chuckled softly. "A good thing indeed. But if she ever returns . . ."

A woman approached, and the two men fell silent. Abinadi moved on. *Please stay where you are, Raquel,* he thought.

He moved to a set of mats that were loaded with maize. His mother usually set up near this area. A man sat perched on the side of his mat.

"Do you know a seller named Esther?" Abinadi asked.

He flicked the straw he was chewing onto the ground. "Who wants to know?"

Abinadi handed over an onti of silver. "I do."

The man tucked the silver into the folds of his clothing. "Haven't seen her for a couple of days."

"When did you see her last?" Abinadi asked.

The man remained silent.

Abinadi handed over another onti.

The man said, "Day before last. She left early . . . left her produce, too. Strange, says I. Haven't seen her since."

Abinadi's eyes flitted along the next mat. It was his mother's. A pit formed in his stomach. Why had his mother left her things? Why hadn't she returned? He drifted along the street from one seller to the next, asking questions. Others must have known her, seen her that morning. Maybe she'd taken ill and someone had offered her a place to recover. But even as he thought it, he doubted.

O Lord, my God, Abinadi's thoughts turned to prayer, *please guide me. Show me the way.*

He watched the bustle of the market, scanning the crowd for anyone he recognized—anyone who might have known his mother. An elderly lady sat across the way, guarding cages of parrots. The birds periodically called out to passing strangers. Abinadi approached the woman, hesitant but determined. Each time he spoke with someone, he took an additional risk.

"Do you know a woman named Esther? She used to sell maize and other vegetables nearby," he asked.

The woman slowly raised her eyes, and Abinadi was surprised to see that one of her eyes was green, the other brown. She slowly shook her head.

Deflated, he turned away, looking for anyone else. But the truth was that he didn't know who his mother was acquainted with. He walked through the market as slowly as possible, listening for any snatches of information. A few times he looked over his shoulder, wondering if the man behind in a dark brown kilt was following him or just happened to be stopping the same times as he.

Finally, he left the market area deflated. He had one more source to check, although he knew it would be the most dangerous of all. His mother's cousin lived near the palace, and though he hadn't seen her for many years, he hoped that she might know something . . . anything. He walked along the paths between the close-set houses. He didn't want to take the most direct route, since more people traveled the main road through the city. The closer he came to the palace, the nicer the homes became until most of them had decorative gardens surrounding large courtyards.

Just as he rounded another corner, someone grabbed his neck. Before he could cry out, a hand clamped over his mouth. He struggled to get free, but the arms of two men dragged him between a pair of houses. Abinadi blinked at the eyes staring at him. By their fine kilts and breastplates, he knew they were the king's soldiers. He tried to move beneath their grip. One of the men said, "Don't make a sound, or we'll be forced to kill you."

"Which wouldn't be much of a loss," another voice added.

Abinadi raised his gaze and saw the towering figure of Amulon. The man looked as if he were fresh from battle—his breastplate was still on and his face was dirty.

"Stand him up," Amulon commanded the soldiers.

Abinadi staggered to his feet as the men lifted him. *I'm going to die,* was the only thought that went through his mind.

"Where are you going?" Amulon asked.

Abinadi gazed at the man—wondering if he knew about Ben's escape. If not, it wouldn't be long. He decided that his best option was to ask about his mother. "My mother didn't come home the other day. I'm merely looking for her."

"I knew you would come for her eventually," Amulon said.

Abinadi's heart raced. Amulon knew something . . . or had *done* something.

"I find it interesting that you chose this particular row of houses," Amulon continued, his voice a near snarl. "Had you inspected any of these homes, you might have discovered something."

Abinadi strained against his captors and leaned toward Amulon. "What did you do with her?"

"Nothing . . . yet," Amulon said, a smirk on his face. "It's what I *will* do to her that you should be worried about."

Abinadi lunged for the priest, but the other men held him fast. His face was just a breath away from Amulon's. The stench of perspiration and sour wine emanated from the unwashed man. "Where is she?"

Amulon laughed, then circled Abinadi. "I want to trade. Your mother for my daughter."

"Raquel?" Abinadi said before he could stop himself.

"Ahh. So you do know her." Amulon's lips were next to Abinadi's ear. "She has escaped her fate for now, but it is only a delay. I will not rest until she meets her punishment. I want her returned. And only then will you see your dear mother."

"I don't—" Abinadi started.

"Oh, but you do. And you will." Amulon faced Abinadi, his dark eyes narrowed. "I know that Gideon has a secret settlement. I knew there was no way she could survive on her own. I told myself that someone took her in. Someone was protecting her." He brought two fingers to his lips and whistled. Almost instantly, a man appeared.

Abinadi stared. It was Izehar, who'd attacked them at their campsite.

"Yes," Amulon said, "I thought you two had met before." He shoved Izehar forward, and Abinadi was surprised to see fear in the man's eyes. Amulon had used them both.

"Izehar and his friends will be waiting at the south pass. When you deliver my daughter, he will release your mother."

Abinadi knew he couldn't trust Amulon. Even if he did deliver Raquel—which he wouldn't—he doubted this man would keep his end of the bargain.

"Tell me where she is," Abinadi said. "Tell me if she's well."

Amulon appraised him with arched eyebrows. "She is well enough." His expression darkened again. "Now go! If I see you again, empty-handed, I'll let my men do what they are trained to."

The grip on his arms tightened momentarily, then relaxed. Abinadi backed away, his heart thundering in his chest. Amulon's request was sickening, maddening. Abinadi couldn't bring Raquel back and deliver her to her death. He wouldn't ever tell her of this turn of events. For if he did, she would insist on returning.

Abinadi turned and fled through the streets, ignoring those who stared after him. He slowed as his breathing came in gasps. He hadn't slept much and had eaten little, but he knew he couldn't leave his mother in this city. Every moment that passed was another moment of horror for her. Abinadi skirted the market and walked along the roads, wondering *if* his mother managed to escape, whether she'd return home. But how could she escape?

He must find her. Utter helplessness wracked his body. He found a place to rest between two homes that seemed deserted. They were in a dilapidated part of town . . . perhaps the owner had died and the rest of the family had moved on. He leaned against a reed wall and, lowering his head, he thought of Gideon's latest teachings about Father Lehi and the journey across the high seas. When Laman and Lemuel had danced for pagan gods, the Lord had sent his wrath in the form of a tumultuous storm. Nephi had been tied up and the rest of the family cowered in sickness and fear of the great waves.

What had Nephi done? He prayed of course. *But will a simple prayer lead me to my mother?* It seemed impossible. Yet Abinadi was the first to acknowledge that he didn't understand the power or the knowledge of God like Gideon. It seemed so simple for the Teacher. *He* never questioned. He just knew and acted.

That's what I need to do. I know, *and now I need to act.*

Abinadi moved to his knees on the rocky ground. "Oh Lord," he whispered. "I am nothing without Thee. I am lost and broken. I cannot meet Amulon's demands. Give me Thy strength to know what to do. If it be Thy will, lead me to my mother. Preserve her. Have mercy on her. I will do anything that Thou asketh of me. I am Thy servant forever. Amen."

He let the tears surface as he sank against the wall and buried his face in his arms. He knew the Lord was real. The Lord had preserved Nephi's life again and again. The writings on the brass plates showed the Lord's mercy time after time. But Nephi was a prophet—an instrument in the Lord's hands. *Who am I to warrant such miracles?* Abinadi's only hope was that the elders were praying for him now . . . Gideon was a righteous man—his prayers would certainly be heard.

Abinadi continued to kneel and listen—that was what Gideon had taught. Pray, then listen.

Time crept by until night settled in the narrow alley that Abinadi occupied. His chest hurt from worry, and his limbs were stiff and cramped. Drops of soft rain fell on his head. Abinadi ignored his hungry stomach as he stood and stretched. He wiped his face with his turban. The night air, accompanied by the moisture, had brought a measure of coolness.

I don't know what I'm doing or where I'm going, Abinadi thought as he began walking through the streets again. But he couldn't leave without his mother. He steered clear of the palace, knowing—hoping—that Amulon hadn't put his mother there. He let his mind shift to Raquel. There was no way she would ever know about this. Even if he had to sacrifice himself to secure his mother's release, Abinadi would not give Amulon what he'd asked for.

He passed by the homes of the wealthier citizens of the land. As he neared Amulon's home, Abinadi had a sudden urge to storm the house and hold someone hostage. Then he realized that if Amulon valued his daughter so little, there was probably no one that Amulon cared much for—even his wife. When Amulon's courtyard came into view, Abinadi hesitated. Something tugged at the back of his mind. It was as if he should remember something, but he couldn't quite grasp it.

He walked to the wall that surrounded Amulon's estate. *If I am caught . . .* he pushed the thought away and tried to focus. When Raquel had come to deliver the herbs for his wounds, she'd said something about her parents not seeing her leave. Abinadi rubbed his head. There was a way out of her home where she wasn't easily observed.

The hut in the garden.

That was it. Warm adrenaline surged through Abinadi. Could it be possible? Was it that simple? He hardly dared to breathe, but he knew what to do.

Abinadi walked along the outer wall until he found a place completely concealed by trees. The rain petered off, and the trees dripped with the last of their moisture. He started to climb. The wall wasn't high, but he knew there could easily be guards—or even worse, vicious dogs. Abinadi peered over the wall, taking in the surroundings as the moon peeked through the fast moving clouds. A large courtyard, intermingled with trees and groupings of plants, covered most of the front property. The house was dark, but to the side, Abinadi saw the beginning of a garden. The hut was back there somewhere . . .

He took a deep breath and pulled himself over the wall, then scaled down the other side. For once, he regretted his height. It would be difficult to stay hidden. He half crawled, half walked along the edges of the wall to the back. Every so often he paused to listen.

The light of the half-hidden moon made the view of the garden dim at best. He sidestepped the more delicate flora, arriving at a row of miniature plants. *Herbs*—these were Raquel's herbs. For a moment he stopped and stared. It was as if she were close by somehow. Then he raised his eyes and saw the hut situated on the opposite side of the garden. He tried to move slowly and carefully, but it was hard to restrain himself. He leaped over a row of bushes and ran to the hut.

"Mother?" he whispered, gently prying the reed door open. Even in the dimness he saw it was empty. His heart sank. She wasn't here. How could he have been so foolish? He'd wasted all this time pondering and then coming to Amulon's own home.

Suddenly something struck him on the head. He staggered against a row of jars, sending them crashing to the ground. Several fell on top of him, adding to the pain.

A petite woman stood in the doorway, a large clay jar in her hand. "Who are you?" she demanded.

"Abinadi . . . I've come—"

"I know why you're here," the woman said.

"Y-you do?"

The woman grabbed his arm. "Come. I'll take you to her."

Abinadi followed the woman inside the house as he rubbed his head. For someone so small, she'd delivered a significant blow. The corridors were dark, but the woman moved quickly. She finally stopped at a door, then swung it open. A platform bed stood in the middle of the room.

A form huddled on the bed. When Abinadi entered, he saw that it was his mother. "Mother!" He crossed to the bed and knelt by her side.

"She's ill," the woman said, hovering in the doorway. "She has the fever. My husband would be very displeased if he knew I brought her into the house, but I couldn't leave her in the hut like an animal."

Abinadi turned to look at Amulon's wife. "Thank you," he said. "You may have saved her life."

The small woman shrugged. "I have done nothing. She didn't look well when my husband brought her." Her gaze shifted away. "I don't understand everything my husband does . . . but to lock up this poor woman . . ." Her voice cracked, and she took a deep breath before continuing. "I have stood by him in many things. But not this."

She leveled her gaze at Abinadi. "Take her from here and make haste. My husband may return at any moment." She withdrew as if she were afraid to remain in the room any longer and said from the doorway, "I don't know if she'll make the journey . . . wherever you are going." She paused. "Take an alpaca from the stable since it will be gentle enough to carry your mother. It's the least I can offer."

Abinadi nodded and turned to wrap the covers around his mother. She seemed to be sleeping, but her breathing was shallow. He carefully lifted her in his arms, surprised at the light weight.

Amulon's wife backed out of the doorway, allowing him to pass. "Wait," she whispered. "If this has anything to do with my daughter," her voice trembled, "and if you know where she is . . . please tell her that . . . I'm sorry." She turned away.

"I will," he said, but she was already halfway down the hall. He gripped his mother tightly and followed the woman. Amulon's wife led him outside to the stables south of the house.

"Take what you need." She met Abinadi's gaze a final time in the dim light, then turned and hastened away.

He wasted no time throwing a rug over the alpaca and loading his mother upon it. She murmured incoherently. He touched her face and felt the heat of her skin. Her hair was damp with perspiration. She tried to speak again.

"Hold on, Mother," Abinadi said. "I'm taking you to safety." He led the alpaca out of the stable. As they traveled out of the city and into the night, he realized he'd just witnessed his first miracle.

Fourteen

Blessed is the man that trusteth in the Lord, and whose hope the Lord is.
(Jeremiah 17:7)

Raquel's mind was still clouded with sleep when she woke in the late morning. Slowly, the events of the prior night came into focus, and she turned to look for Ben. But he was gone. She rose and pulled a coarse-fibered cape about her shoulders—something that Gideon had provided her. Then she combed through her hair and plaited it again.

Stepping outside, she saw that her tent was the only one standing. The others had been packed. Ben worked alongside the other men as they tied bundles together with rope. Raquel crossed to Gideon. "Why are we leaving so soon? Abinadi hasn't returned."

Gideon finished tying a bundle, then faced her. "He'll find us."

Raquel folded her arms. Was he just trying to appease her? She glanced at Ben, whose expression was somber. "What if he doesn't?"

Gideon said, "If the king's men aren't after you still, they're certainly after Ben . . . or me. We can't just wait for them to appear." He let out a breath of frustration. "I don't want to leave any more than you do. But our best hope is to leave a trail that Abinadi will be able to pick up."

Raquel took a step back, her mind reeling. They were going into the wilderness, someplace secret that only Gideon knew of—what were the chances of Abinadi finding them? Her stomach churned as she thought about never seeing him again. This wasn't how she'd planned her escape from her home. Well, she hadn't really planned any of it, but when Abinadi had entered the picture, everything had seemed so . . . right.

She turned away from Gideon so he wouldn't see her eyes smart. A couple of elders were already striking her tent. Her belongings had been tied into a bundle and placed on the ground. She crossed to the bundle and snatched it up, securing it across her back.

Within moments, the group was ready to leave. Raquel followed, walking next to Ben. He remained quiet for the most part, and Raquel was in no mood herself to try cheering him. Every so often, she stopped and plucked leaves or flowers she recognized as useful herbs. They were walking through a rather dense forest section when she noticed Gideon marking the trees with his dagger.

"What is he doing?" Raquel asked Ben.

"Leaving a trail for Abinadi."

Raquel's mouth formed an *O*—perhaps Gideon did know what he was doing. Not that she would question his judgment. Her mood lightened immediately. Gideon was no fool—he was just looking out for all of them.

By mid-afternoon, Raquel's lack of sleep caught up with her. She struggled to keep up with the others.

The terrain started to change, and the trees thickened. They passed by a group of willows clinging to each other. Raquel stopped at one and stripped a few lengths of bark.

"What are those for?" Ben asked.

"The bark of a willow helps relieve pain," Raquel answered. She opened the piece of cloth in which she'd laid the other leaves and flowers she'd collected. "See? All of these plants have medicinal uses."

"What's that one?" Ben asked, pointing to a thick leaf.

"It's called curaiao." She removed the leaf from the satchel. "Here, let me show you." She made a slit in the center of the leaf, and a liquid substance oozed out. "Let me see one of your scratches."

Raquel pressed the oozing leaf against a long scratch on his arm.

"Ooo. It's cold," Ben said.

Raquel smiled. "It feels that way at first. But after a moment, the skin will soak in the gel, and it will heal faster." She removed the leaf from his arm and tossed it away.

"You can't use it again?" Ben asked.

"No," Raquel said. "It's no good when it dries. You can help me look for more curaiao plants."

"All right," Ben said, his grin returning.

They increased their pace, easily catching up with the elders. Raquel noticed that Gideon had stopped marking trees. Ben noticed too. He ran to Gideon and asked him why.

The Teacher turned his kind face toward Ben. "We are nearing the settlement now. If anyone else picks up the trail, we don't want to lead them right to it."

"What about Abinadi?" Ben asked.

Raquel scurried closer to hear.

"We'll have to post a watchman at the end of the trail. Good or bad, we need to know who's following us," Gideon said.

Ben nodded, his eyes filled with excitement. "Can I be the watchman?"

Gideon chuckled and ruffled the boy's hair. "I think one of the elders should do it."

"I can help too," Raquel said. "I'll keep watch with Ben."

Gideon turned and looked at her with surprise. "Neither of you are strong enough to fight a soldier."

"But if there are two of us, Ben can run and warn the others—"

"And *you'll* fight?" Gideon pursed his lips.

Raquel fell silent. She wasn't afraid.

Ben continued to pester Gideon with questions as they traveled up a hill. At the top of the crest, they stopped. Below, two ridges sloped into a narrow valley. In the center of the valley, by a river, sat half a dozen huts.

"We're home," Gideon said.

Raquel was surprised to see smoke coming from a cooking fire. She hadn't expected others to be living here already. As they descended from the ridge, Ben chattered, telling her that Gideon had a wife and two daughters. They'd been living in this valley for several years. Three other elders also lived there with their families, and more were said to be coming.

The settlement was very primitive, but it was situated in a beautiful valley. As they neared the first hut, a woman emerged. She was short and stout, but she wasted no time in hurrying to Gideon. She threw her arms about his willowy neck and planted a kiss on his lips. He laughed, and Raquel felt a little embarrassed at witnessing such affection.

"I knew you were coming today," she announced. Her gaze landed on Raquel. "Who have you brought?"

Gideon introduced Raquel to his wife, Tia. The woman bustled over and drew Raquel into her arms.

Surprised, Raquel awkwardly returned the woman's embrace.

Tia pulled away, her eyes shining on her round face. Her black hair stuck out beneath a scarf, which sat haphazardly on her head. She was a woman with little care or time for preening. "You'll get used to us yet. Now come and eat something. My girls will be back from the fields soon, and they'll want to ask a dozen questions, I'm sure." Tia threw a look at her husband. Raquel was sure the woman wanted to know the answers herself.

Tia ordered the elders around, directing them where to place things. "You'll sleep in my home," she told Raquel. "The men can sleep under the stars. A little rain never hurt anyone."

Raquel was about to protest, but Tia took the bundle from her and disappeared inside. Raquel followed her into the dim interior. The hut was only one room, although it was clear that sections had been created for the sleeping quarters and the eating area.

She offered to help Tia prepare the food, but the woman insisted that Raquel rest.

As Raquel waited with the others, she scanned the area. Several patches of maize and bean fields spread through the valley. From her vantage point, she watched the laborers working in the heat of the day. She narrowed her eyes against the slanting sun. Women and children worked in the fields as well. It made sense, though—it seemed that this was a community that had to work together unlike the people of King Noah's court, who worked little, benefiting from the taxes from others.

"Come," Tia said, touching her shoulder. "You need to eat."

Raquel was suddenly grateful for Tia's motherliness. Although her mother was different from Tia in almost every way, Raquel had missed the feeling of being taken care of. Her throat constricted as she thought about her mother. She tried to push the thoughts away as she followed Tia to the cooking area.

Raquel ate the simple dish of boiled beans and chilis, relishing the excellent food. It wasn't lavish, but nothing had tasted so good in days. Tia hovered over the elders, her hands on her wide hips, encouraging them to eat their fill. Raquel noticed a tall man who was completely covered in clothing—even his hands. She couldn't quite catch a glimpse of his face beneath his hood, but she realized it must be Abinadi's brother, Helam.

When she finished, Helam approached her. He bowed and said, "Welcome."

She hastily stood and said, "Thank you." He regarded her for a moment, not revealing much in his hooded gaze.

Ben sidled up to him and tugged his arm. "She knows how to make healing pastes," Ben said.

"Very good," Helam said, ruffling Ben's hair. Just then Gideon stood on the other side of the circle and asked Ben to accompany him to the lookout point to watch for Abinadi. Raquel watched them leave, trying not to let Gideon's earlier reprimand affect her. She busied herself cleaning up, despite Tia's protests.

"My daughters will take care of all this," Tia said, waving her hand toward the leftovers.

"Your daughters have been working in the fields all day."

Tia laughed, her brown eyes merry. "I like you."

Raquel smiled, straightening as she lifted a stack of clay bowls. "And I like you."

Another chuckle came from Tia. "You'll fit right in with my brood." Her gaze was curious, but still the woman didn't question Raquel.

Tia finally had her way, and Raquel crept into the house for a short nap. What seemed like moments later, she was awakened by loud whispering.

Raquel rose on one elbow, blinking back the haziness of her vision. Two girls knelt together, peering at her. They looked almost identical, their curious faces dusty. Both of them had midnight-black hair, twisted with strips of cloth. One looked older than Raquel by a couple of years, the other about ten years old.

The younger one spoke first. "Where did you get your tunic?"

Raquel touched the embroidery edging. "My mother made it."

"Oh!" The ten-year-old touched Raquel's hem. "I've never seen anything so beautiful."

The older girl nodded, but her gaze wasn't as intent as her sister's. Her dark eyes seemed to assess Raquel in a different way.

"What are your names?" Raquel asked.

"I'm Adriel," the younger sister said. "She's Neriah."

Raquel looked at Neriah. "How old are you?"

"Seventeen."

Raquel nodded. "Me, too." She was surprised Neriah was not a year or two older. Her figure was as developed as a grown woman's, yet her skin was as flawless as a child's. She was quite beautiful, Raquel thought.

Neriah's gaze shifted.

Raquel suddenly felt awkward. She was probably on Neriah's mat. Raquel rose to her feet. "I hope I didn't take your sleeping quarters."

Neriah shrugged, remaining quiet. But her sister wasn't afraid to speak. "Mother says you'll stay with us." She took Raquel's hand and tugged. "Will you tell us about the city of Nephi?"

"Of course," Raquel said, glancing at Neriah. "Haven't you been there yourself?"

"Neriah went once when she was very small, but I've never been," Adriel said.

Raquel looked about the house. Had these people lived here so long? She knew King Noah had been ruling for about eight years . . .

Adriel looked at her eagerly, waiting for an answer.

As Raquel began to describe the many homes and the market, Neriah turned away, straightening things about the home. Raquel told Adriel about the vast fields, the massive wine presses, and the king's palace.

Adriel kept a hold of Raquel's hand. "Mother says you know Abinadi. That's why you're here."

Raquel's face warmed as she nodded.

Neriah suddenly turned and looked at Raquel. "You know Abinadi?" Her face was unreadable, but her tone didn't sound too pleased.

"My sister's in love with him," Adriel announced.

"Hush!" Neriah said. Then she walked out of the house, her head high, eyes averted.

The breath went out of Raquel as she stared at the retreating figure of the beautiful girl.

Fifteen

Even by the God of the father, who shall help thee; and by the Almighty, who shall bless thee with blessings of heaven above.
(Genesis 49:25)

O God, give me strength, Abinadi pled as he walked beside the alpaca. *Deliver my mother from this illness.* He wiped the perspiration from his brow. He needed another miracle. Or, at the very least, an angel. His mother barely clung to life, her breathing shallow, her words incoherent. Every so often she cried out. That was what tore at Abinadi's heart. He couldn't bear to see her suffer.

Yet he had no choice but to continue their journey. Outside the city, Abinadi had knocked on the home of a healer but was refused service. It seemed that Amulon's influence spread far and wide. Or maybe it was Abinadi's lack of gold. Regardless, his only hope was to reach Gideon's settlement and see if Tia or one of the other women could assist.

After he painstakingly crossed the river, he found the markings—hopefully left by Gideon. Abinadi was fairly certain of the direction, but some elders had become lost in the past.

He really couldn't complain about his own discomforts. He might be exhausted and footsore, but his mother was worse off. Still, it had been a true answer to prayer to have her at his side—and alive.

Could he really ask more of the Lord? He had to try. Again he prayed silently as he pushed himself to continue walking. Going on little sleep wouldn't stop him; he could sleep later, after his mother was settled. *If...*

Abinadi shook the thought away. Perspiration soaking his clothing, he pushed forward. The markings were gone now, but he recognized enough of the terrain to know that he was close to Gideon's homestead. The man and a few of the elders had lived there since Zeniff's death. Abinadi himself had visited once before.

Something sharp hit his back, and he turned, his hand going to his dagger.

A dark form fell from a nearby tree.

The person stepped into the sunlight, then yelled, "Abinadi!" and ran full tilt toward him. Laughing, Abinadi grabbed Ben and swung him around.

Then Abinadi looked up to see Gideon emerging from the shadows. The two men embraced.

"You're safe," Gideon said.

Abinadi nodded, his gaze flickering to his mother on the alpaca.

"What happened?" Ben asked immediately. "Is she all right?"

"She has made it so far," Abinadi said, sharing a worried glance with Gideon. "We must hurry though." The three started walking together, and Abinadi touched Ben's shoulder. "The important thing is that she's safe again. Perhaps Tia can help her get better."

"I know who else can help," Ben said. "Raquel collected all kinds of plants and herbs. She told me what some of them were for, and I'll bet she can find something for your mother."

Abinadi patted the boy's shoulder. "I'll bet she can." He thought of Raquel's surprise visit to his home and the herbs she'd brought for him.

"I'll tell the others you're here at last," Ben said. He looked up at Abinadi eagerly. "And I'll have Raquel prepare something that will make your mother better." Ben turned to Gideon. "Do you think we should say a prayer?"

Abinadi couldn't help but smile at the boy's simple faith.

"Of course," Gideon said. "In fact," he said, his gaze meeting Abinadi's, "we should anoint her and pray over her when she's settled."

Abinadi nodded, his throat thick. He hadn't realized what a heavy burden he'd been shouldering as he traveled with his mother alone. Now there were others to help and care for her.

Ben sprinted away, his agile form leaping over bushes and scurrying up slopes.

"You'll have a mob waiting with rugs and hot bowls of lemon-grass tea by the time we arrive," Gideon said with a wry smile.

"I'll take anything at this point, mob and all." Abinadi glanced at his mother, perched precariously atop the alpaca. Her breathing was even, but her skin was still pale and yellow. *Please, Lord,* he prayed in his heart again, *preserve my mother.*

Gideon's words were more than fulfilled. As the sun tipped the horizon, several men met them, Helam included, carrying a sturdy litter. Abinadi embraced his brother, then together they loaded Esther onto the litter, and she was able to sleep as they carried her the rest of the way to the settlement.

When they crested the final rise, Abinadi was struck by the beauty of the small valley. The fields had been laid out in patterns. In the center, the huts circled around a main cooking area where the fire crackled merrily. The scent of cooking food made Abinadi's mouth water.

Esther stirred on the cot, mumbling. Abinadi squeezed her hand. "We're almost there, Mother."

Helam and Gideon ushered them into one of the huts. The men anointed and prayed over her. As soon as the blessing was finished, the women hurried in and took charge—Tia, her daughters, the wives of the other elders . . .

He looked for Raquel and was relieved when he saw her emerge from one of the huts. True to Ben's predictions, she held a bowl and was mixing a poultice with a stick.

In the rush, however, he didn't get a chance to greet her. He was pulled in one direction to eat supper, while the women disappeared with his mother, Raquel included.

Abinadi was ravenous, and for a brief moment he forgot all but the steaming bowl of food in his hands.

"Would you like a drink, Abinadi?" a soft voice said above him.

He looked up to see a young woman. "Neriah?" He was astounded by the change in her. The last time he'd seen her she'd been a girl . . . and now, she was a woman. Her striking features couldn't be obscured by dust or hard labor in the fields.

She smiled shyly and held out a gourd of water.

"Thank you," he managed to say. He stared at her, realizing that it was probably impolite. But it was as if he saw her for the first time.

Neriah laughed. "Aren't you thirsty?"

"Oh, yes," he said, then took a drink. When he looked up, she was gone.

The women kept him out of the hut for the next several hours.

When evening had set in, Tia came to fetch him. He had nearly fallen asleep next to the fire. "Come," she said. "Your mother is asking for you."

Abinadi rose to his feet, his energy absolutely depleted, but he forced himself to walk the short distance to the hut in the gathering darkness. Helam stood at the entryway, wearing a long, hooded robe. "She's waiting for you," he said, motioning for Abinadi to go inside.

Abinadi's mother was sitting up in a makeshift bed when he entered. Her smile was full of courage when she saw him.

"Mother," Abinadi said. He shuffled forward and knelt by her. It was then he noticed Raquel sitting on the other side. She was periodically dabbing a wet cloth to his mother's brow, then rewetting it in a bowl of water.

He wanted to ask Raquel so many questions—about the journey, about what the women had done for his mother.

"Thank you for bringing me here, son," Esther said.

Abinadi turned his attention back to her. Her face seemed to glow in the soft light of the oil lamps. "How are you feeling?"

"Much better, but it will be a few days before I'm able to cook your meals again," she teased.

"I'll cook your meals from now on," Abinadi stated.

Raquel smiled. "They *are* half decent, Esther."

"I'm sure they are," Esther said. She patted Raquel's hand. "I am grateful that this young woman was here. She works a miracle with the herbs."

"I know." Abinadi met Raquel's gaze. "Thank you," he said in a quiet voice.

She held his gaze for a moment. "It is I who must thank *you*."

"For what?" he asked.

She looked past him. "For . . . for everything." She looked down at her cloth and dipped it in the water again. Esther closed her eyes as Raquel moistened her forehead.

Abinadi caught the scent of the fragrant liquid. "What is that?"

"A brew of wild papaya sap," she said. "It eases the fever."

He watched Raquel for a few moments as she continued to cool his mother's face. He'd never felt so . . . peaceful. He had finally completed his journey, his mother was recovering, his stomach was full . . . He looked at Raquel. He wasn't sure he could put into words what he thought about her. But having her in the same room, and caring for his mother, made him feel more secure than he ever had in his life. It was like a part of him had been restored—a part he hadn't even known was missing.

"I saw your brother," Raquel said.

He nodded. "Did he speak to you?"

"Only a few words."

"Sounds like him. I have to pry words out of him myself. Unless he's speaking of the things of God—then you can't get him to keep quiet."

Raquel smiled, glancing at Abinadi. "Brother like brother?"

"I only answered your questions," he said.

Raquel lifted a shoulder. "You may preach to me all you wish. I don't mind."

Abinadi stared at her, seeing her cheeks flush. He wanted to say something significant, important, but words failed him. For a moment, he wished he had his brother's talent.

"Look, she's fallen asleep," Raquel whispered.

Abinadi watched his mother's breathing deepen. The lines on her face had somehow softened in the flickering light. She looked younger, happier, as if her cares had been lifted for a time.

"We should let her rest," Raquel said.

He met her still-warm gaze. "We should." A long moment passed, and it was as if they were the only ones in the room.

Finally, she cleared her throat. "You must be tired."

"I am." He tried to break his gaze, but he was mesmerized. Entranced. The same light that made his mother look peaceful had touched the ginger of Raquel's hair. It absolutely glowed.

"Your injuries—are they healed?" she asked.

He nodded, for some reason unable to speak. The room had definitely grown too hot and his head felt light, his mind unclear. Raquel spoke again, but her voice was too far away to hear. He tried to ask her to repeat her words, yet he couldn't make his mouth work. Suddenly the room pitched, and Abinadi reached out for something to hold onto. But everything went dark.

* * *

Days turned into weeks as Alma learned his responsibilities through observing the others and heeding the mentoring from Amulon. As a high priest on the judgment bench, Alma spent his time listening to petty arguments over land ownership, wandering cattle, and injured sheep—all the cases that the king had no patience for. The attacks from the Lamanites became more frequent, so the king had soldiers posted night and day at the borders of the land. Alma's evenings were late, filled with wine, dancing women, and food.

Most days, Alma existed in a blissfully numb state. Other times, he woke feeling physically ill and miserable for no logical reason. He was living the life that most citizens of the land only dreamed about, and his job was easy; he'd learned to keep his head down and do what was asked of him . . . Alma didn't want undue attention.

That was the key, Alma discovered—not to bring attention to oneself. King Noah was either extremely pleased or extremely angry. His emotions fluctuated continually, sometimes on an hourly basis. So if Alma stayed in the right place, doing his duties, he rarely came into conflict. He had only seen Jahza in passing once or twice since their first days together. The woman who frequented his room now was Bethel.

This morning, Alma awoke to an empty room. Bethel must have left before dawn. The first thing Alma did was reach for the wine jug. He had become accustomed to the strong wine and noticed that when he didn't drink, he felt worse, so he kept a goblet nearby whenever possible. After a few swallows, he was ready to rise for the day. The early light had just touched his room as he dressed.

The past few weeks, the Lamanites had been quiet, so the king had taken the opportunity to travel to Mormon, a place known for its fine hunting. He would be gone for a few days. Consequently, this morning court would be slow, and in the king's and several of the priests' absence, Alma was in charge of the daily sacrifices.

He dressed in full high-priest attire, complete with a beaded cowl about his neck, a bird headdress, and a cape of quetzal feathers. When he emerged from the palace, worshippers were already lined up with their squawking animals. Alma strode to the public altar that sat directly in front of the main temple. Two stone statues of the jaguar flanked the altar—symbolizing *additional* gods that were revered.

The first devotee approached, his head bowed, eyes lowered. Alma took the struggling turkey and slit the animal's throat. Holding the flinching bird over the altar, he offered a prayer, then let the blood drip on the heads of the jaguar idols as he'd been instructed. The sacrificing had become routine, and Alma was able to push the laws of Moses from his mind—the ones his father had so carefully followed. Turkeys would never have been accepted as proper sacrificial animals in King Zeniff's time, but King Noah insisted that a larger variety of animals, considered unclean before, were now acceptable. After the blood had fully drained, Alma handed the bird to a lesser priest, who would section the meat and deliver it to the cooking room in the palace.

The worshipper thanked Alma and left. Another man came forward, holding a young tapir—another unclean beast. The animal squealed ferociously, but Alma ignored its cries and quickly made the sacrifice. A short time later, a commotion arose at the back of the line, and Alma peered past the several dozen people in front. An older man held a young girl by the wrist. She struggled to get away, but the man's grip was firm.

Alma wiped his hands on the cloth provided by the lesser priest and strode to the back of the line. "What is this?"

The girl looked up at him, her eyes wild, filled with fear.

"She has refused her betrothed," the man stated in a harsh voice.

Alma's stomach tightened at the father's words.

"She has dishonored our family and will now offer her own heart as penance."

The girl let out a cry, but the father clamped a hand over her mouth.

Mind reeling, Alma tried to decide what to do. He was afraid to think of what King Noah would do—probably let the sacrifice happen or take the girl for himself. Alma straightened and met the man's eyes. "A fat peccary is sufficient for this offense. And another fat peccary should be delivered to the former groom's home."

The man's mouth fell open, then shut into a grim line.

Alma took a step closer, noticing that the girl had finally stopped struggling. "Take your daughter home and confine her for the period of the betrothal."

The man moved out of line, dragging the girl with him. He shot a curious parting glance at Alma.

With determined steps, Alma took his place at the altar again and finished the rest of the sacrifices. He knew the incident would be retold to the king. But he would worry about that later.

By early afternoon, the sacrifices were finished, and Alma took advantage of the free time to wander through the gardens surrounding the palace. He'd almost forgotten about his previous encounter here with Maia until he heard someone singing. Her voice was unmistakable—as beautiful as it had been on her wedding day. The song was low and mournful but exquisite all the same. He moved toward the sound and stopped on the outside of the small grove of trees. Sure enough, Maia knelt by a small pond, her hand trailing in the water as the first rays of sun lit her dark copper hair.

He watched, entranced by her voice—and her beauty, but he told himself to ignore that. She was the king's wife. She wore only a tunic, so her arms were bare. Alma frowned as he gazed at her arms and what he could see of her shoulders, which had several dark bruises. He wondered what type of work she'd been doing to sustain such injuries. To his knowledge, the women of the court did little besides embroidery and visiting the sweat baths.

He didn't realize he was staring until she turned and saw him. His mouth fell open at the sight of her face—the skin around her right eye was dark and nearly swollen shut. Abruptly, she stopped singing and rose to her feet. She seemed as uncomfortable and surprised as he—although for different reasons, he guessed.

Alma extended his hand and walked toward her. "I didn't mean to startle you. I . . ." He couldn't take his eyes from her face. "I'm sorry to intrude. I heard you singing."

Maia moved a lock of hair forward, concealing most of the bruised eye. Then she took a step away from him, twisting the beaded sash about her waist as if she were nervous—or embarrassed.

"What happened to you?" Alma asked, still moving toward her. Then he stopped, realizing she was cowering. She had backed up against a large tree, her hands gripping the sides of the trunk.

Alma lowered his hand and spoke in a tender voice. "I won't hurt you. I saw the bruises on your arm and wondered . . ." He stopped, his throat suddenly dry. She stared at him, her eyes wild with fear. "It's Alma. Remember? Your father is my father's cousin."

The wildness faded, and she nodded. She released the trunk and wrapped her fingers around her arms, covering up most of the bruises. "Tell no one," she whispered.

Alma cocked his head, wondering if he'd heard right. *Tell no one what?* "I won't say anything." He hesitated. "Will you let me help you?"

She shook her head, her wary gaze still on him. "He didn't mean it." Her voice was barely a whisper. "I'll be all right. A few days and my face will return to normal. It always does." She looked at her feet, causing more of the copper hair to spill over her shoulders.

Alma stared at her—she looked so frail, so thin, so *miserable*. The king would be furious when he found out that someone had hurt his wife. Who would dare touch the king's wife? It was the first rule of the court—punishable by immediate death. A sudden lump formed in his throat. He understood. The *king* had done this. Alma's mind reeled. Anger rose as he thought about what type of despicable man would beat a woman.

He turned from Maia, trying to control his emotions. Utter rage threatened to erupt, and the wine he'd already consumed this morning didn't help. He felt ruthless, bold, ready to take on the king himself. He thought about Amulon's daughter, Raquel, and her escape from King Noah. The young woman had probably saved herself from a life of abuse. Alma's heart twisted in pain. As the one who'd negotiated the bride price, he was responsible for Maia's marriage.

After several deep breaths, he faced her again. "I can help you leave," he said, his voice urgent. "You can return to your family and together find a new city—a new life." He took a deep breath. "There was another, Raquel, who fled. She is somewhere safe. I'm sure—"

"No," Maia's voice cut through quietly. She stepped forward and laid a slim hand on his arm. "I can't. He would track us. He would kill my parents. I must endure this life to preserve theirs." Tears spilled onto her cheeks. "Thank you for your kindness."

She passed him without a sound and was gone. Alma put a hand over his arm where her fingers had been. "Maia," he whispered, turning to scan the gardens. He hurried out of the tree enclosure. "Maia," he called as loud as he dared. Where had she gone? Was there a side gate? He examined the vines covering the outer walls but found no opening. He walked back to the enclosure by the pond, then crouched near the water and touched the surface. The face that stared back at him looked tired, haggard, empty. In the few weeks he'd lived at the court, he already had the look of a hardened man—someone who lived a life of debauchery.

"There you are," a lilting voice spoke behind him.

Without turning, Alma knew it was Bethel. He shoved away his tumultuous thoughts and stood. She crossed to him and took his arm. "You have a free afternoon and you choose to spend it by yourself?" Her full lips formed a pout. "I've missed you."

Alma forced a smile.

"Come, my sweet," Bethel said. She interlaced her fingers with his and pulled him alongside her—back to the life that didn't have room for concerns about the king's wife, young boys tortured and sent to prison, or hunted daughters.

Sixteen

*Ye shall even warn them that they trespass not against the Lord, and
so wrath come upon you, and upon your brethren.*
(2 Chronicles 19:10)

Passing the shuttle along the loom, Raquel thought about Abinadi. He
had fallen ill the night of his arrival. He still had the fever and, although his
mother said he was much better, she hadn't seen him outside of the hut yet.

Esther was back to her old self and spent her days at Tia's side. The pair
of women were involved in all the day-to-day details of the camp from plan-
ning meals to shepherding children. No one complained; everyone
complied.

And no one seemed to notice that Abinadi's main caretaker was
Neriah—no one but Raquel. In the beginning, she tried to help by making
poultices and different types of tea from lemon grass and ginger root. But
each time she entered the hut where Abinadi lay, Neriah was there. And it
became too awkward to stay in the same room with her, both of them
hovering over him.

So Raquel kept her distance, sometimes thinking of the way Abinadi
used to look at her, other times chastising herself for even carrying hope.
Clearly, the rest of the group favored Neriah and Abinadi as a couple. Their
names were often mentioned together. Tia fussed over him like a mother—
or future mother-in-law—would. Esther seemed happy to go along with
what everyone else assumed.

This made Raquel even more determined to be self-sufficient. She
worked hard in the fields every morning until the sun was unbearable. She'd
quickly learned how to plant kernels of seed corn, beans, and squash with a
sharp stick—although she'd suffered terrible blisters from the sun in the beginning. She also quickly learned to cover her shoulders and face. In the afternoons, she settled beneath her favorite tree and weaved lengths of cloth using a

back-strap loom attached to the tall trunk. When she tired of that, she spent the remaining hours turning vegetable fibers into thread with a hand spindle.

She was enjoying the quiet of the afternoon when she heard someone running toward her. She turned to see Ben.

"Raquel!" His face was red from exertion.

Her heart hammered at the urgency in the boy's voice. "What's wrong?"

Ben shook his head. "Nothing's wrong." He took a deep breath. "At least I don't think so, but Abinadi is asking for you."

If Raquel's heart had hammered before, now it practically leapt from her chest. "For me?" she managed to say. She rose and hurried after Ben along the path. With a twinge of guilt, she wondered what Neriah's reaction had been when Abinadi asked for her. Maybe it was nothing, but perhaps it meant his illness was fading.

He asked for me, Raquel thought over and over. Then regret washed over her. She should have insisted on staying by his side, administering to him, even if it meant working next to Neriah. Their differences were nothing compared to Abinadi's health.

Ben entered the hut before her, and it took Raquel a few moments for her eyes to adjust to the dim interior. What she saw surprised her. Abinadi wasn't awake at all. He moved restlessly on his mat, turning his head from side to side. Periodically he mumbled, but it was incoherent.

"He called your name, I know it," Ben said.

Disappointment surged through Raquel. Abinadi didn't seem any better, and his calling her name wasn't significant.

"Where's Neriah?" Raquel asked.

Ben lifted a shoulder. "She told me to fetch you."

Raquel wondered why. She crossed to Abinadi and knelt next to him. Placing her hand on his forehead, she was relieved that his fever was cool today. She picked up an abandoned bowl filled with water and an herbal mixture. Lifting the bowl, she smelled the contents. They were turning stale.

"Ben, bring me fresh water from the river," she said, then heard him shuffle out of the room.

Raquel stared at Abinadi for a moment. He had almost a full beard—not having shaved since his illness. It made him look older somehow, fatherly. *He will make a good father.* Raquel tried to block out such thoughts. She looked about the room for any herbs that had been used recently. She rose and busied herself organizing the plants and leaves she found.

"Raquel," a guttural voice said.

She turned to look at Abinadi. His eyes were closed, but his lips were moving. "Raquel."

She crossed to him and knelt. "Abinadi?"

Suddenly his eyes opened, and he grabbed her wrist. "Raquel, I have to tell you something."

"What?" she breathed. "What is it?"

His expression was wild, his gaze intense.

"How is he?" A woman's voice spoke behind her.

Raquel turned as Abinadi's hand fell from her wrist. Neriah stood in the doorway. "He's trying to say something," Raquel said.

Neriah folded her arms, and when Raquel turned back to Abinadi, he'd closed his eyes again. His breathing evened out as he sank back into sleep.

"Looks like he just wants to rest," Neriah said.

"Yes, well . . . apparently," Raquel conceded. She stood and moved away from Abinadi, feeling as if she were encroaching on someone else's territory—an intruder. "Ben said you sent for me."

"I did," Neriah said, eyeing her. "Abinadi was mumbling so much that I thought you might know what he was speaking about."

Raquel shook her head. "What did he say?"

Neriah looked up at the roof for an instant, then leveled her gaze at Raquel. "Something like, 'Save Raquel.' I would have ignored it, but he said it over and over." Her eyes narrowed. "What do you need to be saved from? Is there something you aren't telling everyone?"

Taking a step closer to the entrance, Raquel thought about how Abinadi had found her in the cave that day. But she said, "No. I—I don't know what he meant."

Neriah didn't look convinced. "I believe you do. I believe you ran from something, and it will catch up with you. I believe you've brought our village bad fortune."

"No," Raquel said. "It's nothing like that." Or was it? What if King Noah's wrath never ended and his men tracked her to this place?

"Abinadi is in fine hands," Neriah said. "You aren't needed here any longer."

Raquel's face heated, and her eyes stung. She blinked rapidly and looked down as she passed by Neriah. As upset as Raquel felt, she conceded that maybe Neriah was right. She didn't know how much Gideon had shared with the others, but spending hours alone each day spinning and weaving hadn't been truly her choice. Maybe it was because everyone avoided her. As she walked through the settlement, she kept her eyes downcast, thinking hard.

If Abinadi didn't recover, she'd no longer have a reason to stay. Not that she really had one in the first place. She had tagged along, saying she was willing to earn her keep. But she couldn't live with the hostility from this girl.

She swiped at the hot tears that stung her cheeks. She wouldn't cry. Not about this. Neriah had more claim on Abinadi than she, and for all Raquel knew, Abinadi had feelings for Neriah.

Raquel passed by the loom, ignoring the unfinished work. She felt lost, out of place, and extremely lonely. Why couldn't she be happy like the others around her? They seemed so . . . pure. Raquel knew the answer—they hadn't made the mistakes she had, hadn't lived lives of idolatry and excess.

She stopped in a grove of trees on the far side of the fields and wrapped her arms about her torso. Was this the best it would ever get? Was she doomed to a life of feeling like she didn't belong?

Pray.

Raquel turned around. Had someone spoken? Was she hearing things? A gust of wind riffled through the trees, stirring the leaves.

Pray.

Raquel shook her head. She was going mad. Maybe she was ill. But she felt all right as long as she ignored the anger in her chest and the slightly nauseated feeling in her stomach.

Wind touched the fallen leaves at her feet. She looked down at the flittering leaves as they were tossed along the ground. The earth, the trees, the sky above—all were created by someone. Was it Abinadi's god?

Pulled by compulsion, Raquel dropped to her knees and clasped her hands together like she'd seen Ben do. Then she closed her eyes and bowed her head. She didn't know where to start or *how* to start. But she knew she had to repent, somehow, and then ask the Lord to heal Abinadi. When the words finally came, it was as if she couldn't stop the flood.

* * *

Where is she? Abinadi tried to open his eyes, but the effort was too great. He was hot, then cold, then shaking. He wanted to tell her . . . tell her everything. How he felt, what he knew, and most importantly, what he'd heard.

The Lord's voice. It was unmistakable when the quiet words pierced his soul. The Lord had spoken to him during the night—or was it day? Abinadi wasn't sure.

Abinadi, go forth and say unto this people, Wo be unto this people, for I have seen their abominations, and their wickedness, and their whoredoms; and except they repent I will visit them in mine anger.

The words whispered in his ears still filled his whole being. The warmth of the Lord's presence coursed through his whole body, lifting him, holding him. Again, Abinadi tried to open his eyes, but they wouldn't budge. So he waited for the words he was sure would come.

Except they repent and turn to the Lord their God, behold, I will deliver them into the hands of their enemies.

Abinadi thought of the Lamanites—their enemies. The people of Noah would be delivered to the Lamanites by the Lord Himself.

Yea, and they shall be brought into bondage; and they shall be afflicted by the hand of their enemies . . . They shall know that I am the Lord their God, and am a jealous God.

How could Abinadi return to the city of Nephi? Amulon would surely discover him and throw him into prison. But the power pulsing through him left no room for argument or doubt. The Lord's command was clear.

The voice continued, soft but strong. *When they shall cry unto me I will be slow to hear their cries; yea, and I will suffer them that they be smitten by their enemies.*

This was more than a prediction, a reprimand, a cursing from the loss of the Spirit. This was a promise—no, a severe warning—that they would be destroyed by their enemies.

Abinadi, go and prophesy . . . for they have hardened their hearts against my words; they have repented not of their evil doings; therefore, I will visit them in my fierce anger.

His mouth was dry, and his body trembled. The Lord had spoken his name twice. Abinadi had been commanded to prophesy to the people, to warn them of the afflictions that would come if they didn't repent. His thoughts unfurled in his mind, flashing to the teacher of the elders. Why hadn't Gideon been chosen? Or his brother, Helam?

But the Lord's voice echoed, rising in his mind: *Abinadi, go and prophesy.*

The Lord had chosen *him.*

Abinadi struggled against his weakened body, but it would not cooperate. *I must prepare myself for the journey. I need my strength to return.*

"Raquel," he called out, not sure if the voice he heard was in his mind or spoken aloud.

Someone was nearby; he felt the breath on his skin. He opened his eyes and thought he saw her face. Was she really there? "Raquel, I have to tell you something," he managed to say.

Then her face faded. He reached his hands out, trying to find her, but he could see nothing but black. *The Lord is waiting for me,* Abinadi thought. *I must get up now.* Then suddenly the room was light. Brilliant white.

Abinadi blinked against the brightness. It was as if the sun filled the entire hut. *Abinadi, go forth and prophesy.* He rose to his feet. He didn't know how long he'd been on this mat, but strength coursed through every part of his being.

"Abinadi," a woman said. He looked at her. It was his mother.

"Where is she?" he asked.

"Who?" Esther said. "Neriah's right here, and Tia—"

"Raquel. Where's Raquel?" Abinadi said, looking at the women standing in front of him but not really seeing them.

"In the fields," Neriah said in a quiet voice. "I last saw her walking north."

Abinadi nodded and moved past the women and out of the hut.

Esther followed. "Son, you're ill. You can't possibly walk that far. Stay here, and I'll fetch her."

But Abinadi continued walking. Outside the sun was a brilliant orange, casting its web across the golden fields. With long strides, Abinadi set across the fields in search of Raquel. She would be the first he would tell of his call. He wanted to tell her of the Lord's voice firsthand. He wanted her to *know,* as he did, that God was real—that He wanted a message brought to His people.

The energy seemed to burst through him, and he felt as if he could run and never stop. He crossed two fields before he saw a shape against the line of trees. He started to run toward it. She was just emerging from the trees and stopped when she saw him.

When Abinadi reached her, he was out of breath but far from tired. He'd never felt so full of strength in all his life. Raquel looked radiant as the late afternoon light reflected off her hair. Her face was practically glowing. It was almost as if . . .

"Abinadi? You—you're better?" Raquel stared at him, her eyes incredulous. "You've changed—"

Abinadi's hand went to his face. "I know. My beard."

She shook her head. "No, it's something else. Your countenance is different."

He stared at her, his heart pounding, and she stared back. "The Lord spoke to me," he squeezed out in a whisper.

Raquel brought her hand to her chest.

"He answers our prayers, Raquel. I—"

"I know," she said in a quiet voice.

"You do?"

She nodded and swiped at the moisture on her cheeks. "I prayed today. I prayed for forgiveness, and my heart was lightened." She tried to smile through her tears. "I don't think I've ever felt so . . . free. He answered my prayers."

Abinadi grinned as his heart leapt with joy. "Really?"

She nodded, then her expression sobered. "What did He say to you?"

"He gave me a commandment."

Raquel's eyes widened, but she said nothing.

"The Lord wants me to go into the city and preach repentance to the people." He exhaled slowly. "God has promised to visit the wicked with His anger."

She brought her hand to her mouth. "Visit the wicked? What does that mean?"

Abinadi looked down for a moment, then raised his head. "He said that if the people don't repent, they'll be brought into bondage and be smitten by their enemies." A combination of warmth and awe passed through him as he spoke. Warmth because the Spirit flooded his being, awe because of the magnitude of what might happen if the people didn't repent.

Raquel clasped her hands together. "Then you must go."

Abinadi saw the conviction and the trust in her eyes. "There's something I need to tell you—something that I didn't have a chance to tell you before I became ill."

Raquel gazed at him with curiosity.

"Your father was the one who imprisoned my mother, in his own house."

She gasped. "No."

"But it was your mother who cared for her and, when she took ill, gave her a bed." He rushed on. "Your mother helped me escape. She sent a message for you."

Raquel arched a brow, the pain and shock evident on her face.

"She said to tell you she was sorry."

Raquel nodded, and her eyes reddened with tears. "I'm sorry too." She shook her head. "I'm sorry that my father was so awful and that your mother endured so much." She fell silent for a moment, several emotions flitting across her face. "Tell me why. Why would my father do something like that?"

Abinadi hesitated.

"It was about me, wasn't it?" Raquel's face reddened with shame, then paled. "How could he?" She turned from him, covering her mouth with a hand. "Everyone must hate me."

"Raquel," Abinadi said, touching her shoulder and leaning to look into her eyes. "No one hates you. We know—*I* know—that you are not your father. You are opposite in every way."

She kept her eyes lowered, not responding.

"Raquel," he said again. "Even before I met you, I knew who you were. But in my grandest dreams, I never hoped that I could get to know you. It was like you were unattainable, a beautiful sculpture that only the privileged could see." He paused. "But you have one of the kindest hearts I've ever known. You might be stubborn, but you are fiercely loyal, even if it means putting your own life in danger."

"You don't know all that happened in the king's palace." Her voice trembled as she spoke.

Abinadi stared at her. "What do you mean?"

She turned to face him, her eyes rimmed in red. She looked down at her twisting hands. "I know the Lord has forgiven me, but I must tell you something. When I met with the king, my father left us alone . . . at the king's request." She took a shuddering breath. "The king made advances on me and even started kissing me. It was then that I kicked him and escaped."

Abinadi tried not to smile, but suddenly he did. Raquel looked at him, startled. He stopped when he saw the pained expression on her face.

"You must think me a fool," she said. "I've been tarnished by the king's touch. No amount of repentance can change what happened."

"You're wrong." He stepped toward her. "I think you made your intentions clear to the king." He waited until she looked at him, then said, "You were just another victim of a vile man. You're not to blame."

Her chin started to tremble, and her eyes filled with tears. "I was so surprised . . . and scared. I didn't know what else to do."

Abinadi put his arms around her and drew her close. After a moment, she pulled away.

"You're not tarnished, Raquel," he said. She nodded, but he didn't know if she was entirely convinced. "What else were you praying for?"

She folded her arms and took a deep breath. "I wanted to know whether or not I should remain here."

Silence stretched between them for a moment.

"And what was your answer?" Abinadi asked.

She wiped her cheeks and lifted her gaze to meet his. "It came walking across the fields."

He smiled and tilted his head, studying her. "You don't mind this rudimentary way of life?"

"I love this place. It's so beautiful and quiet. You must think I miss the wealth," she guessed, "but it came with a heavy price—as you now know. In truth, I've never felt so at peace. And after praying, I know this is where I'm supposed to be. I know that I made the right decision in turning down the king." She looked at the ground as if embarrassed at her sudden confession.

"I think you made the right decision, too." Abinadi hesitated, then said, "We haven't known each other for all that long—" He moved slightly closer. "But the Spirit also whispered something else to me."

She looked up.

"If you really don't mind living here, perhaps I can give you a more concrete reason to stay." A small smile touched his lips. "I know you turned down a proposal of marriage from a king, but I wondered if you might possibly accept one from a simple farmer."

She let out a slow breath, then said in a quiet voice, "I couldn't leave if I wanted to. Forgive me for being so bold, but my heart will always be where you are."

She had spoken the last words so quietly, he wasn't sure he'd understood correctly. He stared at her, his heart pounding. "Are you certain?"

Raquel's gaze slid back to his, and she nodded.

His breath stopped for a moment, and he had to consciously inhale. "Well, then." He reached for her hand and enveloped it in his. "I can't offer you a palace or jewels or servants. But I can offer you my heart."

The golden flecks in her dark eyes danced as her smile reached her eyes. "That's all I need."

"Then I forgive you for being bold." He brought her hand to his lips. "I am going to preach in the city of Nephi, but I'll come back as soon as I've delivered the Lord's message. Will you wait for me?"

"Yes," she whispered.

With his other hand, he touched her cheek. "When I return from the city, everything will be different. I'll build you a home, and then if you're sure you'll have me . . ."

She nodded, a smile lighting her face.

"Come. We must make haste. Gideon will want to know about the Lord's commandment. And my mother . . ." He gazed at her tenderly. "She will want to prepare for a wedding."

Still clasping her hand, he led her across the field toward the huts.

Seventeen

Is any among you afflicted? let him pray.
(James 5:13)

The harvest festival was in full swing. No one in King Noah's court suffered from lack of wine—Alma included. Drinking through half the night was the only way he could dispel the recurring dreams he had of his childhood. They were becoming quite a nuisance, and most times he awoke in a cold sweat, calling out for his mother—not something that many men would admit to. It had happened once when Bethel was in his room, and now there was nothing he could say that would stop her smirking.

Their relationship—if it could be called that—had died out. So now, according to the court gossip, he was available again. Not that he was ever tied to one woman anyway. None of the priests were, and especially not the king.

It became quite ridiculous having the women vie for his attention, so he continued to drink heavily and watch the others dance from where he lounged against cushions. He wasn't sure if Bethel had told anyone about his sleep talking, but he had his suspicions. The women who approached him to dance always held a good dose of amusement in their gazes.

Why do I care? Alma thought as he brought the goblet to his lips again. But he did care. More than anything, he wanted the dreams to go away. Maybe if he visited his parents' home, where they were buried beneath their house—as was the custom—and paid his respects, their memories would fade once and for all. His new life didn't have room for those kinds of memories.

He scanned the dancers. Every once in awhile, one of the king's wives would appear in the circles of dancing. Not often, because they were usually with child or nursing one just born. But whenever a wife appeared, Alma watched more carefully, searching for Maia. Try as he might, he couldn't stop thinking about her. Was it because the times he met her in the garden she'd been upset? Or was it because of her incredible beauty and unmatched voice?

I don't know, Alma admitted silently. It was probably because she was forbidden. The king didn't tolerate his wives' wandering in any form, although that didn't apply to Noah himself. And no priest would ever dare cross the king in that way.

But that's not what Alma wanted. He didn't want to capture her in a love affair, bringing shame to them both. No . . . he had a strange sense of protection whenever he was around her. He wanted to shield her from anything unsavory, which in his more lucid moments he saw as practically everything that went on at court. How did someone so pure and innocent as she endure being surrounded by this lifestyle?

Maybe that's why he rarely saw her; she was keeping to her quarters. Then another thought came to him. Perhaps she was with child, and she was in confinement. How could he find out? Asking another woman would just fuel a round of gossip. *Amulon would know.* Alma scanned the rhythmic bodies for his tall mentor. Sure enough, Amulon was in the thick of the dancers, at least one woman clinging to each arm. He wore a birdlike mask of Wuqub Kaquix—representing the gigantic bejeweled bird-god.

Alma rose and steadied himself, being careful not to slosh the wine in his goblet. He focused on putting one step in front of the other until he cleared the low table. The king laughed at something behind him, but Alma didn't turn. A woman, whose name he couldn't quite remember, touched his arm.

"Joining us at last?" She giggled in a lilting way.

He kept moving, barely offering her a glance. "Amulon," he said as he drew closer. His tongue felt thick, and he was sure his words were slurred. "I need to ask you a question."

Amulon turned and peered through the gaping beak of the mask. He grinned when he saw Alma. "Ask me anything, anything at all, my friend."

Nodding, Alma placed a heavy hand on Amulon's shoulder for balance. "Not here. Alone."

"Ahh," Amulon said, his eyes brightening.

The women with Amulon laughed merrily.

Alma grabbed Amulon's arm. "Come outside with me—"

"It will have to wait. I can't desert my beautiful guests."

Alma looked from the priest to the women hanging on him. What was he thinking? He didn't want Amulon to be suspicious. "All right," he said.

"We'll meet later." He muscled his way back through the crowd, but instead of heading toward the king's table, he turned and left the great hall. He needed some fresh air, away from the throngs that always seemed to surround the king. The noise made his head ache.

Once outside of the main rooms, he exited the palace, reveling in the early evening air. The air felt crisp tonight—sharpening his senses. It seemed that lately he'd often let food and wine become too much of an indulgence. His sandals scraped at the ground as he walked, and Alma decided that he'd walk to the market to purchase a new pair. He hadn't spent much of his high-priest silver or gold. It was time he did.

The farther he walked, the more his head cleared. He missed being among people and walking the streets. He waved to several children as he passed their homes, but they simply stared. Alma looked down at his clothing. Did he have something spilled on his cape? No. Then he noticed that he'd walked into a rather destitute section of the city. The children were all barefoot, and most wore little more than a scrap of cloth. Alma suddenly felt uncomfortable. For what his feathered cape cost, he could clothe more than a dozen children.

Relief washed over him as he left the scraggly homes and entered the north side of the market. Things had slowed for the day, and only half of the usual vendors were still set up. He stopped before a display of green jade necklaces. The merchant—a large, over-dressed man—immediately pounced.

"What do you like?" he asked, his grin showing a large gap between his teeth. "These come straight from the great river. I collect the pebbles myself. Very precious."

Alma stepped back. "They are nice."

"You want one for your wife, eh?" The merchant's gaze ran over Alma's clothing. "Or your concubine? Or both?" He laughed, his belly vibrating.

Heat crawled along Alma's neck. "No, thank you." He gave the man a curt nod, then turned away. The jewelry had been beautiful, and he could well afford it. But there was only one woman that he could picture wearing it. And she belonged to the king.

Within moments, he stood before a leather merchant. The pigskin sandals were crudely fashioned. Alma lifted one and examined it. The word *blisters* popped into his mind. The leather-maker stood from his work spot and waved his hands. "Not for you. I have something special." He rummaged through an oilskin bag and produced a pair of nearly black sandals. "Alligator."

Alma reached for them and examined the workmanship. The leather was surprisingly soft and supple. After a moment of haggling over the price,

Alma strode away in his new sandals. The market seemed even more deserted than before. Then Alma realized that a large group had formed at the west end. They were laughing at something. As he drew closer, he heard a man's voice rise above the crowd. Alma stopped along the fringe of the group and listened.

"The Lord has seen your abominations and your whoredoms. And if you don't repent"—the voice sailed over the crowd—"He will visit you in His anger."

Alma worked his way farther into the group until he had a good view of the man. He was uncommonly tall, with a full beard befitting an old man. But this man was young, perhaps only a couple years older than Alma himself. His clothing was decent—unlike some of the disillusioned people who took to shouting in the streets. But it was his voice that was captivating. He wasn't screaming or shouting—raving as others had done. He spoke calmly, yet his voice carried.

"The Lord has said that if you don't repent and turn to Him, He will deliver you into the hands of your enemies." The man licked his lips and gazed at the crowd. For an instant, his gaze met Alma's.

Alma drew behind another man, uncomfortable with the preacher's expression of calm authority.

"Lamanite!" somebody shouted.

"You've come to scare us, but we won't back down!" another hollered.

"No," the preacher said. "Nephite blood runs through my veins."

"Traitor!"

Alma backed out. The man was certainly a lunatic for arguing against a crowd. As Alma turned away, the preacher said, "My name is Abinadi. The Lord your God is a jealous God, and if you don't repent in sackcloth and ashes, He will not hear your prayers or deliver you from your afflictions."

"Where's *your* sackcloth?" someone called out. The crowd laughed along with the caller.

"What afflictions?" a woman shouted next to Alma. He looked at her and saw that her clothing was similar to that worn at court. Bracelets lined her arms, and earrings dangled from her ears.

As Alma exited the crowd, he saw another woman—a completely different type of woman. She was elderly, her clothing obviously repaired over and over with squares of cloth covering the holes. Her hands were gnarled and the lines on her face pronounced with age. She stood on the outside of the crowd, her hands clasped together, her eyes wide with wonder. For a moment, Alma just looked at her. Here was a woman who looked afflicted. Here was a woman who could have very well been his mother—had she lived.

"The Lord has commanded me to call you unto repentance," the preacher who called himself Abinadi said.

Alma's gaze stayed on the elderly woman. Was it possible she believed his words? She seemed to soak in every word he spoke. Alma turned back toward the crowd. They were restless, shouting insults again. Someone yelled, "Take him to the king!"

Alma turned away from the yelling, from the soft-spoken preacher who continued to tell the people that they needed to repent. Alma had seen enough of the city today. There was no reason to stay.

He made his way back to the palace quickly, this time avoiding the streets with those most afflicted—paying taxes so heavy that they could barely feed their children, giving their sons into the service of Noah's army, hiring out their children to work in the vineyards for next to nothing . . .

As Alma walked it seemed suffering was at every corner, around every bend. Perhaps the preacher had been right about that. But it really depended on who he was talking about. *Not me,* Alma decided. Dark had fallen by the time he reached the palace.

When he entered, he avoided the great hall and strode directly to his room. He was tired, and every trace of wine had worn off. He'd have to drink at least half a jug to keep away the dreaming tonight. Once inside his room, he threw off his outer cloak and sank onto the cushions.

If you don't repent in sackcloth and ashes, He will not hear your prayers or deliver you from your afflictions. Alma shook his head, trying to get the preacher's voice out of his thoughts. *Maybe I should go back to the music and dancing.* But he didn't feel like being around anyone right now. He reached for the jug of wine next to him. It was nearly empty, so he took a long swallow, draining it.

He sighed. He'd have to go to the cooking room and get it filled. Rising, he pulled his cloak back over his shoulders. Just as he reached for the door, a rapid knock sounded. Surprised, he opened it a crack.

"Hello there!" Amulon's voice boomed. It was followed by several giggles.

Alma opened the door wider to reveal Amulon with three women. One was Bethel.

"Hello," Alma said in a flat tone.

"We're here at your request," Amulon said, swaying toward Alma as he spoke. "Ask any question, and I'll answer." He laughed, and the women joined in.

Alma plastered a smile on his face. He refused to inquire about Maia in front of the other women. "I found the answer already," he said. Bethel slipped into the room and stood behind him.

"All right then," Amulon said, not the least bothered. "I'll go and offer someone else my service." He pulled the door shut.

Alma stared at the door, then turned. Bethel set down the jug of wine she carried and wrapped her arms around his waist. "I missed you."

"I'm sorry—"

"Oh, I'm sorry too. I promise not to tease you again about calling for your mother in your sleep." She covered her mouth as a giggle erupted. "Oops. There I go again—"

"No," Alma said, grabbing her hands and firmly moving them off his waist. "I'm sorry, because I have to ask you to leave."

Bethel's lips pursed. "Oh, Alma dearest—"

"I'm sorry," he said again. He opened the door wide and waited.

After a moment's hesitation, Bethel folded her arms, her eyes burning. "Is it Jahza? Am I too old for you?"

Alma gazed at her. "It's not Jahza, and there's nothing wrong with you, Bethel. You're beautiful. I just can't . . . I don't . . ."

Her eyes hardened, and her hands tightened into fists. "I know your secret, Alma. You talked about more than your dear *mother* in your sleep." She smiled in a conniving way. "You reject me, and I'll tell the king about your little infatuation with his *wife.*"

Alma stared at her, his stomach churning. Had he really said Maia's name in his sleep? If Bethel said something, he would be ruined. "I . . ." He hesitated. *The Lord has seen your abominations and your whoredoms.* "I'll have to accept that possibility."

Bethel's eyes widened, then she slowly smiled. She turned from him and glided out of the room. Alma shut the door behind her and leaned against it. His skin was suddenly clammy—his heart thundering.

He slid to the ground. Burying his face in his hands, he shuddered. He was a man of affliction now. That preacher—Abinadi—had been right about a few things, it seemed. Alma raised his head up, stunned at himself. Did he really believe anything the foolish man had said? The jug of wine caught his attention. Alma reached for it, suddenly glad that Bethel had made her untimely appearance. It had saved him a trip to the cooking rooms. He brought the jug to his lips.

If you don't repent in sackcloth and ashes, the Lord will not hear your prayers or deliver you from your afflictions.

Alma lowered the jug. Could the Lord deliver a wayward priest from King Noah? One who had broken the first rule of court? Alma shook his head. No one had that kind of power. Not even the preacher's so-called God. Bethel was likely on her way to the king right now. One word or suggestion from her, and Alma would be ruined. He threw the jug of wine against the far wall and watched the red liquid spray across the wall and onto the floor. The nearby cushions were drenched, but he didn't care. Within minutes, he expected to be summoned to court. But this time he'd be on the opposite side of the judgment seat.

As the room darkened with the night, Alma leaned against the wine-soaked cushions, waiting for the call.

Eighteen

*And he shall turn the heart of the fathers to the children, and
the heart of the children to their fathers.*
(Malachi 4:6)

Raquel was in love with a man who wanted to marry her. And soon—
she hoped—he would return and do just that. Since the first day she'd
prayed in the forest, it was almost as if she couldn't pray enough. She
wondered how she'd ever made it through the day without it. She found
herself praying for every tiny thing in addition to her regular prayers
morning and night—and meals and Sabbath and . . .

She'd caught Neriah gazing at her several times, and each time it ended
in an awkward glance away. Raquel alternated between elation and guilt
whenever she was around Neriah. Raquel was happy that Abinadi had
chosen her over Neriah, but she felt sorry for the woman and wished she
could ease the strain between them.

On an afternoon a few days after Abinadi's departure, Esther sought out
Raquel at her usual weaving place. "Tia wants me to speak with you," she
said.

Raquel's heart rate sped up. She sensed Esther had come to talk about
Neriah.

"We need to discuss your wedding clothing and the mohar."

Raquel's hands stilled against the loom as she looked at Esther with
surprise. "I will wear what I have. And as for the bride price . . . there is no
need. Everything that can be spared should be put to use within the settlement."

"Nonsense." Esther crossed in front of Raquel and stood facing her.
"This is a celebration indeed. I have some things that I'd like to pass on to
you." She reached out and tucked a strand of hair behind Raquel's ear. "It's
not every day that I gain a daughter."

Raquel smiled, but her stomach churned. "I don't want to be a bother to anyone, and I don't want anyone to have to work an extra moment on my behalf."

"And what are you doing right now?" Esther asked, her gaze steady.

Raquel looked down at her hands. "Weaving."

"For whom?"

Raquel remained silent.

"Just as I thought. You're weaving cloth that you will never wear. Yet you won't let anyone else do a thing for you." Esther settled next to Raquel, keeping her voice low. "You don't have to keep paying for fleeing Noah and his men, dear."

"I—I don't know what you mean," Raquel said. She hadn't thought about Noah's soldiers for days. Although she prayed for Abinadi's safety each day, she felt a sense of peace about his journey that she couldn't explain.

"You don't have to pretend like you don't exist. Never taking more than you absolutely need to survive, never asking for help, working more than any other woman in the settlement . . ."

What's wrong with living as minimally as possible? Raquel thought. The others had been doing it for years.

Esther caught her gaze. "Your needs are just as important as anyone else's. You have the right to joy as much as any woman."

"But," Raquel started, "if it weren't for me, Neriah might have been betrothed already."

"What?" Esther looked surprised.

"Her sister told me that Neriah was in love with Abinadi . . ."

Esther was quiet for a moment. "It was on her side only, then. Abinadi has never thought of her in that way."

"Are you sure?"

"Of course. She's a beautiful girl, but a mother knows these things," Esther said with a knowing smile. "I'm his mother, aren't I?"

Raquel clasped her hands together. "But I feel like I intruded in her life."

"Dear," Esther said in a stern voice, "you were an answer to my prayers. My son has made his choice—and it's the *right* choice. Neriah will come to understand that."

Raquel hung her head. How long would it take for Neriah to forgive her? If she hadn't interfered in Abinadi's life . . .

Esther's voice broke into her thoughts. "What else is troubling you?"

"It's just that I feel responsible for Abinadi having to leave the city of Nephi. If I hadn't run away, then my father wouldn't have threatened him."

"Things would have happened in a different order, that's all. The Lord would have still asked Abinadi to call His people to repentance." She chuckled. "That will get him into enough trouble."

"Do you think he'll be all right?" Raquel asked.

"I wouldn't have let him go if I didn't."

Raquel nodded, knowing Esther was right on that account. But guilt for other things had eaten a hole in her heart. "Ben would never have been imprisoned if he hadn't known me. And how can anyone ever forgive me for what my father did to *you?*"

Esther clucked her tongue and put an arm around Raquel's shoulder. "Look at me." When she complied, Esther continued. "It's unnecessary for me to forgive you—you've done nothing wrong. You're not to blame for your father's actions."

"But you could have died."

"I've lived a full and happy life. If it had been my time to go, the Lord would have taken me," Esther said. "But it wasn't. Here I still am, to pester you and fret over important things like wedding clothes."

A small smile turned up the corners of Raquel's mouth.

"There. That's better." Esther paused. "I want to tell you something else—something you may not fully understand until you are older, much older. But if you start to learn it while you're young, you'll always be able to feel peace from the Spirit of the Lord."

Raquel saw the soft lines in Esther's face harden.

"I know you care for Abinadi a great deal. I sensed it when you came to our home that first night with a parcel of herbs. But your love is in its infancy. What you are and what he is may not be what you both will be in the future," Esther said. "Love grows and love fades. We don't always know which will happen to us."

Raquel drew back, wondering why Esther would speak this way. Abinadi had told her that his father had abandoned the family, but Abinadi would never do something like that.

"You can't base your happiness solely on a man or a marriage," Esther said quietly. She pointed to Raquel's chest. "And I'm not just speaking of love. You need to find happiness that comes from within—deep inside your soul. Love, pain, joy, sorrow—all of these are centered within you. Some women marry evil men, some never have children, while yet others carry the curse of sorrow with them."

A shudder ran through Raquel as she thought of her own mother's misery.

"You're blessed to have found Abinadi, and he you. But my other son . . . he may never see such fortune." Esther's voice trembled. "You may think my greatest sorrow is with my husband, but my greatest sorrow is with my son."

"I—I'm sorry," Raquel whispered, aching deep inside for this woman's struggles.

"Don't be sorry for me," Esther said, her tone adamant. "The Lord will suffer all things. He has carried my grief, and He will carry my future sorrows." Esther clasped Raquel's hands. "The Lord will redeem all who obey . . . all who desire. He will break the bands of death, heal the sick and oppressed, and we will be saved at the last day and be made whole."

Raquel exhaled, letting the words soak in.

"I have given my burdens to the Lord," Esther said, "and so should you."

Silence stretched between them, then slowly all the guilt that Raquel felt ebbed slightly. Hope seemed to trickle in. Maybe it was possible . . .

"If I can find happiness—despite the curved journey my life has taken—*you* can too," Esther said.

Raquel blinked rapidly. She wanted to be happy. But she didn't know if she deserved it. Abinadi's proposal of marriage was the one moment in her life wherein she could claim pure joy. Even when she'd prayed and felt a sliver of the Lord's presence, it had been marred with feelings of unworthiness. "I'll try," she finally said.

"Excellent. I can't ask for anything more." Esther leaned over and kissed the top of Raquel's head. "I'll tell Tia that you said yes to everything."

Raquel drew back. "But, I didn't—"

Esther chuckled, rising to her feet. "She won't know that," she called over her shoulder as she hurried away.

Raquel watched Esther leave. Everything that the woman had said seemed to make perfect sense. Could Raquel really turn her burdens over to the Lord? Would He really carry them for her? She lowered her head into her hands and let the tears drip into the dirt next to her feet.

Then she heard a rustle coming from the trees. Instantly she was on guard. She rose to her feet and clutched the weaving shuttle. Taking quiet steps, she approached the thicket. She moved through the trees, stopping to listen every so often. When she reached the top of the low hillside, she gazed over the valley. In the not-too-far distance, she saw the cloaked figure of Helam walking toward the fields.

She stared at him. He was too far away to have been the one to make the sound. But if he had run, perhaps he could have covered the distance. Had he been listening to their conversation? And if so, why?

The wind picked up, stirring the grass at her feet. She had been counting the days since Abinadi's departure: four. She hoped he would hurry home.

* * *

I must have fallen asleep, Alma realized as he awoke to pitch black. He stumbled to his feet and walked to the window. The moon was high in the sky—he had only slept an hour or so. It was still early enough for the harvest festival to be in full swing. Maybe Bethel hadn't broken the news to the king yet. Or maybe she would dangle it over Alma's head to get her way.

He groaned and turned from the window. Either way, he was doomed. He should leave the palace now . . . but go where? Join the other outcasts from the city of Nephi? The idea was laughable. Although he'd been a high priest for only a short time, he'd never settle for living a second-class lifestyle now.

Alma began to reason within himself. He was a high priest in the greatest court in the land. He would do as the others did. *Lie.* It was just that simple. The king would believe a high priest over a harlot.

Alma decided to return to the great hall and make sure the king saw him entertaining one of the harlots—he didn't care which. His mind made up, Alma pulled on his cape, grateful it had been spared the spilt-wine episode. His stomach rumbled as the craving for wine reared its head.

When he exited his room, he heard shouting coming from the front courtyard. Hovering near the wall, he peered around the corner. The king stood on the steps, a mass of people gathered in the courtyard. One of the guards was yelling.

Alma held his breath, listening. The guard was telling the king about the preacher in the market—how the preacher named Abinadi had told the people to repent of their iniquities.

Noah's fists clenched and his face reddened. "What gives this man a right to judge my people?"

The guard continued, his own face red. "He also said the Lord will bring punishments on this people."

"The Lord?" the king scoffed. "Who is the Lord that he can bring destruction to my people? *I* am the king of this land."

The crowd cheered, and King Noah raised his jeweled fist, shouting over the cheers, "I command you to bring the preacher here. I will slay any man who dares to stir up contention among my people."

A guard's voice sailed over the crowd. "He's already fled."

"Find him!" Noah commanded. "And when you do, tell him he will answer for his crimes." He scanned the crowd. "The reward will be great for whoever brings this traitor to me."

The crowd roared in response, and several men took off running. Others organized into groups, shouting excitedly.

Alma stepped behind the wall just as Noah turned. Too late. The king had seen him.

"Alma!" The king's voice bounced off the stone walls.

Alma moved into view. "I was just on my way to gather my things for the search." *The first lie.*

"No time for that. You need to leave now." The king glowered at him. "Find the preacher!"

He nodded. "Of course. I'll do my best—"

"Now!" the king yelled.

Alma hurried past the king and out into the courtyard. Only a few women remained now, standing in groups. The men had all fled, hoping to claim favor or title from the king for bringing in the preacher. Alma moved past the women and ran too, pounding the road in his new sandals. The supple leather conformed to his feet as though he'd been wearing them for weeks. He had no idea which direction to go but assumed that if the preacher had escaped the angry crowd, he hadn't stayed long in the city.

Alma slowed his pace once he was out of view of the palace. As he gulped for air, he realized that he hoped the man had escaped. Incurring the wrath of the king was no small matter; Alma knew—he was on the verge of it himself. Although Abinadi had stirred up the people, was this a cause for death? Lesser crimes had been harshly condemned, Alma realized—like the young boy who'd been whipped and imprisoned for *not* speaking.

The moon was high in the sky by the time Alma reached the outskirts of the city. Across the expanse of fields, he saw torchlights bobbing through the crops. The people were even searching the rows of maize. Alma's heart sank. The preacher stood little chance . . . unless he was already gone. And if he chose to return, the people would certainly take him to the king immediately.

Alma turned away from the frenzied searching and walked the paths between the larger homes of the city. Some of the high priests, such as Amulon, lived along this road. Alma slowed his step as he passed by Amulon's home. It was a massive dwelling with many rooms—obviously for servants and relatives, since he and his wife had only one child, and now not even that.

A light came from the entrance, and Alma hesitated, noticing two people in the doorway. Their movements were quick yet seemed almost furtive as the shorter figure gestured the taller one inside. *Strange,* he thought. Curiosity pulled at him, and he entered the courtyard, careful not to make noise when opening the gate. He moved to a large, overhanging cashew tree and hid beneath its shadows. He doubted one of the figures had been Amulon; he was most likely searching for the priest himself.

Alma tried to steady his breath as he waited. After a few moments, the shapes appeared again. One was clearly a small woman dressed in neat, fashionable clothing. Amulon's wife? But who was the man? Alma stared—it was the preacher. There was no mistaking the tall form and thick beard. Even in the silhouetted light, it was most certainly Abinadi.

Alma watched with fascination. Was there some connection between the preacher and one of the most premiere high priests in the land? *If Amulon is mixed up with the preacher, maybe I don't have as much to worry about as I thought I did,* Alma thought. Then the woman's hushed voice carried across the quiet of the courtyard.

"Tell her I am so happy—for you both." The woman smiled at the preacher yet somehow still looked sad. "I can't express my sorrow for what we made her do. But I can find peace in knowing that she is happy now."

Abinadi took the woman's hand. "I wish you could be there with us when we marry."

The woman raised her other hand to her eyes and dabbed at them. Then, in a swift motion, the woman embraced the preacher. When she pulled away, she wiped her eyes again. "You must go now. The servants have already heard about your preaching. It was not well received."

"No," Abinadi said, his voice soft, yet powerful. "I didn't think it would be. But I couldn't turn down the Lord's admonition. The crowd threatened me, so I fled, but I had to pay a visit to you before leaving. I'll be camping in the forest for a few days, and I'll return again soon."

The woman furrowed her brow. "Only if it's safe. But be careful. My daughter is blessed to have found you." She looked around the courtyard. "Now, go."

Abinadi turned away and hurried to the gate. As the door shut to the home, Alma slipped out of his place. The man was crazy to plan a return to the city.

I have to warn him, Alma thought, then froze. *What am I doing? I'm the one who's mad.* But he continued to follow the preacher until well past the outer wall. Then he called out, "Abinadi!"

The man whirled around in the moonlight; Alma detected his wariness. "You don't need to fear me," Alma said. "I've come to warn you."

Abinadi stayed in his place, poised to spring away.

Alma took a few careful steps forward. "The king has promised a reward to the man who brings you in. He wants to slay you for stirring up contention."

Abinadi laughed. "If that's all I've done, then I haven't completed the work I came to do." He walked hesitantly toward Alma. His gaze took in Alma's appearance and recognition lit his eyes. "Why are *you* warning me?"

"I—I don't know," Alma said. He stared into the clear eyes of the strange, bearded man. "I suppose because . . . my father once spoke of similar things."

"Who was your father?"

Alma didn't want to give out names, so instead he said, "A high priest in King Zeniff's court."

"Ah." Abinadi's face softened into a smile. "I give you my utmost respect then." He stooped and bowed low.

"You're mistaken," Alma said. "I didn't say that I *believed* my father."

Straightening, Abinadi locked gazes. "Everything your father taught you was true." He placed a hand on Alma's shoulder. "Remember that, above all else. No matter what happens to this people."

Alma flinched—it was if he'd been touched with fire. He grasped his shoulder and rubbed it. How could this man know all that his father had taught? The preacher didn't even know his father's name. Alma opened his mouth to question him, but Abinadi had already turned and was moving in a steady run across the fields.

Alma watched the figure grow smaller in the moonlight, noticing that all the torch lights in that area were now completely gone.

Feeling suddenly dejected, Alma heaved a sigh. He had very possibly saved a man's life, but all he could feel was sorrow. As he walked back to the palace, he was tempted to turn away and follow the preacher. But that was ridiculous. What he really needed was an unbroken wine jug filled to the brim. Then he would feel back to his own self.

Another crowd was gathered in the palace courtyard when Alma arrived, but it was subdued this time. Alma found Amulon in deep conversation with a group of men. Did the man never rest? Alma slipped by unnoticed and wove his way to the main cooking room. A handful of women bustled about the room, preparing yet another feast of fish, fruits, and maize tortillas with beans and squash—a meal that would probably be served at midnight.

Alma pulled a jug of wine from one of the storage shelves. One woman glanced at him, but no one said anything. By the time he reached his room, he'd already drunk half of it. He shut the door and walked to the window. Staring at the moon, he drained the last of his wine.

Then he fell against the cushions, barely awake. He didn't mind the stale stench of spilt wine as he let his eyes close. The image of the preacher stayed in his mind, but within moments, Alma was sure it would be obliterated by his dreams. The man couldn't have been right about his father. The preacher didn't even know him. No one knew his father like Alma did. The man who always criticized. The man who was too busy to play games or hunt with his son. The man who spent his time at home poring over scrolls of scripture.

If I'm ever a father, I'll never let my tasks come before my children, Alma thought. *I'll spend long days with them—teaching them. I'll let them carve whatever they want. I won't force them to memorize bland words of long-dead prophets. And most of all, I'll smile and laugh with them.*

His mind finally dulled, but not enough to keep the dreams away this time.

Alma stood in his childhood home. It was as if he was an observer, watching himself as a boy of eleven. His father came home from court unannounced. The harvest was complete, so there was no work for him. But he was on a different errand this time. Alma hid behind the door as his parents spoke.

He watched his mother's face as his father broke the news.

"Ruth, the king is sending soldiers to defend our farms against the Lamanites." His father paused. "I'm going with them."

His mother reached for the low table to steady herself. "No. Oh, Cephas, no," she whispered, gazing at him in shock. "You are in your fiftieth year—those soldiers are not yet twenty. And the Lamanites are bloodthirsty."

He smiled in a sad way. "I know." He took a step toward her, reaching out. "This is our land, our farm, and I must defend it."

His mother leaned against his father, resting her head on his chest. "I couldn't bear it if something happened to you."

He pulled away and touched her chin, lifting her face. "It's in the Lord's hands."

She nodded, tears bright in her eyes. "I'll pray for you every moment until you return."

When his father had packed his things, Alma watched him leave as he waved at his wife.

Then his father returned with both legs severely injured. His mother stayed by his side, day and night, pleading with God to spare her husband. God didn't listen. His mother's heart died a little more each day until it too stopped.

God had taken both of his parents. Alma was eleven, an orphan. God must not exist . . .

Alma awoke, soaked in perspiration. He was sick to his stomach. His father had sacrificed his life for his family—when he didn't have to. He could have let the younger men fight. Instead he had died, taking his wife with him.

And here I am, Alma thought with disgust. Drunk day and night. Caught up in senseless court politics. Surrounded by harlots. He rubbed his suddenly moist eyes. His throat burned with unshed grief. *I am nothing. There's no reason for me to pretend anymore. I'm no better than the next high priest.*

This was his life now. No matter what he'd been taught in his youth. No matter what sacrifices his parents had made. God hadn't protected them, and He certainly wasn't protecting Alma.

Alma didn't have the power to change his life—not unless he was willing to live in hiding like that mad preacher. Alma threw open the door to his room, letting fresh air blend with the stale. He called out to the first servant who passed. "Come here. I have an errand to ask of you."

When the boy approached, Alma handed him an onti of silver. "Please fetch the woman Bethel."

He watched the boy leave, then turned back to his room. He had only a few minutes to clean himself up and prepare an apology. *A second lie.*

Nineteen

*Serve him with a perfect heart and with a willing mind: for the
Lord searcheth all hearts, and understandeth all.*
(1 Chronicles 28:9)

Abinadi's heart hammered as he ran, but not from exertion. The high priest had been right—King Noah did have an order for his death. Mobs of men seemed to come from every corner, every road. *Raquel will kill me if I am caught,* Abinadi thought with irony. *Now we have one more thing in common—both of us are hunted.*

After he sprinted across the fields, away from the high priest who'd warned him, he saw a block. Men were stationed along the line of trees where the forest began. Abinadi spent the next hour retracing his steps and finding another passage through the forest. The safest way was to stay near the river, wading or swimming when necessary. And now he was soaked.

Regardless, he continued to run, his clothing clinging to his body and the water dripping down his legs. He'd spent only one day preaching in the city. He thought he'd noticed a few people listening with interest. But that was before the crowd had started to argue and call out insults. Still, as he preached to them, the words flowed into his mind as if the Lord were guiding his every sentence.

He traveled most of the night until he finally collapsed in sleep in the early hours of the morning. Worry prevented a deep sleep though. He was anxious to see Raquel and the others, yet his heart was heavy. He'd done as the Lord had asked him to but felt as if his mission weren't complete. Was there more he could have done? Should he have tried to befriend citizens in small groups, and only then share the message he had to give?

His shoulders felt weighted with an incredible burden. It had been up to *him* to warn the people. Yet they hadn't listened. They'd run him off, and the king had ordered his death. Surely if they could be made to understand—

even a few of them—they'd change their ways. And one could influence many.

Did I influence anyone? he wondered. That high priest had done something out of the ordinary, and Abinadi had seen something spark in the man's eyes. And even though the priest had denied any belief, he had been reared to believe. *Perhaps . . .*

Abinadi let out a breath of frustration as he walked. He hoped he'd reached at least one person. He looked up. The sun was at its zenith now, and he should come within view of the settlement soon.

He'd done what the Lord had asked, but was it enough? Had he succeeded or failed? Abinadi shook his head. Would the Lord flee from an angry crowd or persecution if He still had a mission to complete? *So why did I?*

His thoughts turned to Raquel, and the answer came. Because he wasn't willing to sacrifice her. He wanted to marry her and raise children together.

A form dropped from a tree behind him. Abinadi turned, reaching for his dagger, then relaxed. "Ben!"

The boy ran to him, wrapping his arms about Abinadi. "I knew you'd come today."

Abinadi squeezed Ben. "How did you know that?"

"I just knew," Ben said, his wide grin revealing his missing teeth.

"How is everyone?" Abinadi asked as they walked together over the last rise.

"Tia and your mother are preparing for the wedding," Ben said, starting to skip. "Raquel is mad, and Neriah is mad."

Abinadi grabbed Ben and stopped him. "About what?"

"Well . . ." Ben stalled, seeming to enjoy the attention. "Raquel is mad that everyone is ignoring the real work and making wedding preparations. She keeps saying, 'I don't need that. I don't need this.'" He imitated a girl's high-pitched voice—although it wasn't much of a stretch for him.

Relief washed over Abinadi. That sounded like Raquel, and he could deal with that type of anger. "And . . . Neriah?"

"She's mad it's Raquel getting married and not her."

Abinadi smiled. "She'll have her turn soon enough, I'm sure."

Ben scrunched up his nose. "That's not what she wants. She wishes that you had asked *her* to marry you."

He stared at the boy. *Neriah?* "Who told you that?"

"Adriel teased her about it, and Neriah chased her out of the fields." Ben lifted his hands. "Now she snaps at everyone and won't talk to Raquel."

Abinadi let out a breath. He'd known Neriah for years yet had never seen her as more than one of Gideon's daughters. Yes, she had turned into a beautiful woman, but how could she expect to marry him? He thought over any interactions they'd had, but his mind came up empty.

"I'm going to tell the others you're here," Ben shouted, running ahead.

Abinadi laughed at the boy's endearing, dependable enthusiasm. Too bad Ben wasn't older, then Neriah would have someone . . . Or too bad Helam was so standoffish on the subject of marriage. His brother was a good, decent, and hard-working man. There had to be a woman who could overlook his appearance, but Helam wouldn't even show his face to give a woman that chance.

Soon he arrived at the settlement. Several people were working to clear the fields, but his mother was waiting to greet him. After embracing her, he looked around for Raquel.

"You'll find her weaving this time of the day," his mother said. She studied him closely. "How was your message received?"

"Not well," he said in a quiet voice. "I was chased out of the market-place. When the king heard of my message, he placed an order for my . . ." He glanced away.

His mother brought her hand to her mouth. "No . . . Oh, Abinadi."

"It's all right. I'm safe," he said.

"You can never return to that place. None of us can. The people will be destroyed because of their—"

"Shhh. I know." Abinadi placed a hand on his mother's shoulder. "Still, I worry that I could have done more to soften their hearts."

"No, son. No." Esther's tone was adamant. She reached up and placed both of her hands on his face. "You risked your life to deliver the Lord's message. You did what was right in leaving."

Abinadi looked at his mother, hoping she was right. But he wasn't entirely convinced. The burden of failure still weighed on his shoulders.

"Now go and find Raquel," his mother said. "Put some happiness on that long face of yours."

Abinadi's mouth lifted at the corners. "Yes, Mother." He kissed her cheek then turned away. He knew the place where Raquel weaved—a clearing set away from the group of huts. It was on the opposite end of the ridge that he'd just crossed.

As he approached, he paused, watching her while she was still unaware of him. Her hands worked swiftly, nimbly, in a steady rhythm. Her beautiful hair was pulled back and tied with a strip of cloth.

Suddenly she turned, startling Abinadi. He hadn't realized she'd heard or sensed him.

"Hello," he said.

Her eyes brightened, but she didn't smile. "You're back."

He walked toward her. She looked down at her lap, staring at her hands. *Why is she acting so strange?* he wondered. He wanted to reach out to her, embrace her like he had his mother. It was a relief to see Raquel sitting here, in peace, away from the tumultuous city of Nephi.

Abinadi crouched so that his face was level with hers. "Not too glad to see me? I can leave for a few more days, but I don't think the trees need to hear my message. They're probably even more stubborn than the people in the city."

She finally raised her head. Her eyes were rimmed in red.

Abinadi was taken aback. "What's wrong? Are you feeling well?"

She shook her head. "I—You . . . You're all right?"

"Yes," he said, trying to understand.

She sighed and looked past him. "I had a terrible feeling last night, and I couldn't sleep. I thought something had happened to you."

"It wasn't a pleasant night. I didn't sleep either." Abinadi moved to her side and took her hands. "The king put out an order for my life."

Raquel pulled her hands away. "I knew it." She was silent for a moment. "Promise me you'll never go back there."

"I—" Abinadi hesitated as Raquel met his gaze again. He didn't know what the Lord wanted. He didn't know if he'd accomplished his mission. He didn't know what might come next. "It's not that simple."

Grabbing his hands, she squeezed. "Promise me!"

Abinadi looked at her hands. He wanted to make that promise. But somehow he knew he couldn't. If the Lord spoke again, was he supposed to ignore Him?

She dropped his hands and turned away.

"Raquel, I'm sorry."

She wiped at her eyes but wouldn't look at him. "I understand. It's foolish of me to even ask such a thing." She cast a sideways glance at him. "It seems that you have a decision to make."

What kind of decision? Would she demand that he never return to the city or else not marry her?

"You have an admirer."

Abinadi smiled with relief. The subject had been most gratefully changed. He touched the edge of her hair. "I should hope so."

Raquel turned and looked at him. Their eyes locked for a long moment. Abinadi was tempted to ask if she'd marry him right now, right here— Gideon could perform the ceremony with the loom as a backdrop . . . But his mother would be furious.

"Not me," she said.

Abinadi narrowed his eyes. "You said you'd wait for me."

She flushed. "I—I did. It's just that . . ." She looked down, wringing her hands. "Neriah has been very upset these past few days, and—"

"Raquel." Abinadi placed his hands over her fidgeting ones. "I know I didn't say this when I asked you to marry me . . ." He finally had her full attention. "I love *you.*"

Her eyes filled with tears.

"What's wrong now?" he asked. "It's true. I love you. Not anyone else—not Neriah. Not any other woman for as long as I've lived . . ." He touched her cheek. "Or will live."

She shook her head, causing tears to slide along her cheeks.

"Tell me what's wrong."

"Nothing," she said. She threw her arms around his neck. "Absolutely nothing."

Abinadi nearly lost his balance. He wrapped his arms about her waist for a brief moment, then drew away.

"Sorry," she said, a sheepish look on her face. She picked up the shuttle and turned it over in her hands.

"I'll take that apology anytime," he said.

She laughed, and he joined in.

"Am I missing a good story?" a male voice cut in.

Abinadi turned to see Gideon. He stood to greet his friend, and the two men embraced.

"You've arrived safely," Gideon said. "Your mother told me what happened. Are you all right?"

Abinadi rubbed the back of his neck. "As well as can be expected." He glanced at Raquel. She'd gone back to her weaving. He and Gideon walked a few paces away, then Abinadi said, "One of the high priests warned me."

Gideon lifted an eyebrow. "Which one?"

"Never saw him before. A younger man, about my age."

"Alma maybe—the newest priest?" Gideon said. "What did he say?"

"He said his father taught the same things."

"It was Alma then. His father was a high priest in Zeniff's court—I remember Alma as a young boy. His parents both died tragically," Gideon said.

Abinadi remained quiet for a moment. Then he said, "Can I ask you something—man to man?"

"Of course," Gideon said.

"Did you or your wife have any expectations for me and Neriah . . . perhaps marrying some day?"

Gideon rubbed his chin. "Tia may have mentioned it once or twice." He clapped a hand on Abinadi's shoulder. "You know how women speculate. Tia didn't mean any harm." He cast another look at Raquel. "When I first saw you two together, I suspected. And I now know you found the right woman."

Relief passed over Abinadi. "So I haven't upset things?"

"No," Gideon said with a smile.

"Then I'd be honored," Abinadi said, "if you'd perform the marriage ceremony."

"I'd be honored to oblige."

The men clasped arms as Abinadi grinned.

Twenty

Nevertheless neither is the man without the woman,
neither the woman without the man, in the Lord.
(1 Corinthians 11:11)

The days plodded along agonizingly slow for Raquel. Four weeks had passed since Abinadi's return, and their wedding day had finally arrived. Typically, their betrothal would have been longer—several months at least—but since there were no relatives traveling, no bride price to pay, and no parents to give her away, it made sense to create the union of husband and wife sooner rather than later.

Raquel woke at the first sign of dawn in the new hut that Abinadi had finished just days earlier. He'd slept in a makeshift tent until the time of their wedding. She couldn't believe it was *today*. The thought both excited her and made her very nervous. She looked about the spare room with its two low stools, short table, and stout mat-covered pole platform—a bed. Raquel had woven the mat and stuffed the coverlet herself.

Tonight, she thought, *tonight Abinadi will be here with me.* She wrapped her arms around her torso, thinking about him. She'd hardly touched him, except for that first day he'd returned and she'd practically knocked him over. What would it be like to be in this room, alone with him, with no one to see? They would be husband and wife.

A shiver traveled along her arms. He was so good, so kind, she almost felt guilty wondering if her mother and father had ever shared this tenderness. She knew their marriage had been arranged, but there were moments when she'd witnessed tenderness and loyalty between them.

But not in the last few years, she reminded herself.

Raquel shook her head, hoping to free her thoughts from her parents. She didn't want anything to dampen the day for her. After all, it was her wedding day. And her mother had sent her blessing with Abinadi. Raquel held no hope for her father—a man who'd never approve. But he wasn't a part of her life anymore, and she'd do everything in her power to forget him.

A rapping sound came from the back of the hut. Raquel turned and saw a hand push away the square of cloth that hung over the window. Her heart momentarily stopped until she realized that it was Abinadi. She hurried to the window, reaching it just as his face appeared—clean-shaven. "You cut off your beard!"

He grinned. "Especially for you."

She laughed, reaching up to touch his smooth face before realizing what she was doing. "I'm sorry." She tried to pull away, but Abinadi caught her hand, his eyes intent on hers.

"You won't have to apologize anymore after today."

Her heart hammered as he kept her wrist firmly in his grasp. "I suppose not."

"You *suppose?*" He laughed. "I want a better answer than that."

"All right, *almost* husband," Raquel said with a grin. "I'm *not* sorry. Is that better?"

"Much better," he whispered. "You'd better get ready fast." He dropped her hand.

"Why?" It was barely dawn. "We still have hours before the ceremony."

"Not anymore," Abinadi said with a wink. "I told Gideon that I'd do his share of work one day next week if he'd get up early and marry us. He's on his way over right now."

"You're teasing," Raquel said. "Your mother would never allow it."

Abinadi laughed, and Raquel reached up to swipe at him, but he ducked out of view. She heard him whistling as he walked around the hut and out of sight.

Moments later, another rap sounded, this time on the side of the hut. Raquel was about to yell at Abinadi to let her get ready in peace when Esther came inside. In her arms she carried a wrapped bundle. Raquel looked at her in surprise.

"I hope you don't mind," Esther said. "I thought you might need some assistance."

"Oh," Raquel said. "Of course."

The woman dipped her head and smiled, genuine happiness flitting across her face. "Very well, then. Let me show you what I've brought." Esther laid the bundle on the table and carefully unwrapped it as if it contained something fragile. Inside was a collection of various objects. First, Esther lifted a piece of delicate white cloth. The edges had been intricately embroidered. She held it up for Raquel to see. "It's a marriage veil—the color denotes purity and faith in God."

Raquel didn't dare touch the square of cloth. "It's beautiful."

"I've been working on it by night the past few weeks."

Raquel's mouth fell open. "You made it just for me?"

Esther nodded, her face breaking into a smile. "This veil is a traditional custom brought over by Father Lehi. When I was married, I didn't know of it. But I wanted something more for my son and new daughter. A true, traditional wedding."

Raquel reached for the cloth and reverently turned it over in her hands. "Thank you," she whispered. The wedding clothing her own mother might have created would have appeared garish next to this delicate white veil. She embraced Esther, careful not to crush the cloth. When she pulled away, she asked, "Do I wear it the entire ceremony?"

"Abinadi will remove it toward the end. Gideon will tell you when," Esther said. She turned back to the table and lifted up a smaller bundle, then unwrapped it. Two gold bracelets, a jade anklet, and a pair of gold earrings shimmered against the cloth. "These were from my mother, given to me on my wedding day." She met Raquel's gaze. "I no longer have use for them, and I'd like you to have them as my new daughter."

Tears stung Raquel's eyes. For Esther to part with something so dear when she had so little was too much. "I can't possibly—"

Esther pressed them into her hands. "Take them. Nothing will make me happier than to see you wear this jewelry as a symbol of making our family whole." She smiled. "And perhaps it will bring you fortune in begetting children."

Raquel's face warmed, but she reached for the jewelry. She examined the fine workmanship for a moment. Esther turned to retrieve the next item.

"You've given me so much already," Raquel protested.

"These will be part of the ceremony," Esther said, holding up a strange-shaped ring with an engraved square on top. "This is the ceremonial ring. The shape represents the home that you and Abinadi will create together."

A tingling sensation spread from Raquel's toes all the way to her fingertips.

"He will place it on your finger during the marriage service," Esther continued. "Gideon will conduct the kiddushin—the rite that will bind you as husband and wife." She unwrapped a piece of cloth stretched around a woven palm garland. "Each of you will wear one of these during the ceremony, and a bowl of water will be brought to dip your hands into."

Raquel set the jewelry on the table and took the garland in her hands.

"Gideon will bestow blessings upon the both of you, then we'll cele-brate with dancing and a large feast."

Raquel smiled. "It sounds wonderful, but—"

"But, it's no trouble," Esther said in a firm voice. "This wedding is as much for all of us as it is for you and Abinadi. We want something to forget the awful circumstances that brought us here. We want to rejoice in some-thing good."

Taking a deep breath, Raquel nodded. "I don't know how to thank you for all of this. You've been so kind. I wish I could repay you somehow . . ." Her voice trailed off as she felt her emotions surface.

"A grandchild would do."

Raquel laughed, hoping to cover up her embarrassment. Regardless, she loved Esther's forthrightness. So opposite of her own mother. "We'll try." Then her entire face flamed. She couldn't believe she'd just said that aloud.

Esther put a hand on Raquel's arm, concern in her eyes. "Did your mother speak to you about . . . the wedding night?"

"A little," Raquel said, not able to look at her.

"Good," Esther said with a chuckle. "Because Abinadi won't let me get a word in. One of you needs to know *something*."

Raquel thought her face might combust into flames. But Esther didn't seem to notice. She turned to the bundle and rearranged some of the items to take with her, leaving the jewelry and the veil for Raquel.

"I'll come after the morning meal to help you with the washings and the dressing," Esther said as she securely tied the bundle.

"Washings?"

"Oh," Esther said, pausing. "It's part of the traditional marriage. It's very symbolic and beautiful in its own way. You'll feel like a new woman when it's finished." She bustled over to the doorway. "Now you're not allowed to help with a thing today. It's your one chance to relax." She waved then passed through the doorway.

Raquel sank onto the stool. The earlier excitement was replaced with a sense of awe. She stared at the jewelry on the table. She was becoming part of a new family, creating a new future. Esther had already mentioned grandchildren. Raquel took a deep breath, wondering if she were ready for all of this. Back at home she'd run from two marriages. They had never seemed real or genuine. But this was real. This was serious. By marrying Abinadi today, she was taking a permanent step toward determining her future.

Looking up at the thatched roof built by her future husband, Raquel knew she needed more faith—faith like his. She clasped her hands and slid to the floor onto her knees. She had so many expectations to meet and didn't want to let anyone down. She didn't want all their preparation to be for naught. But most of all, she wanted her life to stay this way forever: Abinadi, Esther, Ben—safe.

When she finished her prayer, she rose and crossed to the window. The sounds of preparations had already begun. Tia and Esther hovered over the cooking fire, and Raquel heard the faint chopping of wood somewhere in the distance. She wondered where Abinadi had gone.

Raquel didn't leave the hut for the morning meal. She didn't want to face Neriah, who bustled about the common area with Tia and Esther. But she didn't want to sit and do nothing either, lest they think her idle.

She was about to slip out of the hut in search of a task when Esther and Tia arrived, Neriah following.

"Come," Esther said. "We will start the washings."

Tia tugged at Raquel's hand.

"Where are we going?" Raquel asked.

"We can't exactly tell you," Esther said. "The men don't know where our hideout is, although they're curious enough about it."

Raquel walked alongside Neriah. She cast a couple of sideways glances at her but didn't get a response. They passed the fields and cut north until they reached the upper river. Raquel was surprised to see a small hut and a fire roaring to the side of it. Ezra's wife, Naomi, was tending the fire. Naomi grinned when she saw the women approach. "Everything is ready. I have two more jugs of hot water to carry in."

Esther nodded with approval.

"Come," Tia said, motioning to Raquel to follow her inside the hut.

Stepping into the darkened interior, Raquel was surprised to see a huge stone basin—big enough to sit in. It took up most of the space, except for a high table where clay jugs had been placed.

"This is where we wash and cleanse ourselves after childbirth or on other occasions," Tia said.

"You will be the first bride to bathe here," Esther said, coming in behind them. "First you remove your clothing, then step into the basin. We'll pour the hot water in, and you can soak for as long as you like."

"We have an endless supply of flower petals that scent the water," Tia said. She edged around the basin and lifted a basket from the table to demonstrate.

Raquel looked around. She supposed it was similar to the baths at the palace that she'd heard about. Her mother had her own cleansing basin . . . but this was so unexpected. And in the middle of the wilderness at that.

Naomi came in carrying another jug, and Tia went to help her bring in the final one.

"All set?" Tia asked, and Naomi nodded.

"Neriah and I will keep watch for those pesky men," Naomi said. "They know not to come this direction, but you can never predict if one of them will."

"Very well," Tia said with a smile. When they were inside, she turned to face Raquel, an expectant look on her face.

Raquel looked at the basin, then at the two women.

Tia smiled. "Don't be afraid—it's just water."

That's not what I'm afraid of, Raquel wanted to say. But she undressed as the two women filled the basin with steaming water. The first step into the water startled Raquel. It was absolutely luxurious. She slowly immersed herself, relishing the warm water as it cascaded over her body. Tia tossed in flower petals until the water's surface was covered, their heady fragrance blending with the steam, and Esther rubbed a coconut oil mixture into Raquel's hair.

Raquel closed her eyes, soaking in the subtle scent and the enveloping warmth of the water, hundreds of petals caressing her shoulders. It was easy to forget all of her other concerns. Tia started to hum, and Raquel nearly drifted to sleep.

Esther's fingers worked through the lather in Raquel's hair, massaging her scalp at the same time.

"I need to come here every day," Raquel said. Her voice was slow and measured—she felt as though speaking required too much effort.

"Yes," Tia said with a chuckle. "It would be wonderful."

Raquel was glad that Neriah hadn't joined them. It was nice to be alone with the two matriarchs of the settlement and under their intimate care.

All too soon it was time to leave. Raquel pulled the wadded cloth from the drain and stepped out of the basin. Esther handed her a swath of cloth to dry off with, then wrapped her in a fresh cape. Tia combed through Raquel's hair, then Esther stained her fingernails and toenails with red hibiscus.

"I won't be recognized," Raquel said with a smile.

Tia clucked her tongue. "The men will be impressed. The women, envious." She laughed.

The women slid thick leather shoes onto Raquel's feet. "We don't want all our work to go to waste," Esther said. When they finally exited the hut, Neriah hardly glanced at Raquel. She just yawned and bid farewell to Naomi.

When they arrived back at the settlement, Raquel was surprised to see it deserted. "Where is everyone?"

"At the huppah, of course," Tia said.

"The huppah?" Raquel looked around her, wondering what Tia meant.

"It's a canopy that represents the temple," Tia said. "Everyone must already be there, waiting."

Raquel peeked at the sky. "I didn't think we were late."

"We're not," Esther assured her. "Like I said, this is a grand occasion."

Neriah left their side and continued south.

Raquel tried not to feel shunned. Tia seemed to notice, because she said, "Don't mind her. In a few weeks, she'll be back to her old self."

Raquel hoped so. This community was too small for two members of it to keep ignoring each other. Tia went ahead of them to inform everyone that Raquel was ready.

Raquel dressed quickly in a simple tunic the color of maize. The yellow hue set off the warm colors in her hair.

Esther helped her with her veil and jewelry. "Ready?" she said, examining Raquel for the tenth time.

"Yes, I think so," Raquel said. She clutched Esther's arm, and they walked together along the path. Music from a flageolet greeted them. As they reached the first grove of trees, Raquel saw the top of the canopy that Tia had spoken of peeking through the trees. When they entered the clearing, Raquel was surprised at the crowd. She hadn't realized how many people lived in the settlement until they were all gathered in the same place.

Abinadi and Gideon stood at the far side of the meadow beneath the canopy, which stretched between four poles. Both of them turned expectantly. Through her veil, Raquel met Abinadi's gaze. Her heart hammered as she soaked in his dark eyebrows, angular chin—all so familiar and dear now. He wore a prayer shawl over his shoulders, one that Raquel had seen him wear when the elders conducted altar sacrifices.

To the left, Tia held a tray that contained a cup of wine and the washing bowl.

Ben stood on the other side, playing the flageolet, and the people broke into song. Raquel hesitated, but Esther prodded her forward. "Take your place next to Abinadi," she whispered.

Raquel continued toward Abinadi. She lowered her eyes against his intense gaze. It seemed the veil offered little protection. She stopped next to him, and he took her hands in his.

She inhaled sharply at the warmth of his touch. It was as if their hands blended together into one.

Gideon cleared his throat and began the kiddushin with a smile. "Abinadi, will you take this woman, Raquel—daughter of Amulon and Itzel—to wife according to the law of Moses and Israel?"

Abinadi looked at Raquel, his gaze searing through her veil. "Yes."

Gideon turned toward her. "Raquel, will you take Abinadi as your husband according to the law of Moses and Israel?"

She took a deep breath, trying to calm the tremble deep inside her chest. "Yes, I will."

Abinadi's fingers tightened around her hands.

Tia stepped up, holding the cup of wine. First Abinadi took a sip, then he handed it to Raquel. With one hand she lifted her veil, and with the other, sipped the wine. Tia took the cup and moved away.

Gideon produced the ceremonial ring and displayed it on his open palm. "This ring symbolizes the consecration between man and woman." He handed it to Abinadi, who slipped it onto Raquel's finger.

"With this ring, you are consecrated unto me according to the law of Moses," Abinadi said.

His voice touched her heart as she thought of truly belonging to him. The weight of the ring was solid and secure.

Gideon continued to speak. "From the beginning, God created male and female." He looked at Raquel. "You will now circle your husband seven times."

My husband, Raquel thought. She walked around him, counting to seven. When she stopped, Abinadi lifted her veil.

The fresh air touched Raquel's face, and Abinadi's gaze was no longer filtered. She thought her heart had left her chest. He moved closer to place the hem of her veil on his shoulder. Slowly, he removed his prayer shawl and placed it upon her shoulders.

"What God hath joined together," Gideon said, turning to the crowd, "let no man put asunder!"

The power behind the words warmed Raquel. Her chest constricted, making it nearly impossible to take a deep breath.

Esther stepped forward, tears bright in her eyes, and put the palm garlands on each of their heads. Tia held out the bowl of sanctified water, and both Raquel and Abinadi dipped their fingers into it.

Gideon retrieved a piece of parchment—the marriage contract. He read it, then held it out for both of them to mark. Gideon bowed his head and prayed, blessing Abinadi and Raquel with companionship, children, and happiness.

After he finished the prayer, Gideon continued, "Jacob said, 'And let my name be named on them, and the name of my fathers Abraham and Isaac;

and let them grow into a multitude in the midst of the earth.'" Gideon raised his hands. "Praise to God!"

The gathered group raised their hands and repeated, "Praise to God, the Almighty!"

A sob escaped Esther, but her face beamed with joy. Ben started playing the flageolet again, and the people formed a circle for dancing. Abinadi pulled Raquel into his arms.

She melted against him for a moment, her heart thundering in her ears. They were finally married. Abinadi released her, and their eyes met. Gently, he took her face in his hands as he leaned toward her. Her eyes widened as his lips touched hers. Cheers broke out around them.

"Would my new wife like to dance with me?" Abinadi whispered in her ear.

Raquel wanted to pull him to her again, but instead she said, "I'd love to."

They were swept up into the circle and jostled into place as everyone moved in rhythm to the music and the clapping.

Everything around her seemed to move more slowly than normal, as if she were dreaming. *It's amazing,* she thought. *I'm married!*

After the dancing, the group moved to the feast that Tia and Esther presided over. Compared to what they usually served, the food seemed abundant—squash, avocado, tamalitos, cassava bread, amaranth seeds soaked in honey, and a thick brown beverage made from cacao seeds.

Abinadi stayed close to Raquel during the meal, and every time he brushed her arm she became distracted. All the guests were smiling and laughing, and even Neriah seemed to be enjoying herself. As the evening started to close in on them, the celebrations died down. When the women started to clear the food and dishes, Abinadi leaned toward Raquel. "Pack your things for an overnight stay. I have a place to show you."

Raquel looked at him with surprise. "Where are we going?"

He just winked, then stood and held out his hand. She took it and stood next to him. "I'll meet you at the hut shortly," he said.

The men around them started singing, and several people congratulated them again. The women surrounded Raquel, guiding her to the home she'd share with Abinadi. Girls and women alike giggled, making Raquel feel even more nervous.

"May the Lord bless you with many children," Tia said as they reached the entrance to the hut. She embraced Raquel.

"Thank you," Raquel said, trying to keep the tremor out of her voice. Where had Abinadi gone? Was this part of tradition, too?

"We'll see you in the morning," Esther said. She pulled Raquel into a fierce embrace. Raquel clung to her for a moment. In the distance, the men's singing grew louder. They were coming this way.

Raquel released Esther and waved to the women. She wanted to be inside before the men reached the hut. Slipping inside quickly, she lowered the door-covering and held her breath, listening.

As the laughter and singing drew closer, Raquel remembered Abinadi's request to pack something for the night. Where was he taking her? She lit a lamp, causing the twilight shadows to shrink. She wished she could make her pounding heart calm down. Her breathing came rapidly as she thought about facing Abinadi alone, and she hoped her nerves wouldn't make a fool of her.

With trembling hands, she tied a bundle with clothing and an extra rug. The men's singing was right outside the hut. She sat in the corner, the farthest she could be from the entrance. Any moment, Abinadi would enter.

The singing and laughing seemed to go on forever. Then suddenly the door skin was raised and lowered swiftly. Abinadi stood in the doorway. Raquel met his gaze, and he put his finger to his lips. After a few moments the sounds from outside faded.

Abinadi strode forward and pulled Raquel to her feet. He wrapped his arms about her and spun her around. When he set her down, he was grinning. "Good evening, *wife.*"

She smiled, trying to conceal her nervousness. "Good evening, *husband.*"

He just stared at her, making her feel even more awkward. She looked down, unable to hold his intense gaze.

"Raquel? Are you all right?"

She nodded, still not looking at him.

"What's wrong, then?"

She took a deep breath. "I—I'm just . . . nervous." She twisted her hands together. "Everyone has been teasing me all afternoon about our wedding night. I just feel like they're all watching us."

Abinadi laughed. "Every newly married couple gets the same treatment." He touched her face, making her look at him. "Don't think about them. In fact, there's only one person I want you to think of tonight." He leaned down and kissed her.

It was quite easy to forget the teasing after that. When Abinadi finally pulled away so they could both breathe, he said, "Do you have your things?"

"Yes," Raquel said, surprised that she could come up with a coherent response. "Where are we going?"

"Away from all those prying eyes and ears," Abinadi said. His hand slid to her waist. "It will be just the two of us."

Raquel nodded and went to gather her bundle. She felt a little more relaxed, although her heart pounded loudly in her ears. Then she moved to the oil lamp to extinguish it.

"It can burn itself out," he said. "Let the others be surprised to find us missing in the morning."

"But your mother might be upset."

Abinadi took the bundle from Raquel and grasped her hand, amusement in his eyes. "We're married now." He lowered his voice. "My mother doesn't have to know *everything*."

He tugged her with him and out the doorway. After looking left, then right, he said, "Let's go." They hurried around the hut, off the main path, then picked their way to the first field. The moon had risen and provided a silvery light for their journey.

The night air stirred Raquel's hair from her face and she closed her eyes briefly, relishing Abinadi's warm grasp and the fact that the wedding festivities were over. When they reached the other side of the field, Abinadi turned south and led Raquel along the river.

After several moments, he stopped. She caught her breath as he gazed down at her.

"We'll have to cross the river here," he said.

She looked at the rushing water, and then suddenly Abinadi's arms were around her, lifting her. He carried her to the edge of the river and plunged in. The water hit his knees instantly, and Raquel tightened her hold around his neck. He nearly stumbled on a rock halfway through.

"Don't drop me," she said.

"Then stop breathing on my neck," he said, laughing. "You're making it hard to concentrate on my footing."

She smiled and blew on his neck. His grip tightened as he laughed. "You'd better be careful." He held her threateningly close to the water.

Raquel clung tighter, breathing in his scent. Her nerves relaxed a little. It was just Abinadi—the man she trusted. The man she loved. She had nothing to fear.

He stepped onto the bank and set her down. Then he stretched his arms over his head. "That was tough. I'm glad I'm so strong."

Raquel took a swing at him, but he caught her hand. She tried to wriggle away as he reached for her other hand. But it was too late. He'd trapped her. Then he kissed her again, for the third time that day. Yes—she was counting.

"Let's go. I don't think I can stand this anymore," he said, breaking away.

"Stand what?" she asked.

"Your teasing."

"I'm not teasing you," Raquel said, hiding a smile.

Abinadi nodded. "Then *torturing.* Come on." He held out his hand, and Raquel took it. They walked for a few more minutes until they arrived at a clearing, well lighted by the moon. In the center was a tent.

Raquel dropped his hand. "What's this?"

"Our residence for the next day . . . or two," he said, studying her. "Do you like it?"

She stared at the tent for a moment. No one would find them here. There was no singing, no laughter, no teasing. Only the two of them. It was perfect. She turned and saw concern on Abinadi's face. Smiling, she grabbed his hand. "I love it."

A smile touched his lips. "Really? It's not as lavish as our hut. I didn't know if you wanted to be surrounded by more luxury or—"

"Shhh," Raquel said. "You know I didn't marry you for your wealth."

He threw his head back and laughed. When he met her gaze again he said, "You really like it?"

"As long as you do the cooking, I'll be happy anywhere," she said, feeling more relaxed by the moment. She glanced at the surrounding trees—their leaves flittered gently in the breeze as if welcoming them. "I love it here." She looked at him and moved closer. Taking a deep breath she put her arms around his neck. His expression was so tender that her heart almost stopped. "And I love *you,* too. Thank you for thinking of this."

He smiled, leaning down until their faces were only a breath apart. "Thank you for saying yes." Then he kissed her for the fourth time.

Twenty-one

And ye shall seek me, and find me, when ye shall search
for me with all your heart.
(Jeremiah 29:13)

TWO YEARS LATER

The scene Alma stumbled upon sickened him—six "friends" had over-taken his house, living off his wine and good food, spending his fortune, and spoiling his luxurious furniture. And tonight was the worst yet. As he entered his newly constructed home, they welcomed him with sloppy greetings. It didn't take long for Alma to notice the broken carved cups, the pile of *his* gold they were gambling over, and the two underdressed women—one of whom he recognized as his new neighbor's daughter.

Did these friends of his have no boundaries? *No,* he thought sadly, *nor did I a short time ago.* But lately, he'd felt restless around his riotous friends, disgruntled with his position as a high priest, not to mention impatient with the city of Nephi's continual lust for destruction.

Every week there was a new campaign to slaughter the Lamanites. Before, it had been in defense of the borders and vineyards. But over the past year, the Nephites had become unduly aggressive, being the perpetrators instead of the victims. The tales coming from the battlefield were horrid—the things the Nephites had done to defenseless women and children unthinkable. It made Alma shudder just hearing about the atrocities.

"Alma! We've been waiting for you," one man called.

The neighbor's daughter rushed to his side, tugging at his arm. "My father sends you his best," she said with a flattering smile.

Everyone wanted something from him, it seemed. His influence had grown at court, but not for the reasons others might expect. He wasn't the king's pawn. He had his own opinions and frequently voiced them. But the king seemed to love him even more for it. King Noah had doubled Alma's pay. Now, even the other high priests went out of their way to indulge him. And Alma was tired of it all.

He slammed through the room, ignoring the jeering remarks from his drunken friends. But before walking down the hall to his bed chamber, he grabbed a jug of wine. He would drink alone tonight. He shut the door against the voices that called for him to join them.

Today, Maia had given birth to a son. Suddenly, she was the king's favorite wife again. The news had spread all over court moments after the child's arrival. The king had been ecstatic all day. Alma pulled off his outer cape and tossed it onto the floor. He sat with a heavy thud on his pile of cushions and tipped the jug of wine back, taking a long swallow. He'd moved out of the palace the day he'd found out Maia was with child.

He couldn't bear to hear about her confinement. No matter what other women surrounded him, he couldn't stop thinking of her. So he'd left. He groaned as he hung his head. If anything, the news about her son had made his heartache worse. Her tear-filled eyes sprang up in his mind. The king had beaten her, but now she would be his favorite again, for a time—until the next displeasure.

Alma squeezed the jug, watching the ceramic crack in his hand. A burst of laughter came from the front of his house. They weren't leaving. His head pounded as anger surged through him. He just wanted to be left alone.

He stood and left his room, striding down the hallway.

"Get out!" he yelled before reaching the gathering room. Silence fell among his uninvited guests. "Get out!" He threw the jug of wine, and everyone watched it sail across the room. As it smashed into the wall, his friends scurried to their feet, scooping up their winnings and making grand apologies as Alma shouted, "Leave! Now!"

Seconds later, Alma stood alone in the room, surrounded by wreckage—overturned tables, spilled food and wine, soiled cushions, haphazard drapes . . . all for what? He was twenty-three. He had no wife, no children, *no dignity*. He sank to the floor and leaned his head against the wooden wall. His eye caught the carved figure of a feathered serpent above the doorway. He'd carved one for every room in the house. Then he'd carved them for his friends, his neighbors. Everyone who saw them wanted one, but he'd taken no gold or silver. His payment was defying his father again and again.

Father was a liar, Alma thought. He scrambled to his feet, seeing the destroyed room with new eyes. *If it weren't for his lies, I wouldn't be here. If it weren't for his God, I wouldn't be alone. Mother would still be alive. I would have found a nice girl who wouldn't be repelled at the sight of me. I wouldn't be forced to favor the wealthy over the poor. I wouldn't watch the king torture innocent people. I wouldn't watch my friends delight in bloodshed.*

He kicked at a table, sending a half-filled goblet flying onto the rug. *If God were real, I wouldn't have to listen to the soldiers talk about the children they beheaded and the women they violated. If He were real, His wrath would surely punish those soldiers. If He were real, peace would be established. The king would be compassionate. If God were real, I'd be an honorable priest.*

Alma picked up another jug of wine. He studied it for a moment. "If God is real, why did He take my parents? They were innocent," he whispered to himself. "And why doesn't he take me? I've committed unmentionable sins." He took a shuddering breath, then put the jug of wine back in its place.

"Help me," he said. Then his voice grew louder. "Help me, someone!"

A knock sounded at his reed door. Alma whirled around, stunned. He stared at the door for a moment until the knock came again, this time more urgent. Alma crossed the room and flung open the door.

A woman stood there, her graying hair sticking out from beneath a scarf. The deep lines in her face made her look ancient, but when she spoke, Alma guessed she was no more than forty.

"Alma?" she said, her voice timid.

"Yes?" He was so stunned he didn't think to invite her inside.

"The baby is dead, and she said to come for you. She said that only you could change the king's mind."

"What?" Alma's mind spun. "Come inside, woman. Explain yourself."

She stepped in, not saying anything about the wrecked room if she noticed. "The king wants to kill her—says it's not his child and that's why the gods took it. The gods are punishing her."

"Maia?" The word came out as a horrified whisper.

She nodded. "The king will accuse her of treason. He's assembling the high priests right now."

Alma stared at her. It was unbelievable—dragging a woman who had just given birth into court. Her days of purification hadn't even begun, yet she'd have to stand before a collection of men. Of course, from what he'd heard, the king didn't give much heed to things like a woman's purification.

"Tell her I'll be there." He ushered the woman from his home, then dressed in his finest cape. He needed all the influence and favoritism he could muster. Before leaving his home, he took down one of the feathered serpents. The king always enjoyed a gift.

Alma hurried through the night, weighing his options. He was certain the king didn't know of his feelings for Maia. Time and again, Alma had paid off Bethel with a favor or a privilege to keep her quiet. A few months ago, she'd actually married and left court—a desired fate for a harlot super-seded by younger women.

Yet he still needed to make sure he didn't appear to favor Maia in any way so that the king wouldn't grow suspicious. He must find a way to influ-ence the king without him suspecting. It must appear to be King Noah's own idea. Alma gripped the wooden idol in his hands, wondering how far he would go to save this woman's life.

But she's not just any woman, Alma reminded himself.

The front of the palace blazed in the torchlights—a sure sign that a notable event was taking place. Alma brushed past the guards with a nod and entered the grand hall. A group of women huddled together in quiet conversation. Their gazes followed Alma as he crossed the hall. Just as he reached the entrance to the throne room, someone called his name.

"Alma!"

He turned to see Amulon. Over the past couple of years, the man had grown positively huge, nearly matching King Noah in girth. But where the king was just heavy, Amulon was still strong—a formidable image of the warrior he was. Tonight, however, instead of the usual expression of lust and greed, Amulon's expression was sober.

"We have to convince the king to change his mind," Amulon said in a low whisper when he reached Alma.

At least they agreed on something, Alma thought. "What happened to the child?"

"He was sickly when he was born—never did lose his blue coloring." Amulon glanced at the group of women who watched them with fearful eyes. "Don't you understand the precedence this will set? Every woman who carries a child will now fear for her life."

Alma followed Amulon's gaze and looked at the circle of women. He could very well see Amulon's point. They may be conniving at times, temptresses by their own design, but no one deserved to die for the tragic loss of a child. Alma was glad he wasn't the only high priest who doubted the king's judgment. Of course, Alma also knew that Amulon had special interest in at least one of the women.

"Be prepared, my friend," Amulon said, placing a hand on Alma's shoulder. "I've never seen the king in such a rage, at least for some time. The last time he was this angry was when my daughter . . . I mean . . ." His voice faded.

For an instant, Alma thought he saw a flash of regret in Amulon's eyes. Then the steel gaze was back. "We need a plan."

"Definitely," Alma said, lowering his voice. "Tell me, is there any credence to the king's accusations?"

"No," Amulon said. "Absolutely not. The woman had never been around the other men. I've questioned some of the other women. They say the only man who has been inside Maia's chambers is the king himself."

Alma tried to suppress a shudder. *To beat her, among other things.* "Is she well enough to be tried?"

Amulon cast him a puzzled look. "I think that's the least of her concerns." He glanced again at the women. "We must enter the court room separately, so it doesn't look as if we're conspiring. Maia will be brought soon."

Alma nodded. "We have to find a way to change the king's mind." He waited outside while Amulon went in. In a moment, he regretted letting Amulon go in first.

The women gasped, drawing his attention. Coming into the hall was Maia. A guard was leading her, gripping her arm.

Her face was deathly pale, her hair a tangled mass spilling over her shoulders in confusion. She walked with a limp, as if every step was painful. But it was her eyes that were the most disturbing of all. Alma would have guessed they'd be swollen or at least red from crying. But they seemed vacant, as if she'd already given up hope and accepted her fate.

She'd just given birth, lost a child, and now this. Alma wanted to push the guard away and take Maia from all of this. They could run, hide somewhere, and start a new life together. He stared as she drew closer—she was but a shell of the woman who had first come to court and sung for the king, entrancing everyone with the beauty of her voice.

Alma stood in front of the door to the throne room, forgetting to move aside until Maia came to a stop in front of him. With great effort she looked up at him. A glimmer of recognition registered in her eyes, but then they were dead again. Alma stepped toward her, knowing it was probably the most foolish thing he could do, but his heart took over his mind.

He leaned close to her and whispered, "Have faith."

She blinked, but nothing else. He wasn't even sure she'd heard him, and he wasn't sure why he'd said it. As the guard reached for the door, Alma backed out of the way. He watched her enter, and immediately the ranting started. The king's accusing voice carried into the hall, causing the women to cower together.

Alma's hand involuntarily closed around the dagger at his waistline. It would be so simple, he thought, to attack the king. Everyone would be too surprised to stop him fast enough. The king's life would be over, and so would his reign of terror. Alma would surely lose his life in the process, but it might save countless others.

Have faith. The thought entered his mind again, echoing the words he'd just spoken to Maia. He wasn't sure where the words had come from. But they felt right. And for the first time in more than two years, Alma realized that he was completely sober. He looked down at the wooden idol in his hand. *Give me strength,* he thought.

Alma opened the door and strode into the room. The first thing he noticed was Maia standing in the middle of the room, her head lowered. The king was circling her like she was some sort of prey. He glanced over at Alma.

"You took your time."

Alma dipped his head in acknowledgment. "I ask permission to speak, O Highness."

Noah arched a brow, his face red from his earlier ranting. "Speak."

"I was waiting to be summoned."

The king sighed. "So you were. We are casting lots."

"For what?" Alma asked, raising his head. He glanced at Amulon, but the man's expression was a mask of stone.

"Whoever wins gets to decide her manner of death."

Alma moved his gaze back to the king, trying to look nonchalant. He walked over to his usual seat and sat down. He withdrew his dagger and picked at his nails. "And what exactly is her crime?" he asked without looking at the king.

"My son is dead!" the king roared.

Alma glanced up, one eyebrow arched. Instead of feeling flustered like he sometimes did when the king yelled, Alma felt surprisingly calm. "I'm sorry to hear the news. It seems the court should be preparing for your son's funeral." He put away his dagger and leaned forward. "The death of your infant son is certainly tragic."

The other priests around him froze, waiting for the king's reaction.

The king stared at him, his jaw working. Alma didn't know if the king was astounded or enraged, but the answers seemed to tumble into Alma's mind and he rushed on. "The entire city should be in mourning. Seven days spent in mourning for your son whose spirit is too pure for this world." He lifted the wooden idol. "Or . . . perhaps we should be celebrating."

Maia's head snapped up. Her eyes focused on Alma, finally listening.

"The gods have sanctified your son's soul and taken him into their circle," Alma said, his own explanations surprising even him. "Your son has become one of them."

Noah's mouth fell open, and his eyes gleamed. "You think my son is a god?"

"The son of the greatest king in the land and the most fair wife—what god wouldn't want such a child?" Alma stood, keeping his gaze locked with Noah's. Warmth spread through Alma, giving him courage as never before. "The gods sent this son to you only to capture the breath of life. Then they took him, not able to spare him a moment longer. They have exalted him so that he may forever protect you and bring prosperity to this court."

The king nodded, the redness in his face turning from anger to puzzlement. He was like a small child, soaking up the praise of his parents.

Alma pointed to Maia, seeing her incredulous face and knowing he felt just as incredulous as she. "Let this woman return to her chambers, where as the mother of an infant god, she will rest and be fed until her full health returns. Let your people pay homage to her. Let them celebrate this miraculous event." Alma focused his gaze back on the king. "Let the people come to bring you gifts and declare their adoration."

Noah's face shone and a grin erupted. "Let it be done," he said, then, turning to the other priests, he added, "Declare it throughout the land!"

Alma strode toward Maia, all eyes on him. He bowed his head and knelt before her. Then he took her hand and kissed it. "Praise to the queen mother."

The king clapped as the other priests left their posts to pay tribute to Maia.

In the excitement, Alma arose and slipped out the door without a backward glance. He'd just told the greatest lie of his life. The king would never know that he'd just been manipulated. Alma's father would disapprove of the lies, but Alma hoped the outcome justified the means. Alma thought about the king's change of heart and wondered how he'd been able to come up with just the right explanation to thwart a possible execution. It was as if another person, or another power, had dictated his words.

The women in the hall watched him in stunned silence as he passed by. He smiled at them, then left the palace. The sun had disappeared behind the horizon, its orange remnants streaking the sky. Warmth expanded Alma's chest. He'd just saved a woman's life. The feeling was incredible. He'd done something *good,* something useful . . . something righteous.

He looked at the people on the streets with new eyes, realizing that God didn't cause His people to be afflicted. They had brought it upon themselves. If he, a flawed priest, could alter the mind of a king, then there must be a greater power at work. Greater than any king or man on the earth. Someone had spoken the words to his mind. Someone had guided him to change the king's temperament.

The breeze stirred his robes just as his mind whispered, *God is real.* Alma stopped as the words seemed to spread through every part of his soul. *God is real.* His heart thundered. He could no longer deny that the Lord was the supreme ruler—not Noah, not the high priests of the city of Nephi, not some serpent creature with feathers.

Alma took a step, then another; soon he was practically running. Something greater was at work, and he had spent too long denying it. He'd spent too long lying to himself and others. Tonight he'd told his last lie. Even though it had saved another life, he was through lying.

When he arrived home, he started carrying his furniture into the yard. All the luxuries that he'd purchased over the past two years would have to go. They represented who he used to be—someone he despised. He wanted to cleanse everything around him—from the inside out. He piled on rugs, tapestries, fine carvings, and fragile vases. Then he collected all of the wooden idols in his house, feathered serpents included. His father had been right. *The images are offensive.*

The notion that an animal or beast could replace a powerful being such as the Lord was offensive indeed. Alma touched a burning torch to the furniture and watched the flames leap quickly into action. Within minutes, black smoke billowed from the courtyard as all his possessions burned. He sank to his knees, watching the purging—feeling as if his own black soul were finally being purged.

People came out of their homes to rush to his aid, but when they found Alma staring at the flames, doing nothing, they stopped to watch too.

Ashes, Alma thought, *sackcloth and ashes.* The words of Abinadi came again to his mind. *If you don't repent in sackcloth and ashes, He will not hear your prayers or deliver you from your afflictions.* Alma looked around, almost expecting to see the preacher standing next to him, but all he saw were his neighbors staring with wide eyes at the orange glow of the flames.

Alma stood, moving closer to the fire. The smoke and the heat made his eyes water. He stripped off his cape and threw it into the hungry flames. The luxurious cloth and feathers curled then burst into yellow heat.

He took a step back and surveyed the scene. All of his valuables were now in ashes.

Twenty-two

And the Lord said unto me, Go, prophesy unto my people.
(Amos 7:15)

Abinadi looked around the circle of elders, each of their faces illuminated in the dying firelight—Ezra, Timon, Nathan, Gideon's wrinkles of wisdom, Helam's scarred face. They had spent most of the evening discussing salvation and analyzing the words of Isaiah.

"How quickly we forget our Lord," Gideon said, leaning back with a sigh. "King Zeniff was a righteous leader the people followed, then one man changed all of that. Now the people blindly and easily follow Noah."

Abinadi rubbed his sore neck. They had been sitting for hours. "Preaching salvation to the people in the city was like trying to build a hut from leaves."

The men nodded. Helam folded his hands and said, "Take heart, brothers. As Isaiah says, there will come a time when salvation will be declared to every nation, kindred, tongue, and people."

"Declared, yes," Abinadi said. "But embraced?"

"Not yet, not today," Helam conceded. "But eventually all the ends of the earth will see the salvation of our God."

Abinadi nodded. "Isaiah certainly saw marvelous things."

"The city of Nephi is filled with fear—from the highest judge to the poorest farmer," Gideon said. "It's amazing how one wicked man in the right position can lead so many people astray."

"The temples have been sorely desecrated with idols and sacrifices of unclean animals," Abinadi said, shaking his head.

"And yet Raquel believed," Helam said in a quiet voice.

Abinadi looked at his brother. "Yes. She was unique in that."

Helam met Abinadi's gaze across the flickering flames. "Perhaps not. Perhaps there are dozens like her, hundreds . . . who are too afraid to take a stand." He looked at the men surrounding the fire. "Many still remember the teachings from Zeniff's time."

"Many have been put to death for it, too," Abinadi reminded him.

"For some," Gideon practically whispered, "death may be a better option than living amongst such filth."

* * *

Abinadi woke with a start. He sat up as a chill spread through his entire body. Listening in the darkness, he heard only Raquel's steady breathing. Maybe the baby had stirred. Abe had just turned one year old the week before, and as a gift to his parents, he started sleeping through the night. Abinadi hoped it was more than a temporary phase.

But the child slept soundly.

Abinadi wiped the dampness from his forehead, wondering what had awakened him. He couldn't remember dreaming anything. Maybe it was the conversation with the elders earlier in the night. After a few minutes, he gave up trying to go back to sleep and rose, careful not to disturb Raquel. The moonlight jotted across the room from the window, dimly illuminating her peaceful face. For a moment, Abinadi considered waking her, but then he thought better of it.

Crossing the room, he slipped outside. The moon hung heavy and full. Everything was so peaceful. Since marrying Raquel, he relished the quiet life and the mundane tasks, coming home at the end of a long day to his wife and young son. The community had expanded its crops, and some nicer homes had been erected. Abinadi would start on their new home next, in a few months. And sometime soon, he hoped he and Raquel would be blessed with another child. Although if they had another child, he knew Raquel would say he needed to cut back on his study with the elders in the evenings.

Abinadi smiled to himself. Raquel was hardly ever afraid to say what she thought. It kept things lively between them. He walked to the back of the hut. After some fresh air, he should be able to go back to sleep. It was still several hours before dawn, and he knew if he didn't sleep, he'd regret it at midday while toiling in the hot sun.

Suddenly the feeling was back—a shiver traveling the length of his body, and he felt slightly dizzy. *Maybe I'm ill.* He knelt on the ground, prepared for anything. But what hit him next, he couldn't have prepared himself for.

You must return to the city of Nephi.

Abinadi looked around, knowing that he'd see no person standing anywhere near him. He'd heard that voice before. Quiet, yet powerful. There was no mistaking the voice of the Lord.

Go and prophesy among my people, for they have hardened their hearts against me.

His heart pounded as he listened to the powerful tone.

They have not repented, therefore I will visit them in my anger. Stretch forth thy hand and prophesy these things. Teach them the commandments, and teach them the words of Isaiah so that they will know about the coming of Christ.

Abinadi kept his head bowed and eyes closed as the Lord's instructions poured into his soul. The Lord wanted His people to know all about Christ—His Atonement, His Resurrection, and the truth about their salvation. When the Lord's voice faded and was replaced by silence, Abinadi remained kneeling for a long time. His strength had left him, and he was out of breath.

He lay on the ground on his side and stared at the vast sky above. He thought about all the things the Lord had told him and wondered why he'd been chosen. Gideon or Helam could do a better job than he. Besides, he'd already failed once. What had made the Lord come to him again? The Lord surely knew that King Noah had sought to slay him. Perhaps enough time had passed that he'd been forgotten. Or, perhaps, this time he'd be able to soften the hearts of the people.

Slowly, his strength returned, and he staggered to his feet. Dawn was now only a short time away, and soon he'd have to leave his wife and son behind. Abinadi crept into the hut and settled next to Raquel, careful not to disturb her. He wanted to watch her sleep. The days and nights on the road might be perilous at best, and he wanted to memorize her features for comfort.

He knew she would worry about his departure, so he said a silent prayer that she would understand. It would be hard enough to leave without worrying her. Finally, he couldn't stand waiting any longer. He reached out and smoothed her hair from her face.

Raquel's eyes opened immediately. She blinked a few times, then her eyes widened. "What's happened?"

He hesitated, watching her closely. "The Lord spoke to me again."

"What did He say?"

"He has asked me to return."

She wrapped her arms about his neck and buried her head against his chest. She didn't say anything for a long moment. Then, finally, "When are you leaving?"

"Right away," Abinadi said. He tightened his hold as her body started to tremble. He'd expected her to be angry, but not this—not silent.

When she pulled away, her eyes were bright with unshed tears. "We're coming with you."

Abinadi shook his head, touching her cheek. "It's too dangerous."

"We can stay in your old home while you go into the city."

"Raquel," Abinadi said in a soft voice. "It's been two years. The place is either destroyed or occupied." He moved onto one elbow, staring down at her. "And besides, the king wants you dead."

"What about you?" she whispered. "They tried to kill *you* last time. What about that?"

Abinadi didn't have an answer. Instead he pulled her into his arms again. They stayed together like that until the sun crested the horizon.

A loud cry suddenly interrupted Abinadi and Raquel's half-awake state. Abe was up.

Abinadi chuckled as Raquel picked up the squalling child. The boy didn't have much patience when he was hungry. While Raquel nursed the baby, Abinadi rose and straightened his son's bedding. He folded the coverings slowly, already counting the hours to when he'd return home to his little family. He looked at Raquel, who returned his gaze, worry plain in her eyes.

Warmth coursed through Abinadi as he looked at his wife and son. They were both so precious. At the same time, urgency flooded through him. "I should leave soon," he said in a quiet voice.

Raquel just nodded. Abinadi took another glance about the room. "I'll tell Mother and Helam."

"I'll prepare your things," Raquel offered.

He stepped out of the hut. Everyone would still be asleep, but this couldn't wait. He walked the path to his mother's home, which was next door to Helam's. Abinadi saw his brother outside already, arranging wood at the cooking fire.

Helam looked up as Abinadi approached. "You're up early," Helam said.

Abinadi drew close to his older brother. The hood he wore concealed most of his face, except for his chin and mouth, but Abinadi knew the lines of his brother's scars, stretching from his neck upward, his lips not quite coming together in a cohesive line.

"The Lord spoke to me this morning," Abinadi began.

Helam stopped mid-motion, then straightened to face him. "Do you want me to accompany you?"

"No, brother," Abinadi said. "Mother needs you here."

As if on cue, Esther exited her hut. "What's this? My sons are certainly up early." She bustled to Abinadi's side and looked between the two men. "Something's happened. What is it?"

Helam shot Abinadi a worried look. Esther covered her mouth with her hand. "No. Not again."

Abinadi nodded.

"What about Raquel and Abe?" Esther cried out.

"Raquel already knows, and she understands."

"Last time you barely escaped with your life." Her voice started to tremble, and she broke off, covering her mouth again.

"Mother, we have to put it in the Lord's hands," Abinadi said. "Last time I was there, I had a full beard. Now I have none. I'll wear one of Helam's robes with a hood. I won't be easily recognized."

"Or you could shave your hair," Helam suggested.

"Like a Lamanite?" Esther said, her voice rising in pitch.

"It will be more of a disguise," Helam said to his mother.

She nodded, her eyes still wide with worry.

Abinadi looked at Helam, his gaze boring into his brother's. "I have to ask you something before I go . . ." His voice faltered for a moment. "If something happens to me . . ."

His mother gripped his arm.

"Promise me, Helam," Abinadi continued. "Promise me you'll watch over Raquel and Abe. I don't want my child growing up without a father." His voice cracked. "Like we did."

Helam nodded. "I promise."

Esther clung to Abinadi. "Can't you stay? The Lord will find someone else."

"No, Mother. The Lord called me, and I must obey," Abinadi corrected her gently. He wrapped his arms around her and kissed the top of her head. "You must be strong. Raquel is going to need help."

Esther pulled away, wiping her eyes, but her expression was resolute. "I can do that. Of course, that wife of yours won't let me help her much. She can be stubborn, if I may say so myself."

Abinadi smiled. "She reminds me of someone I know."

Esther narrowed her eyes. "What do you mean?"

"Raquel won't stand a chance." Helam chuckled. "She'll be sick of us by the time you return."

"Thank you, both." Abinadi embraced his brother, then his mother again. He turned away, afraid to stay much longer. Urgency pulsed through him, and he still had to say good-bye to Gideon and the rest. Knocking softly on their huts, he offered a quick explanation and received well wishes in return.

Finally, he arrived back at his hut. He could hear the sounds of Abe's babbling coming from inside. He pushed the skin aside, and Raquel turned in anticipation. She'd packed a bundle of clothing and supplies for him.

When Abe saw him, he squealed, "Da!"

Abinadi took the child from Raquel and held him close. Abe laughed, then squirmed to get away. Reluctantly, Abinadi kissed his son and set him down. Then he turned to Raquel and enveloped her in his arms.

She cried as she clung to him. "Be safe."

"I will," he said. He tilted her chin toward him. "I love you."

A tear dripped down her cheek. "I love you too."

* * *

Abinadi made short time as he traveled with only the small bundle on his back. By the time he reached the city of Nephi, he was exhausted but exhilarated. He hoped his newly shorn hair and shaved face would give him plenty of time to share the warning of the Lord. It was midafternoon by the time he arrived at the marketplace. The wide courtyard teemed with people. Abinadi scanned the crowd for a moment, a lump rising in his throat. All of these people would be brought into bondage and treated as slaves if they didn't repent.

And it's up to me to tell them.

A man tapped him on the shoulder. Abinadi turned to see a gangly merchant, his teeth mostly rotted. His mat displayed sweets—delicacies made with honey and amaranth seeds. "Something for your wife and children?" The merchant gestured toward the delicacies.

Abinadi gazed at him, trying to find some light in the man's dark eyes. "I've come to share a message with you, my friend. A message from the Lord."

The man visibly shrank back, his eyes narrowing. "You're a preacher?"

"Yes," Abinadi said, taking a deep breath. He moved closer to the man and said quietly, "The Lord has asked me to prophesy that because of the people's iniquities, they will be smitten by their enemies and brought into bondage . . ."

The man shook his head, a mirthless laugh forming. "The Lamanites are helpless before us. Where have you been, preacher? Every week we capture more prisoners and kill more women and children."

A shudder passed through Abinadi at the crass words. "Your hearts have been hardened." Several others stopped to listen, looking from Abinadi to the merchant. Abinadi included the new people in the conversation. "Because of your evil doings, you will be driven by men and will be slain until the vultures of the air—"

"Our king has the most powerful army in the land. No one will slay us!" a man in a fine indigo cape retorted. "King Noah has built a strong people. No one has breached our borders for months."

Abinadi focused on the man. "The life of King Noah will be valued as a garment in a hot furnace. Even he will know that the Lord is God."

Several more people had stopped, forming a small crowd.

"The Lord will smite you with sore afflictions, with famine and pestilence," Abinadi said, gazing at those who'd joined them. "Even your king cannot stop those."

Two men moved forward, their faces red in anger. "You are the preacher we chased out before."

Abinadi took a step backward, holding up his hand. "The Lord will cause burdens to be lashed upon your backs so that you work like animals. He will also send hail and wind. Insects will pester your land and eat your grain."

The two men grabbed Abinadi. "The king sent a warrant for your capture." Others in the crowd pressed forward, jostling to reach him.

Abinadi wrestled away from the grabbing arms. "The Lord says that except you repent, you will be utterly destroyed off the face of the earth. You will leave a record that the Lord will preserve for other nations so that they may discover your abominations."

"Get him!" someone shouted.

Abinadi moved around the mat filled with sweets. But there were too many of them. He was grabbed from all sides.

"Find a rope!" someone else commanded.

Within minutes, he was tied, hand and foot.

"Take him to the king!"

"He'll die for his treason!"

Abinadi felt himself lifted and carried along the road. The people of the city seemed even more hostile than before. Angry faces floated in and out above him as he was jostled along. The merchant stayed within view, acting as if he were directing the procession as they made their way to the palace.

Hands took him to the temple, and the merchant announced to the guards that he had a delivery for King Noah. The air changed as they entered the cool interior. With the surrounding mass, he could only see the ceiling above, idols propped in the stone crevices. He felt himself being lowered, and suddenly those in front of him cleared.

Abinadi stared at a group of finely clad men seated on a platform and guarded by a body of soldiers. His gaze moved from one man to the next—they were the high priests, adorned in costly feathered capes and gaudy animal headdresses. In the center was King Noah himself. He'd changed over the past two years. His face was rounder, his skin redder, his eyes harder. His jeweled hands rested on his paunch.

What surprised Abinadi the most were the women who surrounded the king and a few of the priests. It seemed they combined pleasure with business. Abinadi's gaze was drawn to the man on the king's right. His father-in-law—although this relationship was probably still unknown to Amulon.

Abinadi tried to tear his gaze away from the massive man, trying not think of how cruel he had been to Raquel. He felt the anger pierce his chest, giving him even more courage to say what he was about to.

The merchant asked for permission to speak to the king. When it was granted, his rapid voice captured everyone's attention. "O Highness, we have brought this man who says he is prophesying in the name of God. He calls us evil and claims that your life will be valued only as a garment in a furnace of fire." The man came to a blundering stop, casting his bloodshot eyes on Abinadi, then back to the king.

The king's emotions played across his face—amusement to annoyance. A man seated beneath the priests' bench squinted at him, then he looked down at a scroll of bark he was writing on. *He must be the king's scribe,* Abinadi realized. The man was well-rounded, his graying beard wildly overgrown.

The merchant continued to prattle on, reporting on what Abinadi had said in the marketplace. "He said we'll be like a stalk in the field, run over by beasts and trodden underfoot."

A few of the high priests smiled, rolling their eyes, and Abinadi glanced at the merchant.

Then a commotion from the judgment seats caught everyone's attention. King Noah stood and brushed off the two women who flanked him. His lazy gaze traveled the length of the assembled priests. "Am I greater than a burning garment?"

A few laughed, others calling out, "Most definitely!"

"Very well, then," Noah said, a glint in his eyes as he focused on Abinadi. "I'll not worry about my worth quite yet." He adjusted the jaguar headdress. A smile smeared itself upon his face. "You think my people need to repent?"

Abinadi opened his mouth just as the merchant cried out, "He said we are like the blossom of a thistle that is fully ripe. And when the wind blows, we'll be driven off the face of the land."

"Enough!" Noah roared, his eyes narrowing at the merchant. Then a smile returned as he looked at Abinadi. "It seems we have a poet in our midst." He started clapping, and the priests joined in, confusion on their faces. "Well done, preacher. Do you have a name, by chance?"

Abinadi swallowed. He knew he was being baited. He looked at the row of priests, each of them leaning forward. Then his eyes rested on the high priest sitting to the left of the king. He looked a little different from how he once had, but there was no mistaking it was the man who'd warned him on that night so long ago. The man Gideon had called Alma. The priest held his gaze for a brief moment, a mixture of curiosity and challenge in his expression.

"My name is Abinadi."

The high priest flinched, and recognition dawned in his eyes.

"Ah. It seems as if you are hard to dispose of," Noah said with a chuckle. "Just as a dog to its vomit?"

The priests chuckled, all except Alma, who stared at Abinadi with astonishment. Next to the king, Amulon sat down with a thud. His gaze had hardened.

"Your preaching precedes your name," Noah said. He glanced at the merchant, whose face was working in spasm. "Speak your peace, citizen." He folded his arms across his massive chest.

The merchant stepped in front of Abinadi, looking furtively at him. Then he turned and bowed to the king, wringing his hands as he spoke. "O Highness, what evil have you done or what great sins have your people committed, that we should be condemned of God?" He pointed to Abinadi. "Or judged by this man?"

Abinadi moved his gaze from the merchant to Amulon—whose expression had gone from anger to outright fury. Abinadi looked then to Alma. The priest's gaze was intense as the merchant continued his flattering speech, "O King, we are guiltless, and you have not sinned."

"Well, thank you for the complimentary words," Noah said, a smile playing on his lips. A gurgled laughter rumbled through the priests. "Are you finished, sir?"

The merchant shook his head quickly. "This man, this preacher, has lied about you and prophesied in vain. We are a strong people and will not come into bondage. We won't be taken by our enemies—we are too strong!"

Noah nodded. "You are right. Our enemies are no threat to us."

"Here is the false preacher you seek, O King. We have delivered him into your hands so that you may judge him as you will," the merchant finished.

Noah stepped down from the platform, walking toward the trembling merchant, the guards tensing. "You want your reward, don't you, sir?"

The man's wringing hands came to a stop. A slight nod of his head caused the king to roar with laughter.

"Toss me a bag of silver onties."

Amulon stood and tossed a bundle to the king. Noah held it out to the merchant, who took it with bowed head and a very red face.

"You are dismissed," Noah said.

The merchant bowed two more times, then scurried from the room, squeezing his way past the group of guards at the door.

As soon as the merchant was gone, the amusement fled Noah's eyes. He glared at Abinadi as he adjusted his headdress again. The jaguar teeth made him look quite formidable. "Throw him in prison!"

Abinadi flinched.

Amulon smiled.

Hands wrapped around Abinadi again, propelling him to the doors. As he was dragged through the doors, he heard the king say, "My priests and I will discuss the things we've seen and heard today. Cancel all other requests."

Twenty-Three

That unto me every knee shall bow, every tongue shall swear.
(Isaiah 45:23)

Rubbing his forehead, Alma tried to make sense of what he'd just seen and heard. The preacher had returned. It was unbelievable. The man knew he was in danger, yet he still came to warn them. Granted, he'd come in disguise, as he certainly looked different with his shaved beard and shorn hair . . .

Alma watched the king pace before the court. Noah had been quite jovial through the whole episode of the merchant's report, but from experience, Alma knew that good humor usually preceded the storm of the king's temper. Surely today would be no exception.

The king's rambling words reached him, and Alma realized that all of the priests were listening intently, their expressions grave.

"Like a garment in a furnace of fire?" Noah said, mostly to himself. Then his voice grew in volume. "The man didn't even speak while the merchant was here. Is he proud enough to condemn in the marketplace, but when he's brought before the court, he quakes with fear?"

The king looked at his priests. "What kind of a preacher is he?"

Alma drew back, seeing doubt and questioning on the king's face. He tried to ignore the churning of his stomach. Since burning all of his belongings, Alma had tried to keep a low profile at court. He no longer spent his silver lavishly. He'd let all but one servant go. He no longer entertained harlots—there was an unspoken agreement now with the women. He might dance with them when the king was watching, but nothing more. He wore the same cape every day over a simple tunic. Gradually, even his troubling dreams had faded. He had been slowly changing from the inside out, and the last thing he needed was for the king to pay attention to him. Someone was sure to notice if Alma weren't careful.

He'd been fortunate to have subtly thwarted the king's intention of slaying Maia without drawing undue attention to himself, but he certainly couldn't risk his life to save Abinadi's. Yet he hadn't been able to get the man's words out of his mind since their brief conversation two years previous.

Alma focused on the discussion around him. The other high priests seemed to be cowering, none offering up satisfying answers to Noah's questions. Amulon tried to make fun of the merchant again, but Noah no longer appeared amused.

Alma stood as he cleared his throat. The king and priests all looked at him. "Why don't we bring him back to court and question him? Without the merchant or without the crowd of people—just the preacher."

Amulon stood too. "Yes! We'll be able to point out his errors. Poet or not, we know the ways of the gods more than he does. We have been made high priests over the people for a reason."

Several heads nodded. The king looked at the panel of men. "All right. We'll question him."

Noah turned to the guards. "Bring the preacher back in." Then he spoke to the portly scribe. "Eli, call together your best scribes. We'll need their counsel."

Eli rose to his feet and bobbed his head. With a flurry involving a dropped stencil and a scattering of scrolls, he fled the room.

Alma sat back down and twisted his hands. He tried to keep his expression calm, although his heart was pounding. He was looking forward to hearing the preacher speak more than he wanted to admit. Had there ever been a man more courageous? Alma didn't think so. Abinadi was either truly called of God or completely out of his mind.

A few scribes hurried in, ushered by Eli. Their pale faces displayed fear and wonder at being summoned to court. Alma knew their days were usually spent cloistered in their rooms, copying text word by word. They gathered in a tight circle, turning metal plates and opening dusty scrolls. It was then that Alma recognized the youngest scribe—Limhi, the king's own son. It had been two years since Alma had last seen him or noticed him. *At my high priest ordination,* he realized. It seemed the hunting trip had done little to turn the king's intellectual son into a warrior or great hunter.

Alma shifted his gaze from Limhi to Amulon, who sauntered down from the bench and entered the circle of scribes, asking questions.

The king again took his place at his seat. The women moved back to his side, and everyone watched the activity of the scribes as they waited.

When the preacher was announced, Amulon resumed his place, a smug smile on his face. He leaned over to the king and whispered in his ear. Alma focused on the prisoner as he was dragged in. Ropes bound his hands in front, and similar bindings cut into his ankles. When the guards set him upright, the preacher stood straight, his back erect, his gaze steadily ranging over the assembled panel.

"Where did you come from?" the king asked.

"I come from a land where men walk free," Abinadi said. "A place where the fruits of our labors benefit our own families and don't line the coffers of greedy men."

Alma stared at the man. He certainly didn't mince words.

"What gives you the right to tell us what the Lord wants?" Amulon asked, rising to his feet.

"The command of the Lord Himself." Abinadi's gaze moved to Amulon. "I'm not here because of my will, but *His*."

Amulon scoffed. "Who are you to tell us what is righteous or what is wicked?"

"I am merely the Lord's mouthpiece."

Amulon frowned and waved the scribe Eli over. The portly man rushed to Amulon's side, holding out a metal plate—apparently what Amulon wanted, for he smiled and snatched it away.

"All right, since you know all about the Lord, what does this mean?" He cleared his throat and read, "'How beautiful upon the mountains are the feet of him that bringeth good tidings . . . The Lord hath made bare his holy arm in the eyes of all the nations; and the ends of the earth shall see the salvation of our God.' Here we are among mountains, fulfilling Isaiah's words. God protects this people. You are a false prophet."

Abinadi looked from Amulon to the other priests. "Are *you* not priests? Why do you ask me what these things mean? Do you *pretend* to teach your people and *pretend* to understand the spirit of prophesying?"

Amulon narrowed his eyes in anger. The scribes put their heads together, whispering furiously.

"You have not applied your hearts to understand the words of the scriptures," Abinadi said, his voice rising. "You have failed to teach your people the ways of the Lord." He paused, taking a deep breath. "Tell me, what *have* you taught this people?"

The king laughed, and a few others joined in. But most of the priests looked perplexed. "We teach the law of Moses, of course," Amulon said, his face still quite red. He pointed at the group of scribes. "You can ask them. It's all there on the metal plates that have been copied from the brass plates brought over by our fathers. We teach what is written. We make animal sacrifices and sin offerings upon the altars for the people, and we teach them to worship the Lord."

Abinadi's eyes pierced Amulon's. "You sacrifice unclean animals. You may say you worship the Lord, but you worship other gods. If you're teaching the law of Moses, why aren't you living it?"

The room fell silent. Noah's face went from amusement to anger.

Amulon's mouth worked as he searched for an answer. Alma clenched his hands together in anticipation. He wanted to jump up and shout, *He's right!*

"Why do you set your hearts upon riches? Where does it say to do so in the law of Moses?" Abinadi's gaze moved to the women surrounding the king, then to the king himself. "Why do you commit whoredoms and spend your time with harlots?"

Noah's hand clenched into a fist, and he pounded the low table in front of him. "Enough!" The women flinched, drawing back.

"You cause your people to commit sin," Abinadi continued, his voice steady. "The Lord has sent me to prophesy against you." His gaze moved from the king to Alma, and his voice softened. "You know I speak the truth, and you should be trembling before God."

Alma felt as if Abinadi had reached inside his chest and wrenched out his heart. Everyone turned to look at him. He knew this man spoke the truth. And he could see that Abinadi knew he knew it.

The preacher's next words took the attention off of Alma. "You'll be smitten for your iniquities! You say you teach the law of Moses, but what do you know about the law?" He glared at the king. "Does salvation come by the law of Moses?"

The king opened his mouth to speak, but several of the surrounding priests stood. "Yes," they shouted almost in unison.

Abinadi nodded, the red of his face fading. "If you keep the commandments of God, you will be saved." He paused. "You might say you teach the law of Moses, yet you forget what God taught Moses."

The priests began to whisper amongst themselves. Alma couldn't take his gaze off the preacher.

Abinadi's voice was low and urgent, his words causing a familiar feeling to cover Alma—taking him back to his childhood. It was as if his father's words had been resurrected from the grave.

"The Lord said to Moses," Abinadi started, "'Thou shalt have no other Gods before me. Thou shalt not make unto thee any graven image, or any likeness of any thing in the heaven above, or that is in the earth beneath.'"

The preacher lifted his bound arms, pointing to the wooden nawals, or guardian spirits, lining the walls of the temple. "You have brought idols into the temple! This should be the most sacred place in the land, yet you have defiled the very house of God." He looked at the king as he lowered his hands. "You have not kept the law of Moses, and you have not taught your people correctly."

Noah stood, pushing the women aside, and stepped off the platform, sending the scribes scurrying out of his way. "Away with this fellow!" he shouted, his hands clenched into fists. "Slay him! He's mad!"

The guards reached for Abinadi, but he lifted his arms and broke the bindings. The guards fell back in astonishment. Abinadi spread his hands wide, shouting above the exclamations. "Touch me not, for God will smite you if you lay your hands upon me!"

The king took a step back in confusion, his body trembling. Alma stared at the preacher, holding his breath, his heart pounding. A searing heat seemed to pulse through the room, bouncing off the walls, then straight into Alma's soul. The Spirit of God was in the room.

"I have not delivered the message which the Lord sent me to deliver," Abinadi said, his voice echoing in the suddenly quiet room. His face was radiant, as if light were coming from his skin. "Neither have I answered your questions." His gaze stayed on the king, his tone sure and strong. "God will not suffer that I will be destroyed at this time."

The king sank onto one of the scribes' stools, his expression a mask of astonishment.

Alma's breath left him, and the strength in his limbs vanished. All he could do was watch and listen.

"You're angry with me because I have told you the truth," Abinadi continued in the dead silence. "And because I have spoken the word of God, you call me *mad.*" He took a step forward, the bands on his ankles suddenly loose. "You can see that you do not have the power to slay me." His eyes roamed the high priests. "Therefore, I will finish giving the message that I came to deliver."

Alma brought his hand to his heart, and Abinadi noticed the movement. The two men locked gazes. "My words fill you with wonder and amazement. After I finish my message, it will not matter where I go or what becomes of me, so long as I receive salvation from our Lord." Abinadi's chest expanded as he inhaled with the next breath. His voice trembled at his next words. "But this I can tell you . . . what you do with me after I am finished will be a type and shadow of things which are to come to you."

No one moved or spoke. All eyes were on the preacher's illuminated face.

Abinadi's words filled the room, his voice shaking Alma to his core. "Thou shalt not take the name of the Lord thy God in vain; Remember the Sabbath day, to keep it holy; Honor thy father and mother . . ."

Tears stung Alma's eyes, though he worked to keep them at bay.

Thou shalt not kill.

Thou shalt not commit adultery.

The tears came anyway.

Thou shalt not bear false witness.

Thou shalt not covet thy neighbor's wife.

Alma hung his head, unable to look at the preacher any longer. Physical pain wrenched his heart. He may have burned all semblance of his outward wealth, but inside he was still rotten.

"Have you taught your people that they should keep the Lord's commandments?" Abinadi asked.

Alma lifted his head, oblivious to his own tear-stained face.

"No." Abinadi's voice was just above a whisper, but it thundered into Alma's heart. "If you had taught the people, the Lord would not have sent me."

Alma found himself nodding.

The preacher looked at him and said, "You have said that salvation comes by the law of Moses. I say it is expedient to keep the law, but there will come a time when you will no longer need to keep it."

A few of the priests broke from their trances and started to murmur.

"Salvation does not come by the law alone," Abinadi continued, his voice commanding silent attention again. "Were it not for the Atonement, which God Himself will make for the sins of His people, we would *all* perish. God Himself will come down among His people to bring about the resurrection of the dead. And He will be oppressed and afflicted."

Amulon started chuckling. "You know nothing of the ways of God— He would not come among men to be afflicted." The king nodded his agreement.

But Abinadi was shaking his head. "Even the prophet Isaiah spoke of the son of God and his mortal life. 'He is despised and rejected of men; a man of sorrows, and acquainted with grief . . .'"

The king folded his arms over his chest, his eyes narrowed, as Abinadi continued to speak.

Alma recognized several of the phrases the preacher quoted from the prophet Isaiah. The scribes sorted through their records, trying to find what portion Abinadi quoted from. Eli finally located the copy of the text and handed it over to Amulon. The king grabbed it from the high priest and scanned through the words.

"He was numbered with the transgressors," Abinadi continued, "and He bore the sins of many and made intercession for the transgressors."

Amulon cleared his throat, glancing at the king. "Ah, so while God is on earth, busy being oppressed, who is ruling the heavens?"

The other priests chuckled at Amulon's remark.

"The Father. The Son of God is called both the Father and the Son because they are of one heart and one mind. But the Son of God will come to earth in the flesh. And after working mighty miracles, He will be led, crucified, and slain."

"Like you?" Amulon said.

Alma looked at Amulon, disgust tightening his stomach. The other priests laughed, gaining courage with Amulon's caustic remark.

"The Lord will break the bands of death. He will gain victory, giving Him the power to intercede for the children of men." Regardless of the jeering, Abinadi's voice retained its calm power. "I am not the only one to prophesy of the coming of the Lord."

The scribes busied themselves again, searching through records.

Alma held his breath at the preacher's next words—ones he'd heard repeated by his father.

"All the holy prophets have testified of the coming of the Lord. And all who have listened to their words—and believed—will be the heirs of the kingdom of God," Abinadi said.

Alma found himself beginning to nod, then stopped, lest others notice.

The preacher stretched out his hands again, and the guards near him backed away. "The time will come when every nation, kindred, tongue, and people will see eye to eye and will confess before God that His judgments are just."

Every nation, kindred, tongue, and people, Alma thought with amazement. Everyone will confess. He hadn't confessed. He wondered what the king would do to him if he did.

The room went quiet again as Abinadi continued. "The wicked will be cast out, and they will howl, weep, wail, and gnash their teeth. They will not be redeemed and will be resurrected to eternal damnation." He looked directly at Alma. "Should you not tremble and repent of your sins, remembering that only through Christ can you be saved?"

Alma mouthed the word. "Yes."

The preacher looked at Noah. "If you taught the law of Moses, you would have taught your people that redemption comes through Christ the Lord, who is the very Eternal Father."

Noah was shaking, his face a scarlet red. "Are you finished?"

The surrounding priests started to murmur. Abinadi's expression was unfazed.

"You accuse us of not teaching the law of Moses," the king grumbled. "I say we do. As the king of this land, I define and amend the law according to the needs of my people. And for your blasphemous words, you will be put to death!" He turned to Amulon. "Take him away and kill him."

The words chilled Alma's heart, and before another instant passed, he stepped forward. "Wait."

All eyes turned on him.

"Do not be angry with this man. He tells the truth," Alma said, his heart pounding furiously. But as he spoke, he felt power and assurance swell within. "Let him depart in peace. His words have done no harm. If anything, they have caused us to dwell on the mercies of God and our own iniquities. We should not be changing the laws of God to serve our own purposes, but abiding by them." For a brief instant, Alma caught Limhi's curious gaze. The young man had risen to his feet, scrolls scattered on the floor about him. His mouth started to move as if he had something to say too.

"No!" Noah shouted, his eyes bulging. "You—I—get out of my sight—you traitor!"

Alma stumbled backward as the other priests advanced. He stepped off the platform and moved toward Abinadi. Their eyes locked for a moment, understanding passing between them—man to man, believer to believer. Abinadi's gaze was triumphant.

"S-stay away from the—the preacher!" Noah sputtered. He whirled around, pointing at Alma. "Guards! Seize him!"

Alma hesitated for a brief instant, stunned. Then he turned from Abinadi and barreled past the surprised guards. Out the temple doors and down the steps he ran, not daring to look back. Noah's voice sailed after him. "After you catch Alma, throw his new friend Abinadi in prison!"

Twenty-four

Blessed are they which are persecuted for righteousness' sake:
for theirs is the kingdom of heaven.
(Matthew 5:10)

Staring at the sunset, Raquel tried to find beauty in the fiery reds and oranges streaking across the sky. But peace would not come. *Something is wrong,* she thought again. *Something is terribly wrong.* She stood from her perch overlooking the fields. It was as if she couldn't quite catch her breath, couldn't inhale deeply enough. Yet at the same time, she wanted to run and never stop until she reached the city of Nephi.

She'd prayed over and over again, but the Lord was silent. She wondered if He had fled with Abinadi. There were no comforting whisperings, no tender warmth in her chest. She felt hollow . . . empty.

Raquel swiped at the moisture on her cheek, then climbed off the rock and headed back to the settlement. Abe should be waking from his nap by now and would surely be hungry. There was only so much a grandmother could do to soothe a one-year-old. Esther had practically smothered Raquel with attention since Abinadi's departure. It was for this reason that she'd had to take a walk by herself, just to think.

Helam had been no better. Whereas Raquel had only seen him in passing before and spoken to him occasionally, now he seemed to be everywhere she was.

I don't need protection, Raquel wanted to say. *I'm not the one in a city that hates me, or running from a king who wants me dead.* But if she returned, of course her life might be at risk again—just like Abinadi's was now. Yet the more Raquel thought about it, the more she felt she needed to try to find him. If there was any way she could ensure his safe return, she'd do it.

As she emerged from the thicket of trees at the base of the hill, Helam stood from his post. "Are you all right?" he asked.

Raquel exhaled with frustration. "You don't have to follow me."

"I—I'm just following Abinadi's wish."

Raquel stopped, her hands on her hips. "I don't think he meant *everywhere*—just to help me if I needed something." She waved her hand. "It's not like I'm going to disappear or anything."

Helam folded his arms. "Fair enough."

She marched past him, not entirely convinced Helam would let up. At least he didn't follow her back to the settlement—that she could see, anyway.

As she approached the huts, the aroma of cooking reached her, making her realize how hungry she really was. She'd hardly eaten since Abinadi had left. She quickened her pace, suddenly anxious to see her son. When she arrived at the hut, Esther was sitting outside.

"He's still asleep?" Raquel asked.

Esther smiled and nodded.

"He's going to be starving when he wakes up," Raquel mused. She glanced over her shoulder—Helam was waiting several paces away.

Putting a hand on Raquel's arm, Esther said, "I'll bring you a bowl of food so you can stay here and listen for the baby."

"Thank you," Raquel said. She leaned in and whispered, "You can tell Helam he doesn't need to camp outside my hut tonight. If I need something, I'll pound loudly on *his* hut."

Esther's eyes narrowed. "You know he's just concerned, don't you?"

More like he's guarding me, Raquel thought. *What did Abinadi tell* him? "I know. But Abe sleeps pretty well through the night, and you're just a stone's throw away," she said as politely as she could.

"All right," Esther said. "I'll tell him, but he won't like it." She turned away to bustle off. Helam had disappeared.

Helam is taking the charge of "watching over" me far too seriously, Raquel thought. She went inside her hut and breathed a sigh of relief. She was alone—well, except for the wide-eyed boy staring at her from his pallet. She must have awakened him.

"Hello, dear," Raquel said, crossing the room. Abe grinned and held out his arms. She picked him up, and immediately he curled against her. As she made herself comfortable on the mat and started to nurse him, she closed her eyes and tried to relax. But the anxiety for Abinadi's safety wouldn't leave.

The walls of the hut seemed to close in on her and she gulped for air. She felt so helpless. She tried to picture her husband's face, and pain seared through her as she thought about his laugh, the warmth of his touch, his gentleness, the love in his eyes each time they looked at each other . . . She looked down at Abe, seeing the curve of his eyebrows—exactly like his father's.

Oh, Abinadi, I miss you more than I could have ever imagined. Her eyes burned with tears, but she wouldn't give in to them yet. *Come home to me.*

The door covering lifted quietly, and Esther crept in. With a knowing smile on her face, she set a bowl of beans and squash beside Raquel. Esther hesitated for a moment, gazing upon her grandchild. Raquel felt a twinge in her heart as she sensed the bond between grandmother and grandson. She wished her own mother could know Abe as well.

When Esther left, Raquel finally let the tears spill. She felt so much at home in this settlement with her son, her mother-in-law, Tia . . . But she could never be truly happy with Abinadi gone. He was a part of her, and nothing was the same in his absence.

She dried her tears just as Abe finished nursing. She ate quickly, hardly tasting the food. As the room darkened, Raquel lit some oil lamps. Abe scooted along the floor, content to play by himself. But Raquel was far from content as she watched her young son play and babble, her mind far away. Her parents didn't even know they had a grandchild. Maybe her father would finally forgive her and welcome Abinadi. If her father could just lay eyes on this precious baby.

As Raquel watched her child, her heart softened. He was so sweet, so innocent. Did he have the power to unite a broken family? Abinadi had told her he would try to see her mother—tell her about Abe. But the news would be even sweeter if her mother could see the child in person.

Raquel took a deep breath, letting her mind wander. Fear and excitement filled her thoughts as she considered making the journey to the city of Nephi. It shouldn't be too hard to locate a preacher in the city; surely many people had heard his message already. She paced the room as Abe scuttled after her, laughing each time the hem of her tunic brushed him. She wouldn't need many supplies, just what she could carry. She'd probably be able to complete the journey in less than two days.

She stopped, and Abe stopped with her, reaching up. She lifted the boy and swayed with him, wondering what to do about Helam and Esther. They'd never let her go. One part of her worried a little about traveling with such a small child. Maybe she could ask Gideon to accompany her. He traveled back and forth quite often, meeting with elders from the city—those few who practiced their religious beliefs in secret.

Mind made up, she wrapped Abe and went outside. True to Esther's word, Helam was nowhere in sight, but Raquel knew he wasn't far away. She walked along the path, passing several huts, until she reached Gideon's. Light glowed from within, and Raquel hesitated briefly, wondering if Neriah would come. Their interactions had been civil over the past two years, but nothing more than that.

Abe started to hiccup, and with a smile, Raquel knocked.

Tia came to the entrance, and when she laid eyes on Raquel, her brow furrowed. "Is something wrong with the babe?"

"No," Raquel said. "I've come to speak with your husband."

Tia studied her for a moment, curiosity in her eyes. Finally, she nodded. "Come in."

Again, Raquel hesitated. Beyond the entrance, Neriah and her younger sister sat together as they embroidered. Raquel wanted privacy. Her heart raced as she said, "Do you think I can speak to him outside?"

"Certainly. I'll send him out," Tia said.

A moment later, Gideon towered over Raquel, familiar concern in his eyes.

When Raquel explained what she wanted to do, he shook his head. "I understand that you want your parents to meet your son . . . and that you worry about Abinadi." He looked away for a moment. "Truthfully, I've been quite unsettled about him also."

Raquel rushed on. "I can't dispel my worry. It's different from last time . . ."

Gideon met her gaze, his eyes darkening. "Even so, I cannot allow you to travel into danger. Abinadi would never forgive me."

"If you came with me, or one of the other elders, I wouldn't be in danger . . ."

Gideon's jaw clenched. "You're risking your own life and your child's by going. If something happened to you, imagine how your husband would feel."

Raquel looked down as tears threatened. She had to do *something*. "If we put together a large group, I could disguise myself . . ."

Gideon's hand touched her shoulder. "No. I'm sorry, Raquel. I just can't allow it."

She nodded, feeling numb. Taking a step back, she said, "Thank you for listening." Then she turned away, a painful lump in her throat.

She rushed back to her hut, clutching Abe as she blinked back the stinging tears and tried not to stumble on the dark path. Abe started fussing as soon as she entered her hut. She fed him a quick meal of mashed beans, then settled him down for the night. But she couldn't relax. Her head hurt, but her heart hurt worse. She listened to Abe's even breathing. She paced.

She looked out the narrow window. She lay down. She slept for a few restless hours. She rose again.

She couldn't stand waiting and not knowing. With or without Gideon, she had to try, or she would never forgive herself.

By the light of the moon splashing through the single window, Raquel rolled her mat into a tight bundle, then made a pack of food. She poured water from a jug into a goatskin. Then she made a sling and tied it around her waist and shoulders. Carefully, she lifted her sleeping child and settled him against her torso. He stirred for a moment, then relaxed again.

She tied the goatskin and food bundle to the rolled bedding, then strapped it to her back with rope. After taking one more sweeping look at the hut, she left.

Outside, the air had cooled and clouds had moved in front of the moon, making the darkness blacker than usual. Raquel glanced up at the sky, seeing thick clouds swirling. It would surely rain by morning, but she'd be in the confines of the forest before a drop would hit. She hoped. She crept silently past the huts, noting that all were dark.

Her eyes smarted as she thought about Gideon's refusal. She hoped he would understand in the morning when she was discovered gone. She also hoped he would forgive her. *I'll be home in less than a week,* she told herself. There will be plenty of time to make amends then.

She traveled as fast as she dared, trying not to jostle the baby too much. He grew heavy after a while, but the adrenaline coursing through Raquel kept her moving. She'd grown strong during her time in the elders' settlement. But she knew she couldn't keep up a rapid pace for too long.

The rain started just as she entered the thicket of trees. The branches and leaves above offered little protection, and the drops pinged all around her. She adjusted her cape so that it covered the baby's head, protecting him from most of the moisture.

When her breathing came short, she stopped to rest for a few minutes. Intermingled with the pattering of raindrops, she thought she heard something else. An animal? A human? Raquel held her breath, listening, grateful that Abe slept soundly. *His* cry would alert everyone.

Her heart pounded as the crashing sound grew closer. Whatever it was, it headed straight for her.

Then something touched her shoulder, and Raquel whirled around with a scream. She came face-to-face with Helam.

All at once Abe started crying.

"Helam?" Raquel gasped. "How did you . . . ? When did—"

"What are you doing?" His breath was hot on her face. Beneath the hood, she could see his eyes boring into her.

She clutched Abe tightly and tried to hush him. As his cries faded, she continued to stare at her brother-in-law. "Do you never remove your hood?" She gestured to the trees. "It's the middle of the night, and you're away from all civilization."

He inhaled sharply, ignoring her criticism. "Where are you going?"

Desperation pounded against her chest. Had Gideon told him anything?

She took a step back, shaking her head. "No one is going to stop me, especially you."

"Raquel," he said in a quiet but piercing voice. "Don't do this."

She hesitated, surprised at his plea. "I have to, Helam." She bounced Abe, who had started to fuss again. "My son deserves to know his grandparents. It will bring my family together."

"You aren't seeking Abinadi?"

She looked away, unable to meet his gaze.

"You are." Helam's voice was calm, but he stepped toward her, as if ready to stop her flight.

Helam was a lot bigger than Abinadi. Both brothers towered over her, but Helam carried more bulk than her husband. There was no way she could outrun him. Plus, Abe's cries would give her away.

"Just leave us," she said, feeling panic rise in her chest. "Tell the others what I've done, if you must. But I . . . can't sleep, can't eat . . . can't breathe." She looked at him, her voice trembling. "I can't even pray anymore. I have to see my husband."

"I promised my brother I'd keep you safe." He patted Abe's back. "And that's what I'll do, whether here or in the city."

Raquel exhaled. "Really?" She thought she saw the shadow of a smile beneath his hood.

"Really."

* * *

The traveling is faster now, Raquel thought with Helam by her side. She felt grateful for the company. Besides, he insisted on carrying Abe, who at first protested but then warmed up as Helam made silly animal noises. Raquel smiled to herself as she listened to the two of them. If Helam would just rid himself of his reserve and his strange idea that no one could see his face, he'd make a great husband and father. Maybe he could talk Neriah out of her sour mood by proposing. He had many of the same attributes as

Abinadi, although Helam's personality was a notch higher in intensity. It probably came with being treated like an outcast for so long. But in Gideon's settlement, he was well respected.

They rested for a few hours in the early morning. Helam insisted on keeping watch while Raquel slept, Abe nestled in her arms. When she awoke, the foliage radiated a brilliant green. The rain had rejuvenated the plants and flowers. After Raquel nursed Abe while Helam kept a discreet distance, they were ready to travel again.

The day passed quickly as they made their way toward the city, hope brightening Raquel's steps. Since Helam had come along, she knew that Esther wouldn't worry so much and Gideon would be more likely to forgive her. They reached the outskirts of the city just as the sun settled against the western horizon.

They waited until it was nearly dark before continuing. She led Helam and Abe through the familiar streets, her eyes soaking in every feature, every road, every house. When she turned on the path to her former home, her step slowed. There was the courtyard where she'd spent day after day weaving. There was the beginning of the herbal gardens that wrapped around the back of the house. They had overgrown, and many of the plants could use a good pruning.

And there was the tree on the south side of the house that shaded her former room on the hottest of days. Everything seemed smaller, foreign somehow. She had left a girl and returned a woman.

"Let's go," she whispered to no one in particular. But Helam nodded and stepped forward to open the gate. Raquel reached out for Abe, taking him in her arms. "This is your grandparents' home," she said, trying to fend off the threatening tremble in her voice.

There was no use waiting any longer. It had been more than two years already. She crossed the courtyard and knocked boldly on the reed door.

One minute passed, then the door opened. Her mother stood there. Her swept-back hair had gray strands in it, but her face was as unlined as ever. She opened her mouth, staring at Raquel.

"Mother?" Raquel said. "I brought your grandson to meet you."

Itzel's mouth twitched.

Not sure if her mother would smile or frown, Raquel held up Abe, but he turned shyly away from the woman in the doorway.

"I can't believe it," her mother said, covering her mouth with her hands. Tears brimmed against her lashes. She reached out and touched the top of Abe's head. Then she looked at Raquel. "He's beautiful."

Raquel nodded, tears filling her eyes. Then, in one motion, both women stepped forward and fell into each other's arms, Abe between them.

This was the first time Raquel remembered her mother embracing her since childhood, and the first time she ever remembered seeing her mother cry for joy. After a moment, they released each other.

"Come in," Itzel said, glancing furtively behind Raquel. "The city is in unrest . . . It would not be good to have curious people see us."

Raquel and Helam stepped into the home, and Itzel led them to the common room.

Raquel set Abe on the floor where he immediately scooted around, although he kept one eye on his mother. "Is Father here?" Raquel asked, sitting on a low stool.

Itzel's expression tightened. "No. He comes home rarely." Her smile was watery, not quite reaching her eyes. "Always something at court." Her gaze traveled to Helam.

"This is my brother-in-law, Helam," Raquel said. "He traveled with me since . . . Abinadi is here in the city."

Something shifted in her mother's gaze, and she looked quickly away.

"What is it, Mother?" Raquel asked in a quiet but firm voice.

"I . . . it's Abinadi."

"Have you seen him?" Raquel asked, rising to her feet.

"No," her mother said. "But I've heard he's in prison."

The silence in the room was palpable. Even Abe's babbling didn't seem to reach Raquel's ears. "Prison?"

Helam was by her side immediately. "Your father might have enough influence to release him."

But Raquel was already shaking her head. "He wanted me dead, so why would he save my husband?" She looked at her mother. "Does Father know about my marriage?"

"I never told him," Itzel said, pain in her eyes. "He refuses to speak of you. It's as if you are—"

"Dead?" Raquel asked.

Her mother nodded.

Raquel brought a hand to her heart as if she could somehow stop it from breaking again. "What is my husband accused of?"

Itzel hesitated.

"Mother, tell me!" Raquel shouted, her voice startling Abe. He crawled over and latched onto her leg.

Itzel's eyes were wild, and her hands trembled, but she took a deep breath and said, "The servants say he's accused of treason. King Noah has gone into more than one fit of rage and demanded Abinadi's slaying. The servants say it is only a matter of time."

Raquel's knees gave out, and she sank to the floor. Helam knelt next to her as Itzel rushed forward and took her hands. "Oh, my dear. I am so sorry."

"What can we do?" Helam asked Itzel.

"It's best to do nothing," she whispered. "The longer he's in prison, the more time the king has to cool his temper."

Raquel tightened her hold on her mother's hands. There had to be something she could do. Anything.

Twenty-five

*He was oppressed, and he was afflicted . . . he is brought
as a lamb to the slaughter.*
(Isaiah 53:7)

Alma waited in the hills above the temple, hiding, watching as night fell upon the great city. It had been a full three days since he'd fled King Noah's court. The first day he'd run until he couldn't run any more. On the second, he chose a cave in the hills above the city. He spent the night there, but the next morning he felt compelled to return to the city of Nephi to start sharing Abinadi's teachings in secret. He worried about the preacher, and he didn't want him to die, but with each hour that passed, hope faded a little more. *It is up to me,* Alma thought, *to continue teaching Abinadi's message.*

Before returning to his mountain hideout, he had visited his home, unearthing all the gold and silver onties that he could pack with him. He'd also brought along writing supplies—ink, brush, and bark paper, feeling a need to write down the preacher's words.

From his perch, Alma wrote Abinadi's prophecies and teachings. Although it had been three days since he'd been cast out, it was as if he'd heard Abinadi's words only moments before. They flowed into his mind, almost faster than he could write them.

Darkness settled on the land, making writing nearly impossible, but he was too afraid to light a fire. He carefully wrapped his things and hid them, then settled down for the night. Alma didn't mind sleeping out in the open. It was cleansing to his soul to go from suffocating luxury to the simplicity of the forest. Here he would not be surprised by harlots, bullied by the king, or guilted into something by Amulon. Here, in the trees, he could think clearly. As darkness deepened, his thoughts returned again to Maia. He wished he could share the truth with her and teach her about the way things should be. The correct way to practice the law of Moses—what it truly represented—and the salvation that was promised to all who were faithful.

He hadn't seen her in weeks—not since that day in the throne room. For all he knew, she was in the king's favor and with child again. Perhaps if he could teach her parents, then someday the word would spread to her and her children. Alma sighed, content with his plan. *But are my motives pure?* he wondered. *Thou shalt not covet thy neighbor's wife.*

Alma sat up, his heart thudding. *I must repent. I must ask the Lord to forgive me.* He moved to his knee, bent his head, and began to pray. "O God of our righteousness, forgive me of my sins," his voice whispered, urgent in the stillness. The wind stirred the leaves of the surrounding trees as his voice grew louder, until his pleas reached to the heavens. "Forgive me for disobeying my parents." His voice cracked as his heart ached with sorrow. "I miss them so, but I have only let myself feel anger."

Hours passed as Alma prayed, one confession leading to another—the improper sacrificing, the coveting, the drunkenness, the women . . . Each agony slowly softened until peace flooded through every part of his body. When he lifted his head, he realized he had been curled into a ball on the ground and the night was nearly gone. The black sky had softened into gray; dawn was but a couple hours away.

He rose, limbs sore, throat parched, but he knew what he had to do. Regardless of the sentence given to the preacher, Alma needed to prove his sincere repentance through continuing the Lord's work. Alma had begged for mercy, he had promised to change, but he now needed to live worthy of the Lord's forgiveness. The Lord's work was far from finished. Alma wiped his eyes, focusing on the lightening sky. He knew the Lord wanted him to continue what Abinadi had started. There was no more questioning, nor more doubt. Just acceptance. Pure and simple.

But instead of standing in the marketplace and proclaiming repentance, Alma decided to continue to teach in secret, going from house to house, sharing the message with acquaintances, one by one. He would invite them to leave the city with him . . . but first they needed to find a place to set up camp. The place called Mormon was on the Lamanite border, a three-day journey. It was near a lake, and wild beasts roamed the surrounding forests.

For now, it might be the only option, he thought. After hiding his belongings, Alma vacated his hiding place and walked toward the city.

He kept a hood over his face as he quickly moved through the still-darkened streets. Maia's parents' home was in an older section of the city. Although her parents were not wealthy, they kept an ordered homestead. Alma paused before entering the small courtyard, seeing a light coming from within. Like most industrious families, this one rose and began its work before the light of day.

He was just a stone's throw from Maia's childhood home when someone rushed up behind him. Alma turned, his hand going to the dagger at his belt.

"Don't run," the man said. "I won't hurt you." He wore a simple cape, but the fine quality of the cloth was visible in the growing light. When he stopped in front of Alma to catch his breath, Alma stared. It was the king's son.

"Limhi?"

The young man took a shuddering breath. "I hoped to find you . . . I've been searching every morning and night." He looked around as if expecting someone to appear.

"What do you want?" Alma said, his grip firm on his dagger.

"I want to come with you—wherever you establish a new settlement," Limhi said. His light brown eyes were steady.

Alma grimaced. "How did you know?"

"I spoke to those you've taught. I believe. I want to be taught the truth as the Lord would have it. I want to escape the rule of my father."

Alma shook his head. "You have a kingdom to inherit."

A smile twisted Limhi's mouth. "What kingdom? When my father finishes his gluttonous reign, there will be nothing left."

Alma placed a hand on the young man's shoulder. "Remember Abinadi's prophecy to your father?"

Limhi's pale face grew even paler. "Yes," he whispered.

"Someday you'll have to take his place and become the king that the Lord needs you to be," Alma said.

Limhi lowered his gaze, varied emotions crossing his face. After several moments of silence, he looked at Alma again, his eyes wet. "You're right. Thank you. And may the Lord be with you." He turned and walked slowly away.

When the young king-to-be was out of sight, Alma proceeded along the path to Maia's home. He opened the gate and passed through, his nervousness translating into perspiration on his palms. He wiped his hands on his cape before quietly knocking.

Maia's father, Jachin, came to the entrance, raising his eyebrows when he saw who it was. "Come in," he whispered, gesturing Alma inside. "We wondered what had happened to you."

Maia's mother, Lael, entered the room wearing a cotton tunic and dusting maize flour from her hands. "Alma? Are you all right?"

He nodded. "I've been camping outside the city."

Lael touched his arm. "We heard about what you said to the court." She lowered her voice. "Do you really think the preacher is right?"

Warmth surged through Alma's chest. "Yes, I do. That's why I've come this morning. To share his message."

Husband and wife looked at each other with surprise, then back to Alma. Jachin lifted a shoulder. "Let's sit down, then."

But before Alma could begin, Lael said, "We must thank you for what you did for our daughter. You saved her life."

Alma's smile was brief. One good deed hardly balanced his numerous iniquities, although he couldn't help asking, "How is she?"

Jachin's mouth tugged into a tight line, and Lael said, "She's as well as can be expected. She thinks highly of you, though, and speaks of you."

Alma stared at Maia's mother. "She . . . does?" He looked at her father, who glanced away. "Do you see her often, then?"

Lael brought a hand to her chest and lowered her voice. "After the death of her . . . son . . . she became ill and came back home. The king wasn't exactly pleased, but eventually he was distracted with a new wife."

Jachin leaned forward. "No one at court knows about this, so if you don't mind . . ."

"Don't worry," Alma said. "I'm not privy to what goes on there anymore." His heart beat faster at the thought of Maia's near presence, but he was not here for her, but on the Lord's errand.

"That's a blessing," Lael said with a knowing smile, pulling him from his difficult thoughts.

Alma returned her smile. "Indeed it is. That's why I've come to your home. I feel that I can share the Lord's wishes without rebuke."

Jachin nodded slowly. "Both of us," he paused as he glanced at his wife, "desire to know more."

Alma leaned forward and linked his hands together. "First, I want to tell you about the death and resurrection of Christ." As he spoke, he was surprised at how easily the words came. It was as if the words of Abinadi had been stamped into his soul and all he had to do was open his mouth and release them. He continued to speak about the Lord's commandments and the plan of salvation. As the sun crested the horizon, the room slowly brightened.

A movement from the other side of the room caught Alma's attention. He paused, looking up.

Maia stood in the doorway, her dark copper hair unbound from having just awakened. She stepped into the room, her eyes on Alma.

He rose to his feet, suddenly breathless.

"You're safe," she said, her gaze pulling him in.

Alma exhaled slowly. He had prayed to forget her. Prayed to be forgiven for thinking of her. But the sight of her tore at his insides.

She walked toward him. Or was she floating like an angel? It was hard to tell.

"I've been listening from the other room," she said in a quiet voice, her eyes still on Alma. "I know that what you're teaching is true. You made the right decision to defend the preacher." Finally, she broke her gaze and looked at her parents. "Wherever he goes, I want to go."

Her father's mouth twisted. "Maia, dear, you have a husband."

Lael rose and stepped toward her daughter, touching Maia's arm. "You don't know what you are saying . . . You're married."

Alma looked between Maia and her parents. What was going on?

Lael turned to Alma. "She hasn't been well lately. Excuse us, please." She led Maia out of the room.

"What's wrong?" Alma asked Jachin as soon as they'd left.

Jachin shook his head, his eyes sad. "She thinks she's in love with you—that's what's wrong." He rubbed his beard. "Her mother keeps telling her that she needs to forget you. After all, she's married to the king. We could all be put to death."

Alma's mind spun in a thousand directions. Maia was in love with *him?* That was impossible. All the years . . . all the times that he'd tried to avoid her, ignore her, or drink enough wine to forget about her, telling himself it wasn't meant to be . . .

Alma looked at her father. "I'll never ask her to break her marriage vows. But for those who believe, I'm inviting them to come with me to Mormon. When everyone who wants to join us has gathered, we will travel together. The hunting grounds are three or four days' travel from here. There I can teach the fullness of the Lord's commandments, and through baptism you can enter into His holy covenant."

Jachin nodded. "Thank you." He embraced Alma. "Thank you for everything. My family and I will be there as soon as we can make arrangements."

Alma pulled away, feeling tears prick his own eyes. On one hand, he hoped that Maia's family would come to Mormon. On the other, he knew it would be impossible to forget about her if they did. He would have to be vigilant.

He left their home, knowing that he had run out of time to teach others today. He'd have to return again when it was dark.

"Alma."

He turned to see Maia coming around the side of the house. He looked for her mother, but Maia was alone.

"I'm sorry I startled you," she said.

He shook his head, too surprised to respond. Did her parents know she was out here speaking to him?

Maia crossed the courtyard. "My parents think I've gone mad."

He stared at her. She looked far from mad, and with his whole heart he hoped she wasn't. "How are you doing since the loss of your son?" he asked in a soft voice.

A faint smile touched her lips. "See? That's what I told my parents. You're just the type of man to always look out for someone else. Here you are, your life threatened by the king, on the run . . . yet you ask how *I* am. I am so grateful for what you did for me, and I think I understand why."

Alma exhaled, starting to feel lost in her eyes. He took a deep breath and stepped back. He had to be strong. He had asked God's forgiveness for his feelings toward a married woman—he couldn't let them creep back into his heart now.

"Alma," she said again, "after the death of my son, I left the king under a pretense of illness. Even my parents believed I was ill."

He looked at her, astonished. "Why?" he barely breathed.

"I'd rather ask the king for a divorce than continue living at the palace in such degradation, my heart dying little by little each day. And there's another reason," she said, then hesitated, looking at her hands. "I could no longer live with the king when I love another man." She looked up, her eyes moist.

Alma opened his mouth, but he was too stunned to speak.

"Please don't worry about me, Alma. I'm not asking you to love me." She looked away, her voice quiet. "Whether or not the king grants a divorce, nothing would make me happier than to see you marry and have your own children." She blinked rapidly, as if trying to hold back tears. "I know there is no future for us together, and I'll never stand in the way of your happiness."

"Maia, don't risk your life," Alma said, shaking his head. "The king would never grant you a divorce—his temper is too fierce. You must not make such a request or your very life will be in danger."

"Then I will be free of the king whether through divorce or through death." She swiped at a stray tear on her cheek and met his gaze. "I cannot follow the Lord's teachings and live in the king's court at the same time. Leaving that lifestyle is the only way I can live as the Lord wants me to." With a trembling smile, she turned from him.

"Please," Alma said. "Live outside of the palace if you must, but don't incur the king's wrath."

She stopped, her back still to him. "If you wish it. You once risked your life for me . . . I will not make your sacrifice in vain." She glanced a final time over her shoulder. "I'll not seek a divorce. But somehow, I'm going to make it to Mormon." Then she disappeared around the side of the house.

Alma stood there for a moment, heart pinging. Maia would be safe. Married—but safe from the king. His heart would be filled just knowing that. He left the courtyard, his purpose renewed. He'd find a way to free Abinadi.

* * *

I'm giving up on trying to sleep, Raquel decided. She'd been awake most of the night, feeling absolutely sick. Now her mother's and Helam's voices rose and fell in the next room, intermingled with exclamations about Abe. If Abinadi hadn't been in prison, everything would seem so normal.

But it was far from normal. Raquel hadn't come all this way just to wait inside her parents' home. She dressed quickly and walked into the cooking room. Helam and her mother looked up.

Raquel's expression said it all, and Helam rose and crossed to her. "You're not going."

"Yes, I am." She bit her lip. "The court will be entertained and distracted by me for a short time, and while the king is mulling over my punishment, you can get Abinadi and our son far away. I'd rather trade my life for his . . ."

"No," her mother said. She bounced Abe on her knee as he laughed, but the concern in her eyes ran deep.

Raquel took a deep breath. She was terrified to go to court, but she saw no other option. She crossed to Abe and kissed the top of his head. Then she grabbed him and squeezed tight. "I love you, dearest."

She gave him back to her mother, trying not to think whether or not she'd see her son again. Then she walked out of the room and down the hall.

"Raquel," Helam said in a quiet voice. She ignored him. He followed her into the courtyard, but she continued walking.

Helam fell into step beside her. *He's oddly comforting, yet exasperating too,* Raquel thought. It seemed they had stubbornness in common. She hoped their stubbornness could have enough combined strength to release her husband from prison.

As they neared the palace, Raquel was surprised at the crowds of people. It was still relatively early in the morning, and the market should be just opening. But instead, numerous people milled about, the air charged with excitement.

Raquel's heart sank as she overheard conversation after conversation. "The preacher" had been brought before the king again. He was inside the temple walls this very moment. Raquel looked at the temple just beyond the crowd. It was imposing, intimidating. Her heart ached—she was so close, yet so far. Threading her way through the crowd, she sensed Helam following. Finally, she reached the perimeter of the grounds that skirted the stone temple steps. Several guards stood at the top in front of the massive doors, waving people away. No one was allowed to climb the steps.

The crowd continued to mill about, speaking in hushed tones. Some stood still, as if trying to listen to what went on inside the walls. Raquel stared at all the people in amazement. Why were they so interested in the fate of one preacher? Certainly he'd said something to stir their interest— and perhaps their hearts.

Helam hovered close by, his ever-hooded gaze watchful, protective. Suddenly the doors burst open. What Raquel saw next made her want to scream.

Abinadi staggered through the doors, guards flanking his sides. They held his arms and one guard threw a rope around his neck, tightening it for control. But Abinadi didn't flinch. His expression was resolute, his gaze straight ahead.

Raquel pushed through the remaining crowd, shouting, "Abinadi!"

Helam immediately grabbed her and covered her mouth. "Quiet, or they'll bind you too."

She struggled against his grasp, but Helam held firm. Then the priests came out of the temple. "Father," she whispered. Amulon wore all his finery, magnificent in a terrible way. Raquel turned to Helam. "Look at him. He's positively gloating."

Helam gripped her hand, and Raquel felt the tension radiating from him.

Abinadi was shoved down the stairs, and the guards laughed. Around them the people murmured, some of them calling insults. "Who is being punished now, Preacher?" someone shouted.

"It appears as if *you* are the one heading for destruction, not *us!*" another man yelled.

Raquel's heart raced. How could these people say such things? The crowd jostled for position.

One of the guards bound Abinadi, winding rope around his arms and legs. Raquel was surprised at how much rope they used—twice as much as seemed necessary. She lurched forward. If only she could reach him . . . beg for his life. Begging had worked time and time again in the stories Abinadi had told her about Nephi and his wife.

Even Helam couldn't hold her back this time. She escaped his grip and stumbled through the remaining crowd. "Abinadi!" she screamed.

He turned his head slowly, and their eyes met. His eyes widened in recognition.

She staggered the last few steps out into the open and threw herself against him. "Take me!" she shouted. "Take me instead!"

Hands grabbed her, yanking her off her husband.

"Raquel," Abinadi said, his tone anguished. Then it turned gentle, full of understanding. "It is the Lord's will."

"No!" Raquel struggled against the guards who were dragging her away.

"Release her," a voice commanded. Immediately she was dropped to the ground. Looking up, she saw her father standing over her.

"Leave now, or I will not be responsible for the consequences," Amulon said.

Raquel scrambled to her feet, facing her father. "Abinadi is my husband. By allowing him to die, you kill your own family . . ." Her voice shook. "We have a son—you have a grandson."

A slit of softness opened in her father's eyes, but just as quickly, it closed. "You are no longer part of my life, nor your husband, or whatever children you may have." He leaned close and hissed in her ear. "Remember, woman, *you* are the one who made that choice."

He stepped away and nodded to the waiting guards. They grabbed her again and carried her into the crowd. She struggled to free herself, but they had no problem restraining her. Helam ran after her and tried to fight off the guards. Raquel screamed as one of them released her and lashed out at Helam.

Then the guard suddenly fell away. Both guards stared at Helam, their mouths hanging open. It was then Raquel saw that Helam's hood had slipped off.

His skin hung in pink folds on one half of his face, the other half bare skin that stretched so tight it seemed that his bones protruded. He had no eyebrows, no eyelashes, just fleshy sockets surrounding his eyes. The deformity of his face was enough to cause the crowd to shrink away from him. The guards also backed away. Neither of them wanted to go against a man so large and hideous.

Raquel heard shouting, and it took her a moment to realize it wasn't because of Helam—a group of guards holding flaming torches were heading straight for Abinadi.

Helam put his hood back on, then pulled Raquel to his side, trying to cover her eyes, but she shook him free.

The crowd fell back as the torture began, some turning away, others watching in fascination. Raquel stood dazed. She had a clear view of her husband. Guards surrounded the area so that no one could interfere. One of the guards hit Abinadi across his shoulders with a burning torch. Then another guard stepped forward and started striking his legs.

At the top of the temple steps, King Noah watched, sitting on a bier, his arms folded across his chest as he nodded. Raquel's father moved to the king's side. Surrounding them, the high priests in all their decorum, watched. Then someone emerged from the crowd, throwing off a dark cloak. He shouted above the beatings, "Enough!"

Raquel's heart leapt. Someone would put this madness to a stop. She'd find a way to rescue her husband.

"Well, well, Alma. You couldn't stay away long, could you?" Amulon called over the exclamations of the other high priests.

The king glared at the former priest.

Several guards started moving toward Alma, but he didn't seem deterred. "The preacher is right." He took a few steps away from the guards, keeping his gaze on the high priests. "Each of you was there. Each of you felt the power of the Lord. How can you deny it?"

Raquel watched their expressions change from surprise to hostility. Her father came down the stairs and stopped in front of Alma, putting a hand on his shoulder as if they were good friends. "You don't want to do this," Amulon said.

Alma jerked away. "Everything the preacher said is found in the holy scriptures. How can he be accused of treason? It is we who should be accused of blasphemy against God!"

Noah raised his hand, his face red with fury. "Seize him!"

Guards scurried up the steps, but Alma lunged away and ran toward the crowd. The guards gave chase. In her heart, Raquel pleaded for Alma's escape. It seemed that at least one person believed her husband.

"I want the preacher dead now!" the king roared, his voice silencing the crowd.

Raquel struggled to be free of Helam, but he held her back. He gripped her tightly as the guards advanced on Abinadi once again.

One of the guards kicked him in the stomach, and Abinadi gasped for air. The guards beat him with the flaming torches until his clothing caught fire. He cried out, "Even as you do this to me, so it will come to pass that your seed will cause many to suffer as I do, even the pains of death by fire."

A shudder ran through Raquel. Sobs wracked her body.

"You will be driven and scattered as a wild flock is driven by ferocious beasts," Abinadi shouted. "You will be hunted and taken by your enemies, and then you will suffer even as I suffer."

The crowd started chanting, "Kill him! Kill him!"

Raquel's stomach clenched, and she fought off nausea. Helam drew her tighter against him, protecting her from the jostling crowd.

But Abinadi's voice curtailed all. "God executes vengeance on those that destroy his people! O God, receive my soul!"

Raquel caught a glimpse of Abinadi collapsing to the ground, flames consuming his clothing. "O God," she moaned, "take my soul with my husband's." She sank to her knees, feeling the air go out of her. Helam's arms encircled her as he lifted her.

"Take me to him," she sobbed.

"He's gone, Raquel," Helam said, his voice cracking. "We need to leave here. Think of Abe."

"Please," she said, her voice barely above a whisper.

She walked with Helam as he pushed his way through the onlookers. The chanting continued, pulsing through her ears, although her husband's body was clearly no longer moving.

The guards formed a barrier between the crowd and Abinadi's burning body. As if sensing she wanted to break through, Helam held her firmly. Her legs gave out, and she clung to Helam, watching the flames twist grotesquely along Abinadi's skin.

She shuddered. How could this have happened to such a good, sweet man? Nausea raced through her, and she covered her mouth, hating the entire city, the king, her father. "Why?" she whispered. Then louder, "Why him, O Lord?"

Helam's strong arms started to pull her away.

"No," she screamed. "I will not leave him." She clawed at Helam to let her go—she cared little what the guards did to her now.

But he warded off her blows and continued pulling her through the crowd until she could no longer fight. Finally, she collapsed, exhausted.

Twenty-six

We have redemption through his blood, the forgiveness of sins,
according to the riches of his grace.
(Ephesians 1:7)

It was some time before Raquel comprehended that Helam was carrying her through the streets. Everything was a blur. She couldn't get the horrifying image of her husband's death from her mind. Bile rose in her throat, and she turned away from Helam. He seemed to sense her need and set her down.

She fell to her knees, wishing she could purge more than her stomach. Time and time again her stomach revolted, until she was almost too weak to walk.

When they reached her parents' home, Raquel was shaking all over. Helam carried her into one of the bed chambers and set her down on the platform bed.

Her mother hovered above, her image fading in and out.

"We need to recover his body," Raquel said in a rasping voice, reaching for her mother.

Itzel clung to her hand. "Helam has gone with silver to bribe the guards."

"Silver?" Raquel said, not fully understanding what her mother meant.

"Yes," her mother said. "Your father will be paying for the burial whether he knows it or not." She lowered her voice. "You need to leave here as soon as possible. If your father returns . . ."

Raquel tried to sit up, but her head spun. "I told him about Abe, but still he allowed Abinadi to be killed—" A sob choked off her sentence. "I can't believe he's gone."

Her mother pulled Raquel into her arms. "Shhh. All the more reason to leave this place. When Helam returns, we'll have to be ready to go."

We? Her mother was coming too? Raquel must have heard wrong. But her mind was too numb to make sense of it. She closed her eyes, thinking of her beloved husband. The way he so readily accepted her from the first time she brought him herbs. The way he looked at her when they were married. The way he loved her. The way he understood. The way he served God.

She had always known he had been too good, too pure. Every action had been selfless. He had loved beyond a capacity that she could comprehend. And now she was left alone.

Raquel turned onto her stomach and moaned. Why did he have to die? He'd done nothing wrong. He only followed God's commandment to preach. She pressed her hands against her eyes, trying to block out his suffering, his cries. No one deserved that.

Fresh sobs racked her body as she thought of the pain he'd endured. Suddenly his image appeared in her mind—when he came out of the temple, tied like a helpless animal. His face had been so calm, so serene. And when he saw her, he'd simply said, "It is the Lord's will." How did he know?

Raquel sat up in the bed, astonishment pulsing through her. Had her husband known he was going to die before he'd left? Abinadi *had* known. And had accepted it. She buried her face in her hands. But she couldn't accept it. How did he expect her to go on without him?

Suddenly, Helam was in the room, his arms around her. She leaned against his chest and let the tears come. Her husband had told Helam to watch out for her . . . Did Helam know what would happen? Did Gideon know? She thought of Esther, of Ben, of her own son . . . How would she tell them?

She didn't know how much time had passed before she realized Helam was speaking to her. "We don't have much time. We need to leave right away."

She tried to focus on the sounds he made. "I can get up," she said.

Strong hands helped her, and she took several deep breaths to steady herself. When she walked out of the room, Helam following, her mother was dressed for travel and held Abe in her arms.

Raquel crossed to Abe and clung to him. She kissed his cheeks, over and over, wetting them with her tears. "I'm so sorry, baby," she whispered.

After a moment, Helam guided Raquel outside and through the courtyard where a bier sat. Several rugs were piled in it.

Raquel stopped, gripping Helam's arm. "Is that . . . him?"

He nodded.

In silence, the small group left the courtyard, Helam and one of Itzel's servants carrying the bier holding Abinadi's body. Raquel walked arm in arm with her mother, each step more painful than the last. She wondered if she were in a dream—a horrible dream.

Abe babbled as if nothing had happened. His innocence gave Raquel courage as they kept moving and skirted the city until they reached the hills above the temple. Helam found a small grove surrounded by thick foliage.

When the servant left, Helam cleared an area, pulling up plants by their roots. Then Raquel watched her mother and Helam gather rocks. She kept an eye on Abe, but her gaze was drawn again and again to the bier that held her husband's body.

Her throat constricted when Itzel came toward her and gathered Abe in her arms. "We're ready . . . when you are."

She nodded and stood.

Helam picked up Abinadi's covered body and carried him to the spot he'd cleared. He set the body next to the pile of rocks that would create the tomb. Raquel stepped forward and placed a handful of flowers on top of her husband's enshrouded body. Itzel followed, then Helam.

For several moments, the three of them stood together, staring at the covered form. Helam cleared his throat. "Abinadi was the only man I knew who had such absolute faith in the Lord. He would walk to the ends of the earth for his beliefs."

"And he did," Raquel said in a quiet voice.

Helam nodded. "He died because he refused to deny his knowledge that the Lord is the only way to salvation, even if it would have saved his life."

Raquel took a deep breath. Then it came. The feeling she'd been waiting for since Abinadi had left the elders' settlement. Warmth surged in her chest, spreading through her torso, then to the rest of her body. Peace whispered to her heart, and she *knew*. She knew that her husband was in the arms of the Lord. His salvation had been made sure. His death had not been overlooked.

Raquel sank to her knees. Then she leaned over the covered body and pressed her cheek against the rug. "Good-bye, dear husband. I will see you in heaven."

Her mother and Helam both knelt beside her, each taking one of her hands. And then Raquel wept.

* * *

Alma kept to the edge of the forest as he walked. The river twisted and turned before him, leading him on a long-ago familiar path—to his childhood home. He didn't know what to expect upon seeing it, or if it even still existed, but he wasn't prepared when he cleared the final field.

His former home was only a shadow of what it had once been. Stately in its day, it had now fallen into ruin. The heavy timbers that had held up the intricately thatched roof had toppled. No one had bothered to make repairs or take over the homestead. It was as if it had been . . . forgotten.

Alma took a few more steps toward the decrepit structure as a flood of memories swept over him—the last being his father arriving home, seriously injured. Alma blinked back the sudden burn in his eyes as he walked to where the door had once been. Grass had grown wild, blending the neglected floor with the adjacent field.

The wind bent the tips of the long grass at his feet, and Alma felt compelled to kneel. He bowed his head, thinking of his parents resting beneath the home. It had been more than ten years since their deaths, yet the same sense of acute loneliness he'd had then drove into Alma's heart.

"Father, I'm finally following your counsel . . . after all these years," he whispered into the stillness. "And Mother, someday I hope to be the man you raised me to be."

He rose to his feet and took one last lingering look at the tumbled walls. The breeze picked up and stirred his clothing, surrounding him with a gentle caress, as if to say all was well.

Alma turned away, his heart peaceful, yet regretful of so many years lost. So many years living in anger and denial. Wasted.

He lifted his head and trudged uphill, skirting the city of Nephi until he reached the base of the first hill where he'd hidden his things. As he hiked up the steep terrain, he stopped every so often to rest. Then, for the first time in more than two years, he allowed his mind to open as he thought about Maia.

She loves me.

It made his breath come shorter than usual as he hiked. *If* the king were to grant a divorce . . .

Alma shook his head. He had too much work to do and couldn't put energy into *ifs*. He paused, looking over the valley that extended below him. He couldn't allow himself to dwell on Maia right now. Or ever.

Alma took a deep breath and knelt on the rooted ground. "O Lord, this I leave in Thy hands. The love I have for Maia, I give unto Thy care. I will follow Thy will in all things. Amen."

He rose, somewhat unsteady. The only way he could focus on continuing Abinadi's work was to give his other burdens to the Lord. He continued to move up the hillside, turning his mind to the work ahead of him.

His short experience had already taught him that he would gain plenty of teachable people by word-of-mouth. In just one day he'd visited several families who'd been referred by each other, and before he knew it, yet another entire family had agreed to come to Mormon. After a quick estimation, Alma calculated that at least twenty people had committed so far.

After he had scouted an area for them to gather in Mormon, he planned to return and preach in the homes each night, quietly sharing the Lord's message with as many as would accept it.

And Abinadi's death would not be in vain.

Alma reached the leveled ground and started walking through the trees, thinking about teaching the people in secret. It was the least he could do for the preacher who had changed his life. Alma wished he hadn't been so stubborn for so long. He could have found all of this years ago, but instead, he'd ignored the sweetness of the Spirit.

Voices reached Alma, and he hesitated. The sounds came from the clearing near his cave hideout.

He crept closer, straining to listen. The sound of a small child's cry reached his ears. *That rules out Lamanite warriors,* he thought. He drew closer and was surprised to hear a woman's voice. Feeling more bold, Alma walked to the edge of the clearing.

A man and two women, one holding a child, stood around a pile of rocks.

Alma furrowed his brow. It appeared they stood over a hastily made tomb. The people in the city buried their dead beneath their houses . . . a mounded stone tomb was something that only their ancestors had used.

The man turned, and Alma drew back. The man was extremely tall, wore a hooded robe, and looked quite menacing.

Then the women turned, and both of them gasped.

"Alma?" the younger woman said.

How does she know my name?

She stepped forward, balancing the child on her hip. "I prayed that you'd escape." She offered a faint smile, tears forming in her eyes. "Thank you for trying to change the king's mind."

Then Alma realized who was buried beneath the rocks. "Abinadi?"

The three adults nodded.

A reverent hush fell over them as he walked into the clearing. He took a few hesitant steps toward the tomb, then he sank to his knees in front of the mound of rocks. He stared for a while before speaking quietly. "His words touched my heart. I didn't believe at first . . . My father tried to teach me when I was a child, but later I blamed God for my parents' deaths."

Someone touched his shoulder. "But when Abinadi came into the temple," Alma said, "I felt the Lord's presence as if He Himself had entered the room. I couldn't remain silent any longer."

The younger woman knelt beside him, wiping at her damp cheeks. Her voice trembled as she spoke. "My husband would have done anything for the Lord. Even though it meant losing his life."

Alma looked at the young widow in her grief, marveling at her strength. "I am continuing Abinadi's mission by teaching the people in secret. I've invited the believers to leave the city and join me in Mormon—the hunting grounds near the border." He looked up at the other woman and the hooded man.

"My brother would be pleased," the man said.

Alma rose and stared at the man's shadowed face. "You're his brother?"

The man nodded.

"This is Helam," the young woman said, standing. "And my mother, Itzel. My name is Raquel."

Alma's eyes widened. "Itzel . . . Raquel? You're Amulon's family."

Itzel nodded.

"I—I am so sorry about all the pain." He glanced at the tomb again. "I wish his message could have softened Amulon's heart too."

Raquel stepped toward him, her tears coming again, and placed a hand on his arm. "My father has made up his mind. But for me . . . and my mother . . . we hope to make a new beginning."

"Tell us more about this place called Mormon," Helam said.

Alma looked at them in surprise. "There are about twenty people who plan to join me there. I expect more to come as they receive the word of God into their hearts. I will travel there soon and prepare a place for the others. I don't think this location will be safe for long." He glanced about the area. "The king's guards spread out more with each day."

Helam nodded. "We're leaving here soon to return to our settlement. I expect many will join you in Mormon. Our leader is Gideon, but we've struggled to build a settlement. Perhaps if we joined you . . ."

"I've heard of Gideon—he was greatly respected by my father." Alma looked at Raquel, then back to Helam. "It would be an honor to have people such as you join us in Mormon."

"Consider it done," Helam said, clapping a hand on Alma's shoulder.

The young child babbled in Raquel's arms so she turned him to face Alma. "This is my son, Abe."

Alma's eyes started to burn. "Abinadi's son? May I?"

Raquel nodded as she bit her trembling lip, and Alma reached for the child.

Abe didn't protest as Alma took him, but merely gazed at the stranger. "It's an honor to meet you, Abe." Alma's voice caught, and he waited a moment for his emotions to calm. Then he kissed the boy on the top of the head and handed him back to Raquel.

"I look forward to seeing each of you in Mormon," Alma said. He then bade the small group farewell, leaving them to their privacy.

As he walked, his heart felt as if it would burst. The compassion he'd seen in Raquel's eyes made him feel even closer to the Lord. If a woman who'd just lost her husband didn't judge him for his past or treat him with bitterness, he knew that it was possible for him to help many others convert to Christ.

* * *

The days passed swiftly as Alma traveled. On the third day, he arrived at the place called Mormon. Three massive mountains flanked a large lake that stretched across the entire valley. White ibis birds dipped and screeched above the rippling water, while a black-beaked jabiru stalked the shoreline. Alma turned from the lake and walked along the shoreline, looking for a place to rest for the night. It was evident that no one lived in the immediate area, good news for those who would settle here.

Alma paused when he saw a freshwater spring leading into the lake. It looked quite shallow—perfect for baptisms. He crossed to the grassy shore-line and felt the temperature. Mild. Alma stood for a moment, overlooking the spring. Clumps of trees surrounded the water, providing good places to conceal himself from the king's guards, should they choose to come this far. This place was not frequented by either the Nephites or Lamanites because of the wild cats and beasts that roamed through the forests. Coming here to hunt was usually a great challenge or a dare—something that King Noah might do with a full hunting party to protect him. But Alma felt confident that the Lord would watch over His disciples here.

Alma didn't know how long they'd be able to live here, but at least the lake provided a place for baptisms. He folded his arms over his chest. The quiet was interrupted only by the buzzing of insects and flittering of birds. He'd never felt so alone, yet so fulfilled. The shadows around him length-ened, and he realized he had only a few hours before the sun set. In the morning, he'd begin the trek back to the city of Nephi and continue his preaching.

He found a place to sit within a thicket of trees. If anyone came, he could quickly conceal himself. But in the meantime, he gazed over the water, watching the ever-changing colors in the clear surface. The blues, violets, and greens reminded him of the dresses that Maia wore. He thought of the times he'd seen her upset and injured because of the king. She deserved so much more.

He dropped his head into his hands, wishing it could have all been different—Abinadi spared, Maia protected from the king . . . But Alma couldn't change it now. All he could do was move forward and be the person he was born to be. After years of stubbornness, his heart was finally in the right place. Tears rose in his eyes as he realized his mother and father would be pleased with who he was becoming.

Alma lifted his head and gazed across the water as the sinking sun cast its golden net over the ripples. Golden like a new promise. Golden like the forgiveness he'd received.

He rose to his feet, warmth progressing through his body. Here, in this quiet land by the Waters of Mormon, the true believers of God would join him soon.

Here, in this preserved stretch of country, he'd bring people unto Christ.

It was time to finish Abinadi's work.

Chapter Notes

PROLOGUE

Scriptures Referenced: Mosiah 16:17; 17:7–12

A cape was a common article of clothing for the Mesoamerican people. John L. Sorenson says that the cape was worn by "tying the upper corners into a knot or wrapping a kiltlike piece around the body then tucking in a corner or the end at the belt line" (*Images of Ancient America: Visualizing Book of Mormon Life,* 93). Cotton was worn by people of rank, while commoners wore clothes of coarser fibers such as agave or bark cloth.

Mesoamericans used obsidian extensively for tools and decorations. Swords were made with obsidian blades mounted into a wooden base, which became a deadly serrated weapon. In Alma 47:5, the Lamanites flee to Onidah—a place where an obsidian outcrop exists (see *Images,* 53).

Certainly the Nephites and Lamanites lived in the heart of Mayan country and civilization. The Mayas occupied various colonies throughout Mesoamerica well before Lehi's arrival. Idol worship was an integral part of the Mayas' religious structure. We hear mention of idol worship in the Book of Mormon era as early as 420 BC by Enos, son of Jacob (see Enos 1:20). Michael D. Coe points out that the Mayas believed in the underworld as the final place of rest (see *The Maya,* 218).

Trees are an established sacred symbol in Mesoamerican culture. The ceiba tree was very useful in Mesoamerican life. It was revered by ancient Mayas, who considered the ceiba to be the center of the universe. Often temple complexes or plazas were built around the tree. The ceiba is mainly cultivated for its fiber that resembles cotton, called kapok, which is used for making floss and stuffing bedding and upholstery, etc.

Sorenson documents the excavation of the city of El Mirador by BYU archaeologist Ray Matheny. El Mirador sits near the northern border of

Guatemala. It reached its peak around 200 BC and was known as one of the most spectacular cities in Mesoamerica. The architecture was a system of temples, civic buildings, and homes (see *Images,* 103). Joseph L. Allen points out that the Nephi–Limhi time period (578–121 BC) is the late Preclassic period of Kaminaljuyú. A series of impressive mounds has been uncovered dating to this era—in what may have been temple structures or something else equally impressive (see *Sacred Sites: Searching for Book of Mormon Lands,* 30–31).

Throughout ancient America, tributes and taxes supported governments. People such as priests, archivists, military leaders, clerks, and engineers received income through government taxes on the common people. Taxes, or tributes, may have been in the form of labor, food, clothing, liquor, dry goods, or precious materials (see *Images,* 114).

CHAPTER 1

Scriptures Referenced: Mosiah 9; 11:14

In Mosiah 9, we learn that Zeniff travels back to the land of Nephi around 165 BC. Author S. Kent Brown notes that this places the reign of Zeniff's son, King Noah, between 140 BC and 121 BC, and Abinadi's first stint of preaching about 130 BC. (See *Voices from the Dust,* 217).

Prior to King Zeniff's reign, the city of Nephi was possessed by the Lamanites. When Zeniff arrived, he struck a deal with the king of the Lamanites to possess the land of Lehi-Nephi and the land of Shilom. Years passed and war became inevitable. Eventually Zeniff was able to hold onto the city of Nephi. This is the kingdom that his son, Noah, inherited, although it was threatened by Lamanites pressing along the borders (Mosiah 9–10).

Horses are mentioned in the Book of Mormon (2 Ne. 12:7; 3 Ne. 3:22), but horse bones discovered haven't been conclusively identified as having been from pre-Columbian times (see *Journal of Book of Mormon Studies,* 10:1 [2001], 76–77). Given that we aren't sure what type of horses were used, I focused on known breeds of pack animals; such beasts of burden used throughout Mesoamerica include the alpaca or llama. Sorenson points out that "most goods were moved on human backs. The rest went by boat." Even after the Spaniards brought over large animals, the Mesoamericans continued to transport sizable loads, up to one hundred pounds, on their bent backs. "The load was held in place by a band across the forehead. They often traveled at a near trot and for up to ten hours a day" (*Images*, 56).

Maize, or corn, was an agricultural staple throughout Mesoamerica. Most of the population lived in villages surrounding the main cities so that they could be close to their farms. It was the duty of the men to prepare the land for planting. They hand-cut trees and bushes, then burned the dried debris, using the ash as fertilizer. Corn, beans, and squash were often planted together since they matured at different rates. A woman could expect to spend time every day grinding cornmeal and making foods such as tortillas or tamales (see *Images*, 32–33).

Freestanding looms or back-strap looms were used by the ancient Mesoamerican women. Weaving was a revered talent and considered an integral skill among the women. Even as late as the Aztec period, Sorenson notes, "the life of a woman from birth to death centered around the production of beautiful, well-made textiles" (*Images*, 92). The women turned fibers such as cotton, henequen (agave plant), bast (vegetable fiber), and bark into cloth. In Helaman 6:13, we learn that "their women did toil and spin, and did make all manner of cloth, of fine-twined linen and cloth of every kind, to clothe their nakedness."

In King Noah's time, the vineyards and wine that are named in Mosiah 11:15 refer to the agave plant from which an alcoholic beverage—pulque—is made. Wines were also made from bananas, palm, and fermented tree bark (see *An Ancient America Setting for the Book of Mormon*, 186–87). The agave nectar is harvested from a hollow that is scooped out. The nectar then ferments, resulting in a sweeter and thicker juice.

Plants used for herbal remedies throughout Guatemala include orange leaves brewed into a tea to treat the common cold, custard apple leaves made into a poultice to treat broken bones, sap from the aloe vera plant used to heal sunburn or skin abrasions, tea made from the hibiscus flower used to alleviate cold symptoms, and leaves from the wild tobacco plant used to treat headaches and to ease pain.

CHAPTER 2

Scripture Referenced: Mosiah 24:32

Singing and dancing were an important part of the Mayan culture, as well as present in Nephite and Lamanite practices (see 1 Ne. 18:9; Mosiah 20:1). Songs were sung or chanted on important occasions, including songs of "love and flirtation." Mayan art and sculpture depict dancing and musical instruments. Sorenson notes that the most common musical instruments were drums, scrapers, and rattles. Others included whistles, flutes, panpipes, horns, and wood and shell trumpets (see *Images,* 178–79).

During the late Preclassic period, the Maya highlands and Pacific Coast experienced magnificent cultural growth with "massive temple centers" rising up from the jungle floor (see *The Maya,* 76). In Kaminaljuyú, a monument depicts "three successive rulers seated on thrones, each flanked by kneeling captives; all have different headdresses, apparently emblems of their names" (ibid). This parallels the judgment seats in King Noah's court: "And the seats which were set apart for the high priests, which were above all other seats, he did ornament with pure gold" (Mosiah 11:11).

King Noah "built many elegant and spacious buildings. . . . He also built him a spacious palace, and a throne in the midst thereof" (Mosiah 11:8–9). This depiction is similar to Coe's observations: "Temples arranged around plazas, construction with limestone and plaster, apron moldings and frontal stairways on pyramids, tomb building, and frescoes with naturalistic subjects" (*The Maya,* 84).

Chapter 4

Scriptures Referenced: Alma 1:15; 2:1; 14:8, 17; 62:9; 3 Nephi 5:4

We know that the Nephites and Lamanites had many weapons of war— bows, arrows, swords, cimeters, clubs, and slings (see Mosiah 9:16). Sorenson explains that the obsidian-edged sword (*macuahuitl*) was the most fearsome weapon. Its owner could sever the head of a horse. Mesoamericans also used axes, spears (*atlatl*), and armor such as helmets, shields, and breastplates. Sorenson notes that "the most common type [of armor] seems to have been a garment composed of two layers of cloth, quilted, between which salt, kapok, or some other buffering substance had been placed" (*Images,* 130). Matthew Roper notes that "all weapons cited in the Book of Mormon text have parallels among Mesoamerican armaments" ("Swords and Cimeters in the Book of Mormon," *Journal of Book of Mormon Studies,* 8:1 [1999], 43). These similarities would also explain the scripture in Alma 24:12: "Since God hath taken away our stains, and our swords have become bright, then let us stain our swords no more with the blood of our brethren." Obsidian is known for its fine luster—or brightness. And blood would stain the wooden blade of an obsidian-edged sword or a sword made only of wood (ibid, 39).

Most homes throughout Mesoamerica were made of sticks, reeds, or cornstalks, with thatch roofs. Sorenson notes that "the spacing between the sticks might be left open, allowing smoke from the cooking fire to disperse" (*Images*, 60). If the temperature was cool, mud was plastered over the sticks for added protection from the elements. Homes of the wealthy consisted of a home with a courtyard and elaborate gardens (ibid).

Tortillas, tamales, squash, and boiled beans were the most common foodstuffs in Mesoamerica. Roots such as manioc, jicama, and sweet potatoes were also consumed. Fruits such as cherries and guavas, tomatoes and avocados were also common (see *Images*, 36). Maize was the staple of all Mesoamerican diets, although other grains were grown and consumed, such as wheat, barley, neas, and sheum (see Mosiah 9:9). Allen points out that all of the crops mentioned in Mosiah 9:9 are indigenous to Guatemala. Interestingly enough, the corn was planted first, then the beans, so the cornstalks could serve as beanpoles (see *Sacred Sites*, 33–34).

Sweet foods were reserved for special occasions. Honey was a rare treat and was combined with peanuts, amaranth seeds, or popped corn to make delicacies (see *Images*, 45). The cacao bean was also a luxury. Sorenson says it was used as a "form of currency, [and] consumption of chocolate was mainly limited to people of wealth." The cacao tree grows in the foothills, and the seeds from the cacao fruit are ground into powder to make chocolate (ibid, 42).

Prisons and prisoners are both mentioned throughout the Book of Mormon text (see Alma 14:17; 3 Ne. 5:4). Sorenson explains that there were also routine executions (see Alma 2:1; 62:9) and ritual executions (see Alma 1:15; 14:8). Some of the ritual executions included the burning of victims, hanging them from the top of a tree, or casting them into wild animal dens (see *Images*, 117).

CHAPTER 5

Scriptures Referenced: Mosiah 11:11–12

The tradition of juggling traces back to ancient times. Sorenson reminds us that "under the Mosaic law the Israelites assembled frequently to celebrate certain Sabbaths with sacrifices and feasting" (*Images*, 101).

Community games that were played included a basic ball game and the patolli game (ibid).

Routine sacrifices throughout Mesoamerica included blood sacrifices such as animal and human blood (autosacrificing, or removing the head or heart). The sacrifices were made by the priests in behalf of an individual or community. The smoke that rose from a sacrifice was believed to be sweet to the "nostrils of the gods." Quails or turkeys were typical animal sacrifices. The turkey would have been considered unclean under the law of Moses (see *Images,* 142). Autosacrificing was a form of bloodletting, or giving back life to the gods who created the sky and earth (see *The Maya,* 13). Sorenson suggests that human sacrifice might be a part of the "abominations" that Nephi prophesied of in 1 Nephi 12:23 (see *Images,* 142).

Although concubinage existed in biblical times, the inclusion of harlots was against the law of Moses. Abinadi prophesies to King Noah's people by saying, "Wo be unto this people, for I have seen their abominations, and their wickedness, and their whoredoms" (Mosiah 11:20). Ze'ev W. Falk states of biblical times, "The main reason for desiring more than one wife must have been childlessness" (*Hebrew Law in Biblical Times,* 127), though clearly King Noah would have had other reasons.

CHAPTER 7

Scriptures Referenced: Jacob 2:23–28

CHAPTER 8

Scriptures Referenced: Jacob 2:27; Mosiah 13:22

Valuables among Mesoamericans included green jade from the Rio Motagua (locally called Silbapec) and tail feathers of the quetzal from its habitat in the forests of Alta Verapas and the Sierra de las Minas in Guatemala. Above all, the red and white thorny oyster was prized. Conch shells were "used as trumpets in ceremonies, in warfare, and in the chase" (*The Maya,* 23, 57).

CHAPTER 9

In Mesoamerica, clothing was worn mostly to indicate rank. Living in the tropics required little clothing, so clothing became a part of a person's identity. According to Sorenson, "The wealthy used sumptuous fabrics and inventive decoration to place themselves visually atop a hierarchy of prestige and privilege and to display icons that signaled their social roles" (*Images,* 88). This meant that kings, rulers, priests, or warriors could be detected by sight alone. Materials such as quetzal feathers were used only by those of privilege.

CHAPTER 10

According to S. Kent Brown and Richard Neitzel Holzapfel, in addition to the Sabbath, the Mosaic Law included five festivals: Passover (Pesah), held in the spring; Pentecost (Shavu'ot), celebrated in the summer (fifty days after Passover); New Year (Ro'sh ha-Shanah), held in the fall; the Day of Atonement (Yom Kippur), celebrated in the fall; and Tabernacles (Sukkot), held in the fall (see *The Lost 500 Years,* 154).

From ancient times to the modern day, the Maya have practiced a court system with judicial patterns similar to those used by the Book of Mormon people. Cortez described a large building that contained ten to twelve judges who made the decisions in the cities. In the modern city of Zinacantan, a similar court still operates. Four judges sit on a bench during the day, passing judgments on civil disputes (see *Images,* 116).

CHAPTER 11

Scriptures Referenced: 1 Nephi 15:11; 16:1, 5; Mosiah 15:26–27

In Mesoamerica the men's work consisted mainly of farming. During the off season, "wars were fought, trading journeys were undertaken, and houses were built or repaired" (*Images,* 33). Women spent at least part of their day hand-grinding cornmeal with a flat stone, then preparing tortillas or tamales (the wet ball of dough could also be diluted with water and drunk). Women also wove cloth, gathered firewood, carried water, repaired household items, reared children, etc. (ibid).

CHAPTER 12

In the book of Alma (11:21–25), we learn about weights and measures when Zeezrom offers Amulek a bribe of six onties of silver to deny the existence of the Lord. John W. Welch says that "a judge earned one onti of silver for seven days of work. Hence, six onties of silver would equal a judge's salary for 42 days of work." Welch also points out that the physical size of so much silver would have been great ("Weighing and Measuring," *Journal of Book of Mormon Studies,* 8:2 [1999], 38).

CHAPTER 15

Scriptures Referenced: Mosiah 11:6–7; 9:12

Brown and Holzapfel note that "interpreting the written law became the most pervasive religious and intellectual activity in Judaism" (*The Lost 500 Years,* 158). As in Abinadi's era, the temple was central to the people's lives; this included the feasts and festivals that were associated with the sacrifices made at the temple. There are five types of sacrifices outlined in the book of Leviticus: the burnt offering (Lev. 1; 6:8–13), the meat offering (Lev. 2; 6:14–18), the peace offering (Lev. 3; 7:11–21), the sin offering (Lev. 4:1–35; 5:1–13; 6:24–30), and the trespass offering (Lev. 5:14–19; 6:1–7; 7:1–10).

By the time Abinadi came to preach for the first time in the city of Nephi, idolatry was in full swing: "They also became idolatrous, because they were deceived by the vain and flattering words of the king and priests" (Mosiah 11:7). Of course, the irony of this is that Noah's father, King Zeniff, came to the land of Nephi and observed that the Lamanites "were a lazy and an idolatrous people" (Mosiah 9:12).

Sorenson notes that "the God of Israel" had rivals throughout most of the Lamanite and Nephite history. As early as Enos 1:20 we see that the Lamanites had idols and "beliefs and practices related to [other] gods" (*Images,* 140). Some of the worshipped gods and their corresponding idols among the Maya included the Maize God, the Sun God, and the Jaguar God. A "variety of lesser sacred beings or powers and rites connected with them were recognized among the Nephites and Lamanites" as well (ibid). Demons, devils, unclean spirits, idol gods, sorceries, witchcrafts, and magic are all mentioned throughout the scriptural text. Sorenson says, "Clearly the

Nephite record gives us only glimpses of their ritual life and associated beliefs about the supernatural" (ibid).

In 2001, Dr. William Saturno discovered the earliest known Maya painting, which dates to the first century BC. It depicts the Maize God being worshipped, sacrificial offerings such as a deer and fish, bloodletting, and the ruler wearing a headdress (see *The Maya*, 82–84). The famous Bonampak murals are dated later, about AD 800 (ibid, 126).

CHAPTER 16

Scriptures Referenced: Mosiah 11:20–22, 24; 12:1

CHAPTER 17

Scriptures Referenced: Mosiah 11:20–21

Two of the main gods in Maya society were the bird god, Principal Bird Deity, which starts to appear in the late Preclassic, and the Maize God. Coe explains that the creation story is outlined again and again through the "annual planting and harvest cycle of maize, the Maya staff of life" (*The Maya*, 65). Coe also observes, "Small wonder that many Colonial-period Maya identified the risen Christ with the Maize God" (ibid, 66).

One of the twin sons of the Maize God is the Young Jaguar God (Yax Bahlam). J. Eric S. Thompson explains that the jaguar was seen as a protector. The Mayas believed that the jaguar god represented war, sorcery, and the night and stars. Wearing a jaguar skin or head symbolized that a person was of high rank (see *Maya History and Religion*, 292–93). Sorenson also points out that the jaguar acted as a guardian spirit, or *nawal* (see *Images*, 141).

In Kaminaljuyú (proposed area of the land of Nephi), stone carvings have been dated to the late Preclassic era. "A ruler wearing a mask of the Principal Bird Deity (Wuqub Kaquix) is carved on this granite stela" and a stone head of an "aged divinity with jaguar characteristics" also appears. On monument 65, a large relief shows three "enthroned rulers . . . identified by their distinctive headdresses" (*The Maya*, 72–73).

Chapter 18

Scriptures Referenced: Mosiah 11:27–28; 14:3–4

Chapter 20

Scripture Referenced: Genesis 48:16

Kiddushin or *erusin* [meaning "sanctification"] was the first part of the marriage ceremony, in which the bride and the groom were betrothed. The man gave his future bride a ring or other valuable object in the presence of witnesses. In the presence of these same witnesses, the groom would say, "Behold you are consecrated unto me with this ring according to the law of Moses and Israel." Then prayers were said over the wine ("Marriage," *Encyclopaedia Judaica,* 1031).

Ancient Hebrews were married underneath a *huppa*h or canopy, representing the Tabernacle, where covenants were made with God (see *Encyclopedia Americana,* vol. 18, 349). The ceremonial ring is only used for the wedding ceremony. A miniature rendition of a house is built on the ring representing that a new household is being created.

According to the Bible Dictionary, the bride and groom "were crowned with garlands, and a marriage deed was signed. After the prescribed washing of hands and benediction, the marriage supper was held" (LDS Edition King James Bible, Bible Dictionary, "Marriage," 728–29).

According to Sorenson, "Mesoamericans treated ailments mainly through herbal remedies and ritual healing at the hands of several sorts of curers." Also, the steam bath was popular, especially among the men. The women used the steam baths on special occasions (*Images,* 87).

Chapter 22

Scriptures Referenced: Proverb 26:11; Mosiah 12:1–2, 6–14; 13:14; 14:1

Oratory was a practiced and highly developed art in Mesoamerica. The written texts were studied and memorized to be delivered in public to teach and persuade. Sorenson notes that "among the forms of oral literature were epic and lyric poems, hymns, songs, sagas, [and] histories" (*Images,* 174–75).

We see an example of oral presentation when Abinadi speaks to the people of the city of Nephi words that are poetic in nature: "He saith that thou shalt be as a stalk, even as a dry stalk of the field, which is run over by the beasts and trodden under foot. . . . He saith thou shalt be as the blossoms of a thistle, which, when it is fully ripe, if the wind bloweth, it is driven forth upon the face of the land" (Mosiah 12:11–12).

CHAPTER 23

Scriptures Referenced: Mosiah 12:14–15, 20–21, 24–33, 35–37; 13:1–10, 12–28, 35; 14:3, 12; 15:2–4, 8, 11, 28, 31; 16:1, 13–15

Nawalism is the belief that each person has a guardian spirit, usually in the form of an animal. The decorative headdresses of the Mesoamerican dignitaries emphasize these guardian nawals. The jaguar was a common nawal (see *Images,* 141).

John A. Tvedtnes points out that when Abinadi warned King Noah and his priests to touch him not (see Mosiah 13:3), it was similar to other occurrences among the Lord's prophets. When Lehi preached to the people in Jerusalem about the coming of the Messiah, they were angry with him. Therefore the Lord commanded Lehi to flee Jerusalem (see 1 Ne. 2:13–14). Also, when Nephi was threatened with his life by his brothers, the Lord made it impossible for Laman and Lemuel to touch Nephi until his words had been delivered (1 Ne. 17:48–55). Tvedtnes shares Brigham Young's quote from October 1844, "The Lord never let a prophet fall on the earth until he had accomplished his work" ("His Stewardship Was Fulfilled," *Journal of Book of Mormon Studies,* 5:2 [1996], 169–70).

CHAPTER 25

Scriptures Referenced: Mosiah 17:14–20

Record keeping was most likely done on animal skins or tree bark. Papermaking isn't documented until the Classic era (AD 300–900). Sorenson says that books were used even earlier by the "Jaredites, Nephites, and Lamanites from perhaps the third millennium BC until at least AD 400" (*Images,* 163).

At Abinadi's trial, he was accused both of lying about the king—that the king's life would be "valued even as a garment in a hot furnace" (Mosiah

12:3)—and for prophesying falsely. Lew W. Cramer notes that Abinadi's trial first focused on the false prophecy charge when the priests challenged Abinadi to interpret Isaiah's prophecy (Isa. 52:7–10). Abinadi explained that the Lord wouldn't save Noah's people since they had rebelled. The trial was postponed for three days, and when Abinadi returned, he was accused of blasphemy (see Mosiah 17:8). The priests also accused him a fourth time—of condemning the king. This was the final ground on which Noah ordered his execution ("Abinadi," *To All the World: The Book of Mormon Articles from the Encyclopedia of Mormonism*, 1–3).

Royal Skousen suggests that the word *scourge* in Mosiah 17:13 was written incorrectly and should read "scorch" (FARMS "'Scourged' vs. 'Scorched' in Mosiah 17:13," vol. 22:3, Provo, Utah: Maxwell Institute, [2002]). In contrast, Brant Gardner suggests that Abinadi was scourged with flaming sticks, much like a common form of punishment practiced among the Aztecs. Gardner reminds us that in Joseph Smith's time the word "scourge" meant to whip or punish severely. A painting from the *Codex Mendoza* depicts two men beating another person with firebrands (FARMS "Update: Scourging with Faggots," Provo, Utah: Maxwell Institute, [2001]). Robert J. Matthews also points out that the scriptures do not say that Abinadi was burned at the stake, but that he "suffered death by fire" (Mosiah 17:20). Matthews suggests that Abinadi was "bound" then "scourged," and as the flames took hold, Abinadi *falls*—"having suffered death by fire" (ibid.) ("Abinadi: Prophet and Martyr," *Ensign*, April 1992, 25).

CHAPTER 26

Scripture Referenced: Mosiah 18:5

Sorenson informs us that the Waters of Mormon were located "on the Zarahemla side of Nephi." Sorenson also estimates that the distance between Nephi and Mormon was approximately two days of travel (see *An Ancient American Setting*, 176). Allen surmises that the Waters of Mormon may possibly be Lake Atitlan, located ninety miles west of Guatemala City. Allen notes that "Lake Atitlan is a crater, cone-type lake whose depth has not been revealed. It is flanked by three towering volcanoes. . . . Remains of the ancient Mayan city Chiutinamit have even been discovered near the village of Santiago, Atitlan" (*Sacred Sites*, 34).

Selected Bibliography

Allen, Joseph L. *Sacred Sites: Searching for Book of Mormon Lands.* American Fork, Utah: Covenant Communications, 2003.

Brown, S. Kent. *Voices from the Dust.* American Fork, Utah: Covenant Communications, 2004.

Coe, Michael D. *The Maya.* 7th edition. New York: Thames & Hudson, 2005.

Sorenson, John L. *An Ancient American Setting for the Book of Mormon.* Salt Lake City: Deseret Book, and Provo, Utah: FARMS, 1985.

Sorenson, John L. *Images of Ancient America: Visualizing the Book of Mormon.* Provo, Utah: FARMS, 1998.

Thompson, J. Eric S. *Maya History and Religion.* Norman, Oklahoma: University of Oklahoma Press, 1970.

About the Author

Heather B. Moore is the award winning author of the Out of Jerusalem series: *Of Goodly Parents, A Light in the Wilderness, Towards the Promised Land,* and *Land of Inheritance.* The fourth volume in the series, *Land of Inheritance,* won the 2007 Whitney Award for Best Historical.

Heather graduated from Brigham Young University with a major in fashion merchandising and a minor in business management—which has nothing to do with writing novels. But at least she can color coordinate her kids' school clothes and balance a mean checkbook.

Heather is also a member of the League of Utah Writers and the LDStorymakers. She appreciates hearing from her readers, who can contact her through her website, www.hbmoore.com.